CHILDREN OF A NEW EARTH

R. J. Eliason

Edited by Janet Fix at The Wordverve

A special thanks to Janet and her team for all their help and
encouragement.

ISBN-13: 978-0-9885730-9-3

This novel is actually the first novel I wrote, though I've published several later novels already. It's gone through more overhauls and re-writes than anything else I have written. Some of those re-writes have been deep, so deep that readers of the early versions may barely recognize the finished story. The process of editing this manuscript taught me much about the writing process, but for a long time I hesitated to put the final version out. However a small team of friends kept pressuring me to get it out, so here it is.

I dedicate this book to all the friends and family that read various versions of this novel. Thank you for continually poking and prodding me to get it published, long after my motivation gave out.

TABLE OF CONTENTS

PART ONE

FREEDOM RANCH

1

Storm Break

Outside, the thunder rolled on the mountainside. A cold rain beat against the heavy sod roof. Lightning flashed, illuminating an old glass window. Within, a girl stirred fitfully and rolled over in her sleep. She pulled the threadbare quilt closer around her so that only the end of her long, blond braid was showing.

In her dreams, Amy turned her face skyward. Never in waking had she seen a place so flat or a horizon so wide. Her eyes were drawn into the vast blue bowl of the heavens.

"Hey, sister," a female voice laughed, pulling her attention back to the ground. The girl could not have been much older than Amy's seventeen years. She had bright red hair, cut short almost like a man's cut, but with no hint of masculinity about it. She smiled, a small mischievous smile, as she held her hand out toward Amy. Her eyes sparkled.

Again the thunder boomed, this time so close it rattled the window. Amy jerked awake. For a few breathless seconds she stared around the room, trying to see what had woken her. Lightning flashed, lighting her room for a split second.

Mittens, her sister's gray tabby, shot off the dresser and disappeared into the hallway. Nothing else moved as the thunder rolled yet again.

Amy climbed out of bed, wrapping the quilt around herself against the frosty night air. A rough-hewn chair creaked as she settled herself down in front of the window. The thunder was almost a constant now, and the lightning leapt across the ridge over the valley. Amy was no stranger to wild mountain thunderstorms; she saw them every year about this time. But this one was incredible, even by her standards.

A flash lit the far ridge. The outline of her dad's solar array could barely be seen. Amy was filled with a strange sense of foreboding at its sight. Something was wrong out there. That surge had struck close—too close to the array.

Amy peered into the gloom, fearful now. After what seemed a long time, another flash hit the ridge. There was the array, right where it always was. She sat back and sighed, but the sense of foreboding did not leave her. She felt a tingle go down her spine. Was it some sort of premonition?

Amy snorted. She had given up premonitions long ago. It had been a game between her and her sister. They had told each other their dreams, had spoken of what they saw in those moments between sleep and waking, and had even tried to read the crushed mint leaves at the bottom of their tea cups, just like Grandma once did years ago—or so Dad had told them. She was his mother, Elaine. Amy had never known her, had never known any of her grandparents for that matter. All she had were a few faded photographs to offer a glimpse into a world that no longer existed.

She remembered how mad her mother used to get about their games: "The devil's work," "blasphemy," "evil," "witchcraft." Each was a declaration punctuated with an open palm. Somehow, the beatings never stopped the girls. If anything, they were part of the game, making it both a secret and a danger if caught. Besides, they got hit for so many things.

That was years ago. Peering through the gloom, Amy could just see the low mound and chimney pipe that marked Luke's house. On the far side, out of view, was the community cemetery, where her mom had lain for the past five years. Amy had not experienced a premonition since.

She snorted again. She shuffled back toward her bed. *I am nearly a grown a woman,* she thought sourly, *too old for such nonsense.* Tomorrow would be a busy day. With the spring rain here, the whole ranch would soon be busy with planting and working out of doors. She had no business spending half the night on premonitions or dreams about unreal places.

Still, as she closed her eyes, Amy again saw the bright eyes, the upturned nose, the small mischievous grin, and the bright red hair.

The air was acrid and sharp in the small, cave-like building. A dim beam of light danced on the dull concrete.

"Damn, this one is no good either," a voice said as the light faded away. There was a brief smell of sulfur, redundant against the smoky air of the room, as a match was lit.

The brief flash of light was followed by the glow of a lamp. The smell of stale tallow joined the cacophony of scents. "At least these always work," a second voice replied.

The man holding the lamp had a strong, sharp face. His hair, cut in a short buzz, was gray and his face was lined and weathered. His eyes were sharp and his arm was strong and steady as he held the light out to the first man.

The first man could not have been a bigger contrast. His hair was thick and dark, falling almost to his shoulders, his beard just as thick and heavy. His nose was broad and flattened somewhat, his eyes dark. His cheeks stood out red and flushed against the darkness. The hand that reached out for the lamp was broad and thick. Everything about Marlin was heavy and broad—a bear in coveralls.

Despite his size, Marlin handled his tools with a speed and deftness that surprised those who didn't know him. In moments, he had the control box open, peering inside, muttering to himself.

"It's every bit as bad as I feared, Amos," he told his companion. "As soon as I saw the rod down," he sighed and turned back, "I knew it was going to be bad."

"Is it fixable?" Amos asked.

"Not likely."

"You know how important this is?"

Marlin sighed again. "Yeah, I know how important this

is. Don't change a damn thing. The charge controller, the inverter, the batteries—they're all fried."

"What about our backup?"

"That was our backup."

Outside, a tall, thin woman waited for the two men. Her long, gray hair, usually worn in a tight bun, hung behind her in a ponytail. She pulled a faded shawl over her shoulders. She wore a long, woolen dress in light brown, which rustled slightly as she stamped her feet to stay warm.

Later, when the sun had been out for a while, it would be warm, but this early in the year you could still see your breath in the morning. Last night's rain had melted the last of the winter's snow, and the lichen stood out green and bright on the rocks above, lending a feeling of spring, though the ground was still cold and dormant.

Amos Deaton gave his wife, Theresa, a grim look as the two men exited the building.

"How bad is it?" she asked.

"Bad," Marlin replied.

"It looks like we are without electricity from now on," Amos said flatly.

"None?"

"None."

"What about water?" Theresa asked.

"The cistern is full, especially after last night," Marlin said. "That should hold us well into the summer, possibly all the way to fall, if we're careful."

"And then?"

"There's a hand pump. It's a hundred-foot well, hard to pump by hand, but not impossible. There's water farther down that's closer to the surface. We'd have to haul it a ways."

"We did it before," Amos put in.

"What about the locker?" Theresa said, a note of hysteria creeping into her voice. She nodded to the second concrete building, slightly larger than the one they had come out of. It was set even deeper into the hillside so that only the front wall stuck out. It housed a community meat locker, the only refrigeration they had.

"We empty it," Amos replied. "It's mostly empty anyway. Divide up the meat between the families. Everyone should can as much as possible." He shrugged. "Then we feast on what's left before it goes bad."

"With the canned food we have and the first greens coming out of the greenhouses, we can make it until the gardens start producing. That meat was more of a luxury anyway," Marlin said.

"I know, I know." Theresa sighed. "We'll be fine this summer. What about the fall? What about next winter?"

"We can more. We dry more meats. We make do," Amos said. "We did it once before, we can do it again."

"I remember before," Theresa said, her lips a tight thin line. Amos didn't answer; he remembered too.

When the ranch had been established, they had been assured repeatedly that they could be self-sufficient. Dozens of books had been consulted; many of them were still here in their library. More importantly, locals had been consulted. Some, like Larry Gatlin, were still here. His family had lived in these mountains since the days of the pioneers. Everyone said the same thing. They had enough land, enough livestock, and enough days in their growing season to be completely self-sufficient. It was close, this high up and this far north, but they could do it.

They had done it, for several years even. But what no book had warned them, what none of the locals, after almost two generations of modern conveniences, had remembered was how hard it was. They survived the winter, but on a near-starvation diet. When the hunters brought back meat, they feasted. In a few days, however, it was back to nearly starving. The cold and the lack of fresh foods sapped their immune systems. Even a mild cold or flu could mean death. The young suffered the most. The Deaton's had lost both their daughters to those hard years.

Then Marlin had come, the outsider with his solar array and his knowledge of electronics. They had scavenged an industrial freezer and built the meat locker. From then on, they froze choice produce, preserving far more of its nutritional value. Their men hunted the ridges and forests of the mountain, bringing back wild sheep, elk, and deer to fill the locker each fall. The ranch had thrived for over twenty years.

"Where's Marlin?" James asked as Amy came up. He was quickly becoming the spitting image of his father, Larry. Both were thin and lanky, with curly, brown hair and thick, brown beards. He stood beside the old red Farmall tractor, looking thoughtfully at the horizon.

"He's busy," Amy replied, a bit shorter than she had intended. It was, after all, a reasonable enough question—if she had been in the mood to be reasonable.

"How are we going to get the tractor running now?" Mark whined from the tractor's seat. He was broader than James, with dark hair, the straggly beginnings of a beard, and dark sunken eyes. *Hung over again, no doubt*, Amy thought in disgust. She held up her toolbox and stared pointedly at him.

"We can get it to turn over, but it won't start up for some reason. We took the battery pack out and jumped it, but that didn't work," James explained.

"I wouldn't want a girl working on my tractor," Mark voiced loudly.

Amy glared at him, her hands tightening on the toolbox.

James just sighed. "Well, it's a good thing it's not *your* tractor then," he said. "'Cause if we have to wait for Marlin, we'll never get the spring plowing done."

"Fuck the plowing," Mark growled as he hopped off the tractor and stomped away.

Amy gruffly ordered James to take his place on the seat. As James climbed into the seat, two men appeared around the other side. The first was Larry Gatlin, an older, more weathered version of his son. With him was Jacob Clayton, a man with a hawkish face that looked as though it had been chiseled from granite. He had short, gray hair and was clean shaven. His build was thicker than Larry's, but both had the look of men who spent most of their time in heavy, outdoor labor.

"Where's O'Malley going?" Jacob demanded.

James shrugged. "Just stomped off." The tractor chugged noisily as he turned the ignition.

"What pissed him off now?" Larry asked.

Amy stuck her head out from behind the engine block. "Guess."

"Where's Marlin?" Jacob asked.

"Busy," James replied, sparing Amy.

Larry just rolled his eyes. Neither man said anything further as Amy worked. James and his father weren't so bad, but she could almost feel Jacob's disapproval. Not that either of the Gatlins wouldn't prefer Marlin. It made her so mad. Everyone knew she helped her father in the garage. Why didn't they want her to do it out in the field?

She knew the answer, of course. The ranch had definite views about a woman's place. The garage wasn't it. As long as they didn't see her, they could overlook it. They had no choice really. There was too much for Marlin to do by himself, and he had no son to help him. They were not about to admit that most of the work that came out of the garage was done by a woman, however. Amy's face grew hot as she worked, and not from the fumes of the engine. The tractor continued to chug but not start.

A man came walking across the field toward them— nearly a man anyway. He was full grown: tall, lanky, and almost painfully thin. His brown hair was cut in a butch, exposing much of his scalp. His face was a study in awkwardness. It was lean and angular, having lost the roundness of youth, but still lacking the weathered lines that would lend it strength in years to come. His bright blue eyes shone with curiosity and youth.

Amy glanced at him briefly, favoring him with a slightly less disgruntled snort, and returned to her work.

"Thought I'd come see if you were planning on coming to class today," Luke said.

Amy didn't answer at first. She had missed two days this week already; it was a busy time. If she missed too many more, Amos would come have a talk with her father. Then there would be no choice; she'd have to go.

"I got to get this—" she began. The tractor roared suddenly, the beleaguered choke catching at last. She stared up at the tractor like it had betrayed her.

"Good," Luke said. "I'll help you with your tools and then we can walk up together." He reached for her toolbox.

"I am quite capable," she snarled, grabbing it away. She stomped off. With a sheepish look toward the men, Luke followed.

"Men!" Amy exclaimed as she threw her toolbox down.

"What'd they do now?" Luke inquired.

"Mark stormed off because it was me, not Dad, who came out to help," she raged.

"Mark? He was probably just looking for an excuse to leave. He hates to work."

"I hate men!"

"You shouldn't judge all men by Mark. He's an ass."

"He's the worst, but most of them aren't much better." Amy continued to fume. "Jacob barely tolerates my presence. James is civil enough, but he's afraid to be seen with me."

"I'm not."

"I know, Luke, but you're not——"

"I am eighteen."

She stared hard at him. "That's not what I meant, and you know it. You're not like them."

Luke sighed. "Mark certainly has no sense of decency or honor," he said. "Sometimes I wonder why they even let his dad in."

Amy snorted loudly. "I don't think they had a lot of candidates."

Luke shifted uncomfortably. The ranch's school taught that they were elite, sent up here to guard the Nations and their way of life from the infidels and the Jews. The ranch's library had a handful of books, written by various founders of their movement, spoke of the New World Order, the Jewish Conspiracy, and the coming Race War.

Amy's dad had come later, not one of the Nations at all. He told Amy and Luke that the Aryan Nations had, in fact, not been a popular cause before society's collapse. He claimed the collapse had been brought on by a variety of environmental problems, not any race war. Nor was there any New World Order waiting in the ruins of civilization to attack them.

Luke couldn't bring himself to say that the history they were being taught was a lie. Still, he trusted Amy and, more importantly, Marlin. Besides, he had read most of what was in the ranch's library. A handful of general history books barely mentioned the Aryan Nation, or dismissed them out of hand as a small ideology believed by only a few people. Environmental problems, on the other hand, were mentioned frequently in almost every survival, backwoods, or gardening manual they had.

The ranch had been built several years before the collapse happened. By the time things started to unravel, their contact with the outside world was already limited. Could they have been misinformed? And if so, what did that mean for them? Had they lived up in the mountains for years, hiding from a threat that wasn't there?

About half a dozen kids were already lounging in front of the community hall when Amy and Luke arrived.

"Well, look who's joined us today," Mary Gatlin drawled as Amy threw herself down on the steps. Mary was short with curly, brown hair that she wore tied up with a faded red ribbon. She had brown eyes and a short upturned nose on her rounded face. Her eyes sparkled with malevolence as she watched Amy. "The tomboy's come to school. Did Mr. Deaton have to threaten your dad again?"

Amy glowered at Mary but didn't answer.

"Amy did better than you on the last reading test," Luke said in her defense. Mary just snorted.

"Today won't be 'so bad," another boy put in. He was slightly taller than Luke and had the same lanky look about him. His hair was a darker brown; his face less angular. His name was Daniel. "After all, we have Mr. Deaton for third period."

Both girls groaned. Education at the ranch was simple. They had one class where the older kids helped the younger ones. The first two periods were taught by Lucille Posch. She had been a schoolteacher before the collapse. She taught reading, writing, and math. Third period varied, with different people coming in each day. Adrian Posch taught Bible study twice a week. Larry Gatlin taught farm management. Matthew Zachary, Luke's dad, taught social studies (the great American way of life), and once a week Amos Deaton, their leader, taught history.

After third period, they were released to go home for lunch. After lunch, the girls stayed at home and helped their mothers around the house. The boys over thirteen went back in the afternoon for combat training with Isaiah Hall.

"Hey, there's something you agree on," Luke joked, looking at Mary then Amy. "You both don't like history."

He was glared at from both sides. It was true; none of the girls liked history. Luke had read the one history book that the ranch owned. Actually, he had read it more than

14

once. It was one of his best subjects. Amos Deaton didn't often go by the book, however. His version of history was filled with lurid battles, often greatly embellished, and long rants about who hated whom and why. It was one of the most popular classes among the boys.

Luke realized that a few things were missing. He had read about the Civil War. The book mentioned nothing at all about the resistance after the war—the resistance that eventually led to the Nations, and by default, to the ranch. In fact, the book seemed to assume that the North's victory had been complete, and even proper.

It was not a subject he was willing to discuss with Mr. Deaton, however. Surely in time their leader would explain this himself.

Two women were approaching the community hall. The short and plump form of Lucille Posch was flanked by Theresa Deaton's taller form. They were talking in low, worried whispers. They stopped talking as they came up to the children.

Theresa looked at them uncertainly for a moment and then said, "Amy, your father needs you, up by the array."

"But she has school," Mary protested. Mary hated that Amy got away with things that none of the other kids did.

Lucille gave a disapproving look at Amy's already retreating back. "She'll be excused, for today only." She shouted this last part. Amy had already broken into a run.

The second Theresa had spoken, Amy realized what was wrong. Her premonition came back to her full force. She knew exactly what hadn't seemed right. She had subconsciously missed the razor-thin line of the lightning rod on the horizon.

She raced through the tiny settlement. She didn't slow down until she was most of the way up the steep trail toward the array, and even then, it was only because she was out of breath.

Her face was beet red by the time she crested the ridge. There, she met her father's face, almost as red as hers.

I just ran up here, she thought, *but he has just been walking around.* She was worried about him. Even this small change in altitude left him out of breath.

His look brought her back to reality in a flash. "Is it bad?" she asked.

"Worse," he replied.

He was right. The rod was down, blown down by the heavy winds. Without its protection, lightning had struck the array. About half the panels were scorched. Marlin was shuffling around attaching calipers to the sides of the panels and taking readings. He muttered darkly as he worked. "About half of them are still working," he told her.

"Is that enough?" she asked.

He stood silent for a minute, staring up at the skyline. "That's not all. The charge went through. Everything is fried: batteries, charge controller, inverter. Everything."

"A meeting tonight?" Patrick asked as he faced off against Luke again. Patrick was a year older than Luke. At nineteen, he would be considered a man next year and no longer required to come to combat training.

That was just as well. Combat training had taken Patrick as far as it could. He was Luke's height, but broader. He was lean and muscular. Sweat stood out on his bare chest. He was like a mountain cat in brown shorts.

His arm shot out. Luke sidestepped clumsily and swept the larger boy off his feet. Before the dust had settled, Isaiah Hall was among them shouting. "Faster, Luke, you have to finish him faster."

Isaiah pulled Patrick to his feet. "Again," he growled.

Patrick looked at the graying combat instructor. Isaiah's hairy arms bulged with muscles and his wide girth carried no hint of fat. He wore the same brown shorts they all wore, and a faded white t-shirt. He wore his hair cut in a butch and his wide face bore a constant scowl.

Patrick's eyes flickered, and his fist shot out. With a grace born of years of training, Isaiah sidestepped and swept Patrick off his feet. He dropped down, his elbow following Patrick's progress. It stopped inches from Patrick's face.

"This isn't a game," he snarled. "Do you think the terrorists think this is a game?"

"No sir!" Patrick and Luke sang out together.

Unappeased, Isaiah continued. "Do you think the enemy thinks this is a game? Do you think the New World Order is playing around? No. It's kill or be killed. This training just might save your life someday, boys. Remember that. Free sparring," he said, looking at Luke. "You and Patrick are up first."

"Spring dance is coming up," Patrick commented as they faced off again.

"Yeah," Luke replied warily as the two circled each other. He wished he'd been partnered with Kurt or Daniel. That Patrick would win the match was a given. He was the best fighter they had at the ranch. Losing was not the problem.

Luke was never sure which was worse—the fact that Patrick's concept of light-contact sparring often left bruises or that he was a master at taunting his opponent into making a mistake. He exploited Kurt's fear, Daniel's caution, and Shawn's slow wit. Luke knew what was coming. He told himself not to rise to the bait.

"Taking the grease monkey?" Patrick laughed.

"Yeah," Luke replied calmly, though he could feel the heat rising on the back of his neck. *Of course*, he wanted to say, *we've gone to every dance together since we reached "courting" age.* He hadn't actually asked Amy, but they'd surely walk up together and spend the whole evening together.

"I hope you were paying attention. You'll need hand to hand with that one," Patrick joked. Somewhere in the background, Shawn sniggered.

Luke's face burned. What was it? Patrick's smug grin or Shawn's snigger? The two always picked on Amy. They never gave her a chance. He wished, as he always did, that he could wipe that smug expression off Patrick's face.

Patrick dropped his guard. He was midway through mouthing the word "feisty" as Luke darted in.

Luke hit the ground hard. Once again, Patrick had used his anger against him, leading him in and then sweeping his feet out from under him. Luke clambered to his feet chagrined.

Head low, he exited the circle. At a gesture from Isaiah, Kurt shuffled fearfully forward. "At least that won't be the most embarrassing defeat today," Daniel commented at Luke's side. Luke nodded as Patrick squared off in front of his new opponent.

"Grease Monkey again, eh?" Shawn jeered from Luke's other side. "Glad I don't have to take an ugly girl like her to every dance."

What a dumb fuck. With so few kids at the ranch, teasing got pretty redundant. Shawn was too stupid to even see that he had left himself wide open. "You want me to ask Daniel's sister for you?" Luke replied. "She's what, twelve, this year?"

"Shut your face, ass wipe," Shawn growled a bit too loud. Isaiah scowled in their direction. "Ain't going with no twelve-year-old."

"What about Elisabeth?" Jimmy Manualson piped in, referring to Amy's sister. "She's fourteen."

"Kurt's already asked her," Shawn moaned.

They all looked at the scrawny kid trying to dance out of Patrick's reach while still remaining in the circle.

"How did he ever get up the nerve?" Jimmy asked. "I thought he was terrified of the beast she calls her father, not to mention her sister." He gave a worried glance toward Luke, Amy's friend and chief defender, fearing he had said too much.

Luke, his anger spent, just shrugged. "He just did, I guess." He had already told Daniel the true story; no one else needed to know.

In fact, Shawn had lumbered up and asked Elisabeth out. Elisabeth, unsure of how to get out of it, had told him that Kurt had already asked her. Then she tromped off to Kurt's place and announced that they were going together. Kurt hadn't disagreed.

After combat practice was over, Luke rushed toward the low metal building that served as the ranch's garage. He was worried. Amy had never come back to class. That was not terribly unusual, not nearly as unusual as her dismissal had been. Coupled with the rumors of a ranch-wide meeting, however, he was sure something was up.

The entire yard surrounding the garage was littered with junk. Car parts and other less identifiable bits of metal sprouted weeds, and clumps of weeds sprouted bits of metal. Paint peeled from the metal siding of the garage in huge flakes. The whole building was slowly sagging to one side.

Neither the paint nor the sagging was particularly unusual. Most of buildings around the ranch were showing their age in this way. The ranch was at war, against nature and other less visible enemies. Paint and maintenance were not priorities.

The mess was another matter altogether. Most of the houses were fronted with orderly garden rows, reflecting both the lack of space in the valley and living proof that one of the enemies, at least, was being beaten.

The garage and its occupants had always been another matter. Luke had heard some of the older members' murmurs, and had heard the boys repeat it often enough. The ranch had made a deal with the devil, in the name of Marlin Beland. Sure, he too had a small personal garden in front of his house. The house the ranch members had built for him, that is. It was tended by his daughter Elisabeth, when it was tended at all.

Meanwhile Marlin and his oldest daughter Amy lived a life unlike any other at the ranch. They didn't work on the communal farm, help with the hunts, or care for the sheep. They ate the food the ranch provided; wore the clothes others wove and sewed for them. The ranch supported them.

Or so they all say when things are going well, Luke thought. He'd spent enough time in Marlin's company to see the other side. While the men grumbled that Marlin had not helped with the harvest, he was busy pressing the meager soybean crop for oil—oil for cooking and more importantly for biodiesel. He and Amy maintained the tractor and repaired the tools. While the women complained that they got no help with the canning, he was the one who fixed the seals on the pressure cookers. He maintained the solar array and the freezer, and manned the smithy. Amy worked almost as hard, helping her dad in the shop, helping Jaime Hall with the ceramic kiln, and a dozen other chores to boot.

And when questioned about the mess in front of his garage, 'Marlin would just say that he'd get to it. It had been thirty years now, and he was no closer to getting to it. Most had giving up trying, but that didn't keep them from grumbling.

The loud clanging of metal on metal broke his reverie. Amy came bursting out of the side door of the garage, her face red. She stomped off toward her home, taking no notice of Luke. He had to rush to catch up to her.

"Amy?" he said hopefully.

"That bastard!" she fumed. "'*This is important business, little lady,*'" she mimicked.

Luke didn't need to ask who she was mad at. "He's our leader," Luke offered. "Don't you think you should show some respect?"

"No," she retorted. "I will when he does. Dismissing me? I have helped maintain that system for the last five years. I know it as well as Dad. Hell, I was the one who jury-rigged the charge controller after the last one burned out. Why won't he talk to me about anything?"

Luke's first impulse was to say, "Surely your dad will tell

21

you what he says anyway, so why does it matter?" but the impulse was stopped as what he had heard sunk in. "The charge controller?" he said. "Is something wrong with the solar array?"

Amy nodded. "Damn thing's fried. Direct lightning hit last night."

"Is it fixable?" Luke asked. "I mean, what will we do if it's not?"

"It's not," Amy replied. "And I would probably know what we'll do if that bastard Amos hadn't told me off. *'Men's business,'* my ass. He knows Dad will tell me later anyway. They're all like that. They bring all their problems to Dad. They refuse to talk to me. They know damn well that once they are gone, Dad will turn to me. What choice does he have? They expect so much from him. But will even one of them openly admit that I can do the work? No!"

Luke let her vent. He knew it'd be useless to try to get any more out of her until she had calmed down. Just like it was useless for her to expect any of the men at the ranch to accept a woman as a mechanic.

"Do you know about a meeting tonight?" Luke asked as Amy wound down.

She nodded. They had reached her house, and she flopped onto a crude wooden bench by the front door. "Sure, that's what Amos is seeing my dad about now. Trying to figure what they are going to tell people tonight."

"There's no hope of fixing it?" Luke asked.

"The panels themselves still produce a bit of electricity, but all the batteries are gone. The freezer took some damage as well. There's nothing we can do. We might be able to rig something up to draw water during the day at least, but that's about it."

Larry Gatlin strummed a poorly tuned guitar while his wife sang a coarse rendition of Bobby McGee.

"Freedom ranch, just another place with nothing left to use . . ." Luke quipped as they went by.

Amy snorted but didn't comment. Luke was always coming up with shit like that. He had stayed up at her place since that afternoon, talking to her to calm her down, helping her sister harvest spring greens from the family garden for supper, and then staying to discuss things with Marlin when he came home.

Amy shivered as a cold breeze played on her shoulders. Around her, other women were pulling their shawls close around themselves. *I should have brought my coat*, she thought to herself. The days were warm, but it still got cold at night.

Directly ahead of them was a faded, gray, two-story farmhouse. It was a mottled, uneven gray, the color you get when the last remains of a dozen paints are mixed together. It too was falling off in chunks. This building served the ranch as its only communal space. It served as a church, an armory, a school, a dance hall, and tonight, a meeting hall.

Light streamed out of the lower-story windows. The buzz of conversation flowed out of the open doors. Amy paused and pulled back; she was in no hurry to join the growing throng.

Instead, she turned back and looked at the ranch. The rest of the ranch was unlike the two large buildings at the center, the communal space and the garage. The houses of the ranch were mostly underground. They were built into the side of the valley in a wide half circle. Posts of rough-hewn pine logs were set into the slope with earth berm roofs laid over that. All that showed was the occasional window.

Only years of familiarity allowed Amy to pick out those windows tonight. *Flickering tallow lamps should show right about there,* she thought, *where James Derry would normally be reading Bible passages to the kids before bed. And just over there should be the dull glow of Jaime Hall's wood stove. When was the last time the whole ranch showed up for a meeting?*

Amy shuddered and turned away. She was filled with a sudden foreboding. She had an image in her mind of all the windows empty and dark. She shook her head to clear it.

"You okay?" Luke asked.

She looked up at the community building without answering. She hadn't realized that he had stayed outside with her. "Do they even use the second story anymore?" she wondered aloud, looking up at the empty windows.

"Sure, but not much," Luke answered. "The library is up there."

"So you use it, anyway."

He blushed but didn't answer. After a few minutes, he said, "The meeting should be getting started anytime now. We'd better go in."

As they entered the building, Amy could tell by his reaction that Luke had never seen a meeting this well attended. He always attended any public function and took great pains to be involved.

He had managed to drag Amy to one of the other

24

meetings. The six or seven attendees had gathered around one long table. That table had been all that had prevented a fistfight between Amy and Theresa Deaton. Luke had never tried to get her to come to another meeting.

Now, however, the table had been shoved into one corner and chairs of every description lined the main room. The community building didn't have enough chairs to sit everyone, so kitchen chairs and rough-hewn patio chairs had been borrowed from a number of families.

Most of the women had either knitting needles or crochet hooks out and were crafting multi-colored afghans from the last remnants of yarn. All were experienced, chatting while their hands worked. In another month, there would not be so much as a skein of yarn left anywhere in the ranch.

In one corner, there was the rhythmic sound of Larry and James Gatlin running the blades of their shears over a whetstone. In just a few days, they would begin shearing the sheep. The women would trade their knitting needles in for carding and spinning supplies, and the cycle would begin again.

A few of the men wore faded and patched overalls like Amy and her father, while a few had on worn fatigues. Mostly, however, homespun wool and coarse woven flax had replaced these as the standard dress for the men of Freedom Ranch. The men wore pants and shirts of oak brown, and the women long dresses in green or yellow. All three colors represented readily available dye materials.

A few of the men still had short military haircuts, but most had gone the route of crude shoulder-length haircuts and thick beards.

The women wore their hair long. They kept it out of

their way in long braids, as Amy herself did, or up in buns. The fashion of Freedom Ranch could be described in one word: practical.

Amy sank down into an Adirondack chair next to her father, who was perched nervously on a tall stool. Luke, finding most of the seats taken already, sat on the arm of Amy's chair as Amos banged his gavel and yelled, "Order! Order!"

Amos, Minister Posch, and Isaiah Hall all sat together behind a card table. Minister Posch rose as everyone grew quiet. They all rose as he intoned a short prayer. Then everyone recited the Pledge of Allegiance.

Afterward, everyone sat again. Amy glanced nervously at Luke. He was watching Amos intently.

"No point beating around the bush, people," Amos said. "I called this meeting to let everyone know some bad news. There's no way to sugarcoat it, so I'll just tell you. Last night's storm got the solar array and the freezer. Both are beyond repair."

There was a moment of stunned silence. Then the whole room broke out in a dozen separate conversations. Amy heard her father's name mentioned several times. Her head darted around trying to catch what they were saying about him. But there were too many separate conversations coming from too many directions. Nothing made any sense.

Her face burned crimson. She could guess well enough. Twenty some years of loyal service, and they would be grumbling, "Why can't he fix it?" Twenty years of doing his best, and they would merely wonder why he wasn't doing better this time.

Amos's gavel banged for silence. "Listen up everyone. I

know what a lot of you are thinking. Marlin's gotten us out of a lot of bad spots before. He's done his best, better than we could have hoped for." Amy felt a flush of gratitude for Amos's support. "We've already burned out one unit of batteries. This was our backup. There is nothing he can do. Marlin, do you have anything to add?"

Marlin shuffled to his feet. He stared pointedly at them. He was painfully self-conscious under everyone's gaze. "Some of the panels are still producing a charge. We got no battery, but we can run the well pump during the day and fill one of the cisterns. That gets us water, at least."

"Can we run the freezer during the day?" Larry asked from the back. "It should stay cold enough at night, I would think."

"And risk half-frozen meat?" someone asked.

"No, the freezer unit took part of the strike. Even if I could repair it," Marlin answered, "where on earth would we find Freon these days?"

Marlin's pronouncement was taken as the final word. No one even asked what Freon was. Again a dozen conversations started up, and again Amos banged his gavel.

"All right, let's not lose our heads. It makes life a little harder, but we're used to that by now, hey?" he chided them. "Here is what we are going to do. Every family gets a share of the remaining meat. There's not much left anyway, and we could all use a spring feast. Whatever you can't use up, can. This summer we clean out the old smoke house and can more food. We get by."

"No, we can't," a woman moaned toward the back.

"We did it once," Amos growled. "We'll do it again."

"No," the voice pleaded, firmer now.

27

Amy craned her head to see. She was shocked to discover that it was Rebecca Hopes talking. *That's the last person I would have expected to lose it*, she thought.

Rebecca was one of the hardest working women at the ranch. She had organized the harvest for many years now and had a reputation for being able to make even the most recalcitrant of the boys pull their share, at least for a day or two.

She rose as she spoke. "I am sorry, sir, but we can't. Theresa told me earlier about what happened, and I have been thinking about it ever since. We did manage for a while, but that was years ago.

"The canning jars we have are reusable, but the gaskets wear out eventually. Some jars get broken, people drop them or whatever; it's inevitable." There was a note of hysteria in her voice. "We haven't got even half what we had at the beginning. And that was barely enough."

"Smoking more meat?" Isaiah Hall asked.

"We stopped doing that years ago, for a reason," she answered sharply. "It needs salt. We can't get salt to preserve things anymore."

"So what do you suggest?" someone asked.

"I don't know, I don't know," she replied wringing her hands.

"Leave it to the men, missy," Liam O'Malley called. "We'll hunt all winter, put fresh meat on your table every day."

Isaiah Hall scowled and glanced across the room at his daughter-in-law Jaime. A momentary silence fell. "Hunting in the dead of winter on the mountain is too dangerous," Isaiah said coldly.

Amy flushed, as did most in the room, at the reminder.

She had been twelve the winter when Richard Hall had fallen to his death hunting bighorn sheep in the cliffs above the valley. That was the same winter her mother died.

"Besides," Isaiah went on, "more hunting means more ammo, and we ain't got much of that left, either. I was hoping we could start relying on the deadfall traps this year, but I don't relish checking them in deep winter."

"I remember a time when we could just run down to the Get-N-Go and buy a stack of deer slugs," Horace said.

"Well, why don't you just run down and get us some then?" Liam O'Malley jeered. "And pick me up some whiskey while you're at it." His two sons laughed loudly at their father.

"That may be our only option," Amos said. "It may be time to send an expedition down to see what remains of society and find supplies." He stood quickly. "For the moment, orders stand. Everyone gets a share of the remaining meat. Make the most of it. The council will consider this situation some more and get back to you. Remember, ladies and gentlemen, that we are still in a state of war. Keep your calm and keep your discipline. That's all for now." He banged the gavel again and the meeting was over.

"And that is how the infidel nearly ended the centuries-long role of white man's glorious civilization," Minister Posch panted. He wiped ineffectively at his brow with a dull white handkerchief.

It had been quite a lecture. Even the youngest of the children knew it well enough. They had heard it from every one of their teachers in one form or another. Their

29

parents told them about the collapse on long, winter nights by the wood stove.

Today, however, Posch had put an even greater zeal into it. Their current plight, coupled with the possibility of an expedition out of the valley, had no doubt fueled it. He had gone to great lengths to impress on them how corrupt society had become. Racial mingling, women's liberation, even rights for perverts and deviants were all considered progress. Such a society sowed the seeds of its own destruction.

The Aryan Nations had already been busy countering these menaces. They were recruiting and pulling together people ready and willing to fight for their religion, their race, and their moral values.

Then America made its fatal mistake. It allowed itself to become involved with the infidel. Muslim states had held the United States hostage with oil for years. They had destroyed the World Trade Center in one of the worst attacks on the American people.

Even in face of all this, America tried for peace. America fought to give the Muslim people the freedom Americans had long possessed, overthrowing dictators in Iraq and Iran. What thanks did that earn for the United States? More hatred, more terrorist attacks.

Finally, the ultimate retribution: a nuclear bomb set off in downtown Chicago. Millions killed in one fell attack. If ever there was a time to repay hatred with hatred, it was then.

The Nations and many others had done so. America would have been—could have been—cleansed. The dangerous element within could have been eliminated. The citizens of this great nation could have risen up and thrown off the shackles once and for all.

The government would not allow it. Martial law had been declared. Hundreds of members were arrested. Hundreds died in vicious street fights, first with police and then National Guardsmen.

Arguments began about how it had happened, who had set the bomb, and what should be done to them. It was in these arguments, in the slow disintegration that the leaders of the Aryan Nations began to see the true threat, the deeper evil that lay in wait.

Powers deeper and broader than even the American government were at work. The New World Order, a shadowy organization of the world's powers, was manipulating the government. It was pitting whites against whites, Christians against Christians, using them as cannon fodder in their war for power.

The leaders of the Nations were wise and had planned for this eventuality. Camps had been prepared where a few chosen men and women could bide their time, waiting. Let them tear down America. When the time was right, they would be there, ready to rebuild.

Freedom Ranch was but one of these enclaves. Amos Deaton and Adrian Posch had left their homes in the Deep South and had come to these mountains to prepare the way.

They would have failed if without the help of locals. Men like Larry Gatlin and the Zacharys had grown up in these mountains. They were raised on the militiaman philosophy. They were not of the Nations, but they knew the truth when they heard it. They helped build and, later, man the ranch.

Minister Posch had delivered the tale at full tilt today.

Sweat had beaded on his forehead and wetly punctuated much of the lecture. His face had gone red, and more than once, Luke feared he would convulse.

Next to Luke, Kurt sat dazed, his face reflecting Luke's feelings well enough. On his other side, Amy had her hand up. Luke groaned. *This could not lead anywhere pleasant.*

"Yes, Miss Beland?" Posch asked. Amy hated being called Miss Beland.

"My dad says the Muslims didn't do it," she said.

"Of course they did," Posch said dismissively. "Who else would do such a thing?"

"The Chinese possibly," Amy replied, "or Africans. He is not sure which."

"Chinese? Africans?" Posch huffed. "What an active imagination. Why would they do such a thing?"

"On account of the environment," she said.

"What, like the trees and things?"

"Yes, and oil and all that. Dad says we were using up too much of it. The rest of the world was mad at us."

"No commie is going to tell America how much oil we can use," Minister Posch declared. Most of the class sniggered.

They probably think she's talking about cooking oil, Luke thought. Amy was not about to give up yet.

"Apparently they couldn't tell us how much to use," she agreed. "Which is why they bombed us. Anyway, Dad says it was all falling apart anyway. Oil was running out, cities were being destroyed, and people were starving everywhere, on account of the environment."

"I think the trees can bloody well take care of themselves, don't you?" Minister Posch answered. Amy went bright red. Patrick whispered something to Shawn, and they both snickered.

"The bomb was Chinese made," Amy pressed on. "That much they knew before Dad came up here. He says we even went to war with China, but he doesn't know if anything ever came of it. And there were other attacks that were claimed by African terrorist groups. But most of the collapse was due to people right here in this country turning nasty toward each other."

"That's a lie, girl," Minister Posch said.

"It is not!" Amy insisted. She was standing now. To everyone else she may have looked angry and defiant, but Luke could see that she was close to tears. "My dad has been trying to tell you this for twenty years. You just don't want to listen."

"Now, girl . . ."

"No! I don't care if you would rather listen to your own lies instead of the truth. But you are going to send people down there, and they *need* to know the truth! They need to know what really happened." She turned and stormed out the door.

"Well, really," Posch murmured after a long pause.

Luke shrugged the heavy bag, trying to make it rest more comfortably on his shoulder. He stared up at the ridge. Excitement ran through the line of young men. There they were: the barricades.

Something was up, that much was sure. Since the meeting, everyone had been talking about it. Amos, Minister Posch, and Isaiah Hall met daily. They spoke little, and encouraged no rumors. They didn't need to. The rumors ran wild.

Already there were clear signs of what the leaders were

thinking. Jacob Clayton, Matthew Hopes, John McKurtz, and William Jones were all out of camp on various errands in the mountains. It didn't matter what excuses Amos gave, everyone could guess the real reason. They were checking out the passes, seeing if they were clear. Any expedition would have to leave as soon as the passes cleared. Otherwise, they could get trapped down in the lowlands when fall closed the passes back up.

And now this. Isaiah Hall showed up at combat training and announced the first ever overnight "field training" session at the barricades.

The barricades were midway through the eastern pass out of the valley. Across the remains of the old road, the ranch had constructed a three-foot-high, three-foot-thick stone wall, to stop vehicles and give defenders some protection. There, they had held the pass against local militiamen no less than three times.

Once upon a time, it had been manned by armed guards. They had radio contact with the ranch. It had been years now since there had been any sign of enemies. Manned patrols had slowly fallen off as work back at the ranch seemed more pressing.

It was said that Amos and Isaiah still came up here regularly and watched for signs of human activity. Isaiah certainly picked the way with confidence, even in the failing light.

The boys had never been allowed up here. As teenagers, they already carried a lot of responsibility. Luke gathered wood from neighboring valleys, fished the high mountain lakes and rivers, and went on weeklong hunting trips. Always it was to the west, deeper into the mountains or occasionally to the north.

To the west, three or four mountains away, there was an Indian reservation. Liam O'Malley Sr. claimed to have been in a firefight with one of them once, long ago. "Don't believe a word of it," Luke's father had said. "Liam's just looking for an excuse because he wasted too much ammo. Never been any danger to the west."

The east was another matter entirely. The road that the Barricade Pass blocked led down out of the Rocky Mountains. It was down there that society had fought and died. In just moments, they would crest into the pass, and Luke would see for the first time where his uncles, Henry and Gerald, had fought and died protecting the ranch.

"This is it, boys," Isaiah informed them. It was not much of a sight: a low, stone wall crudely constructed. An abandoned pickup truck pockmarked with a few bullet holes gave it the feel of an old battle scene.

Luke clutched his rifle closer to his chest. He felt as though the battle had been fought just yesterday, not years before he was born. In the deepening dusk, it was easy to imagine enemy eyes peering out of every shadow.

"*If*," Isaiah was always very careful to stress the 'if' whenever discussing this, "*if* we send an expedition down there," he pointed down the far slope, "we will be manning this pass at all times. Given the manpower, you may well be doing this duty. Whoever goes down there may be stirring up a hornet's nest. That's why we are starting to train you guys up here."

"When out this direction, fire is a luxury you cannot afford. You could see a fire up here for miles. We'll be cooking on oil stoves and keeping them out of sight. Daniel and Jerome, you can cook tonight. Luke, Kurt, Shawn, Robert, you guys set camp just back there in that grotto, out of sight of the barricade. Patrick, you come scouting with me."

"Yes sir!" Patrick snapped.

"The rest of you guys, don't be jealous." It was well known that Patrick was Isaiah's favorite. "You will all get a chance. That's what this whole trip is about, teaching you to spot signs of enemy activity up here. Now get going."

"Think there'll be an expedition?" Luke asked Daniel as the others waited for Luke to get the oil stove out from the bottom of his pack.

"Matt wouldn't say before he left," Daniel replied, "but I am sure that he was supposed to check out how the passes are higher up. They're just waiting to see how things are before setting out."

"So they'll go?" Kurt asked.

"You can bet on it," Daniel replied. "Ever see my mom like that?" Rebecca Hopes was his mother. "She has never been that upset. She's sure that we will starve if we don't get that freezer fixed before winter."

"Amos has to listen to her, doesn't he?" Jerome asked. "I mean he's the leader, but she's been doing the harvest for how long?"

"He'll listen," Luke said. "He's no dummy."

The next day, they took turns walking the approaches to the pass with Isaiah so he could explain what to watch for. He taught them how to distinguish the broken branches where he and Patrick had walked the night before from the natural deer trails that crisscrossed the pass.

Afterward, they took turns crawling up the approaches while the rest tried to spot them. The first to spot each man was given a point. The one to get the closest before being spotted was given ten points. The winner had no further responsibilities for the rest of the trip.

Not surprisingly, Patrick won. He got within twenty feet of the barricade by climbing high up one ridge and coming down at them from above. Luke had spotted him just moments before he rushed down. Luke came in second.

Finally, they built a permanent encampment on the near side of the pass. They built a lean-to, filled a metal footlocker with canned and dried goods they had brought, and built the most enormous bonfire any of them had seen. They were not allowed to light it, though. Since the radios had long since quit working, Amos and Isaiah had come up with this as a warning system. One guard up here could watch for signs of approach. Then they could light the already laid fire, which would be seen down at the ranch.

Less than two days after they returned, the rumors were confirmed. Another community-wide meeting was held, and Amos informed them that they had no choice but to send an expedition after supplies. Jacob Clayton, a military vet who had come up from one of the other camps years before, was selected as the leader.

"Time is imperative," Amos informed him. Amos gave him one week to choose a team of twelve men. They would leave the following week.

2

Expedition

A pale half-moon was poised over the jagged edge of the mountains high above Amy as she left the meeting. She watched as the moon sank toward the mountain, dark and heavy, like a tombstone. A sense of foreboding stole over her. *My father will be dead before this is over*, she thought and shivered.

"Should have brought your coat," Luke's voice said at her side. "Here, you can wear mine. I'm not cold." He passed his coat over. She shrugged it over her shoulders but didn't put it on.

"Thanks," she said, returning her gaze to the moon. The premonition, or whatever it had been, was gone, and the moon looked completely natural as it sunk behind the mountain.

"Aw, come on!" he chided, nudging her. "I mean, honestly, the first expedition out of the valley in over twenty years, and you're not even a little excited?"

How am I supposed to answer that? she thought. *Am I supposed to admit that I started having premonitions again? Dreaming of flat places, strange people, and Dad dying?*

She sighed. "I'm worried about Dad. I don't think he's up to this trip." Jacob had not yet decided who he would take, but it didn't matter. Marlin would be at the top of the list.

"Your dad's an ox." Luke replied. "No one will go after him. Besides, Patrick said he overheard Jacob and Amos discuss the possibility with his father. Says they plan on avoiding contact at all cost. They will try to scavenge what we need from abandoned towns and things."

"I know," Amy replied. "Dad told them that."

"You've known about this?" Luke replied shocked. "For how long?"

Amy just shrugged. "Amos has been talking about the possibility since the day after the lightning strike. He talked to Dad about it at length."

"And, of course, your dad talked to you," Luke grumbled.

Amy rolled her eyes. Luke went to every community meeting. He took pains to be involved in "adult" business. And yet his dad treated him like a kid. Amy ignored community politics, but they showed up on Marlin's doorstep, and she was invariably caught up in them, for better or worse.

"I didn't know he'd decided for sure until tonight, like everyone else," she said to placate him. "Besides, that's not what worries me. I don't believe the terrorists, the militia, or anyone is out there waiting for us."

Luke nodded. "You were right the other day, anyway. It

was mostly the environment. I reckon what's left down there are just a few villages like us, struggling to survive."

"My dad's health hasn't been good for a while, you know," Amy said. "This winter has been . . ."

"Hard. I know there have been a lot of bad colds and stuff."

"It's worse than that. Dad's been weak, weaker than I have ever seen him."

Luke snorted. At his weakest, her dad could outmatch anyone at the camp.

"He's always so short of breath, like he's been working too hard."

"Your dad does work too hard," Luke countered. "Always has."

"You don't understand, Luke. He's like that even in the morning."

"They'll look after him."

Amy snorted. "Yeah, right, those idiots."

Luke's eyes shone bright as he leaned in, his excitement barely contained. "Maybe there will be someone along who isn't an idiot," he whispered.

"Like who?"

"Like me."

"You!?" She exploded. "Yeah, right. They won't take any boys."

He looked hurt. "I am seventeen, nearly a man."

"No offense, but by their standards," she pointed back toward the community building, "not nearly."

"Daniel and I discussed this on the way back from our last trip up to the barricades," he went on. "They have to. What other choice do they have? After tonight, I'm sure of it. They want twelve men to go. Which twelve? Most of the men are too old. Isaiah Hall would be a given, but his knee . . . he was limping by the time we got back from the barricades. He could never take the hike."

He ticked them off on his fingers, "Larry Gatlin's sixty-five this year; he's too old. My dad's got two young daughters at home; they won't want to risk him. Same for Patrick's dad. They won't want family men, mark my words. They both have responsibilities around the ranch anyway. Shawn's dad took a nasty spill hunting two winters ago, and he hasn't walked the same since." He shook his head. "The point is they can't come up with twelve healthy men who can make the journey."

Amy stared at him. He was right. Everyone knew it, but no one ever talked about the hole. The Ranch had pre-blast originals, old men and women now. And they had the new generation, young men and women in their late teens. In between was a ragged hole, a testimony to the difficulty of the first few years.

Almost every family had one or two babies buried up in the ranch's small cemetery, died of influenza or simple starvation in those horrible first few winters. Other couples had been left sterile, temporarily or permanently, by the hardships.

"Anyway," Luke went on, "I think I have a fair chance of being selected. I am not as good at hand-to-hand combat as Patrick—he's sure to be in—but I am a better shot. It depends, of course, on just how many of us get chosen."

Amy had an image of herself spending the whole summer watching out the window for her father and her only friend. "Fine, be that way!" she yelled and stomped off.

Behind her she heard his faint "huh?" of surprise. If she allowed herself to look back, she was sure she would see his hurt expression. So she didn't look. She knew how much he wanted to contribute, to be part of something this big. Hell, if it came to that, who wouldn't want to get out of this valley? Who wouldn't want to see what was left of the world, the world they had only heard about but had never actually seen?

For a week, rumors ran wild. Every day at school, the boys got together to gossip. Jacob was making the rounds. Every household was host to quiet conversations between the men. Two questions hung in the air wherever he went. Who could be trusted? Who could be spared?

From a few phrases or sentences overheard, the boys carefully constructed their own lists. Old injuries were discussed and factored in. Families were counted; they surely wouldn't send anyone with young children. Ages were counted again and again.

All of the boys agreed on one thing. The ranch could not possibly spare twelve of the men. At least a couple of them were going. Patrick swaggered around like he had already been chosen, and no one dared contradict him. The others held their breath and prayed.

When the day came, it was a warm one. Larry and James Gatlin insisted on driving the sheep down into the shearing pens, even though they knew no shearing would get done that day. By noon, even they had given up any pretense of work and joined the throng gathered outside the community hall.

Jacob Clayton reported for duty just after noon. He

gave a short speech. He spoke of the need for experience versus the need for stamina. He spoke of the need for speed and stealth versus the need to carry as many supplies back as possible. Both issues required compromise.

He spoke of the strains on the ranch. Twelve men was a lot for a ranch that boasted barely forty adults altogether. The hardship for those who stayed behind, he said, would be nearly as great as for those who left.

The ranch had only four young families, Jacob reminded them. All the rest were either veterans from before the collapse and their remaining children, or youth not yet old enough to be wed. The ranch must be careful of sacrificing any of them. They were the ranch's hope. There was a silent cheer from the boys, for the implication was not lost on them.

Luke and Daniel had discussed the young men in detail. There was more to it than that. James Gatlin, Matthew Hopes, and Bobby Gamelson Jr. were hard workers and invaluable to the ranch. Liam O'Malley and Scott Callahan were worthless and untrustworthy. Jacob would not choose any of them.

Finally, after presenting all the same arguments that the boys had made over the last week, Jacob got down to the real business of offering his solution. He pulled the list of expedition members from his pocket and began to read.

First, after himself, was Marlin Beland. This was no surprise. In fact, Marlin himself hadn't even bothered to show up to hear the list read. Amy had, however. A fact that Luke noted.

Next was Larry Gatlin. His name had often come up and been hotly contested. A five-year veteran of the

Marines, he was in his sixties but still very fit.

He was native to this region and had practically run the farm by himself in the early years. He would have been indispensable, except for the fact that his son was almost his spitting image. Larry's youngest daughter was seventeen now. His son James had a two-year-old daughter, his first. Everyone knew who would be the bigger loss.

Next came Horace Manualson. He was mostly a given. His two sons were both dead. He was a mediocre worker around the ranch. He had no actual military experience, but it was well known that he had been one of the toughest street fighters the Klan had ever seen. This was one last chance to put that to work.

Then there was John McKurtz. Jerome McKurtz had been a founding member of Freedom Ranch. He had gone to prison on gunrunning charges a couple of years before the blast, leaving his wife and twelve-year-old son, John, for the ranch to care for.

John's own son, Jerome, named after his grandfather, had hoped desperately to be picked, despite being only fourteen years old. Now he would wait at home while his father went.

Next came Willie Jones, an old friend of Horace's. He was mildly retarded, but he was in good health, strong, and had no family to miss him.

Liam O'Malley was next. The twenty-year-old had a wife and one-year-old daughter, but it was generally agreed that they would not miss him much. He did little enough around the ranch that his work would not be missed either. In fact, the only thing the O'Malleys were noted for was their home-brewed beer. Since they drank the majority of it anyway, it would be no great loss. Besides, Mark had one very important thing going for him: he was undoubtedly the meanest man anyone had ever met, topping even his father in this. For once that might work to his advantage.

Then came Patrick Callahan, followed by Shawn Gamelson. The two gave each other high fives.

Finally Luke heard his own name called. He made a little victory gesture. Spying Amy's frown, he dropped it. He barely even heard the last two names as they were called out: Daniel Hopes and Kurt Derry.

Daniel patted Luke on the back in congratulations. "A good worker and a stable influence," Daniel's father had been telling anyone who would listen for days now.

Kurt was the only real shock. He cringed as people craned to look at him. It was clear he was as shocked to find his name on the list as they were.

Luke thought he could guess the reason for Kurt being included. Jacob and James Derry, Kurt's father, had been friends for years. They had grown up together in the foothills of these mountains.

James was wiry but strong. Those who fought with him knew him to be a cunning and ruthless warrior. But Luke had once heard Jacob tell his father that it was not always so. He had been nervous and high strung as a child. The years leading up to the collapse and the fighting during the first years had hardened James Derry. Jacob apparently thought this mission would do the same for James's son. Luke hoped it would be so, but he had his doubts.

Jacob told everyone they would have one week left to prepare. Then they would be leaving. Luke knew this was more for those staying than those going. Amos made sure there were rucksacks packed with tents, supplies and rations for an extended trip, all available at a moment's notice. After thirty years of waiting, others might have let their guard down, but not Amos.

Those remaining behind had so much more to do. This was the first such expedition in many years. Likely, it would be the last for as many. They had to make the most of it. Everyone was busy compiling lists of things they might need. Every request had to go through Amos. Most would, undoubtedly, be denied. The expedition would be severely limited as to how much it could carry. Even those requests that were accepted would have to be carefully prioritized.

Amy came over and gave Luke a weak smile and a half muttered congratulations. It was probably as close to an apology as he would get. He could understand her being upset now that he thought about it.

In the end, he was going as much for her as for himself. After this mission, his father would have no choice but to acknowledge that he was a man. Then he could get permission to start building his own house. Before the next summer was over, he and Amy could be wed and living in their own house. Surely that was worth his sacrifice this summer?

Amy wandered off, leaving Luke to celebrate with his friends. Hell, she'd have to get used to him being gone anyway.

She stopped and sighed. What was she going to do all summer with both her father and Luke gone? It would be quiet around their house.

Well, she'd find things to keep herself busy. With her dad gone, she'd be twice as busy with work anyway. She'd have to manage just about anything that took more than half a brain. She'd have to run the biodiesel still, keep the tractors running, and get the well pump back up. That was about the extent of the remaining technology now that the solar array was fried, but it was by no means the end of Marlin's responsibilities.

The shed next to Marlin's house contained the ranch's main smithy. Marlin and Larry took it in turns to work there. With both of them gone, it would pretty much be up to Amy. She could probably get James to help her on big jobs, but he would have double the responsibility with the sheep now too.

Theresa Deaton had been after Amy for a couple of months about blowing some new glassware. Jaime Hall wanted help with the kiln, as she had most of a winter's worth of ceramics that she hadn't been able to fire. She couldn't recruit Luke and Daniel to help dig clay from the neighboring valley, but maybe she and Jaime could handle it themselves.

Still lost in thought, Amy entered her house. She found her dad at the kitchen table, blowing his nose. He shoved the handkerchief into his pocket when he saw her, but not before Amy saw a flash of red against the white.

"What's wrong?" Amy demanded her eyes narrowing suspiciously.

"Sinus trouble." He shrugged. "Another damn cold."

"Bullshit."

He shrugged and looked away.

"Leukemia," she said.

Still looking away, he nodded.

"How long?" she demanded, wide-eyed.

"A while."

"Why didn't you say something? Did you even go to the doctor?" William Pritchard had served as a medic in the Army before the collapse. He was the closest thing they had to a doctor, and after thirty years, everyone had forgotten the difference.

"Nothing anyone can do," he muttered.

"You still could have said something."

"You worry enough as it is. It can't be changed."

Her eyes burned with unshed tears. "Damn it, you could have said something anyway."

"I didn't want to worry you," he repeated.

After a long time, she sat down at the table opposite him. She couldn't meet his gaze, not yet. She thought of the others, her mom for one. It was always the same with radiation-induced leukemia: the bad colds that just got worse, the nosebleeds, then bleeding elsewhere, and finally death. There was no cure. Even before the collapse, there had been no cure.

"Does anyone else know?"

"Just you."

"What about Jacob?"

"He'd have to take me anyway."

"Damn it! This trip could kill you!"

"I'm dying anyway. The ranch needs me."

Amy felt anger rising inside her. *The damn bastards, they don't deserve loyalty like that. They certainly wouldn't repay it. What right do they have to take Dad's last days?* She wanted him here and safe, not out there in god-knew-what sort of danger. Their precious supplies could go rot.

She looked at her father and bit back her tongue. She

couldn't voice what she was feeling; it would only hurt him. Besides, he knew how she felt.

She could only guess at his motives. Her father had a philosophy that was at once naïve and practical. He did what he did because he was the only one able to do it. Whether those who benefited from his labor were good or bad, appreciative or hostile, didn't even enter his mind.

"Harder! Again!" Isaiah barked.

"Yes sir!" Shawn barked back, leaping to his feet and striking out at Patrick. Patrick dodged the strike easily, and they continued to spar.

Isaiah nodded before returning to stalking the practice field. Everyone was training in earnest now. Luke was drilling Kurt in takedowns. Daniel was holding Bobby O'Malley off with a vigor he had never shown before. Now that several of them were going into action, everyone was taking their training serious.

If it weren't for my knee, I might be going as well, Isaiah grimaced. That couldn't be helped, but he was bound and determined that anything that went wrong would not be due to lack of preparation on his part. He was pushing them harder than ever and planned on continuing until the day they left.

His afternoon did not look so cheery. Jacob had asked him to give a refresher course for the older men. *Refresher course, my ass*. It had been twenty-eight years since the last military contact. With the exception of Jacob, himself, and Amos, no one attended the regular training sessions. Trying to get them all back up to speed in one week was not going to be easy.

* * *

Luke punched Kurt. Kurt sidestepped and swept Luke's leg. He was definitely better. He hesitated less. But he was still a long way from where Luke would trust him to be able to do it in combat.

Luke was just glad that he had worked up the courage to talk to Isaiah. He didn't want to question the arms master's strategy, but Kurt was going to be a serious weak link on this mission.

Kurt was just too small and weak to ever excel at Special Forces hand-to-hand combat drills. Luke had found a book in the ranch library, *Judo for Self-Defense*. He and his brother had been experimenting with it for much of last winter. He had talked Isaiah into letting him work with Kurt one on one, teaching him takedowns and throws.

"Do you think we will have to fight?" Kurt asked as he helped Luke to his feet.

"Honestly, no," Luke said. "But we have to be prepared. Really I don't think it's likely we will find much. Some ruins where we can scavenge what we need and be back."

"That's a relief," Kurt said. He never questioned Luke's knowledge in any matter. "That's one less thing to worry about."

"What else is there to worry about?" Luke asked as he closed in again. Kurt swept him to the ground.

"My dad's been going on about the end of the world again," Kurt muttered, embarrassed. It was generally believed that his father was slightly off his rocker. During the collapse, he had sincerely believed the end of the world was at hand (Luke knew this to have been a fairly common belief back then). He thought of the ranch as good Christians fighting the Anti-Christ.

When the world did not end, James Derry had been disappointed. He had expressed many times since that he feared the ranch had been found wanting. When drunk or in moments of deep despair, he declared loudly that the world *had* ended and that they were all in hell and just didn't know it. Luke shook his head.

"Don't worry. I'm sure we will find the world outside the valley," he said.

Kurt gave a sheepish grin and nodded. "You excited?" he asked.

"Yeah," Luke replied. He could barely contain his excitement. The only thing that marred it was Amy. He understood her being upset, but she had barely talked to him since the news had come out. They didn't have much time left together. Why couldn't she forget about herself for once?

"I'm scared," Kurt admitted, "but under that, I am excited too. Whatever is out there, it can't be worse than here, can it?"

The thought startled Luke. He had never thought about it like that. He took the ranch for granted. It just was; there was no other possibility. For Kurt, a scrawny boy with a half-crazed father, always picked on by Patrick, Shawn and the O'Malley boys, it must indeed be hell.

"Well, I think that should work," Marlin puffed as he hoisted the pump. "You want to hook her up?" He gently lowered the pump into a bucket of water while Amy went to attach the wires.

Since she had discovered his condition, Amy was noticing all sorts of things. He held the pump steady with one hand, but his face showed a slight strain. That would be unremarkable in anyone else, as the pump weighed some thirty pounds. Her dad, however, was something of a legend at the ranch for his strength. He had been relieved of most of the farming and gardening duties because he was too hard on tools. Several of the stronger men had snapped spade handles working in the rocky soil of the valley. Marlin had snapped a blade.

She attached the wires, and the pump rumbled to life. Water shot out of its top. Amy shared a relieved look with her father. "Well, that's one thing you won't have to worry about while I'm gone," he said as she killed the connection. "We'll get Luke to help us put it back down later today."

He wiped at his face, which was bright red. "I'll take it up to the pump house," she said, "you head home. Elisabeth will probably have lunch done by now."

Marlin gave her a pained look. "Probably chicken noodle soup again," he muttered. Amy returned a stern look.

She didn't care what he did or did not tell Jacob, Amos, or any of the others. Elisabeth was another matter. She would not let him leave without telling her the truth about his condition. He hadn't wanted to, but Amy hadn't given up.

Elisabeth had taken to following her father around fearfully, constantly offering him chicory coffee and chicken soup, like these small comforts could keep leukemia at bay. Marlin tried his best not show how the extra attention bothered him. He kept busy packing and repacking tools and going over the ever-growing list of things the ranch could use.

* * *

"Amy!"

Amy was halfway back to her house when her sister's cry interrupted her thoughts. She ran the rest of the distance in moments.

Her sister was out in front of their house, bending over her dad. He was on his knees, struggling to rise. His face was white behind the dark beard. His beard and lips were specked with red, and he struggled to breath.

"He just started coughing and went all weak," Elisabeth said. "I saw him go down, and I ran out here."

"Let's get him inside," Amy said after a moment's deliberation. Marlin nodded his agreement. With one daughter under each arm, they helped him to his feet. Amy was shocked at how easy it was. She had always thought of him as a burly man, but the thin body under his overalls showed just how sick he was.

They got him inside and propped him up in his bed. Elisabeth brought him some warm broth. "Dr. Pritchard?" she asked.

Marlin started to shake his head no and began coughing again.

"Yes," Amy said firmly.

Jacob came by later that afternoon. Dr. Pritchard had come to see Marlin and given him some herbs, mainly mint for his breathing. He had spoken quietly to Amy and Elisabeth in the kitchen. He left them a small bottle of valerian root tincture. It would ease Marlin's pain. There was nothing else that could be done.

The herbs helped, and Marlin was sitting propped up in bed fingering the list he had made Amy bring him. Jacob sat stiffly at his bedside. Amy sat in the hall and listened.

"I'm sorry," Marlin said as soon as Jacob entered.

"Good God, man," Jacob replied. "You're not the one who should be sorry, after all you have done for us. If there's anything we can do . . ."

"There's not," Marlin muttered.

"I know," Jacob sighed. "And, unfortunately, this couldn't have come at a worse time."

"Give me a few days," Marlin breathed.

Damn him, Amy thought angrily. *A few days and he'll be . . .* she broke off, not even wanting to think it. *He'll never be in shape to go,* she finished to herself.

Jacob apparently had the same thought. "Not a chance, Marlin. Sorry, but we have no time for pleasant lies. You won't be out of this bed this summer, if ever."

"I'm sorry," Marlin said even quieter.

"It's nobody's fault. We will do what we have always done. We'll make do. You give me the list, and we'll do what we can."

"That'll never work. You need someone who knows the stuff."

"I'm sure whoever we find to bargain with will be able to handle that."

"What about scavenging? I thought we were going to avoid contact if possible."

"So I had hoped," Jacob said. "But plans change."

Marlin shook him off. "No matter. You still need someone who knows the stuff. Even if we find friendly people, we may still have to scavenge. Besides, they may not have what we want, but something else that will work. Someone on the mission needs to know the technology well enough to make a judgment call."

"Don't you think I know that?" Jacob shot back. There

was a pause while he took a deep breath. "I know this will make my mission hard, maybe impossible. But you are too sick, and that's that. There is no way you can come."

"And you know that's not what I'm talking about," Marlin snarled. There was the sound of rustling as he tried to rise. He started coughing and fell back. There was a long uncomfortable pause as he fought to catch his breath. "I taught her everything I know," he said, his voice husky.

Amy went cold as she realized what he was talking about. *Me? On the mission?* Ever since the mission was proposed, she thought about the men leaving the valley and her behind. She imagined working alone in the garage, she and Elisabeth alone in this house, watching out the window for their father to return. She even thought of herself sitting alone in the evenings missing Luke's company. Never once did she think of *going* on the mission.

"This is a military mission," Jacob shouted, slapping his hand on the bedside table for emphasis. "It is no place for a little girl."

Amy bristled. She had dark thoughts of bursting in and yelling at Jacob. Her father beat her to it. "Don't you think I know it's dangerous? Don't you think I would do anything to spare her? Don't you think I have prayed every night for the strength to last long enough?" Marlin broke off as he went into another coughing spell.

"Of course, of course," Jacob said.

Amy didn't hear much for a while after that. Her mind was spinning. Now she understood why her father had tried so hard to hide his illness. She was ashamed of his goodness, his self-sacrifice.

Why had it never occurred to her? It was so obvious, once she thought about it. Luke and Daniel had worked out as much weeks ago. They knew their fathers were no longer able to leave the ranch for an extended mission. They were too old, or they had too many responsibilities. This mission would belong to the next generation, and they had few enough of them to spare.

"I can't approve of this, Marlin," Jacob continued when Marlin had recovered somewhat. "The risks, the resources we would have to use to keep a woman safe out there . . ."

Marlin controlled his anger better after that. He knew as well as Amy how these people felt about women in general, and Amy specifically. He never fought it head on, the way Amy always did. He let Jacob argue. He did not refute a single point. In the end, it made no difference. They had no other choice.

Amy looked down as she heard Jacob rise to go. The knitting she was supposedly doing in the hall had not grown any longer the whole time she had listened. It was a hopeless mess anyway. She never seemed quite able to get it right. Everything came out lopsided.

The door opened, and Jacob came out. He sank down on a bench opposite Amy. "I'm sorry about your dad," he said. "Unfortunately, it doesn't change my mission. I have a ranch to save. I guess I'll be needing you to come with us. I know, I know," he said to the protest that never came, "there will be risks. A woman . . . well, we will do our absolute best to take care of you, see that you come to no harm. Marlin says he can fill you in on what he needs and all that."

Amy stared at him, fighting the anger. He never asked her, for one thing. Then he implied that she would be too scared to go, that they would have to take care of her. Finally he implied that she didn't know what they needed, that she'd have to ask her father. Hell, she'd done most of the work on that damn list.

Her father coughed weakly in the next room. That drained the anger from her. Her father was dying. Still, he remained faithful to his old philosophy. He did what was needed because he was the only one who could do it. Now it was Amy's turn, for him. "I'll be ready," she answered.

After Jacob left, she went into her father's room. "I'm sorry it had to come to this," he said as she entered.

"I can take care of myself," she replied, harsher than she had intended.

"Thank you."

"For what?"

"I heard you in the hall. Jacob may not have realized it, but I know how hard it is for you to help them."

I'm not doing it for them, I'm doing it for you, she wanted to say. "You're welcome," she said. Then she brightened. "Don't worry, look what I've done." She presented him an old mason jar of clear liquid.

He sniffed it. "That's your solution," he joked, "taking up drinking?"

She laughed. "Well, I figured there was almost half a year's worth of corn thawing and rotting up in the freezer and we had that old still . . ."

He roared with laughter, his old self for one minute as he caught on. That started another coughing fit, but he was still smiling when it was done. "And we have that old Jeep out back, just waiting for some fuel," he finished.

"See, we'll be gone less than a week," she said.

* * *

"Haven't seen you in a while," Luke greeted Amy, a wary look in his eye.

It might not have been apparent to anyone else, but Amy could see the hurt in his eyes. What had she done now? She shrugged. "So how's the planning going?"

"It's going," he evaded. He pulled her a little way away from the other boys, who were all waiting outside the communal hall for Jacob. "Look, I'm sorry. I don't want to leave you alone. I don't want to be away from you. I have to go; the ranch needs me. I am sorry there isn't some way for us to be together this summer."

Is that what he is upset about? Well, then again, that should have been obvious. The last thing she had said to him was just that. She'd gotten over it, of course, but then she found out about her father and that had pushed everything else out of her mind. The mission was only two days away, and they hadn't seen each other in all that time.

"Oh well," she said punching him lightly on the arm, "I guess I'll just have to come with then."

He stared at her like she was nuts. He was trying to decide whether she was joking or not. In spite of everything, she laughed aloud.

Luke's expression changed to sheer disbelief as Jacob approached and said, "Good morning, Amy, I am glad you could make it. We will be getting started right away if that's okay."

"Yes sir," she replied with a sarcastic salute.

"Her!?" Shawn exploded. "But she's, she's . . . a girl!"

"Thanks for noticing," Amy replied with a sneer.

"That's enough, soldier," Jacob warned before Shawn could reply. Jacob was acting like a man trapped between rabid raccoons. Since last night, he had come to the conclusion that he was going to have to get along with Amy, somehow. Before the meeting and during his introduction, he had gone out of his way to treat her respectfully. Now the reaction of his men was about to undo all his work.

"Sir, have you considered the ramifications of a girl—" Patrick spoke, calmer than Shawn, but still very hostile.

"Yes," Jacob cut him off. "Just as I have considered the ramifications of not taking Amy."

Amy glanced across at the older men. Larry's face showed sadness; he and Marlin had been friends for years. Horace and John looked like they had swallowed a bug. Willie's face was its usual unreadable blank stare. Mark O'Malley showed open revulsion. He was the next to speak. "But her, of all people."

"That's enough!" Jacob roared. "This is a military operation. I am in charge. Anyone want to question that?" No one did. "Right. It is my decision, and we are taking Amy, understand?"

"Yes sir!" Luke threw out a little too fast and loud. Amy was glad of the support. Daniel followed suit, and Larry even gave her a slight nod as he added his voice.

The rest of the men mumbled "Yes sir" sullenly.

"Good," Jacob said. "Then we can get down to business. We leave tomorrow, so this is our last chance to discuss the mission. We've got some good news as well." Jacob swallowed nervously as he realized that could be taken wrong. When Amy showed no sign of reacting he went on. "Amy, do you want to brief us about this Jeep of yours?"

* * *

"I'm sorry about your dad," Luke said as they left the community hall. The meeting had lasted all morning and when it picked up after lunch it would probably last all afternoon as well. Amy only understood part of what they were discussing. She didn't understand the point. They discussed various strategies for dealing with any number of situations they were unlikely to even face.

"Thanks," she said. "Come up for lunch. Elisabeth always makes too much anyway, and I am sure Dad would like to see you before we leave."

He nodded his agreement. As they rounded the corner, Amy heard several of the others talking.

"You don't think it's a good idea, do you?" Daniel was asking someone.

"It will be bad luck," Kurt replied, his voice sullen. Amy felt betrayed by his lack of support. She had always liked Kurt. "Dad says the mission is cursed as it is. He'll not like this." *That explained a lot.*

"Oh your dad's daft," Daniel said. "He thinks everything is cursed."

"Maybe it is. Maybe we are all doomed."

"Oh, you're just mad because we're taking a woman along and you are still the weak one," Mark laughed. "Look at it this way, boys, it will be kind of nice to have some around to cook and clean for us." Shawn and Patrick both laughed.

"Maybe more than just cook," Shawn leered.

"That grease monkey?" Patrick replied, "Yuck!"

Amy went red but refused to acknowledge that she'd heard any of it. Luke looked away uncomfortably. When they were out of earshot, she exploded. "Those assholes! Who the hell do they think they are? Do they think I wanted to go on their precious mission? The whole damn lot of them could rot, for all I care. If it weren't for Dad, I'd tell them to their faces. And if they think for one second I am going along to cook and clean . . ."

"They're just being immature," Luke said. "Ignore them."

"Most of them are older than you," Amy shot back.

"I know. They just think that they have to talk like that to be considered men."

"And being a woman means putting up with it?"

"No, of course not. They don't understand the great American way of life, honor and decency and all that."

Amy rolled her eyes. Luke looked hurt. "Sorry," she mumbled. "I am glad you don't feel the need to act like a baboon. And if it's any consolation, now I am glad that you were chosen." He smiled and nodded.

When they got back to Amy's house and told Elisabeth what they had heard the other boys saying, her sister was direct. "If they expect you to cook for them," she said, "they have never had your cooking."

"When you get back . . ." Marlin trailed off, not wanting to give voice to the pleasant lie.

Amy stared back, tears in her eyes. Looking at her father, she knew he wouldn't last a week. As much as it would hurt her to watch it, she hated to leave him now even more.

She fell into his arms, crying. In the end, she wiped away her tears and said an ambiguous goodbye, leaving the worst unsaid. She knew she would never see him alive again.

Luke gave her a sympathetic pat on the back, which she

shrugged off. He had come up early to help load her tools into the Jeep, as well as the supplies the men had brought up yesterday. Luke and she had attached a small flatbed this morning for the men to ride on. It would be slow going. Hell, down here in the valley, they could walk as fast as she could safely drive. Farther up in the mountains, it would be a different story. They had chosen this valley carefully. The approach was at a high altitude and treacherous. Even without heavy packs, it would be torturous on foot.

They made their way slowly toward the center of the community. A cheer went up as they rounded the corner and followed the now almost invisible line of the gravel road.

The community hall had been decorated for the occasion with two faded American flags. Two barrels and a couple of rough-hewn planks had been commandeered for a makeshift bandstand. It was small, but then again the dignitaries of the ranch amounted to Amos and Minister Posch, both of whom fit on it fine. The rest of the expedition was already gathered for inspection. Luke leapt from the passenger's seat and ran to join them while Amy parked the Jeep.

Amos called them to attention. The men all snapped into position with obvious pride. Amy stood at the end of the line, unsure what she should do. No one seemed to being paying her much attention anyway.

Amos reiterated the problem the ranch faced and Jacob's mission. Jacob called out, "Orders received, sir! We will do our best, sir!" He saluted. The men all followed suit.

Then Minister Posch stood and intoned a short prayer,

asking for God's blessing on the mission and on the men who were about to "serve the cause."

Amos pulled out an old boom box, wired directly into an old solar panel. It was her own handiwork, she noted, as he tilted the panel toward the sun. A scratchy rendition of the "Star-Spangled Banner" played while the men loaded onto the Jeep's trailer.

Elisabeth broke from the crowd and ran forward to hug Amy. Amy felt a momentary pang of guilt. As bad as it was to be going, how much worse was it for Elisabeth? To be left at home with a dying father?

Scott Callahan Junior was waiting for them at Barricade Pass. A look of poorly disguised scorn passed between him and his brother Patrick. The ranch did not have two more different brothers. Everyone knew why Scott wasn't going, despite being young, strong, and unmarried. He had refused. Nobody ordered him about, he maintained.

He lived in a tiny shack on the edge of the village that he took over two years ago to get away from his father. The only person that had anything to do with him was Daniel's older sister, Ruth. The two talked about building a house in one of the neighboring valleys and having nothing to do with the ranch.

Daniel's father, Robert, had finally made peace between Scott and the ranch. Scott was taking over sentry duty at Barricade Pass for the summer. In return, Robert gave him two axes, a maul, and a crosscut saw. Robert would join him at the pass several times a week, and they would harvest logs from the adjoining valley. By fall, they should have enough for a house.

Scott had lain four rough-cut logs against the barricade

on either side, to serve as ramps for the Jeep. Amy drew a deep breath, aligned the wheels, and drove slowly over.

She stared down the trail. The road had been well-packed gravel years ago. Now, it was almost all overgrown with grass and weeds. It served one essential function though: it still cut a path through what otherwise would be impenetrable forest. The rich, old forest had been all but destroyed in the ecological disaster. Now, thirty years later, a thick scrub forest of new growth had erupted.

This first valley was shallow and short. They were soon rising again. The next pass was much higher, well above the tree line. The altitude of the second pass was enough to make it difficult for the average person to breathe well. It was here that the Jeep would be its most useful.

As they reached the peak, Amy's head swam. The Jeep sputtered, and she remembered with a jolt that combustion engines took oxygen too. Then they crested into the pass, and the road level out. They came out the other side, and she stopped, looking down on a world she had never visited before.

Hundreds of feet below them, she could see the tree line. It seemed the forest stretched out forever. A line of lower mountains blocked her view of the plains that she knew lay below. For that, she was glad. Already it was too much. A lifetime of having the steep walls of their little valley on either side made this view dizzying.

"God, I hope the brakes work," she muttered as she drove slowly over the edge and downward.

The rest of the day passed in a tortuous haze. The Jeep lurched over huge potholes and rain-cut divots with bone-jolting force. She lay heavily on the ancient brakes, trusting neither them nor the pockmarked road. Once they made it down into the tree line, she had to stop frequently for the men to clear dead falls from the road. She wasn't sure what worried her more—the way the temperature gauge rose or the way the fuel gauge dropped.

It was mid-afternoon when Jacob called the first halt. Amy gratefully let the Jeep roll to a stop. She popped the hood and started to rummage through her tools.

"Whatcha going to cook us, missy?" Shawn called out as he climbed wearily off the trailer.

"I am not your cook!" Amy yelled, brandishing a wrench. Shawn took a step back.

"Enough!" Jacob barked. "Put down that wrench," he told Amy before turning on Shawn. "Another comment like that, and you will be doing to cooking for the rest of the mission, understand?"

"Yes sir," Shawn growled.

"Besides," Jacob continued as he pulled a bag from the back of the Jeep, "This one's on me. MREs," he declared. "We need to make time so I talked Amos out of most of our remaining emergency rations."

"MREs," Horace said, "Meals Ready to Eat. Thirty years old and as good as the day they were packed."

"More than thirty years." Larry grimaced. "They were almost ten years old when we got them. And they were awful the day they were packed." Larry had served in the Marines and spoke from experience.

"MREs kept many a soldier alive in the field," Jacob told him. "Soldier's best friend."

Larry's dim view of MREs was not shared by many. For most of the younger men, MREs were the stuff of legend. They had grown up listening to the old men talk of their days fighting, complaining of the many hardships they had endured. Now was their chance. Come what may, they would have earned their right to tell their own grandiose stories of their days serving the cause.

After passing out MREs to the men, Jacob approached Amy with two packages and a battered case. "Let's talk a minute," he said.

Leading her away from the men, he handed her one of the meals. He sat down with a groan. "Damn, that was one bumpy ride," he said. "Pardon the language, Miss."

"I've heard worse."

Jacob laughed. "Yeah, Marlin can cuss a blue streak. I forgot you weren't brought up like most womenfolk."

"I was brought up just fine," she retorted.

"Sorry, I meant no insult," he said, placating. He pulled a battered map from the tattered case. He laid it out on the ground. "Any idea where we are?"

"None," Amy shrugged, looking at the map.

"Everything has changed so much, I can't be sure," Jacob replied and then chuckled. "Well, the mountains haven't changed. We are somewhere between here and here." He pointed.

Amy measured the distance with her fingers, the way her dad had taught her. "Shit," she said.

"Now just because you know how to cuss, doesn't mean I approve," Jacob warned.

"But that means we have only come about twenty miles. We have used almost half the fuel already. We will be out before we reach . . . anywhere."

"Shit," he replied. "I mean, I see your point." He stared at the dark shadows of the forest. Already they were creeping forward. Evening would be short this side of the pass. "Well, that's why I wanted your opinion." He shook his head. "That pass was wicked. I don't think we could walk it, not with packs anyway. What are the chances of finding fuel down below?" he asked.

"Slim to nil," she replied. "Dad always said they were running out when he came up here. I wouldn't count on more."

"Even if we did find some," Jacob went on, "we'd have to pack it back to the Jeep. No, I can't risk it. We need the Jeep to get back over that pass, and we shouldn't need it on any of the lower trails. We leave it here."

"You mean go on foot?"

"We knew it would come to that sooner or later. I guess it just came sooner," he said.

He stood up and went to the others. "Listen up, everyone," he called. "We camp here tonight. Tomorrow, we continue on foot."

"What!?" several voices exploded together.

"You heard me," he repeated. "We go on foot. You all knew it would come eventually. Well, it has come early."

"Why?" Mark retorted angrily. "I thought we were taking the Jeep."

"Jeep's only got enough fuel to make it back over that pass. Unless you would like to lug all the supplies we need back over on foot, we need to leave the Jeep now."

"Why didn't she bring more fuel?" Patrick wanted to know.

"I made all I could," Amy retorted.

"Maybe we can get more down below," Luke suggested.

"Maybe we can trade her for more fuel," Patrick commented to Shawn.

"The decision has been made!" Jacob shouted. "One

day and the discipline is already going to hell! Kurt, start unloading the packs. Shawn, Patrick, you get the tents. Get to work everyone!" He stomped back to his map and went back to studying it.

The men grumbled as they started setting camp. Shawn kept shooting her dirty looks.

"I don't mind walking," Willie said. "That ride was rough."

As soon as the packs were unloaded, Amy covered the Jeep and the trailer with a canvas tarp. She had to search for rocks and sizable logs to hold the tarp down so the wind wouldn't blow it off.

Amy spent the whole evening repacking her tools. She could take only the essentials. They would have to be divided up evenly between all the packs. She knew that the men would begrudge her every ounce.

It was full dark before she was done. She went straight to her solitary pup tent. She collapsed on her bedroll thinking that she would have to remember to thank Luke for setting it up for her. No one else would have.

When Luke's voice woke her in the morning, she was too groggy and sore to be thankful. Clouds had rolled in overnight, and it was cold. She could feel moisture in the air. *It's going to be a horrible day for walking*, she thought as she collapsed her tent. They ate a cold meal of yet another MRE. Whatever the men thought, Amy was not impressed with the rations at all.

Jacob ordered rain ponchos out. He was quickly vindicated. They had barely shouldered their packs when the first drizzle started.

They continued their winding descent along the road.

According to the map, there should have been a more direct route. The impenetrable scrub did not invite them to find it. "We'll get nowhere lost," Jacob said.

Thunder rolled around them, and lightning lit the otherwise dull day. They plodded along, their spirits sinking. *At least we aren't up on the pass*, Amy thought. Lightning could be dangerous high up in the mountains.

The drizzle grew to a steady rain, and their feet became soaked in the growing puddles. The intensity of the storm kept increasing as the day went on. By early afternoon, the winds began to grow fierce. Lunch was dry granola that Larry's wife had made. They walked on.

Jacob tried to keep their spirits up by telling them stories. Stories that Amy was sure he thought were motivational, though more often than not, she couldn't see the point.

The ponchos worked well against the rain itself. But as the wind grew worse, it whipped the edges of the ponchos and blew moisture under them. Amy was soon soaked and cold.

The intensity of the storm continued to grow. They walked closer to the edge of the woods, looking for shelter, until Jacob yelled at them. "It is dangerous to be under trees in this wind."

So they plodded on making what progress they could, sticking close enough to the trees to block out the worst of the wind, but always keeping an eye out for falling branches.

The storm did not abate as night fell. Fearful of getting lost in the dark, Jacob found the most sheltered spot he could and called a halt. They huddled together in a narrow gully, struggling to keep their ponchos both over and under them. It was the wettest and coldest night Amy had ever experienced.

Jacob passed out more MREs. Amy was starved after the long day's march, but she grimaced at the package. The crackers were soggy as soon as they were opened, and there was no hope of heating the main dish.

Patrick grumbled as he spooned cold, wet, chipped beef into his mouth. It was the only attempt at conversation. Jacob sat slightly apart from the others. He had nothing motivational left to say. If anyone went to complain, he gave them such a sour look that they stopped.

The storm ended around midnight. By that time, it was too dark and too wet to unpack the tents. They slept were they were, in a cold, huddled mass. Despite exhaustion, Amy found sleep elusive. She stared off into the night, feeling miserable. Finally, the monotony as much as anything lulled her to sleep.

When she woke up, she was greeted by a vast, shimmering wonderland. *It might even be pretty*, she thought angrily, *from inside a nice warm bed*. Heavy drops of water clung everywhere. Amy shook the worst of it from her hair and stood slowly. She had never been so stiff in her whole life. Her legs were asleep and bore her weight numbly. Her back ached, and her head hurt. Her legs began to burn with pins and needles as life returned to them. She moaned and began to rub them.

"Think it's bad?" Horace muttered unsympathetically. "Try it at my age."

Even the young men, who only a day ago had spoken romantically about the soldier's life, now grimaced as another round of MREs were passed out by Daniel.

"Breakfast in fucking bed," Larry growled as he took

his.

For Amy, hunger had overcome taste. She ate quickly without relish. When everyone was done, Jacob ordered packs made ready.

"Walking will loosen us up and dry us out," he told them.

It has done no such thing, Amy decided as she splashed through the umpteenth ankle-deep puddle. It was nearly noon, and after four hours of walking, she was sore and tired. No one else seemed to be in any better shape. Even Mark and Patrick were so worn out that they forgot to be mean to her. Shawn, possibly not even realizing who she was, had even muttered "'scuse me" when he bumped into her.

Shortly after noon, they came upon an open meadow. The ground rose slightly, and the sun shone on drying grass.

"This is as dry as we are likely to find," Jacob said as he lowered his pack wearily. "We break early and dry out. Let's set camp."

There was a collective sigh of relief as they all lowered their packs. Luke gathered the driest firewood he could find and, with the aid of some fire starters from his pack, managed to get a blaze going.

Amy cursed when she discovered her pack had leaked. She heard many of the others cussing. It had been a common enough problem. She managed to find a set of clothes in the center that was only slightly damp. It was a big improvement over what she had on. She walked a ways into the woods to change.

When she returned, she found that Daniel had taken over fire duty. He had extracted his cook gear, and he and

Larry were working on the first hot meal they had in what seemed like forever.

Luke was setting up his dome tent. Amy cursed again silently. She meant to set his tent up for him, in return for the other night. She was sorry she didn't get back sooner. She went to help him finish.

"Wow, that was sure some storm," he said as she approached. He seemed to be the only one whose spirit hadn't been lost.

"You could say that again," she groused, though she felt better despite herself. "That is, if you are totally insane. I'd say that was the most miserable experience of my life."

"Sure, but think: it'll be a great story to tell the grandkids."

"Grandkids?" Amy snorted. "Sure, Luke, when you have grandkids, I'll come over and tell them the story of the time their granddad got rained on."

Luke blushed and looked away. He didn't speak at all while they finished setting up the tent. Afterward, he mumbled thanks and walked off. He spoke only briefly during dinner.

I don't know what's gotten into him, Amy thought sourly. *Sometimes he can be as moody as, well, as Mom always said I was.* She finally decided there was just no explaining some people and left him by the fire.

The next couple of days went more smoothly. The weather was clear, and the sun was warm. Every night, they laid wet clothes over tree limbs and bushes. By morning, they would be that much drier. They marched through a thick pine forest that had slowly replaced the scrub.

They were still in the mountains, and the road wound over hills and valleys. Despite the occasional climb, their course was generally down. The road often wound back almost on itself, so that at times, it felt like they were making no progress at all.

It was the third day before they encountered their first solid landmark. It was the broken remnants of a bridge across a swift-flowing river. Jacob called a halt for lunch and then sat down a ways from everyone else to consult his map. After a while, he rose and approached them.

"Right then, we have a couple of problems, men," he glanced in Amy's direction, "and ladies, no disrespect."

"The first problem is no doubt apparent: we have to cross this river. We had hoped the bridge would still be serviceable, but obviously it's not. We didn't expected this to be a problem either way, since as far as Amos or I could recall the river wasn't deep."

"Usually no more than knee deep," Larry agreed. "Used to wade in here fishing when I was a youth."

"Well, maybe that's usually true, but the rains have changed things, no doubt."

"And the spring melt farther up," Larry reminded him.

"Anyway, we are going to have to send someone across with a line and make a rope bridge. It'll have to be one of the older men; you younger guys never got a chance to learn how to swim. We didn't have anywhere at the ranch to teach you. No, Luke," he added to the raised hand, "this is not something you can learn from a book."

"Practiced in the tub too," Luke muttered as he lowered his hand, disappointed. Amy had to fight down a giggle at the thought of the gangly Luke flapping his arms trying to swim in a tiny porcelain tub.

"Maybe we can wade?" Patrick asked. "Looks shallow enough."

"That current is strong; you'll get pulled off your feet in no time. Then you have to know what you're doing," Horace warned. "Better be me or Larry. I was a good swimmer once."

"Consider yourself volunteered," Jacob told him. "Good, but now that's the simple problem. According to plans, we had hoped to reach this far in the Jeep the first day."

There was muttering and scowls in Amy's direction.

"Stop that!" Jacob roared at Shawn and Mark. "The decision to leave the Jeep was mine, not hers. Besides, it doesn't matter. Amos and I first planned this mission without the Jeep, and we should have reached this place the second day at the latest. A well-conditioned soldier should be able to hike twenty miles in a day. Maybe down below, we'll get there." He trailed off.

The truth, Amy thought, was that several of his 'well-conditioned soldiers' were well past their prime, and several more were just plain lazy. Granted, she was sore as hell and didn't begrudge a single break, but at least she didn't whine about it like Mark.

"The last time we came down this road, we could drive along at fifty miles an hour," Jacob continued. "We knew it'd be worse now, but we had no idea how bad. Skirting dead falls, boulders in the road, we've been delayed. It might get better the farther we go, or it might get worse."

He added, "If it gets better, great. But at this rate, we are still at least a couple of weeks from any civilization. I am not sure we have the rations for a trip that long."

"Damn it!" Larry exploded. "Surely you'd realized

that! Why didn't you or Amos consult with someone who grew up around here? I hiked around here all the time as a kid. I could've told you it was going to take three weeks of hard slogging to get down to the nearest town."

"Three weeks!" Mark exploded. "And three weeks back? Damn, I didn't think we'd be out here that long."

"Yes, we did realize it would take that long," Jacob bristled, "but what choice did we have? The ranch only had so many rations to spare. Besides, even if we had a whole barn full, we could only carry so much. These packs are heavy as it is, and they'll be heavier still with supplies."

He paused and stared off into space a moment. "You see, the thing is, Amos and I are hoping that we don't have to go quite so far. There's another ranch not that far off."

"Another ranch!?" Patrick howled.

"It was a need-to-know basis," Jacob said. "The fewer people who knew the locations of the others the better."

"You mean there're more?" Shawn gaped.

"Of course, dummy," Luke said.

"And how do you know?" Jacob asked.

Luke shrank under his gaze. "Kind of obvious, isn't it?" he replied. "After all, Amos always talks about the movement, how there were thousands in our cause. Forty some people at the ranch can't be all that's left."

Larry laughed. "Can't get anything past that one, Jacob."

Shawn turned on him. "You knew too?"

Larry just rolled his eyes. "All of us older guys knew," he said. "We helped set things up, remember? Of course, none of us knew the locations. I am glad there's another ranch close. Maybe we can avoid meeting any unfriendlies at all. Besides, it gives me more faith in old Amos." He nodded to Jacob. "Sorry for expressing any doubts earlier, sir."

Jacob accepted the apology with a curt nod. "Amos figures that if the other group is still operational, we will be able to barter for most of what we need. If they've been compromised, aren't there, they may still have hidden supply stashes we can use.

"They are still a week or so away, and even in the best case scenario, they will not have everything we need, so we'll have to go on. They'll certainly not have the technical stuff. Our primary hope was to be able to get more rations for the deeper mission.

"I still hope to do that. We did make some plans for if that was not possible. I thought we could live off the land, hunt as we go." He shook his head. "But I haven't seen any sizable game this whole trip."

"In these thick woods you won't either," Larry replied. "Deer could be three feet away and unless you're lucky you'd never know it."

"I saw a couple of squirrels yesterday," Kurt said.

"Right, but don't go wasting precious ammo on anything that small. We may need that ammo soon enough."

"I got a sling," Daniel said, "and I am pretty good with it."

"Good lad. Keep it out," Jacob said. "We are going to have to forage. It will slow us down even more, but it beats starving."

"I wonder if we can find some acorns," Shawn said, thinking of survival classes.

Patrick rapped him on the head. "Wrong season, moron."

Several people chuckled while Shawn blushed. Horace reached over and rapped Patrick on the head. "These are pine trees, moron."

Patrick was halfway to standing, his fists up, before he caught himself. He sat down blushing.

This trip might be worth it, Amy thought grimly, *to see that bully put in his place.*

Kurt took his turn at fixing a noon meal from their dwindling supplies while the rest watched Horace's progress across the river. He had waded over halfway across and was chest deep before the current took him. He swam clumsily and reached the far bank only a few meters downstream.

After that it was a simple matter to throw him ropes across the river. He tied three to various trees to make a V. After their meal, they crossed the crude bridge. Amy fought nausea the whole way. It was only her determination to not show any weakness in front of the guys that kept her going.

She noted with satisfaction that both Daniel and Kurt had difficulty with the crossing, and it took a great deal of prompting by Horace to get Willie to cross at all.

As they continued on their way, the path leveled out and the trees began to thin. They crested a low rise, and the trees stopped altogether. They looked out over a vast sea of green.

3

Death on the Plains

"A bright clear sky over a plain so wide that the rim of the heavens cut down on it around the entire horizon . . . Bright, clear sky, today, tomorrow, and for all time to come."

Everyone turned and looked at Luke.

"It's from *Giants in the Earth*," he said sheepishly. Everyone continued to stare at him. "My favorite book," he added.

"Oh, right," Shawn drawled.

"Short grass prairie," Larry said as everyone's eyes were drawn back to the vast panorama before them. "Never thought I would see it again."

Countless miles of knee-high grass and a vast blue sky stretched before them. Amy felt her breath leave her. Her entire life had been spent within steep valley walls. This openness was both exhilarating and frightening. You could see for miles. She felt small and exposed.

The grass achieved something the forest did not. It completely obliterated the road. The gravel made poor soil, so the grass grew less robust, leaving a ghost-like impression.

"Damn," Mark said, "anyone else feel like we are the only ones left?"

"It always felt that way out here," Larry said with a sigh. "I used to long for it, this solitude. Not anymore." He laughed dryly. "You know what's funny? This is called the high country."

Even though they had come only a couple of miles from the river, Jacob called a halt while he consulted his map.

"There's good news and bad news," he told them as they prepared to embark. "The bad news is the map is pretty well useless for a while now. I'd swear this is too early to be leaving the forest, but who knows? Maybe things have changed. Anyway, the good news is we shouldn't need the map. Our next destination isn't on it anyway. We head due east."

They trekked on into a sea of green. Amy soon realized that it was not just green. The short growth boasted a dizzying assortment of plants and flowers. What looked from the distance as a bleak monotony of green was close up an array of colors. Black-eyed Susans, blue chicory flowers, yellow dandelions, and a few taller, purple coneflower were among the few that she could name. There were many more that she could not.

The second thing that Amy soon discovered was that the land was not nearly as flat as it appeared. There were gullies and depressions. The land rose and fell in long slow hills. It was as if the land were a sea with its waves frozen solid.

They trekked on for three days without seeing anything bigger than a bumblebee. Then one day, they crested a hill and saw what must have been a thousand bison spread out on the plain below them.

"Holy cow," Patrick said in awe.

"Bison," Daniel corrected him.

"What?"

"They're bison, not cow."

Patrick groaned, and a few of the others laughed.

"They're lunch," Shawn said raising his rifle.

"Stop it!" Jacob barked, knocking the rifle aside. "Look!"

Amy followed his pointed finger and saw a man on horseback moving sedately through the herd. She followed everyone down into a crouch. She glanced at Luke. He already had his binoculars out.

"They don't seem to have noticed us yet," Jacob said from behind his own pair.

"Native American clothing," Luke said. "That's odd."

"Indian," Patrick corrected. "They're Indians." He was squinting through the telescoping sight on his rifle.

"You're kidding?" Horace said.

"Nope," Jacob said. "Indians if I ever saw one. Bows and arrows and everything. What does anyone make of it?"

"Maybe society has been reduced to primitive stuff like that?" Kurt ventured.

"In thirty years?" Larry asked.

"Could've happened," Kurt maintained.

"No way," Luke said. "There'd be some people left who remembered, surely."

"Maybe all the older people died from the blast or something, and the children, like, didn't remember civilization," Shawn said.

"Not possible," Larry said. "Bows and arrows ain't as easy as they look. Somebody had to teach them to make and use them."

"Well, what other explanation is there?" Patrick demanded.

"Maybe they choose this," Luke said.

"What?"

"They choose to live like this. They remember technology, but they refuse to use it," Luke explained.

"Why would anyone do such a damn fool thing?" Horace said.

"One thing is sure, they ain't real Indians," Jacob said putting his binoculars down, "The one on the left is blond and as white as you or me.

"And a couple of them look to be way past thirty-something as well. No, I think I agree with Luke. They've chosen this, though I can't imagine for the life of me why," Larry said.

"Maybe it's because they are mad that technology ruined their world and civilization," Amy ventured, "so they refuse to use it?"

"That's just plain stupid," Patrick sneered.

"Maybe it's easier," Luke commented.

"Correction, *that's* stupid," Patrick replied.

"What do you mean?" Jacob asked of Luke, ignoring Patrick.

"Biodiesel and ethanol are one thing, but with all this

grass, feeding a few horses would be a lot simpler."

"What about the bows and arrows?" Shawn asked.

"Maybe arrows are easier to come by then bullets?"

"And the get-up?"

"Raising Bison would mean you'd have plenty of leather; why not use it?"

"No way," Mark sneered.

"I think you are most likely correct, but it doesn't matter right now," Jacob told Luke. "Right now what matters is what are we going to do?"

"I say we go down there and get some meat," Patrick snarled.

"And if they object?" Larry asked him.

"Then we'll see how their bows do against this." He brandished his rifle. Mark and Shawn both cheered.

Typical men, Amy thought sourly.

"We do no such thing," Jacob declared. "We backtrack and pass behind those hills and go about our way."

"What?" Shawn gaped. "We are going to let this opportunity pass?"

"Yes," Jacob ordered, "head out everyone." He ushered them back down the far side of the hill.

At the bottom of the hill, John stopped Jacob. "Sir, with all due respect, you did say that rations would not hold us. We clearly outmatch them . . ."

"No," Jacob turned back. *John apparently deserved an explanation, whereas Shawn did not*, Amy thought as Jacob launched into his talk. "It's a simple matter of risks versus benefits.

"First the risks; they appear not to have technology, but that is not certain. Even without it, a fight could be risky. I only count four, but they may have reinforcements nearby.

Even given we can overpower them, one survivor could alert every hostile force in the region of our presence."

"Not to mention that attacking people without provocation is wrong," Amy threw in. Everyone ignored her.

"Then there are the benefits. If Luke is right, and I think he is, they have no technology. That means they will not have what we need. They have meat, and that's tempting enough. We would only be able to fill our bellies tonight, though. We do not have the time to stop and dry the meat for storage," Jacob finished.

Amy could hardly believe her ears. She thought she would have believed anything bad about the men of Freedom Ranch on general principal, but she never thought she'd hear them discuss attacking innocent people for a meal. Yet they all seemed to accept this as normal.

"We are assuming they are hostile," Luke put in, "but we have no reason. Could we parlay?"

Amy could have kissed him.

"We assume everyone is hostile until we know for certain otherwise. Even then, we suspect," Jacob replied sharply. "I am taking no chances."

"If they don't like technology, they'll not like us either," Larry told Luke. "Besides, what are we going to parlay with?"

With that, the debate was ended. They moved slowly to the southeast, keeping the hill between them and the bison herd. Patrick and Shawn continued to grumble about how good fresh bison meat would have tasted. Amy felt a bitter fear settle over her. It was not Patrick and Shawn's comments that bothered her so much, it was Larry's.

What did they have to parlay with? Did Jacob or Amos

ever intend to parlay?

Three slow days passed. Jacob had to tighten down on rationing. Each order led to another round of grumbling about the missed bison meat. Patrick seemed to have accepted the decision, but Shawn and Mark had turned sullen.

On the third day, they came to a small river, little more than a stream, really. Its effect on Jacob was way out of proportion to its size. He broke into a big grin. He let them halt long enough to refill their canteens with water and then led them northward, following the river.

They followed him for the better part of the day. He began to move faster, always staying in sight, but ranging ahead of the weary men.

In the late afternoon, the river turned back east. Jacob had gone ahead, northward. As they reached the bend in the river, he came down from a low hill to meet them.

"We're almost there," he said. "Just over the next hill, in . . . well, what around here would be called a valley, though nothing like we have back home, is Liberty Farm. That's another one of the encampments. My first camp actually," He laughed, a note of hysteria in his voice. "Now, we got to be careful from here. We don't want to startle the sentries."

"If they still have sentries," Horace muttered. Sentry duty at the ranch had ended over fifteen years ago.

"They will," Jacob replied. "I knew their leader well. Besides, down here they no doubt saw a lot more action than we did. Probably still do. We need to go in obvious and sure." He withdrew a bundle from his pack and unrolled an American flag. He tied it to the end of his

M-16 rifle. "The rest of you, I want guns out. We don't know if they have been compromised or not. Keep them up but do not show any signs of aggression, understood?"

Amy didn't understand. *How can you have your guns out and not be showing aggression?* She kept her mouth shut.

"I know most of the passwords; Amos taught me," Jacob was saying. "Plus we might get lucky and I might recognize the sentry."

He assigned them each a place in formation. Taking the lead, he led them up the hill. Amy was, of course, at the back, "out of harm's way." Nervous about their first encounter with others, the men made their guns ready.

"Better if the sentry doesn't recognize him," Larry muttered to Horace as they started up the hill after Jacob. The comment made Amy wonder. She had heard the rumors that Jacob had left his first assignment after some incident. No one seemed to know exactly what had occurred, but to have resulted in his expulsion, it would have had to be pretty bad.

Just below the crest of the next hill, Jacob called Horace forward, and the two of them approached the crest together. There they halted, and Jacob used his binoculars for a long while. When the two of them turned and gestured the rest forward. The disappointment was apparent on their faces.

As Amy crested the hill, she could guess its cause. Liberty Farm was still a good half mile away, but even from here it was obviously deserted. A gaping hole in the roof of the main building stared blankly at them. Pigeons fluttered lazily out of broken windows. Several of the houses sagged as though on the verge of collapse. The place had been abandoned for a long time.

"They appear to have been compromised," Jacob said. "Move in slow and careful, no telling what's up there. It could be a trap."

Amy caught Luke's dead-serious look and quelled her snort. The place had been abandoned for years. They had no communication with Freedom Ranch, and no idea that they would ever come, let alone be coming now. Why would the enemy have left some people there for god knows how many years to ambush the next party to come along? *Then again*, she told herself, *isn't that exactly what the ranch was about? Weren't we set up in the mountains to wait for just such an occasion?*

The approach was uneventful. Jacob waved them off in pairs to explore the farm and its buildings. "Report," he called from his position behind the first building.

"This building's clear," Patrick sang out from inside the main building.

"All clear," Luke yelled from a nearby building.

"All clear," came another voice, Larry's.

Excited shouts came from a half-collapsed barn behind the main building. There was a brief crack of gunfire.

"Talk to me! Talk to me!" Jacob shouted.

There was a rustling in some tall weeds nearby, and a deer broke cover. It dashed between two of the buildings and then passed not more than five feet from where Amy hid. It ran toward the river.

Mark and Shawn came barreling after. Shawn had his gun up and fired again, missing the deer. It galloped down the hill at full speed.

Shawn made to shoot again, but Mark pushed his gun aside. "Quit wasting ammo, dolt!" he shouted. "You couldn't hit the broadside of a barn."

A hundred yards away the deer paused and looked back. Amy saw Luke's gun go up. There was a crack. The deer took a step, and its legs gave way. It dropped.

"Good shooting, Luke," Larry whooped. Luke flushed and gave a sheepish smile.

The house-to-house search was forgotten. Luke, Daniel, and Larry went to collect the deer and field dress it. The rest of the men made a more leisurely inspection of the premises.

A second shout of excitement, this time from Horace, was so filled with glee that no one went into combat positions. Amy wandered over to see what he had found. Horace and Willie were standing in front of a large patch of corn. It was already almost as tall as Amy and had big round ears on it.

"Seems a bit early for corn," she said, trying to count the days they had been gone. Had they really been gone that long?

"The stuff we grow, yes," Horace told her. "This is a variety we haven't had in years. It's sweet corn."

"Sweet corn?" Kurt asked as he came over.

"Damn, I forget how long it's been. All you kids have ever had is parch corn," Horace said. "I grew up in Iowa. I bore the fighting okay. I took the hard years okay. I gave up everything for the cause, gladly. But the year that the corn borer infestation destroyed our entire crop of sweet corn, I cried."

Under Horace's directions Kurt went to get a fire started while Amy and Willie helped him gather and husk as many ears as were ripe. Amy was surprised to find big yellow kernels inside.

"I have never seen corn that color," Kurt said when she

brought their harvest to him. He was boiling water in the biggest pot they had.

"I have," Luke said as he came up bearing venison steaks.

"From a book," Patrick finished.

Luke blushed but didn't comment.

The older men, however, had pretty much the same reaction as Horace. They gathered around and watched the food cooking. "Now, boys, this will be a real treat, mark my words," Larry told them.

Only Jacob was missing. By the time the meat was nearly ready, he came out of one of the buildings and slumped down beside John.

"Nothing," he sighed. "The place has been stripped. There is no sign of when, why, or how."

"Do you think the terrorists got them?" Daniel asked.

"Probably," Patrick muttered.

"I don't see any sign of a struggle," Luke objected.

Jacob gave Luke a look. "Luke's right again. I've looked everywhere. No bullet holes that I can see. No bodies, no bones, nothing to indicate anyone died here. Everything of value is gone, but nothing looks to have been broken up. I'd have to say they went peacefully of their own accord," he said.

"Why would they do that?" Kurt asked from by the fire.

Jacob shrugged.

"Maybe things got too hot," Horace ventured. "Just because they didn't fight here doesn't mean they didn't fight."

"A distinct possibility," Jacob said, mulling it over. "They could have taken too many casualties, or seen something big coming, like an army moving into this region. They could have fled to one of the camps deeper in the mountains. That would explain the rest of it too."

"The rest of what?" Luke asked.

"I've been through Martin's house," Jacob explained. "He was our—their—leader. It has been completely gutted. No paper or anything to indicate what this farm once was or where the people went. If they fled, they would have taken all his papers and documents."

"That explains it then," Shawn said.

"Not necessarily," Jacob countered. "Everything's been gutted as far as I can tell. I even found a few old autos stripped of just about any usable part. Unless they added a bunch more members after I left, they wouldn't have had the manpower to take that much stuff, not on short notice anyway."

"Maybe they had enough notice?" Mark said.

"Maybe they left because they didn't need to stay," Kurt ventured as he turned a steak. "Maybe they went back . . . you know, to civilization, because, well, because it was over."

Nobody replied. The more Amy considered it, the more likely it seemed. The thought disturbed her immensely. What if they had been up in the mountains for years needlessly?

Her train of thought was interrupted by Kurt's next proclamation, which was that dinner was done. After weeks on MREs and dried foods, even the smell of venison and corn was enough to drive everything else out of her mind. Within a couple of bites, she had to admit the sweet corn lived up to the praise the older men had given it.

Everyone thought so and expressed the sentiment in

their own way. "Damn, this is good," Mark said.

"You ain't fucking kidding," Patrick agreed around a mouthful.

Kurt glared at the pair of them momentarily, and Amy could almost hear a lecture on cussing. Then Kurt shrugged and went back to eating.

They ate without conversation. The corn was gone in minutes. There was plenty of meat, however, and the men attacked that at a much more leisurely pace than they had the corn. Luke and Larry hoisted a huge spit lined with cuts of meats high above the fire to dry.

The men began to laugh and joke again. The mood was jovial, almost drunkenly so. Then Larry puked.

"Oh, gross," Patrick said.

Before anyone could move to help Larry, John wordlessly joined him in sickness. Amy's stomach lurched, in sympathy perhaps, or at the sight of the others. Jacob was sick next, followed by Horace.

It was soon clear that everyone was affected. It struck suddenly and unrelentingly. Amy had only a moment to wonder what could be happening before she fell sick as well.

Amy paused as she gagged again. It was only dry heaves. She had long since emptied her stomach. She was bent over like an old woman, in part due to the twelve canteens that hung over her neck and in part due to the pain in her gut.

The sun was setting low in the sky. She paused and tried to think. That made it how long? Twenty four hours of worrying, not for herself so much as for the others. She dragged herself upright and walked the last few steps back to the farm.

Shawn was sitting on the steps to the porch of one of the houses. He gave her a ragged smile and thumbs-up. The other ten men of the expedition lay on the porch. They all slept fitfully, if it could be called sleep. Unconscious was nearer the truth.

Why Shawn and she were spared, she didn't know. They'd both been sick, all right, but not nearly as bad as the others. Amy's medical knowledge was almost nonexistent. It would have probably been better if Luke had been the one to remain conscious.

She did the best she could. Without Patrick to boss him around, Shawn followed Amy's directions like a lost puppy. Together they escorted or dragged the men onto the porch. It was not much shelter, but Amy didn't know what else to do. The two of them did not have the strength to set camp by themselves.

Several of the men had turned delirious. Shawn herded them as best he could, stopping frequently to puke himself.

Meanwhile, Amy tended to those on the porch. She rolled them on their sides when they were puking and cleaned them the best she could when they finished.

She was in constant fear that either she or Shawn would succumb next, but neither of them did. She knew she had a fever and her mind felt cloudy, like she was thinking through molasses, but she had remained conscious so far.

She knew the men needed water or they would dehydrate. So she had managed to take all of their canteens to the river twice so far. Most of them couldn't even hold water down, but she tried. She dabbed their foreheads and made them suck on wet rags when she could get them to wake up long enough.

She slumped down on the porch and held a quick conference with Shawn. While she was gone, Jacob, the last of the delirious ones, had passed out. It was a blessing of sorts. At least they no longer had to worry about someone wandering off. They dragged sleeping bags and blankets out of the packs and got everyone covered for another long night.

Amy awoke in the pre-dawn light. A dove cooed somewhere nearby. She couldn't remember falling asleep. She had slept fitfully, waking periodically in the night to check on the men. Now she crawled over to where Luke lay. The rag on his forehead was still damp, and he moaned slightly when she touched it. Had she been awake recently or had Shawn been up checking on the men as well?

She gathered the canteens and walked slowly and stiffly down to the river. There, she washed her face and drank a little. To her relief, it stayed down.

As she returned, she found Shawn up and moving amongst the men. A quick worried gesture brought her over to where he knelt. Her blood froze as she saw Larry's familiar face. There was something unnatural in the way he lay that told her everything. Still, she bent and felt for the pulse she knew she wouldn't find.

Shawn looked at her, his eyes bright with fear. Would they all die out here?

She shrugged off the unspoken question. "We need to bury him," she decided.

It took what little strength they had, but they somehow managed it. They got him picked up and carried him to the edge of the settlement. They dug a shallow grave under the shade of an old elm tree.

Amy thought of Larry; of all the people who would miss him: his wife, his son. All of the things he had done for her dad, for her. There was so much to say about such a man, but in the end neither of them knew what to say. They were so out of breath, so exhausted by their labors, they merely pushed his body in and covered it.

To Amy's great relief, no one died while they were away. Some of the younger men even seemed to be doing better. Luke, her main fear, was less feverish and resting quietly. She got him to suck on a wet rag, and then even drink a little. She lay wearily at his side and slept.

The world spun as Luke pried his eyes open. He tried to recall where he was. He was sure he was supposed to be doing something important. What was it?

Then it hit him: the mission. He had to get going, or he would be late. He struggled to rise and a searing pain went through his head. He fell back and closed his eyes.

He took a few deep breathes and tried to concentrate. This was not right. They had already left, hadn't they? Then it started to come back, the trip down the mountain, the storm, the farm, and then . . .

He opened his eyes again. Light clawed at them. He squinted. Amy's face swam into view.

"You don't look so good," he told her.

She smiled. "You're hardly one to talk," she replied, the relief apparent in her voice. Her face was streaked with dirt and grime, and she had bags under her eyes.

Luke tried to rise again and felt a wave of nausea wash over him.

"Not so fast," she told him. "Drink this."

She held a cup to his lips. It was water, fresh and cool. Suddenly thirsty, he drank deeply. He promptly threw it up. He sat up, his head spinning. He was a frightful mess.

"I threw it up," he said.

"At least you didn't pass out, like last time," she replied.

How long have I been unconscious? He tried to think.

"Two days, more or less," Amy said, guessing his thoughts. "Try again, slower."

He sipped carefully this time. His stomach rebelled, but he did not throw up. It took all of his willpower not to gulp at the water, his body was so thirsty for it, but he managed another swallow.

Shawn appeared and sat down beside them. "Back up, I see," he said wearily.

Luke nodded, looking around. The other expedition members were sprawled out around the battered wooden porch. He looked at Amy.

"We were too sick to do much better," she said with a resigned air. "I don't know why, but Shawn and I were less affected; we didn't pass out, at least. We tried to set camp and all, but it took all our strength to look after everyone."

Another mouthful of water, and he felt much better. He tried to stand despite their warning looks. He got only halfway up before collapsing again.

"Man, you've been out for two days," Shawn said. "Don't push it."

"How bad is it?" he asked craning his neck to see the others.

"Larry is dead," Amy told him, her voice flat. "Everyone else is still alive. You are the first one awake."

"Hooray for me," Luke said. "You two?"

"Been sicker than a dog," Shawn said. "She has too. We

made it though."

"You've done well, all things considered."

"I don't want it, I don't want it," Kurt moaned.

"He's delirious," Shawn said. "Keeps trying to give me back the Bible his dad gave him before we left. Keeps saying it isn't right."

"He hasn't talked since that first night," Amy said getting up. "I think he might be coming around."

Before Luke could crawl over, Kurt was awake, or at least partially so. Amy got him to drink a little bit, and he settled back quietly.

By nightfall both Kurt and Daniel were awake and helping Luke tend to Patrick and Mark, who were just waking up. Jacob had drunk some water, and the others all looked better.

By morning, the stamina of youth was clearly paying off. All of the younger generation were up and about when Amy got back from her morning water run. One MRE was enough breakfast for all seven queasy stomachs, but they all held that much down.

The older generation looked to be surviving, at least. John was up and moving, though he declined his share of breakfast. Jacob and Horace were awake and watching the younger men. Willie was still out but less feverish.

"What do you think happened?" Jacob asked as Amy approached. She merely shrugged.

"Radiation?" Mark ventured.

"If it was radiation you'd be dead," Jacob told him. "Radiation don't go away."

"Could've been the water," Daniel said. "All the survival manuals warn about that, parasites and bacteria and stuff."

"You're still drinking the same water," Amy pointed out. Everyone looked nervous. "And you're getting better."

"A virus maybe?" Luke said.

"From what?"

"I don't know, maybe the deer."

That was as far as they got. They had no medical equipment or any training. There was no way to know what had struck. Worse still, there was no way to avoid another outbreak other than dumb luck.

That night Jacob called a meeting. "I have done a lot of thinking today, men," he told them. "This mission is vital to the ranch. We simply can't afford any delay. Willie's doing better tonight, but he'll be in no shape to move tomorrow. Neither will Horace or me, for that matter."

He paused and looked around. "I fear it will be days, at least, before we can get moving again."

There was a groan. Already they had faced many unexpected delays, now this?

"Time is too valuable to waste. Those who are fit to travel must go on."

"We can't leave you, sir," Daniel said.

"You can and you will," Jacob replied. "John will stay behind. He's still too sick for a full day's march. He'll slow the rest of you down. But he's better off than the three of us. He'll be able to take care of camp until we are back on our feet." He looked at them sternly.

"I can't stress enough how important this is. I know this means sending you younger boys off without our experience. Still, we may be weeks from any civilization. Once there, who knows how long it will take to scavenge, or . . . obtain what we need?"

Amy's eyes narrowed suspiciously. She had noted that the term barter had all but dropped from Jacob's vocabulary. What did he intend?

"The point is, there are too many possible delays ahead to waste time now. If we don't get back up that pass before winter sets in, we could be stuck down here until next spring."

There was a stunned silence. Looking around at the boy's faces, Amy knew they were shocked at the possibility that the mission could take so long.

Kurt was the first to speak. "But sir? If we don't get back to the ranch before fall—"

"The ranch will suffer," Jacob finished. "There will be hunger, maybe even some unavoidable deaths due to starvation, but they'll get through somehow, just like you will complete this mission somehow."

Everyone's faces reflected the same thought: some unavoidable deaths? Whose? Her father's? No, he was most likely dead already, she realized with a pang of guilt. What about Elisabeth, alone? She was young and strong, but their garden had never been large. She had always relied on Amy and their father. Their skills were always in demand and that meant barter. How would Elisabeth fare without that?

At last Patrick spoke. "Of course, sir, you're right. We have to complete the mission and return before fall. We will leave at dawn. Is there anything else?"

"Yes," Jacob held Patrick's gaze. "Luke's in charge."

Patrick turned crimson but did not speak.

"But sir," Shawn spoke up, "Patrick's been class leader for two years."

"This isn't class anymore. It's real life!" Jacob barked at

Shawn. To Patrick he added, "You're the best soldier in your class. I know that. If it comes to fighting, you'll be needed. Our hope lies in avoiding fighting until absolutely necessary, especially now, with just the seven of you going on. That will take a different kind of leader, someone with a level head and quick mind. Luke's in charge. Understood?"

Patrick continued to glare for a moment and then nodded curtly, turning away.

"Sir?" Luke and Jacob were alone in the remains of one of the houses, poring over Jacob's map and making last minute plans.

"Yes, son?" Jacob answered.

"What you said earlier about . . . about me having a level head and a quick mind?" Luke asked. "Is that really why I am in charge?"

Jacob gave him a discerning look. "If you are asking if that's really how I feel about you, the answer is yes," he replied after some time.

Luke was as long in answering. "Thank you, sir, but no, that's not it. It's that . . . well, is there another reason? Daniel's level headed and probably a better diplomat, and —"

"No, that's not true," Jacob interrupted. "But you're right, there are other considerations. You're smart. I never cared much for book learning, but you've shown me its value so far. You're dedicated. You're one of the few who has treated this mission with the seriousness it deserves."

"It's just that Patrick has been the class leader and people respect him."

"People respect you more than you realize," Jacob

replied. "Some more than Patrick."

"You mean Amy."

"She's vital to this mission."

"I know," Luke said. "But if you think that she'd refuse to go because of Patrick, I don't think that's true."

Jacob sighed. "You know her better than I do. That thought hadn't crossed my mind. It's not like that. She does respect you; what's more, she'll help you."

"And not Patrick."

"No. Face it; he wouldn't give her the chance. Hell, a month ago, I wouldn't have given her the chance. She's proven valuable more than once already. Who knows? Maybe Marlin had it right. All I know is that you, with Amy helping, have a lot better chance at completing this mission than Patrick ever will." He paused and then added, "There's just one thing you have to watch for, Luke."

"Yes sir?"

"She's smart and competent, but she's still a woman. She turns squeamish about things."

"Things?"

Jacob griped Luke's arm and gave him an intense look. "The needs of the ranch outweigh everything Luke, everything. Don't forget that."

Luke swallowed. He wished this burden hadn't fallen on him. He knew what Jacob was thinking. He wished it had been left unsaid. "Yes sir," he replied quietly.

The next day they set out. They left most of the rations behind with the older men; they would need them more. They promised to send help, if there was any to send, and to be back as quickly as possible. Luke had inherited

Jacob's map, but for the moment he led them due east.

Amy felt a strange mixture of feelings as they left the older men sitting on the broken porch. There was sadness at leaving them behind, though not much, if Amy was to be honest. There was still a sinking feeling at the thought of Larry's death, but she had little regard for the others. There was a deep dread at the thought of what Patrick and Shawn would be like without Jacob's controlling presence.

Underneath it all though, there was an odd pleasure. They were walking away from any adult supervision for the first time in their life. With that fact came a sense of freedom and adventure that nothing could quite quell. Looking around, she could tell that the others felt it as well.

Even Mark, who had technically been an adult for two years, had an added swagger to his walk. Once out of sight of Liberty Farm, three separate conversations broke out.

Only Luke seemed unaffected. He barked at them to be quiet, as they may well be in hostile territory. No one paid him much mind, and he grew sourer as the day passed.

Their second day out, they surprised a deer coming out of a creek bed. Luke dropped it in one shot. They were all hesitant to eat it. Luke decided that one person should try some, and then if that person did not get sick, they would all eat it. Being the one to come up with the plan, Luke felt that he should be the one to try the deer.

To his surprise, Kurt volunteered. "I'm sick of MREs anyway," he said with a grin. He grilled and ate a small portion while the rest of them set camp.

He did not get sick, and after they had set camp,

everyone ate their fill. Over a breakfast of the remains, the mood became self-satisfied.

"Not so bad, roughing it," Mark laughed. "Fresh venison every other day."

"One could learn to live like this," Shawn agreed.

"As long as he keeps us fed," Mark continued, "we'll let Luke play leader if he wants."

"It was Jacob," Kurt shot back, "Jacob said."

"Sure thing, Kurt," Mark drawled.

The end of the second day's march brought their first sign of civilization. Cresting yet another low hill among the many, they found a dirt road stretching across their path. It snaked from one horizon to the other with no indication of what lay on either side. Tufts of low weeds indicated it had not been used much or recently, but it was still a road.

Luke pulled the map out and laid it out on the ground. "I doubt the road will be on this map. I suspect it has been built since the blast."

"'Built' might be a stretch," Daniel snorted.

"So, where do you think it leads, oh mighty leader?" Patrick asked.

Luke didn't respond.

"Could be between these two towns," Amy said pointing at the map.

"This X is Liberty Farm," Luke said pointing. "From my estimate of how far we've traveled, that would be about right. The real question is which way to go. Vicksburg, here, is larger, and Shelan is smaller."

"Easy then," Mark replied. "Vicksburg is more likely to have survivors, so we go that way." He pointed.

"Right idea but wrong direction," Luke replied. "Our

goal is to avoid contact if possible. My guess would be the survivors built this road to get to Shelan for salvage. That's what we want: salvage."

Mark snorted loudly and muttered, "Wimp."

Luke went red but ignored him.

"I think we should go see the survivors," Shawn declared loudly. "Let them do the salvage work, not us."

"For one thing," Luke said, "we have no idea how many there are or who is in control. There could be some sort of military state. Even if not, even if they are friendly, we would have to barter. That would take time. Time we don't have."

It was Patrick's turn to snort. "I overheard Amos and Jacob back at the ranch. Barter is not our only option."

"Only if there's no other way," Luke replied.

"What are you guys talking about?" Amy demanded. She already had a good guess, but she wanted to force someone to say it.

Patrick did. "The right of seizure. If we outclass our opponent, we should take what we need."

"You mean steal?"

"I mean, little girl, seizure. A necessary right in any war."

"You can't be serious?" Amy demanded, turning toward Luke. He'd surely not go along with that.

"Only if there is no other way to obtain what we need and we know that the survivors are hostile toward us," Luke replied, keeping his voice as even as possible.

"How are we going to know they are hostile?" Mark said. "You going to go up and ask them?"

"Doesn't matter," Luke replied, "because we aren't going that way. We are going to go into Shelan and scavenge what we need and get out."

"I agree," Amy said.

"I don't." Shawn glared at her.

"Too bad. Luke's in charge. In case you forgot."

Shawn just laughed. "You really believe that?"

To Amy's surprise, Kurt leaped to her defense. "Jacob said, Shawn. Jacob said."

"Everyone knows that Patrick is our leader," Shawn insisted. "He's been class leader for two years, regardless of what Jacob said."

Mark nodded from behind Shawn's back. Patrick gave the whole scene a quiet calculated look but hung back.

"You can't go against the chain of command," Daniel jumped in. "Jacob put Luke in charge and that's that."

"I'll show you chain of command," Shawn growled with one fist raised.

"Easy there, big guy," Mark laughed. "Daniel's just standing up for his boyfriend."

Daniel glared at him, but before he could reply, Kurt yelled, "Shut up, that's devil talk. You'll burn in hell, sinner."

"Shut up, Kurt," Mark sneered, low and dangerous.

"Back down, everyone!" Luke shouted with enough force to make everyone jump back a step. Shawn went to step forward. "I mean it," Luke said in a steely voice.

"Cool it, Shawn," Patrick said softly. "If Luke wants to go that way, we'll go that way."

Luke took a deep breath and then said. "Okay, now that that's settled, let's set camp for the night. We will go back down this hill a ways to be out of sight. MREs, I am afraid. We will not risk a fire. We can only assume we are in enemy territory from now on."

* * *

Amy sank down beside Luke. He was sitting at the crest of the hill looking out over the gathering twilight. After ordering the setting of camp, he had assigned sentry duty, giving himself the first shift. Amy knew it was just an excuse to get away for a while.

"That was close," he said after a while.

"You can take Shawn," she said.

"Perhaps, but not Patrick," he replied. "But that doesn't matter. We can't be fighting each other like this. This is what I feared. They don't respect me as their leader."

"Well, they should," she said. "They were all there. They heard Jacob."

"That doesn't mean much out here. I just hope it doesn't happen again."

"It will. One of these days, you are going to have to put Shawn in his place, Patrick too most likely."

"Damn!" Amy cussed. "This one's a bust too." They had reached Shelan late the next morning. It was now just after noon. After a quick reconnaissance, Luke had signaled everyone into town.

At first it appeared to be exactly what they hoped for, row after row of deserted houses. It was strange; the ranch only had one building like these, the community hall. At Liberty Farm, everyone had lived in the tall square buildings. Here, there must have been three or four dozen all lined up in a neat grid work.

"Where did they grow their food?" Kurt wondered aloud.

"They didn't," Luke told him. "Farmers grew it elsewhere, and these people bought it."

"What a strange life," Kurt commented.

The boys quickly lost interest. They lounged in the small park they discovered at the center of town, clearly feeling it was not their responsibility to help with the actual salvaging.

Not that they would have found much to do anyway, Amy thought sourly as she walked down the street. Daniel, Luke and she had spent the last two hours going from one empty shell to another.

"What do you make of it?" Luke asked.

"They're all the same," Daniel said, "just empty."

"This place has already been scavenged," Amy replied, "and very thoroughly. I suppose we should have expected as much. After thirty years, we can't be the only ones running out of things."

Luke sighed. "I suppose not, but it does complicate the mission greatly. Now what are we going to do?"

"Head for that other town, I guess," Daniel said.

"I fear we will find the same thing," Amy said.

Kurt came running up.

"What is it?" Luke asked.

"They found something," he said. "Mark and Patrick. They climbed one of those big metal round buildings at the edge of town, you remember?"

"The silos, yes."

"They spotted smoke."

Minutes later, they were there. With only a brief hesitation about the height, Amy followed Luke up the ladder. At the top, on a short gangplank, Patrick and Mark were taking turns looking through the scope on Patrick's rifle.

"There's your hostiles for you," Patrick said.

Luke looked through his binoculars. "Can't tell much from here," he said. "Can't see what's making the smoke. It's just one line, so it's something small and contained, like a cook fire." He paused and looked at Patrick. "Salvage is a bust. I say we check this out."

"Right on."

The rest were not hard to convince either. Soon everyone was packed up, and they were off. Before long they could all see the smoke. Distance on the prairie, however, can be deceptive. It took them almost three hours to reach the origin.

From the top of the rise, Luke peered through the binoculars. Then he crawled back down to where the rest were waiting.

"I was right," he said. "It's just over this hill, a farm or something, one house and one small barn. Odd-looking house. Can't tell what it's made of. It could be stone or something. Has an earthen roof like back home, though. Anyway, it's one story and not very big. One family down there at most. No sign of any vehicles. Either they don't have one or it's gone somewhere."

He paused to consider his words. "The whole set up is definitely civilian. I think we should go down."

Shawn and Mark brandished their guns.

"Some of us should go down," Luke corrected. "Peacefully."

"To barter?" Kurt asked. "Will they have what we need?"

"I doubt it," Amy said. "Not from that description."

"No, I agree they won't," Luke said. "I saw somebody out front. I didn't get a good look, but I think it was an old lady. She shouldn't be any danger, and she may have information."

"Barter is a waste of time," Patrick said. "But interrogation . . ."

"We are just going to talk," Luke growled. "Three of us will go down. Amy, you're coming. They'll be more likely to believe we come in peace if we have a woman with us."

"You are taking a woman into a potentially hostile situation?" Patrick asked.

"It looks like a civilian outpost to me," Luke answered coolly.

"And if it's not?" Patrick demanded. "If this old lady of yours is the cook for a whole garrison of enemy soldiers?"

"That's why I am also taking you."

Patrick paused to consider. "Okay, but I want to be perfectly clear. This mission is vital. If I think for one minute that your wishy-washiness is threatening the mission, I will not hesitate to correct the situation. Understood?" Without waiting for a reply, he hefted his rifle. "Let's go."

PART TWO

THE QUIET EARTH

4

Roger's story

Amy, Patrick, and Luke crested the hill together. Luke thought the most direct approach was the best. They did not want to startle the people living down there into any rash action.

Daniel took up a covering position at the top of the hill. Amy was glad it was him and not a trigger-happy Mark or Shawn. Luke and Patrick both had their rifles on their shoulders, apparent but not threatening, they claimed. Amy was sure she'd feel threatened, but there was no convincing them.

The house was low with heavy, earthen walls that were not quite square, but not quite rounded either, and a heavy sod roof. A chimney rose out of the roof, but the smoke issued from the other side of the building. Small windows were recessed deep into the walls. It had a cozy feel to it, like it grew out of the plains, Amy thought.

The smell of baking bread greeted them as they rounded the west side of the building. The south side of the building had larger windows. In front of the house was a round dome of earthen material about waist high. It had a small door, and the smoke and smell was emanating from it.

An elderly lady was tending the dome. She had long dark hair and nut brown skin. She wielded a long wooden paddle. She deftly reached the paddle in through a door and removed several steaming loaves of bread and set them on a low table sitting next to the dome. Then she fed several more thick lumps of dough in. She appeared to take no notice of them.

"Do you think the Chinese have taken over?" Patrick whispered.

"No, dummy," Amy hissed back. "There were lots of Asian people already living in the US before the blast."

"Excuse me," Luke said, stepping forward.

The lady turned, showing no surprise, and approached, still carrying the long paddle. "My name is Ruth Akira. May I be of service?"

"My name is Luke Zachary," Luke responded. "We come in peace."

"That's very nice," she responded. A chicken clucked as it strolled by.

"Aren't you afraid?" Patrick demanded. Amy groaned. Luke should have never brought him. She could tell by his look that Luke was thinking the same thing.

"Should I be?" Ruth asked.

"No, of course not," Luke replied, shooting a warning look at Patrick. Patrick ignored it.

"You don't need to be afraid." Patrick said, "as long as

you do as you are told."

"And if I don't?" Ruth asked.

"We have guns."

"Patrick!" Luke hissed, "That's enough!"

"I told you I would not stand for wishy-washiness," Patrick hissed back.

"Not when it comes to interrogations, eh?" Ruth asked.

Patrick spun around and stared at her.

"Sound really travels out here," she said. "Your friend wanted to come in peace. I too practice peace and harmony. Please put your guns down so we can talk."

"You'll learn some respect or— "Patrick slung the rifle off his shoulder.

It was over in a matter of seconds. One instant Ruth was standing stock-still and the next she was gone. Patrick hit the ground with a yowl of pain. The long wooden paddle swept in a graceful circle as Ruth spun back in front of him. It stopped inches from his throat, pinning him to the ground. Her eyes, however, were on Luke.

Luke slowly un-slung his rifle and laid it on the ground. "I regret my friend's behavior very much, and I am sure he does too. I apologize."

With a graceful flick of her wrist, Ruth knocked Patrick's rifle several feet away and stepped back two paces so he could rise shakily to his feet. "We had bandits out here in the early days. We can defend ourselves at need. I trust you will not want a second demonstration?"

"Of course not," Luke said. "Again, I apologize for my friend's behavior."

"He's lucky," Ruth told them. "My husband has a gun trained on you as well. Leave your guns where they are. Tell your friends to do the same and they can come down.

We have little to 'seize,' but we will gladly share a meal or two, and perhaps some news."

Ruth turned and walked away. She used her paddle to scoop up two loaves of bread and went off toward the house. Patrick eyed his gun, but Luke's angry motion stopped him from trying for it. "Get the others," Luke growled. "And so help me if I see one gun down here, I'll shoot you myself."

Patrick turned and walked off. Amy followed the woman into the house.

It was cool inside. As her eyes adjusted to the dark, she looked around her. It was small, but neat and clean. Couches and shelves grew out of the walls and were made of the same stuff. There was a crude wooden table and a few chairs, but not many furnishings. Amy felt at home, as if the house itself calmed her nerves.

Ruth's husband was there, looking out one of the windows. He had a single-shot .22 in his hands that looked as if it hadn't been shot in years. He was a thin man with a pockmarked face. He was, to all appearances, white, or at least once had been. Years in the sun had turned him only a shade or two lighter than his wife. His hair was shoulder length and gray, pulled back into a ponytail. His hairline had receded most of the way back to expose a freckled and mole-covered scalp. His wrinkled hands were covered in liver spots, but were rock steady as he held the gun. Ruth introduced him as Roger.

Luke quickly explained who they were and what their mission was. The couple listened intently. Afterward, Roger seemed to come to a decision. He set the gun down and took Luke's hand.

"Never heard of anyone living up in the mountains anymore, but Ruth and I have never turned down someone in need. We don't have much, but we can spare a meal or two for you and your men. Maybe we can give you some good advice too. Sounds like you have been out of the loop for a long time."

By this time, Patrick was back with the others. "Let's take this out on the porch," Ruth said. "This little cabin isn't big enough for all of us."

They gathered outside the cottage and began to talk. Luke, Roger, and Patrick sat on wooden chairs that Ruth brought out of the kitchen. Amy and Ruth sat together on a small bench that grew out of the house itself, and the rest laid their packs down and ranged out on the ground.

"Tell me more about this disease you ran into," Roger said. "We'll need to warn the neighbors if there is something new going around."

"Well, we don't know much about it actually," Luke said. "We have no medic with us. It seemed like something from the food we ate, but we don't know for sure."

"What was it you ate?"

"Well, we shot a deer that day."

"Did it appear ill in any way?" Roger asked.

"No. It seemed fine."

"There is a wasting disease they get sometimes, but that usually shows. Besides it wouldn't have affected you that quickly. I used to hunt a fair bit and never had any trouble with the deer around here. That's been a few years ago, mind."

"We've eaten deer since with no trouble," Amy said.

"Well, what else was there?"

"Nothing odd," Luke replied. "Some corn. That was

all."

"Corn?" Roger's eyes went wide in surprise. "You ate corn?"

"Yeah, what wrong with that?" Patrick asked. "We eat corn all the time at home."

Roger whistled. "Man, you have been out of touch a long time. You really eat corn?"

"Yeah."

Ruth nodded. "They've been up there at least thirty years, I'd say. Imagine, clean seeds. No plague."

"Plague? What plague?" Luke asked.

"The transgenetic plague," Roger answered.

"Trans what?" Shawn asked.

"The transgenetic plague," Roger repeated. "No one has eaten corn down here in over thirty years. It can be deadly, as you unfortunately found out." He watched their puzzled looks. "You really don't know anything about it? Okay, we need to start from the beginning, and that could easily take some time.

"You kids give me a few minutes here; it's been a long time since I talked about this, and I need to get things right in my head." He sat thinking for a long while.

"It was one year before the blast in Chicago . . ." he began.

"The blast," Luke said. "That was when we broke contact completely. The ranch had already been self-sufficient for three years."

Roger nodded. "I was a commodities broker back then, so I was aware of what was going on almost from the start. We were so arrogant in those days. Thought could do anything we wanted. Our scientists discovered they could put genes from one plant into another. At first, it was simple things, corn that grew its own pesticide or was resistant to certain herbicides.

"Then we found we could use the same plants to grow chemicals, thing we found hard to synthesize in other ways: drugs for drug companies and even industrial chemicals. That was the big mistake. They thought they could control it. They added genes that made the plants infertile, limited their growth. They grew them in restricted places.

"Life always finds a way. A few got out. That's all it took, a few ears of volunteer corn by the roadside. Then, it just took one windy day and cross-pollination took care of the rest.

"We had early warnings; genetic material from modified crops showing up miles from where they had been planted. We ignored it. That is, until Bc-144.

"Bc-144 should have made someone a lot of money. It grew just like regular corn. But its oil contained an industrial solvent, one that was expensive to produce. Now, they didn't have to produce the solvent. They could just grow it.

"The first few deaths were a mystery. Once the autopsies started coming back, the mystery widened. They found the solvent and knew how the people had died, but nobody could figure out how it got into their bodies. Most people didn't even know about Bc-144. The company who made it was silent. They were busy burning records, trying to hide their involvement. They could have saved hundreds of lives, but they didn't." He shook his head.

"The connection was eventually made anyway. Enough people knew that experiments had been taking place, knew what the potential was. It was still a catastrophe. Any product with corn in it had to be recalled and destroyed. Thousands of food items had to be tested or destroyed. Whole fields were burnt.

"It was a disaster the likes of which we had never seen. Most of the population had no idea how dependent we were on our corn crop. Still, we could probably have recovered, probably have controlled it in a few years. But then there was Chicago, New York, the Chinese civil war, everything. It all just started to unravel. So much was going on before and after that, but I really believe the plague was it. It was the one thing that brought everything else to its knees."

"How so?" Luke asked.

Ruth returned with a tray laden with tea and fresh bread. Roger continued. "It all hinged on that corn crop. Nobody realized how interdependent everything had become. Take China. The dust bowl in Mongolia was bad; their crops were failing and had been for three years. That should not have led to civil war, but when America's crop failed as well, there was no relief. Millions starved. Same for Africa, they were highly dependent on our grain. It must have been awful."

"What about the blast?" Luke asked. "There was a blast, right? A nuclear bomb in Chicago?"

"Oh yeah," Roger agreed. "I was there, or as close to there as one could be and still live to tell about it. I lived in Chicago in those days." He scratched his chin thoughtfully. "Everything was so different back then. It's hard to believe that world was real."

"Tell us about it," Luke prompted needlessly.

"As I think I said, I was a commodity broker in those

days. That probably means nothing to you now, but in those days we were . . . we were the rugged mercenaries of corporate America. We traded in thousands of dollars a day. It was a heady business.

"I was something of a big shot too, I don't mind telling you. I was one arrogant son of a bitch. I thought I loved the fast life, fast cars, and women. It ruined my first marriage, though I didn't care about that—not until too late, anyway.

"The transgenetic plague had struck the year before the blast. It had been playing havoc on my life. Commodities were always a risky business. Grain could be bought and sold a hundred times between the field and processing plants. Prices went up and down constantly. Big money could be made, and fast, but it could be lost just as fast. On my best day, I made half a million; on my worst, I lost twice that.

"Then came the plague. There was no telling which crops had been affected and which hadn't. One bad finding at a testing station, and crops for miles in any direction had to be destroyed.

"That didn't deter me or anyone in the business. The more the supply dropped, the more money we could make with what was left. And we were making lots. Untested corn could be had for pennies a bushel; tested and cleared, its value soared as high as fifteen to twenty dollars. If you were one of the few with the resources you could make a bundle.

"I was at a corporate retreat in Wisconsin when it happened. We had been studying and planning new ways to make even more off the plague. We knew by then that other contaminants were showing up, and things were about to get even more unstable."

He sighed. "Did anyone at the retreat ask about the farmers? No. We were paying them a fraction of what it had cost them to plant the crops. A frightening half went bankrupt that year alone. That was not our concern, however. I learned about that later. Did anyone ask about Africa? Or the millions of other places where people were starving? Or even the starving here at home? Food rationing wouldn't begin until the next year, but already there were plenty of people without enough. That didn't matter to us, because we weren't them. We had plenty and planned to go on getting more. Like I said, I was one arrogant son of a bitch.

"Anyway, I was heading back toward Chicago. There was this strange cloud on the horizon. Mushroom-shaped, but I didn't connect that up right away. At first, I thought it was a house fire or something. The longer I drove, the more I realized it was much bigger and farther away than I had imagined.

"I thought about the World Trade Center in New York years before. I still couldn't quite grasp the enormity of what I was seeing, though. I turned on the radio, hoping for news. There was nothing but static. I hit the scan button and waited as it ran through the channels."

"Nuclear weapons disrupt radios and other electronics," Luke said.

Roger nodded. "There was only one station on the air. It was outside of Chicago proper. Its undersized transmitter barely reached me. In a scratchy hiss, the first reports of what had happened came to me.

"Downtown Chicago had been rocked by an explosion so big no one doubted for a second that it had been anything other than a nuclear blast. The shock wave had engulfed the city. There were no reports from downtown at all. The few people making it out of the city told of widespread damage and fires everywhere. They spoke in dull monotones with no trace of emotions. The blast left many like that for years."

He paused and drank his tea.

"Damn Islamics," Patrick muttered. "How many did they kill that day?"

"Islamics?" Roger asked. "Like Muslims?"

"Yeah," Daniel put in. "You know, the terrorists that placed the bomb."

"What makes you think they were Muslims?" Roger asked, shocked.

"Well, they were, weren't they?" Mark asked. "That's what we were taught anyway."

"No one knew, and I am not sure anyone ever found out, but I have never heard that theory. The Middle East had actually started settling down after years of unrest," Roger said. "At the time, the government blamed the Chinese. I think we even declared war on them, but I don't think we ever made good on it."

"America started a war and didn't finish it?" Shawn sneered. "Ridiculous."

Roger gave him a hard look but didn't answer.

"But China? Why?" Luke asked.

"We had refused them aid. They were on the brink of civil war about that time because America had pulled all of its foreign aid to help feed our own."

"How could they blame us?" Daniel asked. "We had to feed our own. Besides communism is bound to collapse; my dad always said so."

"Many did blame us, and not just in China. We kept the Cold War alive for so long. Others blamed us for blocking international efforts to help the environment, and for massive resource depletion."

"Resource depletion?" Patrick asked. "Who gets upset because you use stuff?"

"When the stuff is in short supply, a lot of people do," Roger replied. "When the environmental catastrophe was something that leftist doomsayers talked about, a lot people grumbled that those who used the most natural resources and produced the most pollution should shoulder most of the responsibility. That was us, and we did no such thing.

"When it all started becoming a reality, it went past grumbling. There were UN sanctions calling on the US to help the countries hardest hit by the disaster, and we did no such thing. We had lots of enemies. Who knows who finally acted?"

"What about Chicago?" Amy asked, bringing him back to his narrative.

"Oh yes, Chicago," he mused. "Where was I? Oh yeah, at the outskirts. Oddly, when I heard the news, the only thing I could think about was my wife, Charlene. We had been estranged for over a year. She was filing for divorce. Suddenly that didn't matter . . ."

He broke off, pulling out a handkerchief and wiping his eyes. Ruth leaned forward and patted his shoulder affectionately. "That was another world, dear," she told him.

"I loved her," he went on, "or I thought I did. She had certainly loved me. I was so full of myself that I just treated her like crap. I was so above everything except my own greed. She lived just off of downtown, and when I thought I'd never see her again . . . something just broke inside of me. For the first time, I saw my life as one long selfish scam.

"So, instead of doing the smart thing and turning around, getting away, I sped up. I was going after her. I had some naive image of crashing her apartment door and hauling her to safety, hero style. All the way telling her how much I loved her, how sorry I was." He laughed bitterly. "It was temporary insanity. I knew she was dead, had to be dead. Nobody that close to downtown could have survived. But I drove on anyway.

"I'll never forget that night. It was unreal. I was roaring down an empty interstate with the twilight falling around me. On the other side, the road was jammed with cars, all hell bent on being anywhere else. I was the only one foolish enough to be going toward Chicago.

"Overhead, helicopters thrummed past. It was the National Guard, trying to seal off the city and coordinate the relief effort. They were too few and too late. I drove under their lines before they were even set.

"Just outside the city, I saw the biggest crash I had ever witnessed. It seemed to have just happened or maybe it was still happening when I got there. It was like a mountain of metal. There must have been a hundred cars, or so it seemed. For one second, I was enthralled, distracted.

"Desperate to get out, people didn't even stop. They flung their cars ruthlessly through the ditch and over to my side of the road. Suddenly there were hundreds of headlights coming right for me. I swerved and crashed into the ditch. It was a bone-jarring halt, but the seatbelt and airbag held.

"I got out and looked around. No one had stopped to check on me. I had stopped just a few meters from the pileup. In the dark, I could see that many of the older gas automobiles were on fire. Luckily, most people had converted to electric by then, or it could have been worse. A few people stopped to help. A young lady in a nurse's uniform was shouting directions. 'You,' she shouted at me. 'You hurt? Somebody check him. If he's in shock, he may not know it.'

"I passed inspection, and the young woman grabbed me. The air was rent by a gut-wrenching explosion as one of the gas cars went up. It was like an old war movie. 'Over there,' she shouted. 'See about that man.' I obediently went where she pointed and found a man trapped in an overturned car"

"I managed to get his seatbelt off and pull him out. He staggered free, blood running from his right arm. I supported him, blood running all over my Armani suit. Just an hour before, I would have been pissed about that suit, but right then I barely noticed it. As we started down the ditch and away from the road, I looked back at his car. In the driver's seat was a pretty young woman with vacant eyes and clear fluid running from her nose. She was one of the many that would not find help that night.

"The young nurse commanded me sternly to watch as she bandaged the man's arm. It was all the first aid training I got before being set to work. The night passed as a blur. We tore clothes from the dead to make bandages for the living." He shuddered. No one spoke as he paused.

"We bandaged them as best we could. Then we made crude litters and dragged the wounded to a nearby building, a warehouse of some sort. This whole time we did not see an ambulance or receive any help of any kind.

"The wind was picking up and there was an eerie glow on the horizon. I didn't know it at the time, but a firestorm was starting inside Chicago. Whatever the bomb didn't destroy, the fire did.

"We were in no mood for pleasantries. I found a length of pipe and bashed the lock off the door. We moved inside with our wounded.

"Helicopters continued to pass overhead from time to time. Once, I saw an ambulance race past to somewhere. Our little band, however, went unnoticed in the chaos of that first night. A small number of able-bodied people worked under the nurse's tireless direction to care for the wounded, occasionally venturing out for more. I worked late into the night before I collapsed of exhaustion.

"When I awoke, I was disoriented at first. It wasn't just the strange surroundings. Things had changed while I was asleep. There were more people there, for one thing. Among them was a soldier. We had, apparently, received some sort of recognition.

"I saw the nurse and made for her, hoping to find out what was going on. I don't know if she had slept or not, but she looked years older. She was bent over a young man. Half of his face and most of one side of his body was black. His eyes held an unspeakable pain. 'Radiation burns,' she told me dully. 'The first refugees from the city have arrived.'

"'Is there anything I can do?' I'd asked.

"She looked at me, tears streaming down her face. 'There isn't a damn thing any of us can do,' she said. 'No IVs, no sterile bandages, no room at the hospital, not even a damn shot of morphine for his pain. I'd shoot the poor bastard if I had the heart.' She turned away and went to the next patient, not even bothering to wipe the tears away. In that moment, my old life died. In any event so horrific, you will find two kinds of people: those who retreat into shock and those, like that nurse, who keep trying. You also find out which you are.

"From the soldier, I found out that we were now officially an aid station. That didn't make much difference, since he was the only one left behind, and he didn't have any supplies. He wasn't sure when we would be seeing any real help. The National Guard and Red Cross were being mobilized as fast as possible, but the men on the ground were spread too thin. Judging from what he'd seen over the course of that night, he figured one civilian nurse put us well ahead of most stations.

"I asked where the next station was and he pointed in a vague direction. You could just barely make it out. A small crowd was milling around the warehouse. I waved several of them over and sorted out the healthiest of the lot. We headed off for the next station. I left a person behind every so many feet, creating a human net to catch the refugees. Many were in such deep shock that they wandered right past the aid stations and into the countryside to die.

"Arriving back at the warehouse, I discovered two things had happened. A truck had appeared and dropped a load of supplies in a heap in front of the warehouse. And by virtue of showing the slightest initiative, I had been appointed leader. As I walked up to him, the soldier saluted me. 'Supplies have arrived, sir. What shall we do?'

"I was a bit surprise by the sudden promotion, but there

was too much to do to stop and think about it. I hollered for some people to come over. The activity helped lull them out of their shock. We set up tents and cots for the more severely wounded and organized a sort of triage center for the refugees who were now coming in ever-increasing numbers.

"There was food, military rations." Several of the boys grimaced at the mention. "Despite twenty-four hours without food, I couldn't eat. There was still one horrible chore ahead, the worst I had to see to. The dead had to be buried. We didn't have the strength or resources to do more than a single mass grave.

"The soldier promised that the bodies would be removed and buried properly when the crisis had passed. I doubt that ever happened now. It was only a matter of weeks before New York. With two epic disasters on its hands, the government never quite recovered.

"The days passed," he went on, "It was about the third day, I believe, that the Red Cross finally got to us. Like the National Guard, they were overwhelmed by the task of helping so many refugees. They did their best to supplement our food and supplies, but for the most part the only officials we saw were the list bearers."

"List bearers?" Luke asked, "What were those?"

"I don't know what their actual position or title was; that was just what we called them. They came every few days bearing long lists. They would take down the names of any new refugees. Then, in the evening, they would sit and recite from their lists, first the known survivors and then the confirmed dead.

"Periodically, someone would gasp at the name of a living relative or moan for a dead friend. But Chicago had been a huge city in those days. The bomb had decimated its core. Most of us never knew what became of our loved ones. Not that we held out much hope, given what destruction we had seen.

"The days dragged into weeks. We got regular supply drops from the Guard and from the Red Cross. A few relief workers came and went. They were far too few, and we seemed to be managing better than most aid stations, so mostly they left us alone.

"A few of our number had family elsewhere and left. The rest stayed. Many had lost their entire families and had nowhere else to go, no one to turn to.

"In fact, we managed remarkably well, given the circumstances. There was no real organization, but when supplies came, everyone pitched in. Our survival was on the line, and everyone knew it. We all did our best. No one challenged the nurse's authority over the dead and dying, which were by far the most numerous. None of us had any medical training. She told us what to do, and we did our best.

"A young woman, Maria, I believe her name was, took over the cooking and, by virtue, the food rationing. To my continual surprise, no one ever challenged my leadership either. Of course, it was more coordinating than leading. I never commanded anyone to do anything. I stated what should be done and someone did it.

"The soldiers rotated through the week. We always had at least one guard with a radio. They had little to do as guards went. Despite the widespread fear, there was little looting. There wasn't much left of Chicago to steal, for one thing. Besides, the would-be looters weren't in any better shape than we were. We even did a bit of looting ourselves, with the soldier's tacit approval. It was organized, and we shared what we found. Need outweighed everything those first few weeks.

"But the thing was, our needs were so basic. We looted for food, cloth for bandages, and clean clothes. The first looting expedition I went on stands out in my mind as the other moment that helped kill my former life. I was amazed to realize how little of what was in those stores had any value for us in those days, or in any day since.

"So anyway, there were no bandits, and the guards had nothing much to do. They pitched in when there was work, and they had one thing we desperately wanted: news. They had radios and contact with the outside world. They told us what was going on, and it wasn't pretty.

"The bomb, it was decided, had been Chinese made. The president claimed the Chinese were responsible. There was a big declaration of war. The government was still in the process of mobilization when New York happened, so I doubt we ever did anything. I have always had the bizarre image of a troop of US soldiers stranded somewhere over there."

"I can't believe the way you're talking about our government!" Daniel exploded. "How can you accuse America of starting an unjust war? Surely they had some sort of proof that the Chinese did it?"

"And surely they didn't leave soldiers over there," Patrick chimed in. "The US military does not leave its own behind."

"And how would you know?" Roger shot back. "You and your kind were hiding up in the mountains while the country you profess to love was falling apart and leaving millions to starve here and overseas."

The outburst seemed to drain the men. They looked around for support that didn't come. It was true; they hadn't been there. The ranch had done nothing to prevent the collapse.

Luke was looking thoughtful. Amy knew that look; he was searching his memory for something. At last he spoke. "You mentioned New York. What happened?"

"Someone blew the dikes," Roger said.

"What dikes?" Luke asked.

"Boy, you guys really have been out of touch. They'd been building dikes around New York for almost five years before the blast. They had to construct dikes round most coastal cities, what with the sea level rising," Roger answered.

"From global warming?" Amy put in.

"Yeah, that's right," he answered. Amy shot the boys a triumphant look.

"The sea level had been rising slowly for years. That had been ignored until almost too late. By the time of the blast, the water level was up several meters, and they expected at least another two or three meters before the changes they were instituting would have any hope of halting the trend," he went on.

"What kind of changes?" Luke asked.

Ruth laughed. "It was the same stuff the environmentalists had been talking about for most of my life; solar power, wind power, electric cars, and hydrogen batteries . . . anything to reduce greenhouse gases. They had initiated massive reforestation projects in the Amazon and in the Northwest US, but it was all too little, too late."

Roger took up his narrative again. "New York was only about three meters below sea level. But the terrorists were smart. They planted their bombs in the dikes and waited for the next big storm to blow in. The result dwarfed what happened in Chicago. Parts of the city were under as much as ten meters of seawater.

"While we never found out for sure who did Chicago, the group that bombed New York took full credit. It was an African group."

"Africans?" Luke gasped, "Since when were they our enemy?"

"They felt they had every right to destroy us. Maybe they did. We'd been wasting resources for years while they battled famine after famine. Then after Chicago, we diverted our entire world relief program back to our own catastrophe."

"Nobody could blame us for that," Patrick gasped.

"We left millions, if not billions, to starve," Roger replied. "They could blame us, and they did. After New York, things began to seriously unravel. We knew where the masterminds of the New York disaster were, and we responded against them. Small scale nuclear war."

"Serves them right," Patrick declared.

"You would kill millions because of the actions of a few rash men?" Ruth inquired.

Patrick blushed and looked away.

"Well, after that the news we received got pretty spotty. The government had a collapsing economy, food shortages, two massive relief efforts, and war on its hands. It's no wonder it collapsed. There was civil unrest in every city. Rioting and looting were everyday events. The National Guard was slowly drained away from Chicago to serve in whatever hot spot they were needed most. Ruth could tell you more about that; she was one of the Ten

Thousand Warriors for Peace and in the thick of it. My band and I had other concerns, like our survival."

"Ten Thousand Warriors?" Amy asked Ruth.

"Later," Ruth replied. "After dinner maybe. Let Roger finish his story first."

Roger nodded. "It's quite a story and deserves its own time." He took a gulp of his tea, sighed, and continued. "As for my story, let's see. By the time New York happened, they had shipped the worst of the injured out of our aid station. There were no refugee camps or an area big enough for everyone, so the healthier of us just stayed where we were. Meanwhile, the rest of the country saw martial law. The draft and food rationing started. Then one day, a grizzled old veteran who had recently been drafted back into service drove up with our supply drop. With it came a stack of old Army surplus backpacks. That was their way of telling us there wouldn't be any more supplies."

"He pointed in the direction of the nearest town with a Red Cross food station, and that was that. We held a big meeting and voted unanimously to stay together. By this time there were rumors everywhere of bandits in the countryside. While we were unarmed, there was a certain strength in numbers.

"That winter was the worst for me. It was the next two that were worst for most people, though. War rationing was in full effect. For many, this meant more food, or at least a steadier supply of less. The inequality of the marketplace was gone for the moment.

"Unfortunately, war rations required a coupon book. A coupon book required an address. We were homeless. We numbered almost two hundred at the start of our trek, and nobody would let us stay in one place long enough to get an address. We fell through the ever-widening cracks.

"The Red Cross had aid stations everywhere, but their food situation was critical. What little they had, they shared, at least. In some places, the locals headed us off before we got to the aid station. They didn't want competition for what little food the Red Cross had, and told us so at gunpoint. We had no choice but to move on. Other places let us in, even gave us some extra.

"That winter we lost over half our number to hunger and cold. We heard rumors of bandits frequently at aid stations, but our size and obvious poverty kept most of them away. Only once were we robbed by gun-toting militiamen.

"It was wandering the long stretches between towns when the enormity of what we had done began to sink in. While thousands starved in the cities, the countryside was a ghost town. So many farmers had gone bankrupt. So many old farmhouses lay abandoned and fields of weeds abounded; all victims of the transgenetic plague.

"A few farms survived, mostly by growing large subsistence gardens for themselves. Those close to towns often had a thriving black market going in fresh produce. Mostly, they were unfriendly and armed. We couldn't blame them; without every scrap of food many families would have starved. Besides, news of generosity could bring bandits down on them.

"By spring, we crossed the Mississippi river into Iowa. After that, things got a lot better. Everything from the Mississippi to the Rocky Mountains was Quiet Earth Country."

"What?" Luke asked.

"The Quiet Earth Society," Roger said. "They formed in rebellion against martial law. They were the only really successful rebellion. You'll meet some them yourself."

"We will?" Luke asked, his eyes narrowing suspiciously.

Patrick leaned forward in his chair. "What have you done, old man?"

Roger merely laughed and climbed to his feet. "Settle down, kid," he told Patrick. He went into the cottage and came out with a wooden box. "This is what you guys need, eh?" he asked, pulling out a glass jar with a wire strap lid.

Luke took it from him and nodded. "New canning jars," he said. "Yeah, that and a few other things."

"I'd gladly help you out, son," Roger told him. "I could give you a whole case. Any more, and Ruth and I would be short." He turned to Patrick, "You could invoke your right of seizure. We are just two old people, surely you could take us." Patrick shifted uneasily. "That'd net you maybe six cases. You'd still be way short, if I am not mistaken."

"You're right," Luke conceded, handing him back the jar.

"And we have none of the technology you need. So that means your only hope is to go to the Quiet Earth Society. They'd have what you need and more. You don't need to fear them. They're friendly enough, as long as you don't threaten them."

"Thanks," Luke said. "Tell us about them."

"The Quiet Earth Society is a coalition of environmentalists that knew society was on the brink of collapse long before anyone else. After years of failing to convince people, they started making their own plans.

They recruited re-enactors, buck-skinners, and SCA members."

"Buck-skinners and Scaws?" Kurt said.

"S-C-A," Roger spelled it out. "Society for Creative Anachronism. They were history buffs, went out on weekends and lived like it was the medieval times."

"Why?" Shawn asked.

"I don't know," Roger replied. "It was just some sort of hobby, something they did for fun."

Everyone looked around, mystified. "It does sound interesting," Luke said sheepishly.

"Oh, they were people like Luke," Mark joked. "That explains it." Several of the boys laughed. Luke blushed.

"It doesn't matter why they did it," Roger went on, "but the fact is, we were damn lucky they did. Before the blast, I had only thought as far as the store. If I needed new clothes, I went to a department store. If I needed food, I went to a grocery store. I never thought about where things came from or how they got there.

"That was a big part of the problem. Everybody was like me. Nobody thought beyond the store. When the stores closed, we were lost. When the grocers didn't have food, we got mad at them and rioted. Or we got mad at the government and rioted. Nobody thought of going out into the countryside and growing more. We'd forgotten the whole process. Everyone except the Quiet Earth Society, that is. They gathered a vast collection of skilled people. People with skills nobody had needed in generations. People who knew everything from organic farming, herbalism, wildcrafting, blacksmithing, weaving, you name it. When things started going wrong, they took to the countryside.

"While the militias fought for control and political power in the cities, the Quiet Earth Society was seizing national parks and vast tracts of countryside. They knew where the real power lay. They had primitive weapons and little technology. They lived by the motto that you should never rely on anything you can't replace yourself.

"They were outlawed for objecting to martial law. They fought a long guerrilla war against first the government and then a number of militias. I can't guess how many times the military tried to dislodge them. In the end, everyone who went after them eventually ran out of food, ammo, or both. And they won.

"Despite being a violent revolution, they were a free society. Outside of battle, they practiced democracy and were open to most anyone. We didn't know what they would make of our band of refugees, but they seemed like our best hope."

Roger laughed. "Would you believe that the military actually tried to warn us away at the Rock Island Bridge? Told us we were entering Iowa, and they could not guarantee our safety from those bandits, the Quiet Earth people.

"The truth was that there were fewer bandits in Iowa, thanks to the Quiet Earth Society. A young man took up with us just outside of Davenport. He was a witch."

"A witch?" Kurt asked, appalled. "Like with a tall hat and stuff?"

"No, of course not," Roger replied sharply. "What have they been teaching you up in those mountains? He was a witch, as in a member of one of those neo-pagan groups. Great people. He was trained in herbal medicine and was going to visit a distant relative with a difficult pregnancy.

"After Roderick took up with us, things got a lot easier. He knew a tremendous amount about plants. He taught us to gather wild foods. We learned to identify a number of edible plants, and soon we were eating better than we had in months. At times we even had enough extra to barter with townspeople for clothes and things.

"Roderick was also very well connected. Pagans had been moving to the countryside for years. They were the most successful of the survivors because they had always used mostly organic growing techniques anyway. They always had food to spare.

"As he came to trust us, Roderick used his contacts to get us a meeting with the Iowa Chapter of the Quiet Earth Society. We met them in a park just north of Des Moines. Even though at the time they were just beginning their struggle with the military, they knew they were going to win. They were already thinking beyond it to the future. They were using refugees and other homeless to start a giant permaculture frontier out here in the west."

"Permaculture?" Amy asked.

"Permanent agriculture," Luke supplied. "I've read about it—"

"In a book." Mark finished.

"Permaculture, like the name implies," Roger continued, "is meant to be permanently sustainable. But what they had in mind was greater than anything the founders of the philosophy could have envisioned. They figured if the environmental disaster had been brought on by our misuse of the land, then it ought to be reversible with enough work. They were building a whole new society based on the principles of giving more back to the land then we take.

"It was clearly the best deal going. We were to become the infrastructure for this new society of theirs. We would be trained in permaculture, building homes from scratch with natural materials, etc. We would establish farms all along the plains.

"The ordeal in Chicago had left many with a lasting fear of large cities anyway. We knew, roughly at least, what was going on in the major cities and had no desire to return to that.

"With the military after them, they couldn't work in the open yet. So our group was broken up at last and escorted west in small groups. I served with the society for a year and then went on to one of their training camps. That's where I met Ruth. We came out here together and built this place. We have had adventures enough for a book since we got out here, but that, I think, is enough of my tale for now."

"But what about the government?" Daniel pressed. "You talk like it just stopped working one day. Didn't somebody do something? Or did everyone just decide they didn't need the USA anymore?"

"Some people did," Ruth replied. "But most people were too caught up in their own day-to-day struggle for survival until it was too late. And no, it didn't just stop working. After Chicago, there was martial law. After New York, the civil government grew irrelevant. They didn't have the resources to stop what was going on.

"The military held power for a while. They tried to restore peace in their own way, but what does the military know of peace? In the end, they only made things worse. The states splintered off, and civil war erupted everywhere. Finally militias started to appear, no better than common thugs, for the most part.

"Some people stood up to them, tried to stop them. I was one of them for a while. I will tell you about that after we eat," Ruth finished.

5

Ten Thousand Warriors for Peace

"Dinner, right." Roger stood. "Tell you boys what. We got three goats. More than we need really, we have only put off butchering the one because it's more meat than Ruth and I need. If somebody will give me a hand, we'll have ourselves a feast."

After weeks on short rations, it was the best meal Amy had ever had. They roasted the rack of goat in the heavy clay oven. This fascinated her, Luke, and Kurt. The others ignored the proceedings.

Ruth and Amy built a large fire inside the dome while the men butchered the animal. Kurt helped Ruth gather a number of vegetables from the garden. Once the whole oven had reached the right temperature, the fire was removed. The earthen walls retained the heat and roasted everything to perfection. Ruth explained that while they had a wood stove inside, this time of year it was much better not to heat the house.

They ate on the veranda, the house being too small. Amy sat between a quiet and sullen Shawn and a talkative Luke. Roger sat on the other side of Luke and was explaining how the south-facing windows trapped heat in the winter and the deep veranda kept the hot summer sun off the same windows. It was exactly the sort of thing Luke got excited about, Amy thought.

After dinner Ruth produced two apple pies and warmed them in the cooling oven. Shawn poked at his slice suspiciously. "What did you say it was?"

"Can't grow apples where we live. Too high an elevation, or too short of a growing season, or something. I can't remember exactly, but dad always moans about it," Luke explained around a mouthful of pie. "Never saw what the big deal was until now. It's very good."

There was a chorus of agreement from the others. They were enthusiastic enough to get Shawn to try his piece. He roared his approval.

"Well, honey," Roger said as the final forks fell to empty plates, "are you ready for your turn?"

Ruth closed her eyes in contemplation. "Like my husband, I should preface my story by saying that it is hard to talk about before the collapse . . ." She waved off Luke's attempt at an apology. "It's not that. It's just that it was such a different world. It is all like a dream now.

"My life before the collapse was one of ignorance. I would have told you I was an environmentalist. I would have told you I was up on the latest news. I was even a member of the Sierra Club. When it all started happening I was just as surprised as everyone else.

"The problems seemed distant from everyday life. Rising temperatures could be ignored; hey, that's what air conditioning was for. Rising sea levels could be compensated for: build a dike. The ozone layered thinned, so you avoided the sun. Then the plague came. When your food supply is threatened, you take notice.

"At least for a while, that is; you still have to put food on the table, and in those days, that meant work. The daily grind, as I always referred to it, lulled me into complacency. Life went on.

"With the economy in a major downslide, unemployment was way up . . ." she laughed at her audience. "I imagine that more than half of what I am saying makes no sense. Let's see, unemployment means no jobs. No jobs means no money, and no money means no food. When people have no food they will do just about anything to get some. Violent crime was way up.

"It scared me. I decided that I needed to learn self-defense. I was living in Kansas City at the time and just down the street from me was a dojo—a training hall, that is—that taught Aikido. I signed up.

"I signed up wanting to know how to fight, to defend myself. Quickly it became more than that. It connected me to my Japanese roots. I was enthralled by the grace of the long-term practitioners, but mostly I was impressed with the philosophy."

"The philosophy?" Luke asked.

"Yes. Aikido means the way of peace and harmony," she said. "In Aikido, we use throws and holds to blend with our opponent and defeat him without harming him. We teach punching only as a means of practice. The idea of being at peace in the middle of a violent world struck a deep chord with me.

"It didn't hurt either that the instructor was shorter even than I am. Watching this little woman easily take on men several times her size was inspiring. She'd fight six or seven guys at once. She moved with such grace and confidence. It was amazing.

"When the blast rocked Chicago, I had been in training for almost a year. It had given my life new meaning. I was going four or five times a week and was deeply enmeshed. I was improving, but the art takes years to master.

"Chicago shocked me. It did everyone. I sent what money I could to the Red Cross. I even toyed with the idea of going as a relief worker. But my boss would have never approved it, and I didn't dare lose my job.

"Then New York came. Again I donated what I could; it wasn't much. Food prices were high. I was having a hard time just getting by. The problem seemed so big and far away. What could one little Midwestern girl do?

"As winter progressed the world seemed torn apart by violence. Food shortages and the state of emergency had everyone on edge. The economy was on its final leg, and there were more jobless than working. Utilities were disrupted. Electricity and gas shortages left many without heat.

"Everywhere there were more and more desperate people. At the slightest hint of a shortage, aid stations and grocers were overrun by rioters and looters. Even in Kansas City, rioting had become an almost daily occurrence. To maintain order, the police were using stronger and stronger tactics. They had to, or so they said.

"Several of our members were on the police force. Aikido's holds and nonviolent philosophy was ideal for their line of work. They spent a lot of time discussing what was going on. They were terrified by what they were seeing. Veteran police officers were being worn down and becoming callous. Worse still, they were relying heavily on the National Guard to help out. These young men were trained for war, not this. They, too, were getting callous. When the National Guard was not available, the city hired more cops, poorly trained men with guns and clubs. Deaths on both sides mounted. No one seemed to care.

"At least half of the officers in our club handed in their badges. It was a tough decision. They were still cops at heart, and the disorder all around was hard for them. But they could not go on killing every day.

"It wasn't just us in KC either. All over the Aikido community, the same problem was being discussed. The question went up the ranks: what should we do?

"The answer came back from Japan, from the Doshu, the leader of our system. 'What have you been training for, if not this?'

"That was our call to action. I can still remember the first action like it was yesterday. It was a cold February morning. A club member who had not given up his badge yet tipped us off. A Red Cross station just a few blocks away had announced a major cut in its rations. The cut was necessary but unpopular. The riot squad was being dispatched.

"The crowd was tense and things looked to be getting ugly. Many of them seemed eager for a fight. So were the police. As I said, most of them were newly hired thugs, barely worthy of the title of law enforcement.

"There was a thirty- or forty-foot gap between the two groups. We marched into that gap. We were completely decked out in our traditional garb, the Gi and Hakama: the pant-like skirt that Samurai wore for centuries.

"We spread out in two rows and sat down. I don't know what they must have thought, us just sitting there. Our instructor had a bullhorn and was calmly telling everyone there would be no violence today. We simply wouldn't allow it.

"I sat facing the police. I was still a novice and felt scared. Our instructor had planned it that way; all the novices faced the police. She thought they wouldn't move against us. She was wrong.

"First, they shot mace at us. It stung fiercely, and I could barely see through the tears, but I stayed where I was. When that failed to move us, they advanced. They came slowly with their clubs held high. I was so sure I was going to die. My heart was racing. I remember thinking, 'There are so many dying for no good reason. At least I'll die for a cause.'

"When the line reached me and the first policeman swung, I almost laughed. Compared to what I had seen in practice, this was a simple and sloppy attack. I didn't stand; I just moved sideways. He stumbled, and I pulled him down and pinned him easily.

"Another cop came up, this one a grizzled veteran. He had his club held up, and again I was sure I was going to die. An advanced practitioner of Aikido, or Aikikai, as we call ourselves, can easily handle many attackers. I was a novice. I was afraid that if I let the first cop up to take on the second, I would be killed. I was stuck and didn't know what to do.

"That second lasted a painfully long time, for both us, I think. Then the marshal sounded the retreat, and he pulled back. I let the first cop go as well. I saw that veteran a week later. He sat beside me at another action.

"The rioters sensed weakness as the cops pulled back, and they rushed in. They were met by our most experienced and skilled Aikikai. As the rioters rushed forward, they leaped to their feet and met them. Using graceful spinning throws, they sent the first wave back into the crowd. Each of our warriors became a spinning maelstrom. No rioters got through.

"It wasn't just us either. Dojos around the country had started doing the same thing. Everywhere, people had sat back and wrung their hands and worried. Now we had a chance to actually do something.

"The next day, I was in despair. There had already been another riot and several people had been killed. I thought we hadn't done anything at all. Then, I rounded the corner." She paused and smiled.

"There were hundreds there, all wanting in; they all wanted to join us. My instructor eyed them one moment and then nodded. She led the whole crowd to a nearby park. From then on, the lessons were free. Those with experience helped teach. It was incredible to teach so many at once.

"From that point on, the whole thing took on its own momentum. Often, our mere presence was enough to calm situations. We often could negotiate some sort of compromise."

"Compromise?" Patrick asked. "With rioters?"

"They were just people, scared desperate people," Ruth replied. "Once we got a reputation for being fair, our word that an aid station was doing its best was sometimes enough. That wasn't the only situations we went into, however. We kept the police from harassing the homeless and refugees as well.

Roger nodded. "That they did. More than once, they let us into aid stations when the locals didn't want us there. I'd have starved if not for the warriors. They did a lot of good, if you ask me."

"Our experienced members did a lot of negotiating," Ruth continued, "but they were few and far between. The new recruits often had limited understanding of Aikido and resorted to violence at times. But still, we did much better than anyone else."

"Yeah, but what good are those neat moves against a gun? Will Aikido stop a bullet?" Patrick demanded. "Peaceful intentions can't stop everything."

"We faced bullets twice, once at the beginning and again at the end," Ruth replied. "At the outset, the press gave us the name 'A Thousand Warriors for Peace.' Then there was Dallas. Twenty or so of our experienced members were trying to keep the police out of a shantytown on the edge of Dallas, Texas."

"You were trying to keep them out?" Shawn asked. "Didn't you want law and order?"

"No, we wanted peace and justice," Ruth replied. "Not the same things at all. That shantytown was all those people had, and the police wanted it torn down because the rich thought it was an eyesore. An eyesore. We sided with the protesters.

"The police fired shots over the heads in the crowd. It was soon obvious our people would not move. They knew clubs would be a disaster. Their marshal gave the order to shoot. Most of the police, to their credit, refused to obey. But some did."

"What happened?" Amy breathed.

"That day, the police won." Ruth replied. "Eight of the twenty warriors were killed and many more times that of the protesters. The rest fled. Twelve of the warriors were arrested and taken to jail. The next day, as news spread, the police chief came to work to find thousands of protesters outside the jail. They didn't shout or chant or anything. They just sat there, row upon row of them. Unnerved, he let the survivors go. For him and for the police, it was too late to undo the damage.

"Several major martial arts organizations officially joined the cause. Thousands of police abandoned their jobs for us. Even more individuals joined. From then on we were the 'Ten Thousand Warriors for Peace.'

"What? Just because a bunch of you showed up, he caved in?" Mark demanded. "That don't make no sense."

"Can you imagine thousands of people just watching you?" Kurt shuddered.

"It was the discipline," Roger said. "People yelling and shouting and breaking things was one thing. These were warriors; it must have been quite a sight."

Amy tried to imagine it but failed. Her whole life at the ranch had a grand total of forty some people. Thousands were beyond her.

"You said you faced guns at the end too?" Luke said. "What end?"

Ruth sighed. "Our movement was strong for another year. We did much good, or so I thought at the time."

"You did," Roger said.

"I think so too, but for a long time when I looked back, I thought we failed."

"Failed? How?" Amy asked.

"We held back the tide of violence, but we didn't stop it. Officially, martial law was in effect most of that time. Our practice was forbidden, but the military looked the other way. They had too much on their hands, and we were valuable peacekeepers. If we occasionally disagreed with them, well that was just the price they paid.

"As the states began to splinter off and civil war erupted, things changed. The local militias tried to shut us down. The real showdown came in Boston. The state militia was trying to keep a band of several thousand refugees out of the city. Most of the refugees came from New York and had been wandering the coast homeless for the better part of two years. Over a hundred of our warriors were there. They were trying to avoid a violent conflict as usual. They asked that a share of the Red Cross food within the city be brought out for the refugees. In return, they would march elsewhere.

"While the leaders were negotiating, several of the militia took matters into their own hands. They opened fire with semi-automatics. They killed most of the warriors and hundreds of innocent civilians as well."

"No way!" Daniel exclaimed. "Our government wouldn't do that."

"It wasn't the government anymore," Roger replied. "The military had been in charge for close to a year by that point. Their control was slipping. The local militias ran wild and looked after their own interests."

"My husband is correct," Ruth said. "It was local militia, not the government. Who can say they were wrong? People were starving in Boston too. They thought that sharing food meant that their friends or family might starve. What would you have done?"

"They should have shared," Roger growled. "Like we did. No, I have no problem saying it, they did wrong in Boston. Wrong."

Amy looked around. She knew Luke would share, or even Kurt and Daniel. But what would Shawn, Patrick, or Mark? She thought of the expedition in two factions now. She could easily see Mark opening fire on innocent people.

What if Elisabeth was going to starve or Dad? What would Amy do? She squirmed uncomfortably.

"That was pretty much how it ended," Ruth said. "We knew the military would not respect our rights anymore. They would use lethal force again and again until we were all dead."

"Most of our leaders were already in hiding. They were wanted for terrorism and other trumped up charges against the state. The movement was disbanded. We were given a choice. We could stay in the cities and continue our work under the very real threat of death, or we could bend our ethics and join the Quiet Earth Society out in the countryside."

"What do you mean, bend your ethics?" Amy asked.

"We were committed to nonviolence," Ruth answered. "And many of us followed that quite rigorously. The Quiet Earth Society wanted peace and freedom, but they were no pacifists. When push came to shove they fought to win, even if that meant killing.

"For many of our newer members, especially those who came from other martial arts that had a kill-or-be-killed philosophy, there was no debate. They headed for the proverbial and very real hills. The older members, those who had trained in Aikido for a long time, as well as many who had been attracted by the nonviolent philosophy, would not be party to violent revolution. Many opted to stay.

"I was torn. Many of my oldest and dearest friends were staying. I knew they would be killed eventually. I finally decided I couldn't stay. It wasn't that I was afraid of death; I had seen it dozens of times while working with them. But I felt that I could still make a difference alive. If I died, the evil men who were in power and making the bad things happen would win. They would go on doing horrible things. Alive, I might be able to help stop them.

"I had this friend . . . well, acquaintance, really. She led a women's spirituality course I had taken, and we remained in touch. She was still in town, though I was not sure why . . ."

"Had so many fled the towns by then?" Amy asked.

"No, that wasn't until the next winter," Ruth replied. "It was just that she was pagan."

"Pagan?"

"Yeah, you know the whole earth-worshiping group," Roger said.

They all shook their heads in confusion.

"I don't suppose the survivalists that raised you lot spent much time educating you on alternative religions," Ruth said with a soft chuckle.

"What sort of religion?" Mark asked blankly.

"Alternative," Patrick said, though the look on his face showed he didn't understand either.

"What, like Pentecostals?" Kurt asked.

Roger rolled his eyes. "Not even close. They believe in the Goddess, the mother earth."

"Never heard of that," Shawn said derisively. "Sounds

like some sort of hippie freaks."

"Dad told me there were these hippie freaks living just below us on the mountains before the collapse," Mark leered. "He remembered one young girl being particularly friendly." He sniggered.

Roger looked at him perplexed. "Actually, they are very friendly," he said, "and it turned out they were good people to know."

"How so?" Luke asked.

"About ten years before the collapse, they had a group of visionaries appear in their ranks. They spoke of a coming apocalypse. They said that the mother earth was about to shake off human desecration, as they described the environmental problems, with a violent upheaval.

"They began to travel around their festivals teaching. They taught survival skills, gathering food from the wild, organic farming, herbal medicine, everything they would need to survive. By the time it all started—the plague and Chicago—they had mostly dropped out of society quietly, going off to live on homesteads and communities far from the cities.

"I remember it being a bit of a joke even. One conservative radio host I listened to use to go on about, 'Where have all the hippies gone?' Funny, they seemed like such a small group until they were gone.

"We even had one in our office; a young gay guy. I thought he was nuts. He left about six months before the plague hit. Sold his half-million-dollar home in the burbs, left a successful career, and went to live in the woods somewhere.

"Well, he wasn't the one who was crazy, and it was no joke. When I was traveling, it was well known that if you could find a pagan homestead, they would almost always have something to spare.

"I can recall at the time," he went on, "thinking how weird their food was. They ate lots of drought-resistant crops like Amaranth, and easy-to grow vegetables like sunchokes. That's about all we eat anymore."

"So," Luke said to Ruth. "You went to join the Quiet Earth Society and met Roger. You two came out here, built this, and lived happily ever after."

"Yes, happily ever after," Ruth agreed with a smile. "But it was not quite so direct. I spent a year as a soldier for the society . . ."

"They let women fight!?" Mark roared.

Roger's face crinkled in confusion. "Haven't you been listening? She was already a second-degree black belt in Aikido and a veteran Warrior. Why wouldn't they let her fight?"

"Women can't fight," Shawn said. "Everyone knows that!"

"She beat Patrick," Amy said defending Ruth.

Patrick blushed and looked away. "I wouldn't want anything to do with a woman who fights," he muttered.

There was a tense moment, which was broken by Roger saying, "Good, then I don't have to worry about Ruth running off with one of you strapping young lads and leaving me alone."

Nervous laughter followed.

"While *fighting*," Ruth went on, "I was assigned to guard one of our renewal projects, one that Roger commanded. He was a great leader, and I fell in love with him immediately."

"Baa," Roger returned. "I had to woo her for months.

Besides, I was no leader. We in the renewal projects were mere number crunchers anyway."

"What was the renewal project?" Luke asked.

"We computed the number of trees, acres of wetlands, and whatnot it would take to return the world to normal."

"How many?" Luke asked.

"A lot more than we have now," was Roger's reply. "That's ultimately what drove us out here. The battle for what remained of the old civilization was winding down. It seemed a lot less important than saving the earth."

"We've had plenty of adventures out here as well," Ruth said. "Especially in the early days. There were still bandits about, recyclers traveling back and forth through the little towns, and then there was building this place. Even as small as it is, it was a big chore for the two of us. Then there's the weather these days, massive storms once or twice a year and not much rain besides. It's been hard."

"But worth it," Roger insisted.

"Speaking of this house," Luke asked. "What is it?"

"It's called cob," Roger explained. "It's a mix of clay, earth, sand, and straw. You mix it wet and make a sort of mud patty. You sculpt it into walls, letting it harden as you go. You end up with . . . well, you can see for yourself, it's practically as hard as stone. It's been here some twenty years with no wear and tear.

"It took us almost two years to build the house; we spent the first winter in the back half. Even though the barn is smaller, we went slower, and it was almost three years in the making. There's room for a few goats and a dozen chickens in the front half. There's a small storeroom in the middle, and we built a chapel on the back, small, but room enough."

"Where did you learn to do that?" Luke asked.

"That's what the Quiet Earth Society teaches. By adjusting the clay and sand content, you can build with almost any soil type. Things like bricks and concrete are awfully hard to produce any more, and even harder to ship. Dirt is everywhere.

"We had someone drive us out in an ox-drawn wagon. We brought our roof timbers and personal items. It would have taken several trips to bring enough wood to build. Besides we need every tree where it is, in the living forest."

Ruth added, "They thought of everything. Wood is so valuable that we buried it in a living roof to protect it. This house will outlive us by many, many years."

"And after that?" Daniel asked. He fumbled for the words. "I mean, it's not any of our business, but you guys have been out here for over twenty years. Do you have kids?"

"No, no children," Ruth replied. Roger looked away.

Finally he looked back. "Too much radiation, too much hard living, I don't know which. It's all too common these days."

"Some say," Ruth said quietly, "that we are a dying race."

A chill went through Amy. She thought of the ranch. Forty some adults had barely produced as many children in thirty years. And the next generation?

They spoke no more that night. Ruth's declaration had turned everyone introspective. The expedition camped in the Akira's front yard. Their little cottage was pressed to receive one visitor let alone seven.

When Amy awoke, she climbed out of her tent to find

Luke already up and helping Ruth load wood into the oven.

"She's explained everything to me," he told her excitedly. "How to build one and use it. It will cut our wood use in half, I bet." The ranch did all of its cooking on indoor wood stoves. "Best of all, we won't have to heat our houses up in the summer."

She gave him her sourest "good for you" look and went around to the outhouse. Out behind the barn, she heard Roger's voice, followed by Kurt's. They were just inside the back entrance of the barn, where Amy could only guess the chapel must be.

"It's very nice of you to show me this," Kurt was saying.

"No problem, lad," Roger replied.

"Who is that?" Kurt asked. Amy pulled back, not wanting to intervene.

"That's Mary of course."

"Mary?"

"Mother of Jesus."

"I know," Kurt replied. "I just didn't realize that people . . . you know."

"Worshiped her?" Roger finished.

"There's so much I don't know," Kurt said. "What's this mirror?"

"That's Ruth's," Roger replied. "This side is her Shinto shrine. Look, here's her family. She has all their pictures."

"What's Shinto?"

"It's the traditional religion of Japan. Ruth got into after she started doing Aikido."

"You mean she's not Christian?" Kurt sounded alarmed. "Aren't you afraid?"

"Of what?" Roger laughed.

"Going to hell." It was barely a whisper.

"Didn't Jesus teach us to be tolerant?" Roger asked.

"No! Well, at least . . . I'm not sure anymore. See, Dad gave me this . . ."

"Let me see. Hey, that's an old Gideon Bible, New Testament only. I haven't seen one of those in years. Here's mine; King James, very traditional. I was born Catholic, you know. I'm a bit broader now, but . . ." He broke off and sounded more serious when he spoke again. "What's bothering you, son?"

"Well, at home Dad always read from this big Bible," Kurt explained. "I thought I knew most of it by heart. Now I got my own little Bible, and I've been reading it every night . . ."

"Yes?"

"It's not the same. The stuff my dad reads is in there, but there's a lot he didn't read. Some things sound different when you read it all, not just bits."

There was a heavy sigh from Roger. "I hate to speak against anyone's beliefs, son," he said. "In my day, I've seen it all. There are good people in every religion, and there are bad. People have used the Bible to justify all sorts of beliefs. You just have to read it yourself and come to your own conclusions."

Amy retreated, not wanting to admit having overheard. She found the outhouse and sat there a long time thinking. Was Kurt having doubts?

By the time she got back, the rest of the camp was starting to stir. Kurt was now helping Luke and Ruth make pancakes. They made a stiff batter, more a dough really, which they would pound flat. Then Luke would throw them into the oven. Ruth would wait a couple of minutes and then deftly flip them out with her paddle.

Amy went to Roger, who was gathering up the expedition's canteens. They took them to a small pitcher pump atop a small wall.

"Rainwater catchment system," Roger confided. "We got nearly a thousand-gallon capacity. That storm you told us about hit here too. We've had three storms this spring, and that's all I expect. We have to make it last. There is enough for a few travelers, however."

They ate a solid meal of the pancakes topped by more apples and another fruit the children from the ranch had yet to experience: the peach. On the side, they had a vegetable that looked like a lumpy potato.

"Sunchokes," Roger explained. "Farmers used to spend a fortune trying to get rid of them. Now they're our best crop. They grow practically everywhere, even out here."

Amy took a bite and found it crunchy and not unpleasant. She preferred the apples, however, and told Roger as much. Ruth laughed as the boys all agreed.

Roger was full of advice as he explained the route they would have to take. "Now remember the plague and don't go eating any more corn, you hear?" They all nodded. "And it's affected rapeseed as well." Blank stares. "Canola?" he tried. Again, they all stared blankly at him. "Never mind," he concluded. "You don't know it, and you wouldn't eat something you couldn't identify."

"No sir," Kurt replied gravely.

They had plenty of food now anyway. The village was only a day and half away on foot. Ruth loaded them down with several thick, dark loaves of bread and several cans of everything from apples to tomatoes.

* * *

"I feel naked," Patrick grumbled as the Akira's farm disappeared from view.

"Glad you aren't," Amy muttered. She had felt very comfortable with Ruth and Roger. Now, just a few minutes away, it was back to the same old arguments and fighting.

"Come on," Daniel said. "We all agreed it was for the best."

"More like somebody decided, and you all caved in," Mark said.

"Well, he is the leader," Amy pointed out.

"Like hell," Mark muttered.

Shawn glared around mutinously.

"I don't see how the opinion of a noncombatant and a girl could possibly matter," Patrick said.

"Luke made the decision, and it was a good one," Kurt said. He gestured at the gun that was wrapped in cloth and strapped across his back. "You don't want the villagers thinking we're hostile, do you?"

"Bring 'em on," Patrick replied through clenched teeth.

"What if they're hostile?" Mark demanded.

"They're not," Luke said without looking back. "Roger said so."

"How do you know we can trust them?" Mark pressed. "They are a strange couple."

"Yeah," Shawn put in, "they're outlaws and everything. They could be trying to sabotage the mission."

"They are not outlaws," Amy shouted. "They are just a nice, old couple."

Shawn fell silent but Mark would not give up so easy. "They were outlaws, once."

"So were we," Daniel muttered.

"That's a lie!" Patrick snarled. "Take that back."

"It's not," Daniel insisted. "It's like Roger said, the president declared martial law. All our parents were military, weren't they? Why didn't they go? Why didn't they do something?"

"They had to stay," Shawn said, "to protect the ranch."

"Look, you heard Roger," Luke said. "It wasn't the legitimate government anymore. It's not outlawed if the government isn't legit. Not for the ranch or for the Akiras."

They all fell silent for a long while.

It was Mark that broke the silence. "I still say they're weird. Akira. What sort of name is that?"

"It's Ruth's family name," Kurt replied. "Her family is all dead, except maybe some distant relatives back in Japan. Roger had surviving relatives, but her name would die out. Family is very important to her." He hesitated like he didn't know quite how to say it. "It has to do with her religion somehow. Anyway, Roger told me about it this morning, how he took her name instead of the usual way around."

"So that's why she is so sad about not having children," Amy said. "Her name will die after all."

"I think so."

"What? The man taking the woman's name?" Mark interrupted, "I told you they were weird. There's no way I would ever agree to that."

"Carol's family wouldn't have let you," Amy sneered.

"What's that supposed to mean?"

"You know."

"A man has the right to establish discipline in his own house," Patrick said, jumping to Mark's defense. "It's one of the rights we fought to protect."

"If a bitch don't know her place, a bitch gotta learn," Mark said. "If Luke ain't figured that out yet . . ."

"Enough!" Luke yelled, turning on Mark. Mark blanched but held his ground. Luke turned beet red and huffed slightly but did not speak. Finally Mark looked away. Luke turned back and led them on without speaking again.

Is that what they think? Amy wondered bitterly. *Am I Luke's bitch?* Just let one of them say something to her. She'd pound them flat. She stared around her, trying to figure out whom to be mad at. Mark? Of course him, but none of the others showed any surprise.

He eyes narrowed suspiciously. She and Luke were just friends. Had he been giving the other boys the impression there was something more going on? *If he has, I'll kill him,* she thought savagely.

By late afternoon the wide plain had become dotted with trees and started to slope down into a river valley. At the lip of the valley, a solitary form rose. Luke, still ahead and having not spoken since the earlier outburst, stopped and looked through his binoculars.

"What is it?" Patrick asked.

"Some sort of pagoda," Luke replied.

"What's a pagoda?" Shawn asked.

Luke's brow furled. "It's like a picnic shelter, a roof but no walls."

"Oh. Well, why didn't you just say picnic shelter then?" Shawn asked.

"Because some of us have brains," Amy muttered under her breath. Luke didn't answer.

"There's something in it," he continued. "But I can't

make out what it is from here."

"It's too early to be the village," Kurt said.

"Yes, definitely." Luke replied.

"Could be some sort of border station," Patrick said. "The guards will undoubtedly be armed. Perhaps it would be prudent—"

"No," Luke said firmly. "That's exactly why we put them away."

Patrick looked angry but said nothing.

"I think it's a statue anyway," Luke said putting his binoculars away. "It's not moved at all. Let's go find out."

They made their way forward. Mark and Shawn grumbled to each other about going into danger unprepared. Amy wished they'd shut up. All this talk about hidden enemies was making her jumpy. Enough of it, and she'd be seeing enemies everywhere as well.

As they approached, the pagoda resolved itself into focus. It had a bell-shaped top, like pictures Amy had once seen of China. Inside was a huge black statue of a woman sitting. Her back was to them, but they could see she had her knees up with her hands on them. Her head was thrown back in a silent scream. Amy shivered involuntarily.

As they got closer, Amy noted some rust spots on the statue. Who made statues out of metal? It made no sense. Amy was drawn to see what lay on the other side of the statue.

"Gross!" Mark spat as he circled to the front. Moments later, Amy circled around far enough to see what Mark was commenting on. The statue graphically portrayed a woman giving birth. Between her spread legs was the horned head of a bull.

"What kind of sick thing is that?" Patrick demanded from behind her.

Amy felt something pull at her gut. She was torn. Part of her agreed with Patrick. But the statue also held a strange power. The woman's face, thrown back, was not entirely visible. What showed held an unearthly agony. *Like she's suffered so much,* Amy thought.

"It's ungodly, whatever it is," Kurt said.

"Here's an inscription," Luke said. He read, "In the third year of our fight for independence, 912 people died here. One year later under a harvest moon, 1,317 weapons of mass destruction were sacrificed to make this. Blessed be the Cult of the Iron Mother."

"Cult of the Iron Mother?" Daniel asked. "What's that?"

Luke shrugged. "Well, Roger and Ruth said there were Pagans, and that they believed in the mother earth. My guess is this is theirs."

"But what's it mean?" Kurt asked.

"I don't know. We'll have to ask someone," Luke said.

Amy put one hand on the statue. Though in the shadow now, it was still warm from the sun. Mark and Patrick both made noises of disapproval. "She touched it," Shawn commented. Amy was irritated by their juvenile revulsion.

What did it mean? What were the weapons of mass destruction? How were they sacrificed? Then it hit her. "It's gun metal," she said.

"What?" Luke asked.

"The statue," she replied. "It's made of gun metal. That's what it means by weapons of mass destruction. Someone melted down over thirteen hundred guns to make . . . this."

"What sort of fool would melt down guns to make something sick like this?" Mark demanded.

"I don't care," Patrick replied. "But it creeps me out. Let's get out of here."

After another moment, Luke nodded his agreement and led them off.

They camped at the base of the valley within sight of the river. A serviceable wooden bridge led across. The next morning, they crossed and continued their journey.

After a few miles they came to a crossroads. They went straight, as Roger had directed.

After the crossroads, the road began to look more and more used. Ruts from wagon wheels became more common, and the woods that now gathered on either side had a manicured look to them.

Just before noon, they woods gave way to a rolling land of farms and plowed fields. Sheep and cattle grazed by thatched barns. Amy followed Shawn's wide-eyed gaze to a young lady who casually regarded them from the other side of a low stone wall.

6

The Quiet Earth Society

Seemingly unconcerned by their sudden appearance, the woman watched them as they approached. She wore a simple blue dress and a small corset of dark brown material. The dress and corset combination showed quite a bit more cleavage than the ranch women would have found appropriate. At her waist, a leather belt held numerous pouches and a thick wooden cup. *She could be right out of a medieval fairytale*, Amy thought.

"We come in peace," Luke said. He started to describe their mission.

The woman cut him off. "What's that oaf staring at?" she asked. "Hasn't he ever seen a woman before?"

Shawn went beet red and looked away mumbling. *He's hoping to find a woman*, Amy realized with a start. All her life she had moaned and complained about the ranch, about how she had only one friend. What about Shawn? He had friends, sure, but what was it like knowing there was no woman for him? Amy would most likely end up a spinster, but that was her own damn fault. Should Shawn be forced into permanent bachelorhood by simple mathematics?

"You guys have come from a long way off, by the look of it," the woman said, her demeanor turning pleasant again. "Do you have any news for a poor girl who has never left her valley?"

Luke looked uncertain. Amy stepped up. She felt vaguely jealous of the attention the woman was paying to Luke. She knew that was irrational. "Not really," she told the woman. "We come from up in the mountains and have just left our valley for the first time. I am Amy Beland of Freedom Ranch."

The woman introduced herself as Wren. Amy introduced the men.

Wren looked up at the distant mountains and whistled. "I didn't know anybody lived up there."

"We kind of keep to ourselves," Luke said. "Do you know the way to the village?"

She gave him a long, patient look. "Road only goes two ways, Honey." Luke blushed. "Tell you what," she continued, "I'll escort you in. A bunch of big, strapping, mountain lads shouldn't be wandering around all by yourselves, now should you?" She vaulted the wall easily and took Luke's arm. "Right this way, kind sir."

Amy felt another pang of irrational jealousy and quickly squelched it. Wren led Luke off, chatting amiably. The other boys followed close behind, watching her. *They aren't being suspicious this time.*

Just over the crest of the next hill, they could see the village. It was all laid out in one lane, a collection of thirty or so houses of the same earthen material as the Akira's. While several had heavy sod roofs like the Akira's, most favored second stories of wood and thatched roofs. At the end of the village, the lane bent around a large community hall.

The thatched roofs and smoking chimneys gave the whole village a fairytale look. Amy recalled several swords and sorcery books that Luke had talked her into reading; this would the perfect setting for any of them.

As they approached, Amy saw many distant figures heading toward the village. Their approach had not gone unremarked, and apparently visitors were rare enough to draw a crowd. Then again, how would the ranch handle half a dozen visitors?

At the edge of town, an old man sat on a stool with his back against a tree and his nose in a book. He wore a simple tunic of rusty brown that went almost to his knees and gray leggings. Beside him was an unstrung bow.

"Amos Dietrich!" Wren shouted. "Some guard you make."

"What's that, Wren?" he muttered, looking up. Spying the strangers, he stumbled to his feet, fumbling for his knife. "Friend or foe?"

"Friend," Luke assured him quickly.

"You are absolutely hopeless, Amos," Wren went on. "Just go and get Mr. Quimby, will you?"

"Yes, Wren," he said and was gone.

"I really have to apologize for Amos," Wren said. "It's been years since guard duty meant anything except lazing in the shade. Only the worst of the lazy ones take it."

Amy couldn't help but notice that Shawn was still watching Wren, though more discreetly. She had noticed

167

out of the corner of her eye, after being introduced, he had sounded Wren's name out to himself several times as though trying to be extra sure he remembered it.

An elderly man approached. He was tall with shoulder-length, dark hair that was peppered with gray. He wore a simple brown tunic as well, with gray leggings and a tooled leather belt. Despite the similarities in dress, his bearing couldn't have been more different than Amos's. You could tell he was one of the village leaders, just as you could tell that Amos Deaton ran the ranch. It was something in the way he held himself.

"I am Johnathan Quimby, gatekeeper for the village of Bullhaven," he said in a deep sonorous voice. "I bid you welcome and offer you our hospitality."

"I am Luke Zachary of Freedom Ranch," Luke said, taking his hand. "We gladly accept your hospitality. We are here on an urgent mission—"

"Later, son," the man interjected with a wave of his hand. "First, hospitality. You must be weary and thirsty." He turned to the gathering crowd. "We are honored by guests. We will toast their arrival in the hall, and tonight there will be a feast."

A cheer greeted this pronouncement. Quimby led Luke off, the two falling into conversation at once. Everyone else followed behind. Villagers started plying the boys with question about the world beyond their little valley.

Amy could only guess from their reception that the days of bandits must be long over. No one seemed to doubt their peaceful intentions. *Maybe they should*, she thought as she watched Patrick's assault rifle bounce across his back.

They passed into the community building. It was dark and cool inside. The main room was filled with long, low wooden tables and benches. Cups were being filled behind a bar and passed around. Several were brought their way.

One was pressed into Amy's hand. She eyed it suspiciously. The dark frothy liquid inside smelled strongly of yeast. She was not sure what she was expected to do, so she held it.

"To your health and good fortune," Mr. Quimby told them loudly.

"To your health and good fortune," Luke returned. A cheer showed that he had made the proper reply. Following Luke's and Quimby's example, Amy tilted the mug back to her mouth. She nearly spit the liquid back out. It was bitter and foul, as bad if not worse than it looked.

"What is this stuff?" she whispered to Luke.

"To long life and happiness," someone shouted at the back of the crowd. Luke responded in kind, and there was another long drink.

"It's beer," Luke whispered back as he lowered his mug.

"Beer?" Amy replied. "Doesn't look anything like the stuff Dad drinks."

"That's the O'Malley's home brew," Luke told her. "I've had a taste or two. This is much darker and stronger, but it the same stuff, I'm sure."

The toasting went on for some time. Even taking the tiniest swallows, Amy had drained half her mug. Most people had been through at least one refill.

Amy looked around her. The hall was an amazing re-creation of a medieval feasting hall. It had a large fireplace on one side, which was quickly being filled and a fire lit. Heavy tapestries hung on the other walls and oil lamps were spaced evenly along the wall.

The people helped to complete the image. The men and several of the women wore simple tunics of earthen colors and leggings. Other woman wore floor-length dresses, with or without a corset like Wren's.

Amy felt a tug at her sleeve. How long had she been spacing off? Luke was pulling her through the crowd after Mr. Quimby. She managed to deposit her mug on a table and shake her head to clear it as she followed.

"He wants to discuss our mission," Luke said. They broke through the crowd and were led down a back hallway. They were shown into a small side chamber that housed a short table and a half-dozen chairs. An elderly lady in a floor-length white dress was already seated waiting for them. She rose as they entered.

"This is Irene McKinis," Mr. Quimby told them, "the head of the village counsel. You'll deal with her."

"Pleased to meet you," Luke said taking her offered hand. "I am Luke Zachary of Freedom Ranch."

Amy had thought Quimby was the leader. Now she discovered the village was led by this woman. She was impressed by that fact.

Luke impressed her even more. He didn't miss a beat. If a woman leader surprised him, he didn't show it one bit. After introductions, he immediately began to describe the plight of the ranch, with an occasional nod to Quimby, to whom he had already spoken. Amy listened in silence, unsure what her presence was meant to imply. Surely they had already proved their goodwill?

Luke produced a neatly folded stack of papers, the list of what the ranch needed, and handed it to Quimby. The older man read it intently while Luke finished his story.

"Our village has always been ready to help those in

need, even in the early days when we had little ourselves," the elderly lady told him. "However, charity breeds dependence. That's bad for both sides. We would work a trade, if possible."

"Of course, I agree totally," Luke said. "I've been thinking about that. To be honest, we didn't expect to find any civilization . . . quite like yours. I am not sure that we have anything you would want or need. But we do have six strong men willing to work, and Amy here."

Amy squirmed uncomfortably as she became the center of attention.

"The mechanic?" Quimby asked mildly. Luke nodded.

As if in answer to Amy's unspoken question, Irene said, "Perhaps you think we are too primitive to need your help?"

Amy shrugged noncommittally, not sure what to say. It certainly seemed primitive, even by the ranch's meager standards. Irene chuckled. She drew a flashlight from a drawer on one side of the table and flicked it on, shining it at the ceiling. Deep in the shadows above the sputtering oil lamps were dark, long panels: fluorescent lighting.

"I saw the wind generator on the way in," Luke said. "It was not running, so I took a chance and dropped the hint that we had a mechanic of sorts along."

"The oil lamps are quaint, but I'd really like my real lights back," Irene said.

Amy was startled; she had missed the generator. Lucky that Luke hadn't.

Irene went on. "We don't know what's wrong. It went out during the last storm. We have a backup biodiesel generator. We use it for some things, but it is too resource-intensive for everyday use. We have sent to the

Greenbowes for a repairperson. Spring is their busiest time, and the usual repairwoman is out. It could be several months before she'll be able to find time for us."

Amy was getting the gist of it now. "I can take a look. We had a wind generator at the ranch at one point, so I know the basics. I can't make any promises until I've seen it."

"Understood," Irene assured her. "At any rate, that'll be a big help. If you can even tell us what's wrong with it, then the Greenbowes will know what and who to send."

"Even so we may have a problem," Quimby said, looking up from the list. "We can certainly provide an equivalent to all of the household things on the list, canning jars and whatnot. But there are some technical things here, solar panels and batteries? The Greenbowes produce that sort of stuff. Refrigerant? You'd have to contact the Cyclers about that."

"We had hoped to salvage," Luke insisted. "Are there any abandoned towns nearby?"

"I'm afraid not," Irene said. "Years ago, back in the early days, there were groups that made their livings on salvage. They were often violent, quasi-military groups, not a nice bunch at all. We had enough fighting by then, and it served both of our interests to let them be. We even helped them from time to time. We didn't want abandoned cars and crap sullying the 'natural landscape' we were trying to create."

"And it got them out of our region faster," Quimby agreed. "The three closest towns were reduced to little more than foundations before they gave up. We can check with neighboring villages, but I wouldn't hold out much hope."

"Then it's hopeless?" Luke asked.

"Not hopeless," Irene assured him. "Farther in, you will find more. They may have scavenged the little towns dry, but it will take years to empty the major cities of everything of value. Every major city is home to communities of Cyclers, who live by salvage. We'll pave the way for you even. We'll set up credit with the Greenbowes and with the nearest Cyclers, in Kansas City. They will give you what you need, and we will see that it is paid for after the harvest.

"That just leaves you to settle with us. Spring is a busy time here as well, and we certainly can use six strong men. However, your road ahead is still long, and we shouldn't keep you. So here's my offer—you will work for us for one week, the service of six strong backs and one skilled mechanic. Then you will go on to the Greenbowes and the Cyclers. It is a long trip that we rarely make anymore, so we'll ask you to do some minor business for us as well. Does that seem fair?"

"More than fair," Luke replied. Amy was thrilled. They had completed the mission.

As they returned to the feasting hall, Amy sought out the faces of the expedition members. She felt no great love for any of them, but the sea of strange faces was disconcerting. Then it hit her. How many old people were there here? Everywhere she looked, she saw graying hair and lined faces. Maybe a dozen or less young people could be seen anywhere. Was the human race truly dying?

"So much for a discreet mission," Luke groused.

The expedition had been placed at a central table near the bar. A whole crowd was milling around plying them with questions. The boys, still drinking, were happily telling everyone stories about ranch members and describing the place in great detail.

"An ox-drawn plow?" Kurt was saying incredulously. "At the ranch, we have a tractor."

"Yeah, it was a very long hike, I'll tell you that," Mark was telling someone else. "About three weeks."

Luke pushed through the crowd and drew everyone's attention. He quickly explained the deal to his team.

"A whole week?" Mark groaned. "I didn't know the mission would take so long."

"It's going to take a lot longer than that," Luke replied, irritated. "That's just how long we work for the villagers. Then we have to go to the Cyclers."

"How long will that take?" Kurt asked.

"Most of the summer, by the sound of it," Luke answered. "We're going to be cutting it very fine, I'm afraid. It is quite a trip on foot. They haven't been there themselves in many years. That's why they are so eager to help us. We'll be able to pick up a few things for them as well."

There were groans around the table. "All summer?" Shawn gasped.

"At least from here on out, it will be more civilized," Amy put in. "There will be regular roads and places to re-supply."

"What about Jacob and the others?" Patrick asked. "They don't have the supplies to last that long."

"The villagers will send a party out looking for them," Luke said.

"You told them where Liberty Farm is?" Patrick hissed.

"It was that or leave Jacob to starve," Luke replied. "Besides, it's abandoned. It doesn't matter."

"Do you think Jacob will agree?" Patrick asked.

"He'll have to understand."

"Down here all stinking summer," Mark muttered.

The bad mood left almost as fast as it came. The reason was easy enough to spot. Their mugs were filled again and again. Villagers regularly thought up yet another toast, and the whole hall drank.

Except for Mark, they were all still considered "boys" at the ranch and were not allowed beer. Some of them had a drink or two, when they managed to steal a bottle. Now, they were being given it freely.

It was not just that. Here they were accepted as the men they wished to be. They were heroes of a sort. They were being treated as adults and were reveling in it.

They all drank deeply and long. Mark, it was well known, was rapidly following his father down the well-worn path of alcoholism. Today it seemed that the whole expedition was hell bent on catching up.

The strong brew was having its effect on the boys. A heavyset man with a gray beard was leading Patrick and Mark in the chorus of a rather bawdy song that Amy was sure the folks at the ranch would not approve of.

Amy noticed Shawn, mug at his lips, looking around darkly as if to challenge anyone to try to talk to him. A quick look in the direction of his glances was enough to reveal the cause of his foul mood. Wren sat a few tables away, with her arms around a young man. Again, Amy felt an unaccustomed pang of sorrow for the man she had hated for so long.

Food was served shortly, and to Amy's great relief, water was offered as well as beer. The feast went on for what seemed like ages, building slowly up from salads and vegetables to a main dish of roast beef. After a long, hard day, it was delicious.

Afterward, they were led to an unused cottage at the edge of the village, big enough to accommodate them all. Amy collapsed in her bed almost immediately. She fell asleep to the sounds of the others still drinking and laughing in the other room.

When she woke up the next morning she found Mark, Patrick, and Daniel passed out in the main room. Shawn was puking noisily in the bathroom. Luke's eyes shot daggers at the sleeping forms as he shuffled through, but it was obvious that he too was hung over.

"Can't take your drink?" Amy shouted into the bathroom. Shawn winced and growled angrily as he dragged himself out and flopped onto a couch.

Mr. Quimby strode in. "Good morning, Lady and Gentlemen," he declared happily. There was a chorus of groans. "Don't get much beer up in the mountains, I take it?"

"No sir, we don't," Luke replied.

"No mind," Mr. Quimby went on amiably. "We get that reaction quite a bit, to be honest. Those buck-skinners over the hill are fine people, but they have never been quite the brewers we are. A lot of our visitors comment on the quality and potency of our brew. I trust it will not interfere with working today?"

"No sir," Luke replied, kicking Shawn, who had drifted off again. Shawn glared at him.

Mr. Quimby turned to Amy. "We've got the Greenbowes on satellite hookup this morning. They want to know if they still need to send someone out."

"I'm ready to take a look whenever," she replied.

"Good, good," he replied. "The sooner the better." To Luke he added, "Michael will be around in about fifteen minutes to pick you up, okay?"

Amy snagged an apple and a roll on her way out the door. She'd have to ask later who'd provided them. She munched as she followed Quimby across the village.

"Do you know the Quiet Earth Society?" she asked.

"The Quiet Earth Society?" he said. "What a strange question, child. Of course. I was part of the society, or I am, I guess. We never officially disbanded, even though nothing has been done in years. Why do you ask?"

"These people we met on the way in told us about them —about you, I suppose. They said you had fought the government."

"The military," he corrected. "Yes, we did." He gave her a shrewd look. "Wondering how a bunch of old coots like us took on America's finest?"

Amy shrugged.

"Well, for one thing we weren't old then. We were young men and women in our prime."

"It's not that," Amy said. "It's just, well, bows and arrows against guns? It seems improbable."

He laughed. "Yes it does, and it did. They never could quite believe it. I think that's part of why we won; they never could believe we were actually going to stand up to them, so they weren't prepared when we did. But it's not as insane as it sounds, anyway. Our motto was 'never rely on anything you can't replace.' Our enemies made that mistake, not once but many times. Assault rifles are deadly weapons, until you run out of ammo. Then they are just lopsided clubs.

"I'll tell you a secret, though," he leaned in conspiratorially, "mostly we avoided fighting. We were locals, and they were mostly soldiers shipped in from god knows where. We used our knowledge of the area and the terrain to our advantage. We led them on a merry cat and mouse chase all over this region. After they had used up their ammo and their supplies, we would move in.

"Our real weapon was always food. The early military dictators were a stupid lot. They fought over politics. We went straight for the food supply. Once the countryside was on our side, it was over. They just didn't know it until winter hit."

He chuckled. "I remember this one time, I was on a lone scouting mission when a squadron of KC militia spotted me. They pursued me for miles, doggedly. They finally cornered me in a valley not far from here. I thought my number was up for sure. You know what? They wanted to surrender. They had heard that we had food, and they were starving."

"What did you do?" Amy asked, eyes wide.

"I traded them my pack for their guns. I had to scavenge for a couple of days to make it back, but it was worth it. It was quite a coup."

"I thought you didn't use guns?"

"We didn't, but we liked to get them away from those who did. They were running out of ammo, and the parts factories were shutting down, but each one we destroyed sped the process up. That was important to us; people were dying from the damn things every day."

"So you destroyed the guns?" Amy asked.

"Gave them to the cult," he said.

"The cult?"

"Cult of the Iron Mother."

"Like that statue!" Amy gasped, remembering the inscription.

"You must mean the one up on Bull Creek," he said. "That's the only one in our region."

Amy shrugged.

"Big statue of a woman giving birth to a bull? Arnie Maus did that himself," he said proudly, "to commemorate the battle we fought up there. I was there, and I can tell you it was quite a fight. We'd been chased most of the summer by nearly a thousand soldiers. Regular troops too, not the usual conscripts. They gave us a run for our money. Nearly caught us several times.

"They had vehicles, big armored troop carriers, and even a couple of tanks. Luckily, we'd been operating in the region for a couple of years already. One of the first things we did was to cut up the roads, sabotage them in critical places to slow down anyone in vehicles. That stopped most cars, but the transports they had were merely slowed down. Despite their superior speed and communications, we stayed one step ahead of them. It often meant splitting up and backtracking, but we were used to that.

"Anyway, winter was coming on. We had to get home to get the harvest in, or we'd starve. We knew that, but they didn't think that way yet. So we knew we had to make a stand, end the offensive one way or another."

"Bows and arrows against guns is one thing; now you are going to tell me you took on tanks?" Amy asked. She put her hands on her hips and scowled doubtfully.

He laughed. "That's where knowledge of the terrain comes in handy. We burned out the bridge over Bull Creek and waited on the far side. The river was just deep enough to hold the tanks and transports back. They knew we were gathered in force on the other side, so they risked sending the men across on a smaller bridge, just as we planned.

"The far side was heavily wooded. The thing about thick woods is this: a gun has a longer range than an arrow, but in the woods, your range is as far as your line of sight. It's the same if you have a gun, a bow, or a knife. Also, in deep woods, arrows have a surprising advantage over guns: they are quieter." He laughed again at Amy's expression. "When a gunshot goes off everyone looks in that direction. An arrow, on the other hand, makes no sound until it hits. If the archer is good, and we were, he or she shoots from a distance and is long gone before the arrow lands. The effect is that it appears the arrows just come out of nowhere. Quite unnerving for the enemy.

"It was a bloody battle, and the outcome was far from certain. We lost many good people." He stopped and stared off into the dawn. "We fought well into the night. Just after moonrise, we heard a loud explosion. The far side of the river was lit up, flames leaping high into the air. A friend of mine named Peter Wales had swum across the river under the cover of darkness. He got close enough to drop a grenade into one of the transports, the one carrying the extra fuel. He lost his life, but it turned the tide.

"The enemy withdrew, and by morning, they raised the white flag. Their transports were disabled, and their tanks had virtually no fuel. They didn't have the supplies for the long hike back to civilization. They wanted to barter food for leaving us in peace. So once again, food was the real weapon."

After a moment's pause, they continued on their way. Up ahead, another man awaited them with a large trunk. He was introduced, but Amy promptly forgot his name. He wore the now-familiar tunic and leggings. He hoisted the trunk and followed them.

Amy craned her neck to see the wind generator. It was a small tower, maybe thirty feet high, with a modest unit on top. That was enough out here on the plains. It ran two community buildings; the villagers did without in their houses.

Right now, the unit spun feebly in the breeze. "No good." Amy told them. "I can't see what's wrong from here."

Mr. Quimby nodded to the man, who sat his trunk down. He opened the lid, and Amy saw, chagrined, that she needn't have carted her tools with her all this way. They had everything she could possibly need or want right there.

"The Greenbowes insist that we keep a full set available at all times. It saves their people having to carry very much," Quimby told her.

"It looks pretty bleak up there," Amy said a half an hour later as she descended the tower. Her worst fear, at least, had been avoided. She had been afraid that she would have no idea; wind generators could be very different. However, this one looked almost exactly like the Burgey XP they had at home, except its logo read, in a cursive scrawl, Greenbowes Tech. "It looks like lightning in the last storm fried the whole unit. The lightning rod is down, and there are smoke stains everywhere. I think the whole unit is fried."

The men tsked sadly as they led her back toward the community center. "They'll have to bring a new unit," Quimby said. "Gods know how long that will take."

"Sorry."

"Not your fault; you did your best," Quimby reassured her. "Besides, look at it this way, you've saved us months. They'd have sent the repairwoman out and then she'd have had to go all the way back for a new one anyway. Now she only has to make one trip."

Back in the main hall, she was led to another back room. There she found something her dad had talked about all her life, but she never dreamed she'd see. They had two computers. One was even operational; Mr. Quimby sat down at the glowing screen and began typing at the keyboard.

"I'll try to get the Greenbowes on satellite hookup and see what they have to say," he said. Amy watched over his shoulder but could not make any sense of the changing screens.

"You can do that? Talk to them from here?"

"Sure. We have a half dozen or so communication satellites we can access," he said. "They were all launched before the collapse, of course. What happens when they give out is anyone's guess. Maybe we will have the capacity to replace them by then, and maybe not. Maybe it will all be a moot point."

He did manage to get a hold of someone in the Greenbowes' technical workshop. They agreed to send out a replacement generator as soon as possible. They would need new wiring as well, and that was in short supply. It was added to the list of things to get from the Cyclers.

* * *

That night Amy, Luke, and Kurt shared a quiet supper on the porch of their cottage. The others were down at the main hall for supper and what the men at the ranch would have called the hair of the dog that bit them.

Kurt was still queasy from his first experience with beer and went to bed shortly after supper.

"I'll be so glad when this mission is over," Luke griped. "Leading that pack," he thumbed toward the village, "is like . . ."

"It's like the time I had to babysit the Sunday school." Amy shuddered.

Luke threw his arms in the air. "They're at it again. You'd think last night would have been lesson enough, but no. I hope they don't do anything embarrassing. I wish I knew what they were thinking."

"I don't know about all of them," Amy replied, "but Shawn's looking for a woman."

"What makes you say that?"

"The way he looks at Wren."

"She's engaged," Luke told her.

"I didn't know that."

"Yeah," he said. "That's part of our work agreement, helping her fiancé Devon build their house."

"Anyway, that's what he's hoping: that he'll find someone." Amy said.

Luke thought awhile. "I guess that's not surprising. I suppose it has been hard for him all these years, knowing there was nobody for him. He is not as lucky as we are."

"And how lucky are we?" Amy asked coolly.

There was an uncomfortable pause as Luke realized he had said something wrong, but he was not sure how to get out of it. "Well you know, you and me."

"You and I . . . what?"

"Well, we have been going to dances together for five years."

"As friends," Amy said.

"I thought that I would ask my dad if I could have that old trailer behind our house. Daniel and I were going to fix it up. Then we could, you know, get married," he finished lamely, turning red and looking away.

"You and Daniel have planned this?" Amy was incensed. "When were the two of you going to tell me? Before or after the marriage?"

"It's not like that," he protested. "I intend to propose proper-like, get your dad's permission and all."

"My dad?" she snarled.

He blushed, realizing that he had, again, said the wrong thing. "Amy," he continued to protest, "I care for you and you care for me. Besides, who else are you going to marry?"

"That is none of your damn business!" she yelled, leaping to her feet. "I will not have my fate decided for me. Not by you and Daniel, and not even by my father. Do you understand?" Without waiting for a reply, she turned and fled into the night.

She circled the village several times. She did not want to go anywhere near the main hall with its bright lights and people. She did not want to go back to the cottage and face Luke again.

Why did he have to do this to her? He was her only friend. Why did he have to ruin it by wanting more? The last thing she wanted was to be married and settled down. Tears stung at the corners of her eyes as she thought about being married and cooped up in that old trailer, trapped forever.

After a long while, she saw Luke's form slump into the cottage, defeated. She quietly crept back to the deserted porch and sat down. What really pissed her off was the thought that he was right. *Who else would she marry?* The thought pounded her brain.

She would be a woman soon, by the standards of the ranch. She knew what that meant. Maybe her father could get her out of it for a while. She held back another tear at that thought. He wouldn't be there when she got back. He couldn't protect her anymore.

Maybe my abilities will save me, she thought. She knew it was a lie even as she thought it. They would all go to James Gatlin, whether he knew enough or not. Better an incompetent male than her.

She felt rather than heard Luke's presence at the doorway. "I'm really sorry," he said. "I didn't mean for it to come out like this. It was supposed to be a surprise. Romantic-like."

Amy snorted loudly. Romance was something her sister talked about, not her.

"I should have asked and discussed it with you before making any plans," he admitted.

"Exactly," she said, a little harsher than she had intended. Fighting back tears, she went on quietly, "Sorry. I shouldn't have blown up. You're right as usual. Who else am I going to marry? Get that trailer fixed up, and I'll marry you." She tried to sound jovial or enthused, but she felt hollow and empty. What else was she going to do? She wanted nothing to do with any other man at the ranch.

It's not that I don't like men, Amy thought. *It was supposed to be different, that's all. Some tall, dark, handsome stranger comes into town and my heart will do flip-flops. That's all those romance novels Elisabeth reads go anyway.* She shook her head. *The world's not like that anymore, and I just have to deal with it.*

"I'll make it up to you," Luke said. "It will be perfect, you just wait and see."

Amy felt cold. She could sense Luke's eagerness and knew he desperately wanted her to move closer, to put her arm around him or hug him. She sat there frozen. The prospect of marriage was supposed to be exciting, but it brought her nothing but dread. Drained by the emotional tumult, she excused herself and went to bed. Tired though she was, she lay awake a long time before finally drifting off to sleep.

She was woken by the sound of angry voices. It was still dark. *It must be late,* she thought, trying to hear what was going on. She couldn't make out what the voices were saying. She thought she heard some scuffling and then there was silence.

Concerned, she climbed out of bed and pulled her overalls on. She barely reached the door to her room when Luke came up the stairs. In the dim light, she could see that his face was taut with suppressed rage.

"What's wrong?" she asked.

"Mark and Shawn had a fight," he replied tersely. "Both drunk. I had to break it up."

"Assholes," Amy replied. "Let them fight."

"Damn it!" he exploded, hitting the wooden wall. "What were they thinking? What if a villager had been involved? They could have ruined the whole deal over one night of stupid carousing." He slumped against the wall. "I can't do this. They don't respect me, not like they did Jacob. They don't do anything unless I argue and threaten. How am I supposed to lead?"

Amy sank down beside him. "I think you're doing a great job," she said. "They're just a bunch of immature idiots. Hey, nobody's shot themselves in the foot yet, right?"

Luke snorted. "Shawn would be the one to do that. He did it back at the ranch once. Only a pellet gun, but still. Do you really think I'm doing okay?"

"Okay? The way you dealt with the Akiras and then the villagers here, I was amazed. You're a natural diplomat. I doubt Jacob could have done as well."

"I'm not sure I believe you, but thanks anyway."

The next day Mark had a black eye. He said nothing, and no one else dared comment.

"You get that end," Daniel told Luke. "On the count of three: one, two, three." They heaved the massive piece of limestone up between them. Taking short controlled steps, they moved slowly from the wagon to the growing wall. Its share of the labor completed, an ox watched them, looking content as it chewed its cud.

They placed the stone where the old woman directed them and then headed back for another.

"She sure is something," Daniel puffed as they waited in line for their turn to grab another slab. "Must be seventy if she's a day, yet she moves those stones around . . . she's tireless."

"Plenty of practice," Luke replied as they watched the woman work, climbing up and down out of the meter deep trench as she directed the labor. "Devon says her father was a stone mason back in the old days. She's been doing this kind of work for fifty years, both before and after the blast."

"I've been thinking," Daniel said slowly as they each hoisted a smaller limestone slab and headed back towards the trench, "about our agreement."

"What about it?" Luke replied. They had agreed that Daniel would help him fix up the trailer, and Luke would help Daniel convert a small shed into a house of sorts.

"Well, it's doing this that's got me thinking," Daniel went on. He passed his slab down to the woman who was now stacking the smaller stones on top of the heavy slabs they had placed as footings. "I mean, they've got the right idea, don't they? If there is one thing the ranch has plenty of, its rocks, soil and clay. Why bother fixing decrepit old buildings anyway? We could just build a couple of these."

Luke smiled. "I'm way ahead of you. I talked that old man, Macalaster, into taking me with him tomorrow."

"Where?"

"He's got another house they are finishing on the far side of the valley. So while you guys are finishing this foundation and starting to cob the walls, I'll be helping him thatch the other place. When we get home, we'll each know half the job."

Daniel laughed. "Good thinking. Imagine what they'll think of us? First new houses in how long?" He paused and thought, "You know, it's odd."

"What's that?"

"These people. My dad always said a civilian was a bit like a girl. When action gets hot, they all run and hide. These guys were all civilians once. They didn't run and hide. They fought the damn war and are halfway to rebuilding society. What have we done?"

"What do you mean?"

"Well, it's like I just said. If we build, it will be the first house raised in how long? Years."

"So? We've been at war. State of emergency. Can't expect to build at a time like that," Luke answered.

"These people saw more action than we ever did. They didn't ever stop building."

Luke didn't have an answer to that.

The next couple of days passed uneventfully. Shawn and Patrick complained about mud in their toes—the foundation was finished and the men had begun to mix the earthen material for the walls in the time-honored way, by trodding on it barefoot. Kurt, on the other hand, laughed and demonstrated the "cobber's dance" to Amy one night.

Amy saw Luke occasionally as he perched high on the roof of the other farm, learning the slow craft of the thatcher. He seemed to be a natural. Meanwhile, Amy's respect for the villagers was growing by leaps and bounds. What on the surface seemed a very primitive life was actually quite complex. The villagers simply believed in keeping technology unobtrusive if possible.

Amy got to see most of it, however. They tried to keep everything recyclable on a local level. She helped to recalibrate the electric grinder that turned broken ceramic plates and mugs into a fine powder that could be added to the potter's mix for the next batch. She helped the glass blower fix his methane still, and saw broken jars and cups melted down and re-blown.

The gardens represented years of collective experience. They were carefully planned to not only provide a bountiful harvest of healthy food, but they also had the soil's health in mind. Careful composting of every scrap of waste had slowly rebuilt the local soil to a rich humus many inches deep. Amy discovered just how deep one afternoon as she helped dig up and replace pipes in an underground irrigation system. This ingenious system allowed them to put water at the plants' roots while avoiding any water loss due to evaporation.

On the fifth night since arriving in the village, Luke called a meeting of all the expedition members. Mark and Shawn both grumbled loudly as they ate at the long table. They had spent every night in the village drinking and resented being held back tonight. Amy suspected the real reason for holding the meeting was to try to rein them in a bit.

"As you all know," Luke began, ignoring the two of them, "in two days our week of service will be up. We will be leaving immediately to continue our mission."

"Thank God," Kurt and Daniel muttered to each other. They had both given up drinking early on in the week.

"What's the rush?" Mark asked. "Can't we stay a few more days?"

"No," Luke replied. "The ranch is counting on us, and we have a long way to go yet."

Mark groaned at the thought of another long hike.

Amy felt torn about their upcoming departure. She wanted the mission to be over. She was increasingly worried about Mark, Shawn, and Patrick drinking so much. Something bad would come of it, she was sure. And yet her experience here was something totally unexpected. She'd spent the day helping Gerry, the burly blacksmith who reminded her painfully of her own father, fix several well pumps. Gerry, and indeed all of the villagers, had made an impression on her with their openness, respect, and most importantly, acceptance of her.

She had spent so long at the ranch fighting for this kind of respect. Everyone there went straight to her father, even when they knew he passed most of the jobs on to her. They were too bullheaded to admit she was the one who did them. Here, no one batted an eye at her. She tried to discuss it with Gerry, but without much success. "Your mechanical skills are valuable," he told her. "So, of course you are valued."

"But I'm a girl," she insisted.

"Yep, you are," he agreed, blushing.

She was mystified by the reaction. Having fought so hard for acceptance, she now found it unnerving. Still, she was not eager to leave it either. Especially not to go back to traveling with a bunch of men who mostly treated her like dirt.

Luke raised his hand for quiet. "We have an important issue to discuss," he said.

Is he going to tell them to lay off the booze? Amy wondered. Everyone looked at him expectantly.

"The Greenbowes have extended us their welcome. They are about a two weeks' hike away. Their village is in the same direction we will be going to get to the Cyclers anyway, and they may have more help for us. They are a large and influential community in these parts. They manufacture some light electronics, and their help could prove crucial."

He paused and looked around the group before continuing. "There is only one condition. They will not tolerate guns in their region."

Uproar ensued.

"What are you suggesting?" Patrick snarled as the tumult died down.

"I will not give up my gun," Shawn growled.

"This is not open for discussion," Luke shot back. "We need the Greenbowes's help. The villagers have promised to guard our guns and even give us weapons that are acceptable, like knives and bows."

"You can't expect us to go into enemy territory unarmed!" Mark demanded.

"Don't act so outraged," Daniel replied, coldness in his voice. "It's your fault anyway."

"What?" Mark gasped.

"You and your drinking," Daniel exploded. "The villagers warned them, no doubt, that they'd be hosting a bunch of drunks. Drunks with weapons."

"That's dangerous talk," Mark growled, rising from his seat.

"Whatcha gonna do? Beat him up?" Kurt sneered. "Like you did that William fellow? Then make him swear not to tell?"

"Quiet, both of you!" Patrick barked.

Luke stared hard at Patrick. "What's this all about?" he asked very softly.

"There was a problem, but we solved it. Like men," Patrick said.

"Bullshit!" Luke yelled. He pounded the table with his fist. "I am the leader of this mission, and you will tell me what happened."

Luke and Patrick locked eyes. There was a long tense moment. Patrick looked away but remained silent. Luke turned to Mark, who also looked away.

"He got into a fight," Kurt said, pointing at Mark. His hand shook with suppressed rage and fright. "The first night. With one of the men in the village hall. We all swore not to tell."

"We went outside, away from the hall," Patrick explained quietly. "Everyone swore to secrecy." He shot a mutinous look at Kurt. "Both sides. They won't tell."

Ignoring the looks, Luke rounded on Mark. "How could you? Do you think this is some Sunday picnic? These people are helping us. You remember the ranch? The one we are supposed to be saving? How could you jeopardize that?"

Mark turned beet red but didn't answer. Shawn came to his rescue. "He had to fight. Our honor was at stake."

"What honor?" Amy spat.

"Our honor?" Luke asked.

"Yeah," Shawn explained. "They said we couldn't hold our drink. They were laughing at us."

Patrick rolled his eyes and gave Shawn a look. "Don't bother trying to explain," he muttered.

"You fought because of that?" Luke replied incredulously. "You are dumber than I thought."

Mark turned even redder but didn't speak. His eyes shot daggers at Kurt, who stared back defiantly.

"Lay off him," Patrick groused.

Luke turned on him and yelled, "You are not in charge of this mission!"

"I know!" Patrick yelled back, rising. "I wouldn't even consider letting us be disarmed so easily if I was." He turned and stomped out.

Late that night, Mark was sitting on his bunk. Luke had

ordered that nobody was to go to the hall.

Mark looked up as Patrick came in. Patrick pulled something out of a side pocket. The cool metal handle of a 9 mm was pressed into Mark's palm.

"At least two of us will be prepared," Patrick said.

Mark nodded.

7

Lexa Greenbowe

It was a low-key departure two mornings later. They had spent their last day of work a sullen and quiet lot. Mark shot Kurt angry looks, but he made no move to retaliate for spilling the beans about the fight.

They returned from work to find knives and bows laid out for them. Luke had decided to surrender their guns while the others were still working, to save another confrontation. Mark and Shawn both muttered sourly and glared at Luke all evening. Patrick glared at Luke but refused to speak, preferring to give him the silent treatment. Kurt and Daniel, however, seemed to have taken the change better. They spent the evening studying and discussing their new weapons. Amy wasn't sure which irritated her more.

The sullen and silent atmosphere followed them through the first day's march and into the second. Midway through the second day, they encountered another of the big, dark statues. This one was also housed in a pagoda, but it was less graphic. She was a squat, vague form with a pregnant belly and ample breasts.

Mark made a suggestive comment, which caused Shawn and Patrick to snicker. Kurt lectured them angrily, keeping both Luke and Daniel safely between him and the targets of his anger.

"Oh, stop being such a fag," Mark told him.

Kurt went beet red and shut up.

Amy just shook her head. The statue reminded her that when she had asked about the first statue, the answer she received had been about the battle it commemorated. She still didn't know anything about the statues themselves.

"It's strange, hiking without our guns," Shawn commented that night over supper.

"So we've gathered," Amy groused from the other side of the fire. "You've only mentioned it, what, twenty times?"

"Well, it's strange, that's all," he persisted.

"We have been through this a hundred times," Daniel groused. "It was either leave the guns at the village, leave them in the woods somewhere before we entered the Greenbowes' territory . . ."

"And no one wanted to leave them unguarded," Kurt threw in.

". . . or not go into their territory at all," Daniel finished.

"I would have told the Greenbowes to take a hike," Mark put in.

"You would have been the one taking the hike," Luke said. "About three extra weeks to get around their territory, from the sound of it."

The rest of the meal was consumed in silence.

The next day, shortly before noon, they crested a hill and found a crossroads in front of them. A large gray truck was parked there. Greenbowe Tech was printed on the side of the truck. They approached it cautiously.

Under a tree, just a few feet away from the crossroads, sat a figure. As they approached, she stood. It was a young woman, approximately their age. She wore a one-piece jumpsuit in gray and a wide-brim straw hat. Short, red hair and a button nose stuck out from under the hat.

She beamed at them, the freckles on her face almost a match for Amy's, though the two were alike in no other way. She was almost a head shorter than Amy with a slender body. She had a confident, almost cat-like walk.

The sun was bright, and the horizon seemed to stretch on forever. Amy was struck by a sudden sense of déjà vu. *Is this the woman from my dream?*

"You must be the Freedom Ranchers," she called out. "My name is Lexa Greenbowe. I believe I can pick out Amy. The rest of you, I am afraid, will have to introduce yourselves."

Luke stepped forward. "Luke Zachary of Freedom Ranch," he said extending his hand. "I'm confused. I thought we had several more days to go before we'd reach you."

Lexa laughed. "You do have a ways to go yet, I'm afraid. I was out working on one of our remote power stations when Lady Sapphire got me on short band and told me about you. She thought we might run into each other. I decided to swing by and give you a lift. What do you say? Want to go for a ride?"

The men all looked taken aback. They had never met anything quite like this new girl. *It's obvious what they're thinking,* Amy thought as she watched the smirks and leers on the men's faces.

"We thank you," Luke said after a moment.

"Yeah, sure. I'll ride in your truck," Shawn fumbled out. Lexa laughed.

She took Luke by the hand. "Introductions?" she said, patting his arm. He led the way, introducing each member in turn. They blushed deeply as she looked each of them over appraisingly. Shawn turned beet red and mumbled something that made her giggle.

She's a rather brazen tart, Amy thought. When her turn came, Lexa's smile was so infectious and her voice so sincere that Amy forgot to be offended. "Amy, a fellow mechanic, I hear. I've been looking forward to meeting you." Turning back to the others, she said, "We'll have lunch before we set off, okay?"

She casually switched from holding Luke's arm to taking Amy's and led the way back to the tree. She found her small pack and rummaged in it for a moment. She came up with a smallish jar and broke the seal. "Baba ganoush," she declared brightly.

There was a long perplexed silence.

"Eggplant?" she said.

"Oh," several voices mumbled as she produced a couple of loaves of dark bread. Amy was becoming quite used to the bread down here. It was heavy and grainy, but satisfying.

"Lexa, that's a pretty name," Patrick said sitting beside her, in what he no doubt thought was a smooth move. Amy thought he looked ridiculous.

"Thanks. Patrick, is it?" Lexa replied, pulling out a long knife. "Be a sweetie, dear, and cut some slices for me."

Amy expected Patrick to protest, either at being called a "sweetie" or being asked to do women's work, but to her surprise he did neither. He took the loaves and started cutting them.

Shawn sat down next to Patrick. "Lexa, that's an unusual name," he said.

"What can I say? I'm an unusual gal."

"You're one of the Greenbowes?" Mark asked sitting on her other side.

"In the flesh." She smiled.

"'Cause we're headed that way," he finished lamely.

Amy rolled her eyes as she sat down. She was more than a bit annoyed with the guys, who were casting around for anything to say. *They are acting like they've never seen a girl before*, she thought as Luke and Daniel practically sat on top of one another to be close to Lexa.

"So what brought you out here?" Luke asked as he joined the tight circle of boys. Amy shot him a dark "you too?" look that he totally missed.

"Oh," Lexa waved vaguely northward, "bulldog station had a problem with its charge controller in the photo-voltaic array."

"You have photo voltaics too?" Amy asked surprised.

"Sure, it's one of our specialties," Lexa replied. "You have them at the ranch?" She was making sandwiches and handing them around.

"Sure, they're more reliable than wind generators," Amy replied. "Well, until they get hit by lightning."

Lexa giggled. "Damn straight. Wind is good and reliable, as long as you have the parts. Solar is a much better long-term investment, however. No moving parts to break."

"That's right," Daniel nodded sagely.

The fool doesn't even know what he's talking about, Amy thought. "What do you mean by a remote power station?" she asked. *Someone has to keep the level of intelligent conversation up.*

Lexa rose and carried two sandwiches over, handing one to Amy, then sitting down beside her. The look on the boys' faces, now five feet away, almost made Amy break out in laughter. "We maintain powering stations for EVs every twenty miles or so, for our use and for travelers," Lexa said.

"What's an EV?" Patrick asked.

"Electric vehicle," Amy answered quickly. Patrick gave her a sour look, but what was she supposed to do? Let Lexa answer and think they were all stupid?

"It's a good thing you guys brought one smart one with you," Lexa teased. They all laughed. Amy couldn't believe it. If she had made a comment like that, they'd have killed her.

"So how many visitors do you get?" Luke asked.

"Not so many. You will find ample welcome, I'm sure," Lexa replied. Amy found the tone cryptic. Something had been implied, but Amy had no idea what.

"How long will it take to get there?" Luke persisted. If he had caught the implication, he didn't show it.

"Our EVs are built for rough terrain and heavy loads, not speed," she replied. "It will take the rest of today to reach the next power station. Tomorrow by supper, we will be back in Tir-Na-Nog."

"Tir-Na-what?" Shawn asked.

"Tir-Na-Nog," she sounded out. "That's the name of our village. Let me put out an offering and we can get going."

Without explanation, she disappeared into a nearby bush. She came back presently and led them to the truck. The wide back door rolled up to reveal a mostly empty cargo space.

"Haven't room in the cab for everyone, so in you go," she laughed, grabbing Kurt's bag and throwing it in. They all tossed their bags in and started scrambling in after.

As Amy threw her pack in, she felt a quick slap on her butt. She spun around, ready to pound the man responsible, only to find herself face to face with Lexa's innocent smile. "Ride up front with me, partner," she said. "We'll have some girl talk."

Disarmed by the friendliness, Amy waited while the others were loaded in. "Must be a hoot traveling with that lot," Lexa said conspiratorially after she rolled the big door shut. "One poor girl with six strapping lads."

"It's not like that!" Amy protested, indignant.

"Damn! And I was hoping for some juicy gossip. Oh well, I am glad someone's life is as boring as mine."

Amy doubted very much this woman led a boring life, but she said nothing. As she went around and climbed into the cab, she wondered what the next few hours would bring. A mechanic's daughter, she had never been particularly versed in what you might call "girl's talk." In fact, she had no idea what that might be.

"I want to thank you for saving me a trip out to Boringhaven," Lexa said as she swung herself into the seat beside Amy.

"Oh, that's fine," Amy replied. "I was glad to be of use.

Don't you like it out there? They seemed friendly to me."

"If you go for old skin bags." Lexa grimaced. Amy blushed. She hadn't thought about it like that at all. "They're a bunch of prudes, if you ask me. Every time I go out there, all the girls watch me like chickens guarding their nests. Not that it's much of a nest either. Even the few young'uns out there are only good at two things, drinking and bragging, if you know what I mean."

Amy laughed in spite of herself. She remembered the first night at the feast, William, the one the boys had fought with, had drunkenly told Amy exactly how many inches he was.

"Now, that bunch back there?" Lexa asked speculatively. "What about them?"

"Bunch of immature idiots," Amy muttered, thinking of their behavior at lunch.

"Yeah, I caught that," Lexa giggled. "What was with all those puppy-dog stares? That big one, especially. He's got some nice muscles there, but he's not the sharpest tool in the shed now is he? And that Patrick looks like he could handle himself, and he's got plenty of muscle as well, but I don't know . . . there's something dark in those eyes."

Amy marveled as Lexa continued to describe the expedition members. She was not sure what surprised her more, how quickly and accurately Lexa had sized the men up or how she described them.

"That Luke fellow, he seems to be the only level head in the bunch. The whole lot of you are pretty skanky, mind, but that's to be expected with what you've been through," Lexa said, summing up. "But I suspect he'd clean up pretty nicely."

Here is where I'm supposed to say something like, "Hands off;

he's mine," Amy thought. She didn't voice the sentiment.

After several more minutes of speculation about the boys without getting any response from Amy, who couldn't imagine what to say, Lexa started asking about their trip. "Tell me about this mission of yours."

Amy started slowly. She felt like she was reciting a book report. Finding a receptive audience, she warmed up. In fact, she had never experienced a more receptive and lively listener. Amy found herself talking about the ranch and her life there.

"He said what? Because you're a girl? That right bastard!" Lexa said of Amos Deaton. "Oh, that place seems frightfully primitive."

"Oh no," Amy replied. "We have electricity, or we did. We have a couple of tractors and had some cars, but we don't have any fuel—"

"I meant socially," Lexa interrupted. "All that boy/girl stuff. It's just like you read about in the old days. Do they really think less of you because you're a girl? Mr. Quimby said you did a great job."

Amy glowed at the compliment.

After a moment's reflection, Lexa went on, "So, you and Luke? You two a thing?"

Amy shrugged. "Kind of."

"But you've never done anything?"

"Anything? Like what?"

Lexa just looked at her.

With Luke? Amy was startled. She had never really thought of him that way. Then again, she had agreed to marry him. That would certainly entail *something.* Blushing, she shook her head no.

"Oh my Goddess," Lexa squealed. "You've never done

it?!" Amy blushed even harder. "Women?" Lexa asked.

"I'm not a lesbian." Amy declared indignantly.

"Just asking," Lexa sounded miffed. "It's not like it's a big deal."

Not a big deal? What kind of reaction did she expect?

After an uncomfortable silence, Lexa changed the subject. "So tell me about the generator."

Amy described the wind generator and what was wrong. "It was a pretty old unit anyway," Lexa told her. "We would have had to replace it in a year or two." Within moments, Lexa had seemingly forgotten the earlier incident and was back to rambling like she was Amy's oldest friend.

Amy was not sure what "girl talk" usually consisted of, but she was pretty sure it was not EVs, solar panels, and wind generators. For the first time in her life, she had found someone who shared her interests.

As the afternoon progressed, the conversation turned more personal again. Amy described the men of the ranch. Lexa gave an indignant shriek. "No wonder you're a virgin," she said.

"I've never had to deal with that," Lexa continued, "but I know what you mean about people thinking you can't do stuff. I get that all the time. They say I'm too young, it's too dangerous, you name it."

"Oh God, yes," Amy said. "I hate that."

"Daisy is the worst. She is always after me about these long trips. But I've been out in this old truck since I was a little girl, helping mom."

"You're mom used to do this?" Amy asked surprised.

"Sure, she taught me everything I know. Taught me fractions with her socket set when I was four."

Amy laughed. "Yeah, well, I got you topped. My dad used to get me to sleep by reading old technical manuals when I was three. I'd even trace the circuit diagrams with my finger," She paused. "Of course, he probably wouldn't have taught me if he had a son. Women back home just learn cooking and cleaning and crap."

"Sounds like bizarre pre-blast ideas to me," Lexa said. "They had queer ideas about women, about a lot of things really. Why else would they let the earth get in such a state?"

After some thought, Amy asked. "So who's Daisy?"

"My wife," Lexa answered. "One of them anyway."

Amy stared at her. She was trying vainly to make any sense of the answer. She wasn't even sure which part confused her more.

Lexa saw her look and laughed. "Sorry, did I mention that I am married?" Then she asked, "Is that so surprising?"

"Well, yes, actually," Amy finally managed to answer. "I mean, just a while ago you were talking about the boys like . . . like . . . *a horny tomcat?* . . . like maybe you were interested."

"Well, maybe," Lexa answered. "Not the whole lot, mind, but one. Just depends. Does that have anything to do with being married?"

"Usually," Amy answered. "And did you really say you were married to a woman?"

"Two," Lexa corrected, "and three men."

"All at once?"

"How else?" Lexa laughed again. "I am guessing from your big eyes that is not the usual arrangement up in the mountains?"

"That would be a big understatement. How can you have more than one husband?"

"It's a group arrangement," Lexa explained. "Robin's Nest, that's our family name. There are three men Rowan, Merlin, and Luther. Then there are three women, Daisy, Winnona, and me." Lexa ticked them off as she went. "We have three children. Our Daisy is quite a breeder. She's had two already, Owen and Morrigan. Winnona's had one, Ewan. He's my little doll."

"Where I come from marriage is just one man and one woman," Amy said, trying to assimilate it all.

"Sounds awful. Boredom aside, that would mean doing the dishes every other night. Who could stand that? Ugh!" Lexa wrinkled her nose. "I had a boyfriend once who wanted something like that, just the two of us. I can't imagine why."

Amy was unsure how to proceed with this conversation but was luckily spared. "We're here," Lexa called, pointing at a small red brick building. Behind it, a tall tower and wind generator spun lazily above them.

As the truck rolled to a stop, Lexa turned and studied Amy carefully. "I hope I haven't offended you. I tend to talk first and think second. I know you guys were raised differently."

"It's okay," Amy told her. "It's just so different that I need time to get over the shock."

Lexa opened the back of the truck and said, "It's not much guys. Just a utility shed really. We'll have to camp. But at least there's a well and a pump out back, and an outhouse."

They set camp and made a fire in the permanent fire pit in front of the building. Lexa produced a box of cooking gear and food. She cooked pasta with tomatoes and artichokes. Pasta and tomatoes they had at the ranch, but artichokes were a novelty.

The boys complimented the dish repeatedly, though Amy noticed that several of them pushed the bitter artichokes to one side. Now that she had befriended Lexa, she found their behavior humorous rather than irritating. She had to bite back a laugh more than once at the sarcastic comments that Lexa kept dropping. The boys didn't seem to ever get them.

"I notice you haven't set camp yet," Luke said as dinner ended. Several of the boys eagerly moved forward, ready to be of service.

"I usually just sleep in the truck actually. It's both easier and safer when I am alone."

"I can take Amy's pup tent, and you two can share my dome. It's big enough," Luke offered magnanimously. "If that's okay with you?" he added as an afterthought to Amy.

"Yeah, what do you say?" Lexa asked. "A sleepover?"

"Sure," Amy replied, not wanting to refuse but not sure what she was getting herself into.

They sat around the fire for a long time, the boys shifting about periodically and constantly looking for yet another subject of conversation.

Lexa finally stood and said, "Well, I have to drive tomorrow, and I'm beat, so I'm going to bed."

"Me too," Amy agreed. The boys grumbled a bit, and there was at least one grandiose statement about the night still being young. Amy knew it was all bluster. They all looked dead tired. Once their new subject of interest was gone, they would go to bed as well.

As soon as they were alone in the tent, Lexa said, "They don't get out much do they?"

Amy laughed. "No, I told you it's a small, boring place where we come from. I'll bet they are all dreaming that you'll come scratch on their tent flaps after everyone goes to bed."

"I thought that was wrong—sinful or something?" Lexa asked, perplexed.

"Yeah, but they're boys."

"So it's different?"

"Sort of. It's still wrong," Amy explained. "But it's expected. Everyone turns their backs and says things like 'They're sowing their wild oats.'"

"But girls are not allowed?" Lexa asked, catching on.

"Nope, definitely not."

"So who are the boys doing this with? Each other?"

"Of course not!" Amy was shocked. She would have been offended if not for the confusion in Lexa's voice. "No, that's wrong too. They do it with girls. If the girls get caught, they would be shamed, but that doesn't always stop them."

"I don't understand you people at all," Lexa declared, stifling a yawn. "But I know this: those boys will have to go on dreaming. I am beat." She lay down.

Amy stretched out next to her, stiff as a board. Lexa noticed and commented, "Don't worry, honey. I know you don't swing that way."

Not sure she wanted to know the answer, Amy tentatively asked, "Do you?"

Lexa shrugged. "Time to time, when the mood hits. I wasn't lying though. I am beat. Just remind me to seduce you tomorrow okay?" With that, she rolled over and went to sleep.

Amy lay awake a long time trying to figure out if that last comment was a joke or not.

When Amy woke, Lexa was already gone. That was okay, Amy needed some alone time to sort out all she had learned about her new friend. Lexa's customs seemed strange and disturbing. But seen from Lexa's point of view, so did the ranch's culture. Amy's justifications of the beliefs at the ranch seemed hollow, even to herself.

She didn't get long to mull it over. There was a scratch at her tent flap. It was Luke inviting her to breakfast. Kurt had cooked oatmeal from Lexa's supplies.

They all ate quickly and broke camp. The boys were again loaded into the truck, and Amy was again invited up front. She accepted gratefully. Lexa was strange, and at times her views were disturbing, but it was still better than the boys. If she had to hear Daniel and Patrick argue the merits of various assault rifles one more time . . .

The talk in the front of the truck was lighter this time. Lexa did most of the talking. After yesterday's discussion, she barely mentioned her family. Instead she gave a glowing description of Tir-Na-Nog. It was a place of sprawling earthen houses with deep wooden porches and dense forest all around. Most of the tribe lived in group marriages and some of the houses were enormous.

A large glen at the center of the community was filled with a vast and productive garden, tended by some of the best gardeners left in this world. They grew a huge array of food and herb crops. They had a seed bank that traded varieties of plants with hundreds of individuals and other tribes.

Most impressive to Amy was Lexa's description of the workshop. It was a large, metal building from the pre-blast era. At many workstations, the community produced and maintained solar panels, wind generators, and even some basic computer technology. In this region, people had two options: learn to get along without technology or learn to get along with the Greenbowes.

Not that it would be too hard, if Lexa is anything to judge by, Amy thought. It was hard to stay offended at anything she said. She had a vivacious and quick wit. She entertained Amy all morning with stories about growing up at Tir-Na-Nog. Lexa had grown up there, the daughter of the now-aging Meadow family who had helped found the tribe long ago.

"Roger Akira told us that your people had some sort of vision thing before the blast happened," Amy said.

"Yeah, mom could tell you more about that," Lexa answered. "She was one of the visionaries, believe it or not. They were doing a full moon rite, this standard little piece. Anyway, all of sudden, she starts going on about the end of society and everything. She thought it was some fluke; some weird little subconscious thing. Then they talked to one of their sister covens and found out that they had the same thing happen. It happened all over really. That's when they knew they had to do something."

Amy only understood half of what Lexa said. From group marriages to odd religious beliefs, Amy found her an enigma. *At least she's a friendly enigma,* Amy decided. And despite the wide gulf in their communities and upbringing, they had so much in common.

By noon, they were passing into a countryside of rolling hills and growing patches of forest. They stopped for lunch at another fueling station. "Give the boys a chance to air out," Lexa said. "Besides, I can top the battery off in fast fuel mode."

The boys looked sullen. Amy wasn't sure if they were carsick or if they had another fight about something. They didn't volunteer, and she didn't ask. No doubt Luke would tell her soon enough anyway.

They all brightened whenever Lexa was looking their way. None of them had lost their puppy-dog expression toward her, and only Luke and Kurt even bothered to try to hide it. Lexa continued to flirt with them all, but after two long rides with her, Amy knew it was just part of Lexa's personality.

After a leisurely hour-long lunch, Lexa opened the back of the truck again. As the others loaded up, Patrick approached Lexa. "One of us could ride up front this afternoon," he said. "Keep you company."

For a split second, Amy thought she would agree. It would only be fair.

"Thanks, but Amy and I have technical stuff to discuss," Lexa replied. "You know, PVs and EVs and whatnot."

Amy was glad of the support. She was also relieved not to have to ride with the other boys. That and, well, she couldn't quite call it jealousy, but she did not want the boys after Lexa, especially not Patrick. Lexa was apparently quite worldly, much more so than Amy. Still, she had no idea what the men of Freedom Ranch could be like. Amy already felt protective toward her.

"You know, it just hit me," she told Lexa as they drove off. "I never did tell any of the boys about your custom, marriage-wise, that is. I wonder what they will make of it."

"I thought it was okay for boys, just not for girls?"

"Yes and no. Taking a woman to bed for a fling would be one thing. They'd call that 'sowing their wild oats.' Actual marriage with many partners would be another deal altogether. I don't think they'll understand that at all." Amy paused. "Not that I am sure I understand it. How does it work?"

"Well, every family is different. Some have chore lists, and everyone is assigned a turn. Our family is more casual. I am gone so much that they don't expect me to do much housework . . ."

"I kind of meant," Amy interrupted "you know, the marriage thing?"

"Lexa laughed. "The marriage thing? You mean sex?" Amy blushed and nodded. "That just depends on mood and practicality. Sometimes we swap around, take turns, you know. Other times, we all play together."

"That's carnal!" Amy said.

"I know, isn't it?" Lexa smiled. Seeing Amy's expression she sobered. "Oh, you meant that in a bad way."

"What other way could it be taken? It's sinful, unchristian."

"Is it?" Lexa asked puzzled. Her sincerity disarmed Amy. "Is that what Christians believe?"

"Yes, hasn't anyone ever told you that?"

"No," Lexa answered. "Well, maybe Erin mentioned something in history class. I never paid much attention. I didn't ever expect to actually meet anyone with all those weird pre-blast ideas. I'm sorry if I have offended you. That's the last thing I want."

"It's okay," Amy was even more confused. She had

spent so long fighting the ranch's beliefs. Now that she was cast in the role of defender of those same beliefs, she found herself ill equipped to deal with it. At the same time, she was not ready to abandon what she had been told was right for so long.

"So," Lexa was back to her usual bubbly self. "Who will go for it? Which of the boys will 'sow their wild oats' among the sinful pagans?" She giggled.

"Well, I know that Shawn is looking for a woman," Amy replied, making a sour face.

"Looking for part of a woman anyway." Lexa grimaced. "I swear that boy never gets his eyes up to face level, if you know what I mean."

"He doesn't have anyone at home," Amy explained. Once again, she felt she had to defend someone she had never defended before. She told Lexa about the numbers at the camp and how no one his age was available or interested.

"That's sad," Lexa said. "I hope he does find someone."

"Find someone willing to marry him and go live in the mountains?"

"Not likely, I am afraid." Lexa shrugged. "But I am sure he can find company for a night or two. He's a big strapping lad, if a bit slow on the uptake."

"If it's offered, I doubt he'll stop and question it."

"Okay, so what about the others?"

"Well, Kurt won't. He's big into religion, he and his whole family. A sin's a sin to them, no exceptions. Patrick will in a heartbeat, and so will Mark, even though he is married."

"Okay, but up there, if you're married, you aren't supposed to, right? Is there some sort of exception for him?"

"No, he's just an ass," Amy replied. "Daniel's one I am not sure about. Luke will be polite but not interested, mark my words."

"Damn, he's cute," Lexa said. Then her mouth went into an O. "But you two are a thing, right? I'm sorry. I won't try anything, I promise."

Amy shrugged and waved off the objection. She had no real fear that either of the two would do anything. She did not know what to say; she didn't really want Lexa after Luke, but she didn't want to link herself to him publicly just yet. There'd be plenty of time for that when they got home.

Lexa grinned. "What about you? Will you taste the pleasures of Tir-Na-Nog?"

Amy blushed fiercely. "I . . . I never . . ." she stuttered. She would never. But that didn't stop her from thinking about it.

"I could introduce you to one of my husbands," Lexa put in helpfully.

"What!" Amy exclaimed. "Your husbands? You'd just line them up and say take one?"

"Of course, they're the best."

Amy just stared at her in shock. Lexa laughed. "I'm just teasing. It's okay. It will be okay with all of them." She waved at the back of the truck. "My tribe is lot like me. We talk a lot, but it's mostly talk. No one will push it. If the boys want to, they will be welcomed. If not, that's okay. Just as long as nobody wigs out."

Amy could only hope that no one would wig out.

214

8

Tir-Na-Nog

It was dusk when they arrived. They had spent most of the afternoon on well-established roads in an increasingly dense forest. About a half-mile before they reached the community, they turned onto a gravel road that looked in good repair. Another turn into a long drive, and Amy got her first glimpse of the community.

Straight ahead of them was a vast metal building that could only be the workshop Lexa had described. To her left was a long earthen building that was the community hall, and to her right, a large network of gardens. In the center of the garden area was a low, stone building with ivy creeping up its side. Lexa made straight for it. Behind, and back in the woods, Amy glimpsed a few of the sprawling earthen houses that Lexa had described so well.

As the boys piled out of the back of the truck, two men approached. They were almost a matching set; both were tall, blond, and broad. They wore their long hair tied back and tunics with leggings.

Swords hung at their sides. Lexa had carefully explained at lunch that they were ceremonial weapons only. She didn't want anyone to get nervous or freak over them.

The two men bowed low. "I am Michael," one of them said, "and this is Lorn. We are captains of the guard for Tir-Na-Nog."

"We bid you welcome and well met," the one introduced as Lorn said. "We offer you the hospitality of our community."

"I am Luke Zachary of Freedom Ranch," Luke said, pushing past Amy. "And we gladly accept your hospitality." Patrick was glaring at the sword, as though he was unsure about accepting any hospitality, but he said nothing.

"A feast has been made ready, as have accommodations," Michael told them.

Patrick brightened, and Mark muttered, "That's more like it."

"But first, you are all weary and dirty. Come," Michael finished. They followed him to the low stone building. Three more people awaited them there, one man and two women.

The two women were a stark contrast. One was tall, dark haired, and mousy. She stood silently and patiently. The other was easily two heads shorter than Amy. She had bright blond hair and a round smiling face. She practically bounced with impatience. The man was young, with dark hair and a slender build.

"Lexa!" the blond squealed as the expedition walked

up. She rushed forward, sweeping Lexa into a fierce bear hug.

"Hi, Daisy," Lexa said sarcastically. She didn't look upset, however, and returned the hug. Amy couldn't help but notice the smirk on Patrick's face. *If he only knew the half of it*, she thought.

"Hospitality," Michael said gesturing them inside. It was a rectangular building. The entryway contained a small alcove with hooks on the walls and low benches. The entryway opened into a shower room with low showers and small wooden stools. On the far side of the building, steam curled up from a large pool of water.

Amy heard a gasp and turned back to see Lexa casually stripping off her clothes. She hung her jumper on one of the hooks and turned to them. The men gaped at her slender naked body.

"Well, come on," Lexa said. "Don't you want to clean up for the feast?"

They all stared at her, silent. No one had any clue what to say. Daisy looked concerned. "Is something wrong?" she asked.

"Well," Luke said, licking his dry lips and not taking his eyes off Lexa. "Where we come from, we usually bathe alone."

"You do?" Daisy asked. "Who scrubs your back?"

Lexa said, "Oh, I get it. More of that old-fashioned stuff. No problem. Girls first and then the boys. Acceptable?"

They nodded. "We'll wait outside," Luke said, averting his eyes. Kurt bolted for the door, followed by Luke. The others moved more slowly, Shawn trailing at the end.

Amy hesitated. Misreading her reluctance, Lexa said,

"Right, you too." The young man scampered out as well. Michael and Lorn bowed and made a more dignified exit.

Amy undressed slowly. She had no choice really. These people were doing their best to accommodate them as guests. They simply didn't understand that at the ranch they bathed alone—as in completely alone.

Daisy and the other woman shed their simple robes as casually as Lexa had her coveralls. Lexa sat at one of the stools and began to adjust the knobs, feeling the water for temperature. The mousy woman, whose name Amy learned was Willowshade, meanwhile filled a bucket with soapy water. Taking a long brush, she began to scrub Lexa's back while Lexa washed her own front.

Daisy stood by Amy, making small talk while Amy undressed and followed her to the showers. "I'm so glad to have our Lexa back," she said. "She does take risks, that one. She was told about you guys mostly as a precaution. They didn't want her running into you unaware. I told Lady Sapphire that was the last thing to do. Telling Lexa was clearly inviting her to go take a look. And of course, she did. Oh well, she seems to have had the right of it anyway. You don't seem dangerous."

Amy sat on the stool, naked and feeling very uncomfortable. She wasn't quite sure how to respond. *Are we dangerous?*

Despite her discomfort, the warm water felt good. Daisy's scrubbing massaged the tension from her back, and she relaxed.

"First rinse done. Into the pool with you," Daisy declared. Amy went to the pool. Lexa and Willowshade were already neck deep in water, talking.

There was a stone stairway leading into the water. The

water was almost painfully hot as Amy walked down into it. Standing at the bottom of the stairs, she was about chest deep. A stone ledge ran along the inside of the pool, so that you could sit down and be almost completely submerged.

Amy let out a long sigh of contentment as she sat down beside Lexa. As her body adjusted to the temperature, she felt herself relax even more. "I think someone likes our idea of bathing." Lexa giggled.

"I've never been covered by so much warm water," she said. She thought of the old metal tub back home. Pouring kettle after kettle of boiling water in, you were inevitably either too hot or too cold. "How do you do it?" she asked.

"Back before the collapse, we had a company come in and drill a geothermal well," Willowshade explained. "This bath is actually the cooling tank for the generator. We produce most of our own electricity that way. The generator is in another building behind this. The steam comes up and turns the generator. The water is held in a holding tank until it is below scalding and then pumped in here. As it cools, it flows down an outlet tube at the bottom and back down the well."

"Ingenious," Amy told her. She leaned her body against the stone side and listened while the women talked, telling Lexa news of people Amy didn't know. The three women's casualness was such that she almost felt embarrassed of her embarrassment.

"So how's my favorite man?" Lexa asked.

"Oh, that one's a handful, let me tell you," Daisy responded. "Just this morning, he bonked his poor little noggin but good."

"Oh no," Lexa exclaimed. "How?"

Daisy laughed. "Climbing the kitchen shelves to get at the cookie jar again. He's not hurt. Serves the wee devil right."

"That's my Ewan. He'll be climbing wind generators with his old woman before he's five."

"He will not!"

Lexa shrugged. "Okay, six then."

"No time for a leisurely soak, girls," Willowshade warned. "Out you go, and we'll do a deep scrub this time."

Daisy washed Amy's hair for her. Modesty gone for the moment, she gloried in the deep scalp massage. She broke into giggles suddenly.

"Not ticklish?" Daisy asked.

"No, I was just thinking what our minister, Reverend Posch, would think of this."

"You've got a reverend?" Daisy sounded surprised.

"Sure, don't you?"

"Pagans believe everyone must make their own spiritual connection to the divine. We don't trust reverends or priests, or anyone who claims to know what the gods want for you. Nor do we trust dogmatic faiths that claim it's all written down in some book somewhere. We never went for that, not even back before the collapse," Willowshade told her. "It's just that since then, organized religion has been kind of scarce. I can't think of a tribe or village anywhere near about that has a reverend."

"So what would your reverend say?" Daisy asked.

"He'd say it was awfully sinful," Amy said.

"It's a sin to be clean?"

"No, no, clean is good," Amy answered, "It's the

whole . . ." she gestured around her, ". . . the immodesty."

"What immodesty?" Daisy asked, "I'm not immodest."

"That's the whole point," Lexa told her. "You're supposed to be." To Amy she added, "She doesn't get out much. It's like the villagers I always tell you about. They think it's proper to be embarrassed about showing too much skin."

"Silly way to live, if you ask me," Daisy declared.

"That's why the men reacted the way they did," Willowshade explained. "We haven't had to deal with outsiders in so long, at least not with outsiders that don't already know our ways, that we didn't think about it." Then she giggled.

"What?" Daisy demanded.

"It's just that so many of the men around here spend so much time trying to get Daisy to see them naked. Imagine someone trying to prevent it," she joked.

"Oh, hush you," Daisy scolded.

They had a second short dip in the pool before drying off. The women showed Amy to a series of closets along one side of the building. There they presented her with a kimono-style robe in green. They promised to have her overalls washed and returned later.

The robe was brilliant green with a silver dragon embroidered on it. Unused to such finery, she had to take the women's word that it matched her eyes perfectly. They all seemed to think it looked very good on her. Daisy helped her get her hair brushed and pulled up.

Judging from the strange reaction the boys gave her when she left the bathhouse, the women must have been right. After a long, awkward pause, Luke managed, "You look nice."

The other boys looked at her like she had sprouted wings. "Who'da thought?" Mark muttered as he passed her.

The men disappeared into the shower house. Shortly afterward, there was an angry shout. The young man, Ravencloud, came running out, eyes wide. "I don't think they want help," he said panting.

"No, they don't," Amy told him. "It's okay. They just aren't used to your customs."

"You didn't react like that," he said.

"It's different for me," she told him. *I did inwardly*, she thought, *I just kept it too myself.*

Lorn appeared in the doorway. "I have shown them where everything is," he said. "I expect that is all the help they want or require."

The men didn't take nearly as long. Soon they were strolling out one by one. *They didn't even try the pool*, Amy decided. They had all spurned the robes set out for them. Luke and Patrick had at least had the foresight to get clean clothes out of their packs. The others just put their old clothes back on. Shawn looked like he had forgotten to towel off first. Amy was embarrassed for them, though nobody commented.

Michael and Lorn led them across to the community hall. The land about them was rapidly falling into shadow as dusk gave way to night. The doors of the community hall stood open; noise and the smell of roasting meat and vegetables spilled out into the night. Amy's stomach lurched and grumbled loudly, reminding her that she had not eaten since lunch.

She followed just behind Luke as he entered the hall. The noise died down as their entrance was noticed. Amy looked nervously over a hall-filled room of strange faces and fancy robes, gowns, and jackets. Everything and everyone glittered and glowed with decorations. There was brilliant embroidery on every piece of cloth. Earrings, necklaces, and rings were worn by almost everyone. Amy was unsure what to expect from people who called themselves pagan, but it certainly wasn't this bright gaudiness.

"Visitors have come seeking shelter after a long, harsh trip, help after much struggle, and company after much solitude," Michael intoned in a rich, deep voice.

A woman stood at the head of the hall. She was tall with raven black hair that hung loose past her waist. Long streaks of gray did nothing to mar its beauty. She had a strong, lean face with sharp, dark eyes. She wore a flowing, red dress that was tied with a gold braid. It showed her impressive figure well. Unlike most of the crowd, she wore no ornamentation.

"Do they come in peace and goodwill?" she asked. Her voice was rich and showed long familiarity with public speaking. She could project it clear across the room as if she were next to you, without sounding loud. *There is no need to ask who the leader is*, Amy thought, impressed. She had never seen a woman with such an obvious aura of power and respect.

"We come in peace and goodwill," Luke replied.

"Then may you find warmth and rest here," she replied. "I am Sapphire Greenbowe, and I offer you the hospitality of my tribe. All blessings of love and light be yours."

"And yours," Luke replied.

There was a cheer, and they were led forward. Amy and

Luke were led up to the front table and sat opposite Lady Sapphire.

"Tomorrow we will discuss the detail of your mission," Lady Sapphire said before Luke could open his mouth. "Tonight we feast and celebrate your arrival."

A bottle and a platter of bread were set before the lady. She uncorked the bottle and poured a measure of amber liquid into a shallow cup. She held it up and then presented it to the man on her left. "May you never thirst," she said.

He drank and then passed the cup to the person on his left with the same phrase, "May you never thirst."

Luke took the cup when it reached him and nodded appreciatively as he passed it to Amy with the same words. The amber liquid was sweet and rich, and it left a burn at the back of her throat that told her it was alcoholic.

Once the cup had made its way back to the lady, she broke the bread. The aroma of the dark loaf was intoxicating. It went around with the words, "May you never hunger." That was, thankfully, the extent of the ceremony.

At a gesture from the lady, the table was piled with a dozen different platters, bowls, and tureens. Amy's stomach gave another loud grumble as she followed the lady's example of helping herself to whatever was in reach. She piled her plate high, even though she couldn't identify half of the dishes.

"What was that drink?" she asked between mouthfuls.

"Mead," the lady answered. "Surely you've had it before?"

Amy shook her head.

"No?" the lady responded. "Most unusual. Bear can tell

you much more than I can." She gestured at the man on Amy's left.

With long, brown hair, a shockingly long beard braided into two forks, and dark brown eyes, Bear was aptly named. *There is enough hair on him to comfortably cover the entire expedition with some to spare,* Amy thought. His eyes twinkled mischievously as he turned toward her.

"I have been known to make a batch or two of the stuff," he said. This was greeted by many chuckles across the table.

"Just a few," a voice joked from farther down the table.

"Not that we haven't appreciated your effort," Lorn called out, raising his glass. There was a cheer, which Bear acknowledged with a small bow.

Amy spent the rest of feast hearing about the differences between wine, mead, and beer. Bear told her much about the brewing process, punctuated by stories and anecdotes about memorable batches and how they had affected certain tribe members.

She understood little of what was said. She was unfamiliar with most of the ingredients. Other than one story about Lexa and one about Lorn, she knew none of the people mentioned. She didn't care, however. Bear's genial humor reminded her of her father in the old days, before her mom died.

Once during the feast she wondered where the others were. Other than Luke, who was seated next to her and deeply engrossed in a conversation with someone on their other side, none of the others were seated at their table.

Craning her head around, she spied them at a long table not far away. The conversation looked lively, and they seemed to be having no problems fitting in.

Lexa was harder to spot. Finally she heard Lexa's distinctive tinkling laugh. She was seated toward the back with a brown-haired man who could have passed for Bear except for the fact that he was twice as big.

Must be Luther, she thought, remembering Lexa's descriptions. Lexa looked almost comically small as she sat on the man's lap, laughing and feeding him bits of food. A blond toddler stood on his chair and reached up to help feed the man.

Another bottle was passed Amy's way, and she forgot about the others for a long time. She had a mug of water at her place—everyone did—but the bottles of mead were also being passed around freely. Despite Amy's proclamation that she wouldn't imbibe alcohol again, every time a bottle went past, Bear would make some comment about it, and to be polite, she'd have a taste. So far her water was mostly untouched. Truthfully, the sweet warm liquid was far more to her liking than beer, and her head was starting to swim.

Later, she could never quite remember how long the feast had gone on or how many bottles had passed her by. At last there was a hand on her shoulder. It was Daisy. "We're claiming this one," she said to Lady Sapphire.

There was a brief look between Sapphire and Lorn. Then the lady nodded her consent. Amy looked at Daisy in confusion.

"Each family will put up one of the expedition members," Daisy explained. "To spread out the task and privilege of playing host to all of you. I just stepped in a little early to have my say as to who we would have."

Amy rose and left the hall with Daisy. She was fighting

an odd battle to keep a straight line. Daisy turned to her. "Lexa has already told us a great deal about you, especially your ranch's views on things. You'll not be propositioned in my house, unless you want to be, of course."

Amy giggled. Daisy stared hard at her a minute then grinned. "You're drunk."

"Am not," Amy insisted. "Much."

"Luther, come here," Daisy called and the big man bounded up from somewhere with Lexa on his heels. "She's drunk."

"I am not," Amy continued to insist. She stumbled and fell into the man. Before she could open her mouth again, he swept her off her feet. Amy was no slight girl. The number of men she had met who could lift her easily was exactly zero, until now. It was a strange sensation, to be carried like she was a little girl again, in her father's arms.

What would it be like to spend the night in this man's massive arms? she wondered dully. *Stop it,* she told herself fiercely, *you are acting like one of those silly women in your sister's romance novels.* Still, her mind kept returning to the same thought.

Luther, however, was a perfect gentleman. Amy soon found herself deposited safely on a low couch. Lexa's face swam into view. She was holding a small cup in her hands. "Drink this," she said.

"What is it?"

"It's one of Merlin's hangover remedies. Believe me, you are going to have one whopper of a headache tomorrow without it," she explained. "Bear's mead sneaks up on you."

Despite the tea, Amy woke with a horrendous headache.

She peered around the room, disoriented. She had only a dim recollection of being helped in here. The room was small and made of the same earthen material that was so common down here. Light streamed through a small window that was opposite the bed. A wardrobe and a dresser took up the rest of that side of the wall.

The door on the wall facing the foot of the bed burst open, and Lexa came bustling in carrying a tray. "Rise and shine, sleepy head."

She sat down beside Amy. Amy rolled over with a groan and realized she was naked. She pulled the covers up to her neck as she sat up. Lexa offered her a cup. Amy eyed it suspiciously. "Just water," Lexa told her, "best thing for a hangover."

Amy moaned again and held her head with her free hand.

Lexa laughed. "Don't fret, honey. We've all been there a time or two. You don't think Merlin came up with his hangover remedy by accident, do you? Drink the water first; then try some food." The tray contained fruit, apples, pears, and some bread and jam.

"My clothes?" she asked, looking down.

Lexa giggled. "I take it you don't remember puking then?"

She did now. They'd helped her clean up and get back to bed. *How embarrassing.*

Lexa patted her cheek. "It was your first encounter with mead. It will be better next time, you'll see. You'll know how much is enough."

Amy shook her head and moaned. "No, never again, not ever."

"The times I have said that! If it makes you feel any

better, you were not alone last night. That was quite a feast. Most of the boys and quite a few of our own people overdid it. Sort of makes you want to run around the community with a gong, doesn't it?"

Amy groaned.

"Just teasing." Lexa rose and opened the wardrobe. "Clothes for your stay, compliments of Winnie; she's about your size. Mostly long sleeves for outside work; someone with your fair complexion shouldn't risk too much sun."

Amy peered at the closet. It overflowed with long, flowing dresses, colorful blouses, and long skirts, which seemed to be common apparel at this community. She was pretty sure she'd even seen more than one man wearing such garb last night. She'd have to find her pack pronto.

Lexa left her to drink and eat. After drinking the water, she did feel better, and she ate some fruit as well. She went to the wardrobe and picked out a floor-length, green broomstick skirt and matching cotton top. A wide-brimmed straw hat completed the ensemble.

Amy made her way to the main room at the front of the house. Daisy and Lexa were waiting for her there. "The first order of business is a bath," Daisy declared.

Amy happily agreed. The thought of a warm soak was irresistible. She could almost hear Minister Posch saying, "You are giving in to decadence and sin, girl." *Shut up, you old git.* She followed the two women out.

When they got to the bathhouse, they found Willowshade and another woman already there. Soon all five women were soaking together in the bath and discussing last night's feast. With the warmth slowly seeping into her back and her joints, Amy felt much better.

As they soaked, an old man wandered in and began to undress. Amy looked around nervously, but the other women took no notice. Then she remembered that both sexes usually used the bath together here.

As he shuffled across the shower room, Willowshade noticed him and called out, "Hang on there, Sal. I'll come help you." She climbed out and went to the man.

Amy tried not to watch. She feared they would think she was being rude. Yet, it was hard not to. There was something about the scene, the young woman ignoring her own nakedness as she helped the old man onto the low seat. As she scrubbed his back, he hummed in contentment.

Amy felt something stir inside her. She fought for the correct word to describe the scene but failed. The two were beautiful, but not in a sexual way, and the concept of sensuality was not familiar at the ranch.

Lexa noticed her watching and slid over. "That's Salmontears, but everyone just calls him Sal. He's one of the Laughing Crones. They're the oldest family out here. Started the community years before the blast."

Sal and Willowshade were now shuffling toward the pool. "You are a true blessing, child," he was telling her. "These old bones don't work like they used to, especially not before my morning soak."

Once in the pool Amy and Sal were formally introduced. While Amy's modesty was rapidly disappearing, it was still somehow incongruous to make polite introductions while standing stark naked in chest deep water.

"Salmontears, that's an unusual name," she commented.

"It is a name of mourning," he told her. "I worked the Alaskan fisheries in my youth, long before the collapse. When the Salmon went extinct . . ." he shook his head, "that's when I realized how bad it was. I changed my name and dropped out of society for good, just in time to find a bunch of city witches wanting to move out into the deep woods."

Michael—or maybe it was Lorn; they looked so similar—came in and crossed the shower room without bothering to undress. He leaned down and said, "Ten minutes until council."

Amy waited until he had crossed and exited the building before following the other women to the shower, but she gave only a fleeting thought to Sal as he also followed them.

On the path to the community hall, they ran into Luke. His eyes widened as he looked at Amy. She looked back perplexed.

"Wow," he said, "you look so different."

"Boy, he sure knows how to woo a lady," Lexa teased.

He blushed. "I'm sorry I'm just not used to seeing you so—"

"Pretty?" Lexa supplied.

"Feminine," he mumbled going even redder.

"I am not pretty," Amy declared. She had been described any number of ways throughout her life. Many graphic words had been used, none of which were synonyms for pretty. Still, she could not help but notice the same wide-eyed look from the other men as they gathered. It was a novel sensation, one that she wasn't sure she liked.

Another novel sensation, one that she did enjoy, was the respect the outsiders paid her. As they filed into the community hall, she was again placed at Luke's left. The message was clear. Next to the leader, the mechanic's input was second most important, regardless of her sex. Patrick's angry glare showed that he had read the situation the same way, but was less happy about it.

Lady Sapphire sat the end of a long table with Luke beside her. Amy sat on Luke's left with the others in the expedition behind her. On Sapphire's right sat Michael, Lorn, and the other council members. Sal shuffled in, moving better since his bath, and sat down at the far end of the table. "I apologize for my tardiness," he said.

Lady Sapphire's gaze softened as she looked at the old man. "No apology is needed, Sal. We are glad you could make it."

He pulled out a notebook and opened it. "Let the record show that with my tardy entrance all the council members are present."

"So noted."

"Then I call this session to order," Sal continued. "The purpose of this session is well known to all, but for the record: we are here to discuss the visitors from Freedom Ranch. The villagers of Bullhaven have given us a rather thorough account of their plight and mission. We discussed this last session, so unless there is anything new to add?" He gave Luke a meaningful look. Luke shook his head no.

Amy looked at Lady Sapphire. She was the leader here, wasn't she? Why wasn't she running the meeting? Obviously there were aspects of this community Amy didn't understand.

"Good," Sal went on. "In that case, we can dispense with any further background, since we discussed it less than a week ago.

"The villagers have indicated that they have made a barter arrangement for supplies and parts these people need. If we provide the items we discussed at the last session, the villagers will settle with us at harvest time. They have always dealt fairly with us in the past, and I see no reason to doubt their word now. I see no reason to object to this arrangement."

"Nor do I," Lady Sapphire put in.

"Then I move that we accept the credit of the villagers for the items requested by Freedom Ranch and extend a similar arrangement with the Cyclers," Michael put in.

Lorn said, "I second." There was a chorus of "ayes" around the table.

"Motion carries with no dissent," Sal said. "Duly noted. That was mostly a formality anyway. Now we can get down to the real business. What help does this mission need from us, and can we provide it?"

"But," Daniel burst in, "didn't you just agree to provide us help?"

"Yes," Michael replied. "We will give you the parts and equipment you need from us. Most of your list, however, will have to come from the Cyclers. With both the village and us providing credit, acquiring what you need should be no problem. Actually getting there could be another matter."

"It seems," Sal said. "That you have not yet taken into full account the extent of your mission. The Cyclers are established in what used to be the city of Kansas City. That was maybe a couple days' journey long ago on the interstate highway. That interstate no longer exists. On foot, it could take you several weeks or even months to travel that far."

The entire mission groaned. At each leg, they'd thought they were done, that they'd somehow completed their mission. Then they found there were months more to go. It didn't seem fair, but they'd been forewarned of how long this journey might take. Amy stared at her group in contempt. *Don't they listen?* Jacob had said as much at the outset. The villagers had said as much. Now they were surprised to hear it again?

"We have always helped those in need," Lorn told them. "We will not let you down."

"It's just that charity breeds dependence," Lady Sapphire explained. "We would prefer a solution that leads to interdependence . . . a trade, if you will."

Luke shook his head to clear it. Obviously much of this was going over his head too. "All I know is that fair is fair. We obviously need your help, but we want to earn it in an even trade."

"That is all we want as well," Michael assured him.

"And we have a plan that will achieve exactly that," Sal added.

Lady Sapphire held up a finger. "I want it noted for the record that I have reservations about this plan."

"Reservations or objections?" Sal inquired.

There was a moment's pause. "Reservations," she replied. "I will not stand in the way of consensus, if they consent."

Amy marveled. At the ranch, any hint of Amos's disapproval generally halted all discussion. Of course, the most common hint he gave was when he banged his gavel and shouted. This quiet discussion was new to her.

"What sort of reservations do you have?" Luke asked.

"I worry about your youth and condition," she replied.

"Our youth?" Patrick exploded. "Our condition? I'll have you know we have made it this far without your help."

Michael deflected the attack with a laugh. "Nobody here has any doubts about your stamina or your abilities. Indeed we have marveled at the incredible journey you have made already. If you will listen for a moment to our plan, I think you will understand Lady Sapphire's reservations better."

Patrick settled back with a huff. A middle-aged woman with dishwater-blond hair and a square, masculine face held up her hand to be recognized.

"Yes, Lucy," Sal said with a nod. "You are the best qualified to talk about it."

"The project I have been spearheading is a cleanup project," she began. "The river that flows a few miles west of here has become increasingly problematic. Silt laden with toxic chemicals and radiation has been building up in the sandbars for years.

"There are two major issues. One, that water feeds our water table. Second, if we go ahead with our expansion of the irrigation networks, we may have to utilize that water directly. The only solution we have been able to come up with is to remove most of the silt. The Stewards have agreed to take it."

"Who are the Stewards?" Luke asked.

"A monastic order," Lorn said. "They have taken vows to clean up the mess humans have created. Specifically, they monitor waste sites and have marked off areas where the radiation levels are too high for human habitation. They have agreed to accept the silt and either process it or keep it at one of their sites."

"And they agree with Lady Sapphire on one point," Lucy went on. "These young people should not be directly involved with the waste. We cannot in good conscience expose people of your age and potential fertility to radioactive material. The human race needs every fertile member it can get."

"That is indeed the nature of my reservations," Lady Sapphire said. "And I apologize to you, Patrick, and any of the others who might have misinterpreted it."

"However," Sal interrupted. "The Stewards have provided lead-lined canisters for shipment. They claim that once the waste is sealed the danger is minimal. The levels of radiation should be no higher than normal background level. It should be perfectly safe for you to help with delivery."

"But," Kurt began slowly, "I thought our problem was how long it was going to take to get to the Cyclers. If we help with this delivery first, won't that take even longer?"

"Our first delivery will be ready to go within two weeks," Lucy explained. "Only we can't possibly spare the people. If you take it, with some of our people to help of course, you could then have the trucks on loan."

"It is a considerable detour, but traveling by truck is much faster, so you will end up coming out ahead. It should be possible to complete the whole trip in as little as two months."

"Two months?" Shawn howled. "But we need to be back before fall. We'll never make it."

"My companion is right, if a bit dramatic," Luke said. "We need to get these supplies back before the passes close. It may well be life or death for the ranch if we don't."

"Then it is a race against time," Sal said. "May I propose that we extend the loan of the trucks to the return trip? We could easily send a few of our own people with you to drive them back."

"The roads out that way are almost nonexistent," Luke said.

"Our EVs can handle it," Lucy assured him. "It'd still be close, but they could make it. Hell, our EVs could probably plow the passes if necessary."

"Can we spare the trucks that long?" someone asked.

The woman just shrugged, "They're all committed to this project, and they'll likely sit full of waste all summer if we don't get more drivers. So it's about the same either way."

"So let's make this official," Lady Sapphire said. "I propose that we ask the members of this mission from Freedom Ranch to deliver five trucks of toxic waste to the nearest stewards. We, in return, agree to loan said trucks to the mission for the trip to the Cyclers and back to Freedom Ranch. Any objections?"

There was an immediate second, and the motion carried easily. Lady Sapphire turned to Luke. "Do you understand our proposal sufficiently, or have you any questions?"

"We understand," he replied.

"Then we will give you some time to discuss this amongst yourselves before asking for an answer." She rose. "Food and tea will be sent in; otherwise, you will be given one hour's privacy. We will reconvene at that time to hear your answer."

As trays of refreshments were brought in, Luke unrolled

a large piece of paper. "Michael gave me this," he explained. "It's a map of this region, updated as much as possible. One thing is for sure, they aren't kidding. It could take us months to walk that far."

"Worse still, the parts we need aren't light. I have been dreading the thought of the walk back under heavy packs."

"But I thought we were getting most of the stuff from the villagers?" Shawn asked.

"Yes and no," Luke replied. "They are providing most of the household stuff; bulk-wise, that's the majority. But the rest of what we need is mostly electronics and mechanical parts, such as parts for the tractor and the Jeep. Once we get new gaskets for the still, Amy will be able to keep that Jeep running, with parts, of course. Most of that stuff is metal. Smaller, but a lot heavier. Weight-wise, that will be the biggest share."

This was greeted by groans. "I just don't think we can do it without help," Luke continued. "And I've been thinking: if we have vehicles, we can get even more stuff and not have to do this again."

"That's true," Amy agreed. "I say let's do it." She was hard pressed to feel bad about another two weeks here.

There was a general murmur of ascent. "Well, if Amy thinks it's a good idea," Patrick sneered, "then it must be. Our good old Luke, always doing what his woman wants."

"What did I say?" Amy gasped, her mood deflating instantly.

"Since when do the men of Freedom Ranch go around kowtowing to women?" Patrick continued angrily, glaring at Luke. "I held my tongue at the village. They at least seemed like ordinary folk. These people here are serious freaks. Have you seen how all these long-haired men all meekly follow that witch?"

To everyone's surprise, it was Shawn who interceded. "Hey, even I can I see that we need their help, and they are good enough to provide it. What's wrong with taking help when it's offered?"

"Pussy whipped already?" Patrick responded. Shawn blushed and didn't answer.

Daniel stepped in next. "I don't know where that all came from, but Shawn's right for once. There is nothing wrong with taking help when it's offered."

"Walk or ride," Mark threw in. "That's a damn easy choice, Patrick. Why spoil it?"

Patrick glared around the room. Seeing everyone arrayed against him, he deflated. "I'd rather walk then take help from that bitch," he muttered, sinking into his seat.

"I am tempted to let you," Luke replied. "But we need to stick together. We are going to help these people, and they are going to help us, regardless of what anyone thinks of their leader. Understood?"

"She's got four husbands," Patrick said.

"And two wives," Amy put in with a grin. Luke shot her a dark look.

"Understood?" he repeated to Patrick.

"Understood," Patrick muttered.

"Good," Luke said.

"They're all like that," Patrick continued. "Poly . . . poly whatever it is; group marriage and all that. It's sick. Minister Posch would have a cow. It's wrong, according to the Bible."

Amy found Patrick's use of Minister Posch and the

Bible in defense of his argument suspicious. He rarely had anything good to say about either.

"The Bible says we should be tolerant of others," Kurt replied. Everyone looked at him. He stared back, eyes wide.

"Does it?" Daniel asked.

"It does," Kurt replied, though he looked less sure of himself. "I've been reading it," he ended lamely.

The remainder of the hour stretched into an eternity for Amy. No one felt like talking much.

Patrick fidgeted sullenly with his knife with a look that dared anyone to comment. Daniel and Kurt huddled over the small green book that Kurt carried. "Huh. It does say that. I'll be damned," Daniel muttered. "Wonder why Posch never read that passage?"

Luke and Mark were studying the map together. Mark kept speculating about the other communities along the route and what sort of "hospitality" they might provide while Luke rolled his eyes.

Amy was left to herself. She kept alternating between wondering where Lexa was and wondering who had "pussy whipped" Shawn.

Finally, the council filed back in. Luke gave his approval to the plan, and the details were quickly set. Three members of the community would be sent as guides and to assist. This gave the expedition ten men to drive five trucks. This was more than sufficient, since the Stewards would do the hard part, unloading the waste.

The expedition had approximately ten days before the waste would be ready. In that time, they would have to learn to drive the electric trucks.

For Amy, training began and ended that afternoon. She

was already familiar with both automatic and clutch vehicles and tractors. Electric vehicles were a piece of cake by comparison.

Luke had suggested that she could help teach the others. After one explosion with Mark, Lucy wisely overruled him. Amy was sent off.

So Amy found herself wandering around the community with nothing to do for the next ten days. She found Robin's Nest, but nobody was home. Michael was sitting in the garden as she wandered by. He waved a greeting, and she went over to him. He gestured for her to sit.

"Am I disturbing you?" she asked.

"Not at all. I was meditating, but I am done. How are the lessons going?"

She told him. "Do you know where Lexa is?"

"I believe she is in the workshop. They are quite busy this time of the year. Winter plays havoc on the wind generators."

"Oh, I'd hate to bother her then."

"Are you looking for some company?" Michael asked. "If so, I am free."

She agreed. She enjoyed his quiet manner and frank answers. As they toured the village, he explained much about the how the tribe was governed and how it functioned. It was all so different from what Amy was used to that she understood little.

"Michael?" she said after a while.

"Yes?"

"I feel I can ask you anything, you are so calm and polite."

"You are too kind," he replied with a grin. "Is there

something special you want to ask?"

"Well, yes. I don't really understand the marriage customs that your people have, and I didn't want to ask Lexa anymore questions."

"Why not? Lexa would give you very thorough and descriptive answers no doubt."

"That's what I am afraid of," she replied. He laughed so hard he nearly fell over. Amy blushed and smiled sheepishly.

He sobered after a moment. "I shouldn't jest. I know your people are very conservative. I imagine you don't approve."

"I am trying to be open minded," she replied. "I like your community and all that, but I am a bit confused. Is it necessary for you to, you know, be like that?"

"Necessary, no," he replied. "You came in past the Akiras, I hear. I know Ruth, fought with her years ago. She's tough as nails; so is Roger. Anyway, they're not like us—strict monogamy all the way."

He paused and reflected. "You have to understand, we were always like this. Pagans, I mean. We believed that love was good no matter what form it took. We accepted everyone, straight, gay, bi or transgender. Group marriage was not uncommon among us even then. We were a haven for alternative thinkers of all sorts."

"Yes, but how did the rest of society come to accept this?" Amy asked.

"Oh, not all have. Indeed many of the outlying villages haven't. Bullhaven doesn't have any group marriages."

"But they allow," Amy struggled for the words, "loose sex."

"Oh, that?" Michael replied. "I didn't even think of

that. Your ranch really is conservative. Yes, the sexual ethics have shifted a lot since the collapse."

"There are two primary reasons. Interestingly, they are also totally opposite each other. First off, fertility is way down. As a boy, I remember hearing that fertility was beginning to be a problem even before the blast, due to pesticides and stuff in the drinking water. Then came the blast, the collapse, and whatnot. Radiation and toxic waste have combined in such a way that we are lucky if one in five is fertile.

"So the first issue is the need to procreate. We could be just a few generations from extinction. We all feel it. Many think that the human race is dying. Can we just let it?

"Liberals once argued that we should stop having so many babies because the world was too crowded. Now the opposite is true: the same liberals tell us we must take every opportunity to propagate. It is our sacred duty to at least try." He chuckled.

"Of course, no one listens to liberals much. The second reason is just the opposite. With fertility way down, people have less fear of pregnancy. Those who know they are sterile have no concern. Fertile women know that any pregnancy will be welcomed, not called an accident like it once would have been."

"In my world," Amy said. "A woman who gets pregnant out of wedlock is looked down upon and no one wants her."

"So I remember. But here, she would be even more desirable, having proof of her fertility. Any family would be glad to have her.

"And there is genetic diversity to consider," he continued.

Amy knew the phrase from livestock management. "You mean like breeding animals?"

He nodded. "The same rules apply to humans. Too much inbreeding can lead to serious problems. With so few people left, and those all scattered about, it's a valid concern. To protect ourselves, we must make an effort to mix the gene pool as much as possible."

"So you are saying that group marriage protects the gene pool?"

"No, open relationships protect the gene pool. Being free to mix sexually with any travelers helps avoid inbreeding."

"I'll bet the boys are enjoying that," Amy sneered.

"Rumor has it several of them have," Michael replied. "We placed most of the boys with older families so that their hosts would be aware of how the ethics were in the old days. There have been no unwanted advances, as far as I know."

Amy did not want to think about what the boys were doing. "Anyway, what is group marriage about, if not genetic diversity?"

"Much simpler matters really," he replied. "As I said earlier, before the collapse we already had a number of such arrangements. Others adopted it later because of the chaos that ensued during the collapse. Struggles and grief have a way of building intimacy fast, but what do you do when you discover that your spouse survived after all? Leave the new one or the old? Many of the survivors were familiar with our example and decided to give it a try.

"Also there are distinct advantages. Just look around. Life is hard these days. In subsistence farming, an extra hand or two is always helpful."

"But at the ranch we work together, and there is no group marriage."

"Yes, but how much conflict is there?"

Amy thought about that. She compared in her mind the quiet discussions she had witnessed here with the unruly chaos of meetings back home.

"Sex is not just about procreation. It is about bonding. It helps create a strong emotional bond. It doesn't prevent conflict; in fact, it can create more. But it does provide some cushion, some way around conflict. Take the Dog Boys."

"Dog Boys?"

"Yes, they are the tribe's primary warriors. They are mostly sterile and mostly homosexuals, like the ancient Greeks. Because of their open sexuality, they are a tightknit group. In times of trouble, they have always fought well, in part because they are so protective of each other."

A gong sounded as they walked. "What was that?" Amy asked.

"Quitting time at the workshop," he replied. "Come on."

9

The Dog Boys

They approached the workshop as the workers were starting to come out. Lorn and Lexa were among them.

"Good day to you," Lorn greeted them. "I hope everything went well at the council?"

Michael explained the deal. Lorn nodded. "I had hoped as much. I hate to dash off," he said, "but I need to catch the boys before they return to their host families. We are going to invite them up for a warriors circle with the Dog Boys. Are you interested, Amy?"

"Warriors stuff," Lexa scoffed. "We have better things to do." Amy allowed herself to be pulled away despite a vague curiosity.

Luke studied the circle with some interest. The horrible sinking feeling he had felt when Michael and Lorn revealed they knew the boys had "been a bit rowdy" at the

246

village was finally leaving him. It was replaced by a mixture of curiosity and dread.

At least the Tir-Na-Nog warriors were not, apparently, put off by the reports they had heard. They expected young warriors, out on their own for the first time, to behave that way. Indeed, they had traditions in place to assist. It was only natural to want to test yourself, the warriors believed, and they had found a safe way to do so: the warriors circle. At least that was the theory.

As they had described the warriors circle and its rules, Luke grew calm, even relaxed. It sounded no different from the free sparring they did in their combat training course. It was nothing more than a few friendly matches so they could compare styles and abilities. Afterward, they would feast together, drink, and be friends.

Now that they were about to begin, however, he realized just how different this combat training was from that of the ranch. Several of the Dog Boys gathered up large wooden and leather drums. They began beating them in a deep, booming rhythm. Everyone began to circle slowly. One man picked up a stringed instrument and began to play. He sang a deep, rhythmic song in a language Luke had never heard before.

Lorn was "Maestro" for the evening's game. He would decide who fought, and he would judge the matches.

The boys were all huddled close to Luke. They were intimidated by this.

"There are women," Shawn muttered. "I thought it was warriors only."

"It is. They have women warriors," Luke replied.

"I won't fight a girl," Patrick declared. "It's not right."

"Send in Mark," Kurt piped up. "He'll hit a girl."

Mark snarled savagely at Kurt, who ducked behind Daniel.

"You will go in and fight whoever they put against you," Luke told Patrick. "You are the best fighter we have. Make the ranch proud."

Pride forced Patrick into action. He stepped slowly out of the circle, like they had been instructed. He knelt at the edge of the bare space that was the ring.

Several of the tribe members immediately followed suit, showing their willingness to take the challenge. Among them was a slender woman. She had her hair cut as short as Patrick's. She wore what they had been told was the traditional Hakima: cotton pants and top held together with a very faded black belt. She was short and slender, but her face shone with an intensity that Luke had not seen since Isaiah Hall. Next to her right temple a spider was tattooed.

"At the ranch, we don't fight women," Patrick called out.

"Why? Are you scared of them?" someone asked.

Patrick's eyes shot around, searching for the speaker. Lorn gave Patrick a nod, and he took the center of the circle.

"I'll take whoever made that comment," Patrick declared.

"You'll take who you're given," a voice answered.

"You'll get Spider," Lorn said.

The woman gave a quick bow and leaped into the ring.

Several voices began chanting "Spider, Spider."

"For the ranch," Mark shouted at Patrick.

"For the ranch," Shawn added.

Patrick laughed. Luke knew what he was thinking; Luke

was thinking it too. Why send this little woman up against Patrick? She had no chance. He was twice her size.

Still laughing, Patrick took a ready stance. His fist shot out. She ducked easily. He was fast, almost too fast to see, but she was faster. He threw jab after jab. She bobbed and wove, always just out of reach.

Finally, with a shout he leaped forward, bearing down on her. She fell before him. He pushed her down, overpowering her.

Then, incredibly, as she fell on her back, her feet came up. Her legs twisted, and Patrick was caught. She wrapped her legs around his neck in a very unladylike chokehold. With a simple twist, Patrick was on his back, held helpless. There was a roar from the crowd. "Spider!" they cheered.

So the night went. Other than the rules of contact, there were few similarities between this and the way the boys had been trained. The warriors of the Greenbowe tribe ducked, bobbed, wove, somersaulted, and cartwheeled fluidly around the circle, hitting, kicking, and throwing each other. It was fast and furious, but mostly devious. One moment, they were falling down defeated; the next, a foot snaked out and they swept their opponent down.

After a while, Luke began to be able to pick out several distinct styles. A few people predominately used throws that were very reminiscent of Luke's Judo book. A larger number of others used a more flowing style of throws that Luke guessed from Ruth's description to be Aikido. There were many other styles that Luke had no name for.

The ranch's training was done by Isaiah Hall based on US Special Forces training in hand-to-hand combat. Luke had always firmly believed it represented the best possible fighting style. His confidence was now shaken badly.

One thing that Luke had always wondered about was becoming clear. The Judo book talked about the style as though it were a lifestyle or a life-long discipline. Luke had never quite understood that until now. Now, he was watching people who had devoted years to the perfection of their style. There were many black belts, indicating high-ranked and well-trained practitioners. A couple of the older warriors wore white belts, the beginner's color, even though they were obviously very skilled. Luke remembered what the book had said about that and explained to Daniel and Kurt that these warriors were at the highest possible rank; they had gone full circle.

The biggest surprise of the night was Kurt. Kurt and Luke had drilled in Judo throws for some time before the beginning of the mission. A complete failure at the harder style favored at the ranch, Kurt had quietly taken the lessons to heart. Also, he was less sure of himself and, therefore, more cautious. He did not fall for the more obvious tricks of the Greenbowes.

He even managed to unseat his first opponent, throwing them over his shoulder with a triumphant cry. The Greenbowes cheered as loudly for him as they had for their own, and the tension among the boys dropped dramatically. For all the intensity, it was indeed a friendly game.

The fighting went on well into the night. They each fought several times and often the Greenbowes fought amongst each other. These were the fun matches to watch. They pitted skilled warriors, people who knew each other's style well, against each other. The results were impressive.

Even Patrick appeared to relax and enjoy himself. He had spent nearly a half an hour scowling and glowing red after his first match. Then Spider took the field again. She took on six fighters in turn, many of them much larger. She was fast and clever. She used a combination of fluid throws, "Aikido," Michael confirmed from Luke's side. She also used tighter vicious holds and throws that Michael identified as Brazilian Jujitsu.

"See, Patrick?" Mark said. "It's no shame to have lost to that woman. She's one tough bitch!"

Luke startled at the statement, expecting a sudden flare of wrath from Spider. But she merely smiled at him. "Damn straight," she told Mark. "Want a piece?"

It was over in seconds, and to Luke's surprise, Mark didn't appear the least bit put out as he limped back out of the circle.

Toward the end, Maestro Lorn took the center ring, gesturing to three separate people. "He always waits until the end," Michael explained. "His Tai Chi is fabulous, but it is more impressive after you've seen the others fight."

Luke didn't know what Tai Chi was, but he had to agree. If he hadn't seen the men fight before, he wouldn't have thought much of Lorn's movements, which came off as light and easy. He didn't appear to be doing much, but each of the three fighters went down. It was as though they had suddenly developed two left feet.

All three attacked at once and were repulsed easily. While Lorn's movements were effortless, his opponents were often thrown several feet. It was an impressive demonstration.

"You have us at a great disadvantage," Luke announced when asked how he had enjoyed the circle. "We surrender to your superior skill." There was another cheer at this graceful admission.

"Nonsense," Lorn returned. "You stood against some of our most skilled warriors. Many have more years of training than you have years. It was an honorable match, and you acquitted yourselves well." Another cheer went up followed by the popping of corks as mead bottles were opened.

10

Robin's Nest

Amy had one moment to watch the other's leave for the warriors circle before Lexa dragged her back to her family home. Returning to the nest, they found Rowan waiting for them. He wore tight leather breeches and a light blue tunic with long sleeves. With his long, blond hair pulled back in a tight braid, he looked quite handsome. Amy thought, *I can see why Lexa fell for him first.*

"Hello, my dears," he said kissing both Lexa and Daisy soundly on the lips. "And hello to you," he added to Amy, kissing her hand. She blushed.

"Such a gentlemen," Daisy said a bit too loud, winking.

"And why shouldn't I be?" he replied, "With such a beautiful guest in our house?"

"Don't embarrass her," Lexa laughed.

Embarrass me.

Inside, Luther was doing some knitting. Amy almost

burst out laughing at the sight of that great bear of a man very carefully knitting socks. It was a tight weave in a pattern that Amy recognized but had never mastered, despite her mother's many lessons. *What would mom think of all this?* She pushed the thought down.

Winonna came in next. She was tall and thin with a sharp nose, small hips, and a narrow waist. Despite this, she was quite attractive, as Merlin told her as he kissed her. She had three kids at her heels, two of them little more than toddlers.

"I believe it's your turn with these rapscallions," she told Luther.

Luther put his knitting up and towered over the kids. They stared up at him with wide, amused eyes. "Well, let's get you rapscallions ready for supper," he said, shooing them gently with his massive hands. He led them away, the youngest toddling after and calling "papa woofer" gleefully. They came back promptly, hands wet from washing.

Daisy led them into the dining room. Even though she was the shortest, she managed to give the distinct impression of towering over the others. Merlin went into the kitchen and came out moments later with a tray of roasted vegetables.

As if the sight of Luther knitting hadn't been enough, there was Merlin. He was small, dark haired, and compact, with a dark intensity about him, standing there in a brightly colored apron.

"Is it a holiday?" the older boy asked. Erick was his name, Amy remembered. The girl was Sky and the youngest Ewan.

"Yes," Daisy replied. "It's our first chance to play host

to our new guest, Amy."

The meal was long and leisurely. Despite her day-old promise to never drink again, she took a few sips, and then a glass, of the wine Merlin offered. They ate and spoke lightly of their day.

After the meal was done, they retired to the veranda. Luther produced a small flute from somewhere and began to play. It was a light, airy tune, and the kids danced madly to it.

"A jig, my good sir," Rowan cried.

Luther began a faster tune, and Rowan danced gracefully. Daisy leaped up and joined him. Lexa grabbed Amy by the hand and led her through the steps of the dance.

Merlin disappeared inside and returned with two drums. He sat down and began playing one. Ewan toddled over and beat crudely on the other until Winnie took it from him.

After a while, Daisy took the flute from Luther and Merlin handed him the drum. The two started a slow, stately piece. Merlin bowed deeply to Lexa and Amy, but it was Amy's hand that he took. He led her through the simple but elegant dance.

So the evening passed. As the shadows lengthened across the path and oil lamps appeared at neighboring houses, Luther led the children inside for bed. Merlin lit lamps on the porch, and Daisy produced a small bottle of a rich, red wine.

In the quiet, Amy could hear music from the other houses. It was a comforting sound that wafted with the breeze through the forest. Luther returned, and they sat and talked well into the night.

Amy could just make out an image of dancers at the next house. *These are the children of a new earth*, she thought, and the phrase swam through her head long after she went to bed that night.

"Amy!" a voice cried as people started coming out of the workshop. She craned to see. It was not Lexa, as expected, but Daisy.

"How was your day?" Daisy asked.

"Good," Amy replied. It had been interesting. She had spent most of the day helping Merlin bake bread in the family's mud oven.

"Men cook here?" she had Merlin.

"We eat," he'd replied. "Why wouldn't we cook? Besides, this is more like doing magic."

That answer had intrigued Amy enough for her to offer to help. She wasn't sure what she had expected—him doing incantations and whatnot?

Instead, they had mixed water, flour, and yeast . . . and kneaded and kneaded. Merlin talked the whole time, explaining about the four elements; earth, water, fire and air. The oven was made of earth, fire was built within. Water was mixed into the flour, and with yeast, the bread rose, bringing in air.

It was all very fascinating, and she had learned a lot. For one thing, she now had names to go with the dark heavy loaves she had already learned to love. The dark brown ones were rye, the black loaves were pumpernickel, and the golden ones were barley. The sharp tasting ones were sourdough, made with wild yeasts that were left to work, sometimes for days, before the bread was baked.

Fascinating though it was, it was baking, and that had

never been Amy's forte. By midafternoon, she was bored, so when Merlin had asked if she wanted to go meet Lexa at the workshop, she had quickly agreed.

"My sweety," Daisy greeted Merlin, giving him a kiss. "Lexa's going to be a few minutes. She was working on a nasty problem."

They sat down under a small oak tree to wait. Lexa came out moments later, covered in grease and soot. "I need a bath," she declared.

"What happened to you?" Amy asked.

"Working on an old diesel generator some village sent in. They have been burning straight oil in it, not converting it to biodiesel, for almost a year. It's a mess."

"Yeah, they did that at the ranch in one of the tractors before my dad got there. He was pissed."

Daisy frowned. "I always thought that was okay?"

"It runs okay," Amy explained, "so most of the old books say so. But it's a lot dirtier than after it's been processed. If you run it for long without cleaning . . . well, look." She pointed at Lexa.

"That's going to be awful to clean," Daisy said frowning.

"Me or the suit?" Lexa asked.

"Both, but you are the first priority. Straight to the bathhouse for you. And leave that here; you'll streak grease everywhere."

Lexa stripped the jumpsuit off and smiled at Daisy. "Ready for my bath, Mama Daisy," she joked.

"Get on, you stinker," Daisy said as she herded them off.

No one seemed surprised by Lexa's nakedness, so Amy didn't comment. They apparently had very different views on that.

"Like your outfit," one young man commented cheekily as Lexa passed. She bowed to him. Everyone else ignored them.

Amy was halfway across the shower room floor before she realized she had stripped and joined the others without thinking about Merlin's presence. She was not particularly embarrassed, but rather shocked by her own easy acceptance of their customs.

Amy, being relatively clean, stood beside Daisy and helped, handing her shampoo as she scrubbed and scrubbed. "The worst part," Lexa moaned, "is that it will be at least another two days at this rate."

"One," Amy told her, "with my help."

"Oh, thank you, thank you," Lexa cried hugging her hand.

"Well, that is the last one," Lexa said, sliding the glass plate across the table.

"Good, I'm beat," Amy said. Despite her appreciation of Winnie's loan of clean clothes, she was even more appreciative when Susan, who was teaching the boys to drive the EVs, offered to loan her several gray jumpsuits. They were the almost universal attire within the workshop. It was also an image she was more comfortable with, and like Lexa, she generally wore the jumpsuits home at the end of the day.

They had spent the last several days cleaning the diesel generator and rebuilding a couple of old wind generators. Now Lexa was teaching Amy the finer points of assembling solar panels.

"Thanks to your help, we are ahead of schedule," Lexa

said, peering over a clipboard. "So why don't we knock off a little early and go for a bath? I could die for a long soak."

"Sure," Amy agreed. Her initial reluctance to use the public bath was long gone. She wondered how many of the others had made the same leap. She had seen Shawn down there once, getting his hair washed by one of the Moondancer's women. Surely it had been her idea. She had also spied Kurt leaving the bathhouse one morning, which surprised her.

As they soaked in the hot water, a middle-aged man with graying, blond hair and a short beard splashed in beside them. Amy had met him once or twice and greeted him. "Lars, how are you?"

Lars was one of the driving instructors for the boys. Amy hadn't actually talked to any of them in almost two days.

"Not bad," Lars said, "but I feel grimy. We took the EVs down on the river course, to give everyone some practice on rough terrain."

"How are they doing?"

"Not bad. Driving an EV is not rocket science, as we used to say in the old days," he replied. "They are doing well, though. They'll be ready by the time the cargo is." He looked around. "I'm kind of surprised that I am the only one down here. I wasn't the grimiest one by far."

Amy knew that most of the houses had individual showers and baths for convenience and was sure that Luke and probably Patrick would use them. Mark and Shawn probably didn't care if they were dirty.

An old lady nearby snorted loudly. "That big one, Shawn, he only comes down here when my little Rose suggests it. He's taken to her, I can tell you. Her husbands are trying to be good natured about it, but I don't think they'll be too sad to see him go."

"I saw a couple of the Dog Boys come by for Kurt," Lars said. "So he's up at their little outdoor bath, no doubt."

"The Dog Boys?" Amy asked in surprise. "You mean the warriors?" She wasn't sure what surprised her more: Kurt with the warriors, or the reputation the Dog Boys had at the tribe.

"Yeah, does that surprise you?" Lars asked.

"Well, I mean, don't they, you know, *like* each other?"

Lars laughed. "Yeah, our warriors like each other a lot. I forget sometimes how you were raised. Like the ancient Greeks, our warriors pretty much prefer each other."

"I don't know about the ancient Greeks, but Lexa told me about the Dog Boys. What is Kurt doing hanging around with them?"

Lars just fixed her with a stare. She turned to Lexa, who gave her the same stare. "Oh," she said meekly, "I never thought. I mean, you'd think he'd have said something."

"Think about that little ranch of yours," Lexa said. "Would you have?"

"I guess not."

As they walked home, they came across Lady Sapphire picking flowers in the garden.

"Those are pretty," Amy commented.

Lady Sapphire stood and looked at the flowers a moment. "They are. Funny, I have been growing and using them for years, but it's been a long time since I actually stopped to look at them. They are calendula, a very useful herb. I could tell you more if you'd be so good as to walk with me a ways."

Amy looked at Lexa, who just shrugged. "Luther's making quiche tonight, so don't be late," Lexa said as she left them.

They walked and Lady Sapphire talked. She told Amy about calendula, how it could be used as an antiseptic, how it was a mild mood elevator and good for stress. "I need about a field of that back home," Amy joked. Lady Sapphire gave her a look but didn't comment.

Amy was amazed as always by the complexity that lay just under what appeared to be a simple life. Lady Sapphire named dozens of herbs, told of their medicinal uses, their dye and craft uses, and how they were planted to deter pests or help other plants grow.

She led them to a bench under a large old oak tree. "Even trees play a part, and it's a big one," she said. "They produce oxygen for you and me. They draw water from deep within the earth and release it into the air. They create shade. They have such calming healing spirits . . . so wise."

Amy touched the trunk, for the moment believing. No one at the ranch spoke of trees that way.

"But, as I am sure you guessed," Lady Sapphire went on, "I did not ask you here so I could lecture you about permaculture. I have a question."

"Okay, but Luke is our leader. I am sure he could answer better than me."

"It is not that kind of question," she said. "It is about Patrick."

"Patrick?"

Lady Sapphire sighed. "The first night you came to us, Patrick shared my bed. I thought we both enjoyed ourselves. However, since then he has avoided me. He has even taken to staying at another house with his friend Mark. Among us, this would be considered very rude. Yet, I hesitate to label it so. I fear that there was some rule or custom I transgressed." She shook her head, bewildered.

Amy reeled. Patrick and Lady Sapphire? That did explain a lot about Patrick's attitude, but what to tell Lady Sapphire? She was obviously hurt by his behavior.

Amy drew a long breath and started slowly. "For one thing, Patrick is rude, I'm afraid to say. He is immature and impetuous. That is why Luke is our leader. Also, women back home don't do things like run tribes. Mostly, they sit at home and cook and clean and do what the men tell them to do."

"They brought you along," Lady Sapphire said, confused.

"Only because they didn't have a choice." Her voice held more bitterness than she expected. "My dad was their mechanic and engineer. He got sick and I was the only one who knew how to do what he did. Patrick always calls me grease monkey. He was hopping mad when they choose to take me along."

Lady Sapphire brushed her cheek. "That's horrible."

"Yes," Amy admitted. "It was leukemia. I don't even know if he's still alive. But somebody had to come and I was the only one who knew——"

"That's horrible too," Lady Sapphire corrected. "But I meant the way they have treated you. I was young when the collapse happened, but I remember how some men were, before."

Amy bit her lip. She didn't want to discuss this, not here, not now. "It's just how they were raised. They have a low opinion of all women."

"A strong woman threatens their sense of power," Lady Sapphire said. "That's why they pick on you. But at the same time, it can be a draw. That's why Patrick was so keen that first night." She sighed again. "Well, it's not the answer I wanted, but I have an answer at least. I should have realized. Oh well, I don't want to keep you. Lexa's right; Luther's quiche is not to be missed."

Amy laughed out loud. "Do you know what he looks like to me? He's this big bear of a man, and yet he happily does all these things that the men of the ranch would consider beneath them. It's so strange and wonderful."

Luther's quiche turned out to be as good as promised. Still, something was brewing around the table. It was like a slowly building storm. Eyes shifted back and forth. The children, usually giggling balls of mischief, were quietly rebuked at every turn. Amy caught the feeling that somebody had bad news or at least news that wouldn't be well received. Daisy caught it too.

"All right, out with it," she said, giving them a stern look. Everyone looked around as innocently as possible. "It's no good," Daisy warned. "You all know something you think I won't like, so out with it." She glared at them, setting her fork down. Luther looked away. Merlin drummed his fingers.

Lexa cleared her throat. "Well, you know, I was talking to Susan just the other day. We are sending two of our best warriors on this mission. They're good, and Lorn knows the route. But what Susan really wanted was someone who really knew the route well and, maybe, knew the trucks better too. Well I thought . . . that is, I kind of, sort of, volunteered." Lexa looked down.

Daisy picked up her fork and aimed it squarely at Lexa, "You'll be looking after our Amy, then?"

"You could say that," Lexa squeaked.

The tension deflated suddenly as Daisy resumed eating. "I'd been a bit worried, to tell you the truth," she said between bites. "Our Amy going out all alone on such a dangerous mission."

She pointed the fork at Amy. "You will make sure she doesn't do anything crazy?"

"Yes ma'am," a very startled Amy replied.

"She does take risks, our Lexa," Daisy said. Luther gave a low chuckle.

After dinner, Luther ushered Amy out to the porch where a few of the others had gathered and swept her into a hug.

"That was amazing," Winnie said.

Amy was mystified. Merlin caught her look and explained. "The last time Lexa took a mission like this, Daisy fretted for weeks. Gods, was it awful. You couldn't get near her without her shouting or, worse, crying."

"Daisy loves us all," Winnie said. "But she does worry something awful. It doesn't help that Lexa is such a free spirit. Can't keep her at home."

"Our Amy." Merlin laughed. "You know that's practically an invitation to join our family, one that I don't think anyone would object to."

When Lexa joined them on the porch, Amy ran to her and hugged her.

"You're coming along," Amy said with a wide smile. "That's great." She had secretly been dreading having to say goodbye to the cozy little family. With Lexa along, it wouldn't be so hard.

The next three days flew by, and before Amy knew it, she found herself packed and ready to leave. She had been at Tir-Na-Nog for just over a week and half, but it felt like much longer.

There were five trucks lined up and ready to go. There were now ten expedition members. "Two of their best warriors" turned out to be Lorn, another welcome sight for Amy, and a shorthaired woman named Spider that the men seemed to know. With ten drivers, it would be two to a truck. Not only did that mean they could trade off on the driving, it meant company. On a long trip, that was considered vital. One person asleep at the wheel could spell disaster for the whole mission.

Lexa drove the lead truck. Amy drove the second. Luke rode with her. He looked a bit sullen, but greeted her pleasantly enough. "So how have you been?" he asked.

"Pretty good."

"I was hosted by the Meadows family," he said. "Nice people."

"Yeah, I met Willowshade a number of times. She seems nice."

"Who were you with?"

"Robin's Nest," she replied. "That's Lexa's family."

He nodded. "Didn't see much of you," he said casually. "Of course, we were all busy with training."

"I helped in the workshop. It was very interesting." She knew Luke had a point and wished he'd get to it. But there was no rushing him, she knew.

"They are very friendly people," he said again. "Very . . . open."

She nodded but said nothing.

"Not that I was interested," he said quickly, "in that,

anyway. But I suspect some of our men were. Interested, I mean."

"Some of them were more than interested, Luke," she said, thinking of Patrick.

"Yeah, I know," he squirmed uncomfortably in his seat.

She looked at him. "I didn't do anything, if that's what this is about," she said.

"No, no, I knew you wouldn't," he said, but he did appear to relax.

"Mark," he said after a minute. "Mark did, and he's married."

Amy shrugged. "Mark's an asshole. You can't be surprised."

"Oh, I know," Luke sighed. "To deny his wedding vows like that, that's just mean. The problem is what to do about it. I hate the thought of telling Carol."

"Don't," Amy said firmly. Luke looked at her in shock. "Don't you dare tell her," she said even more firmly. "Carol has suffered enough because of that asshole. Telling her would just make it worse."

Luke deflated. "You're right. I hadn't thought of it that way. I suppose I'll have to keep it to myself. Still what if someone else tells? You know Mark. He's probably bragged to Shawn and Patrick. They did, I am almost sure. Well, Shawn was pretty obvious. I hope that woman comes back and marries him. That'd make him happy."

One look at Shawn's face this morning was enough to tell anyone exactly how that affair had ended. Amy didn't say that out loud. Instead she shrugged.

"I don't think Daniel or Kurt did," Luke said. "Kurt spent most of his spare time training with the Dog Boys. He'll have their fighting style mastered by the time we get back."

Amy thought about Kurt and the Dog Boys. *Where to even begin?* No, she decided, if Kurt hadn't said anything, it was not her place. She was suddenly tired of the whole line of conversation. "Besides sex," she said, "what did you think of them?"

"Oh, they seemed really nice. But as for the group marriage thing, that's really weird." He dropped his voice, "And I heard that sometimes the men . . . you know, with each other."

"And if they do?" Amy asked.

Luke just shook his head. "Well, I can't wait to get back to the ranch and be among normal folk like us. I just keep telling myself that when we get back, no one can possible deny that I am a man. I can have permission to build a house. Then we can start a nice, normal marriage for ourselves. Won't that be wonderful?"

Amy smiled weakly.

Her day only got worse after that. At first, she thought it was just her mood, but that afternoon, the roster had her riding shotgun with Shawn. He blubbered endlessly about his failed attempt to woo his woman away from her husbands. It was pathetic.

By late afternoon, she thought she was getting ill. As they set camp for the evening, she started to count the days they had been gone. It had been almost a month, and *oh my god*, she didn't want to deal with *that* out here.

They camped at one of the last fueling stations in Greenbowe territory. It was there that Lexa found Amy in the bathroom.

"What's wrong?" Lexa asked.

"Nothing, it's just that time of the month," Amy

replied. "It's always hard for me. There are pads in my bag. Can you?"

Lexa stiffened and stomped out. She came back quickly, thrust a cloth pad in Amy's hand, and turned and walked out. That evening she said she was exhausted and went straight to bed after supper.

Amy, who was also exhausted, followed soon after. She crawled into the tent they were again sharing and stretched out. Looking over at Lexa, she saw that her eyes were closed, though she couldn't tell if she was asleep or not. Amy shrugged, exhausted both emotionally and physically. She took some deep breaths, felt her body relax, and soon was asleep.

The next day started no better than the last. Her morning was spent riding shotgun with Mark, who had the gall to brag about the woman he met. She stayed silent and stewed, too miserable to even start an argument.

That afternoon, she drove with Lexa riding shotgun. At first they drove over rough terrain that took all of her concentration. As soon as they hit level terrain, she rounded on the smaller woman.

"What the hell is wrong with you?" Amy growled. "My hormones are already screwed up. Why do you have treat me like some sort of freak? It's not like we don't all have them you know."

"Ha, ha," Lexa said dryly. Tears stood in her eyes.

"What does that mean?" Amy asked, her eyes narrowing.

"Maybe once or twice a year," Lexa answered in a quiet voice.

"I don't understand," Amy said. "What is that supposed to mean?"

"It is supposed to mean, honey, that I am as barren as a rock."

"Oh shit," Amy said catching on.

"Oh, now the big, beautiful, mountain princess gets it," Lexa said. She was weeping freely. "All our lives down here, we hear how we must take every chance to perpetuate the race. It is our imperative to save humanity. And I can't. Sorry, no kids for Lexa. She can put a smile on your face, but that's it, just a toy. She can't give you what we all so desperately need. She can't fulfill her civic duty."

"Is it that bad?" Amy asked. "I mean, I remember Michael saying something, but still."

Lexa shook her head. "I am overreacting, or so Daisy would say. No one would dare say such things out loud, especially not my family. They knew before I came in, and they accepted me anyway. But it's always there, in the back of my mind. We judge people by their breeding potential."

"I'm sorry, I didn't know," Amy said.

"I'm sorry," Lexa said. "I just freaked. I get jealous sometimes, I guess. It's not your fault."

They sat quietly for a while. Then Lexa squealed. "What?" Amy demanded.

"You were fertile when you were at our house." She pointed her finger at Amy, but her eyes sparkled mischievously. "And you didn't even try. You didn't do your civic duty."

"Are you suggesting I should have tried to seduce one of your husbands?" Amy gasped.

"Most definitely," Lexa replied with a laugh. "Luther would have been a good choice; he's very gentle. But no . . . we suspect he's sterile too. So maybe Merlin. He's apt. Very apt."

"I don't want to hear this," Amy said, putting her hands over her ears, but she was laughing too, glad that Lexa was being her friend again. A little voice in the back of her head said that she bet Merlin was quite apt. She ignored it as best she could.

11

The Cult of the Iron Mother

That night they camped at a large fueling station. The Redriver tribe maintained fewer stations, farther apart than the Greenbowes, but theirs were larger. There was a single small cabin, not enough for the expedition, but there were semi-enclosed showers and three pit toilets. There was also another gazebo with a dark metal statue.

"What is it?" Amy asked.

"Durgas, the dark mother," Lexa told her. She opened a small drawer that was built into the gazebo's railing. She pulled an incense stick from within and knelt before the statue.

"Worshiping pagan idols, now?" Patrick murmured and then more loudly, "We don't believe in idol worship where we come from." He stalked off with Mark and Shawn in tow.

"Is he always so cheerful?" Lorn asked mildly.

"Jesus said to be tolerant of others," Kurt yelled at the retreating back.

"Not the way Minister Posch talks," Daniel commented.

"Nonetheless, Kurt is correct," Lorn said.

"How would you know?" Luke asked. "You're a pagan."

Lorn produced a small black book from his pocket. Kurt stared at it in surprise. "Just because the tribe is pagan does not mean that we reject other religions. This Bible was the only gift my grandmother was able to give me, back in the dark days of the collapse. It has been a great comfort to me, a connection to a family long dead."

Luke nodded. "Well, I don't know about worshiping this, but I am curious about it. What can you tell me?"

"Durgas, the dark mother," Spider explained, "is a variation of the Hindu Goddess Kali. She was once worshiped in a week-long festival called the Rites of Durgas in a place called India."

"What I think Luke is after," Amy interrupted, "is about the statue itself. We have encountered two others. At the village, they told me it was something to do with the Cult of the Iron Mother, whatever that was, or is."

"The Cult of the Iron Mother was started by Arnie Mauss," Spider said, "but perhaps that is a story for after supper."

The two tribe members joined Lexa at the statue. Amy was torn. It seemed a harmless gesture and she was sure that Lexa would be pleased, but the men would disapprove. In the end, undecided, she stood and waited.

Instead, she found herself wondering about Spider. Women warriors were not a usual thing at the ranch by any stretch of the imagination, yet the men from the ranch treated her with a respect that bordered on awe. Luke had told her how Spider had so readily beaten Patrick at the warriors circle. She had also apparently let Mark know that the only use she had for men was as training partners. The implied threat had been taken to heart by all the men.

Unable to deal with such a strong female figure, the men reacted the only way they could: they thoroughly ignored any indication that she was a woman and just treated her as one of the men. She seemed happy enough with the arrangement.

There was one practical advantage to her presence as far as the men were concerned. After supper, she brought a set of shears out of her pack and gave Luke, Patrick, and Daniel their first haircuts since the mission began. None of them had thought it would take nearly long enough to warrant bringing their own shears to maintain their short buzzes.

Kurt declined to have his hair buzzed, stating that he was going to wear it a little longer. He stared defiantly about him while he said it, defying anyone to challenge him.

"I think it will suit you," Lorn said as he brushed out his own long hair.

While she worked, Spider talked, telling them what she knew of the Cult of the Iron Mother. "Arnie Mauss was a sculptor, and by his own admission, not a very good one, in the days before the collapse. He was a Canadian who made his living doing blacksmithing. While living on a small farm outside of Montreal two years before the blast, he started to have strange dreams."

"Was he one of the visionaries we've been told about?" Luke asked.

"Not exactly," she replied. "The visionaries had already appeared, and at first he attributed his dreams to their message. However, his dreams were of a different nature. He dreamed of large armies clashing in violent waves. He heard the screams of dying men and saw the blood run in graphic detail. Then a large, dark form rose over the fields of battle, and peace came onto the land. He thought deeply about these dreams but could make no sense of them.

"One day he was in Montreal. He met an old lady. She was crying and holding a small box tight to her chest. He was moved and began to talk to her, asking her story. She told him that her grandson was dead, killed in a senseless act of gang violence. The box contained the gun that had killed him. She intended to throw it into the river to be rid of it.

"Instead, Arnie convinced her to give it to him. He had no idea what he was going to do with it. He took it home to his studio and started to work. He used an acetylene torch to break the temper on the gun's metal. Then he slowly melted it down and worked the metal.

"When he was done, many hours had passed unheeded. In his hands he held a goddess statue, his first. The work was simple but more powerful than anything he had ever done before.

"He gave the statue to the old lady. The news spread by word of mouth and soon people were coming from all over, bringing Arnie guns and the stories of those the guns had killed. He did about a hundred pieces over the next two years.

"He became famous. He was showcased in several galleries. He even published a book showing pictures of the statues he did and the stories behind them."

"We have a copy at Tir-Na-Nog, if you are interested," Lorn added.

"After New York, when the civil government collapsed," Spider picked up her narrative again, "the military declared full martial law and called up all the National Guard units for service. The governor of Minnesota refused. He declared that the state of Minnesota would not be party to a military dictatorship."

"That took balls," Mark commented.

"They let him do that?" Patrick asked.

"No, they didn't," she responded.

"What about the National Guard? What did they do?" Luke asked.

"Some went and some stayed."

"They should have all gone," Patrick declared. "It was desertion. Disobeying a direct order from the president?"

"That was one of the things at issue," Lorn said. "The civil government was in a state of collapse. Supposedly they had approved the military takeover, but it was never confirmed."

"So, those who went felt they were doing the right thing," Spider said, "as did those who stayed. A few men, loyal to the military, tried to stage a coup and take the governor out. It failed and quickly led to a pitched battle in the Twin Cities.

"In the end, the regular military stepped in, as much to enforce peace as to take sides. After three days of intense fighting, almost six thousand were dead. Many were innocent civilians."

"Any hope for peace ended with that battle," Lorn said.

"What does this have to do with the Cult of the Iron Mother?" Amy asked.

"A digression, but a necessary one," Spider said. "You see, the St. Paul Massacre, as it was named, was Arnie's call. He felt drawn to the US, believing he now understood his vision.

"His work was well known by then, and word spread quickly. He was in town just days after the fighting stopped. Survivors came to him in droves."

"You have to understand," Lorn said, "that most of the guardsmen were no older than you guys yourselves. They fought for what they believed was right, but still ended up killing thousands of civilians, their own people. It was a terrible tragedy. Their grief was too much for words."

"Yes," Spider agreed. "They came silently and laid their guns at his feet. Many vowed they would never fight again. Soon Arnie had piles of weapons, everything from pistols to rocket launchers. A local steel works helped, providing torches and operators. All the guns were destroyed, and Arnie began to work on a new scale.

"Now, Arnie was a visionary and an artist. In St. Paul, he met a woman who would change his life forever, Jennifer Orenson. Jennifer was a healer and a born leader. She had an incredible intuitive grasp of human nature. She recognized right away that those who took part in the fighting, regardless of which side they were on, were ticking time bombs. The intense guilt and horrific exposure to death and destruction would give way to depression. Depression would lead to madness. What they would eventually become was anybody's guess.

"What they needed was a way to atone. They needed

an outlet for their grief. Jennifer gave them that. She formed the Cult of the Iron Mother. She trained the men in first aid, herbal medicine, and healing. Her pagan connections kept them supplied with food. Not much food, but no one had much in those days, and they survived.

"Wherever a big battle was fought, Arnie went. Thousands traveled with him. They scavenged or begged what food they could and shared it with all. They healed the wounded when they could, and helped bury the dead. They collected guns for Arnie's monuments."

"Didn't the military try to stop them?" Luke asked. "There was martial law, wasn't there?"

"The military was afraid of them," Spider answered.

"Why?" Mark demanded. "This Arnie melted all the guns down, so they were unarmed."

"And they took vows not to fight," Kurt said. "You said so."

"Yes, both true," Spider replied. "Still, they were feared. Anyone could lay down their arms and join them. Desertion rates leaped whenever a military unit got too close. That was one of the big fears."

"But some units were too hardened to fear that," Lorn said. "They were just armed thugs. They had already lost anyone willing to desert. They tried to take on the Cult more than once."

"Think about it," Spider shuddered. "For all their talk of peace, these were thousands of ex-soldiers. Most were suffering from shock, grief, and near-suicidal depression. In the few cases where they were forced to fight, their death toll was high, but they always won."

12

Sabotage

Early the next morning, Amy, Lexa, and Spider quietly left the camp. There was something Amy was determined to do. She knew the men of Freedom Ranch would not approve, so they would not be told.

On the far side of the hill, they reached a small meadow. Spider silently sat down on her knees and pointed in front of her. Lexa and Amy sat where they were shown and bowed to the woman.

After a short warm up they began. With a gesture, Spider brought Lexa to her feet. Amy watched as Lexa punched at Spider. Spider gracefully moved alongside Lexa's outstretched fist, ending up behind her. She spun Lexa around. Just as Lexa stepped around, regaining her balance, Spider's forearm caught her chin, and she was thrown to the ground.

"Aikido is about blending with your opponent's force,

not fighting against it," Spider lectured. "Now, let's try it, slowly at first."

Amy nodded and rose. Since she had met Ruth and learned that some women could defend themselves, she had resolved to learn. If there was anyone willing to teach her, Spider seemed the obvious choice.

Forty-five minutes later, the three sweaty women made their way back to the camp. Lorn and Kurt were awake and talking, but everyone else was still asleep.

Lorn was cooking breakfast while Kurt showed him passages out of the small Bible he carried. As Amy passed them, Lorn was shaking his head emphatically. "A short reference, made by Paul even. Jesus himself is all but silent. This should be telling, shouldn't it?"

Curious though she was, she did not stay to find out what they were discussing. When she returned from the shower, the whole camp was up. As the girls dried off and ate breakfast, the men made for the showers.

"Really, this sexist shower arrangement is going to take some getting used to," Lorn groused.

"Can you honestly say that you object to showering with six young men?" Spider joked.

"Point taken," he replied and bowed. Amy was glad none of the men heard that.

The day passed slowly. Amy rode all morning with a taciturn Patrick. Her afternoon shift was with a now contemplative Kurt. *The idea is that a companion keeps you from falling asleep*, she thought. *What good does it do if they don't even talk to you?*

They were driving a very long stretch today. Yesterday, they had touched the edge of the Redriver tribe's territory, and today they would cross over into the Roan's territory.

Dusk was already turning rapidly toward darkness as they finally pulled up to the fueling station.

Amy's subconscious mind immediately picked up that something was wrong, but it took her a minute to figure out what. "The pole, oh shit, look at the pole."

Kurt just shrugged. "Looks like an ordinary pole to me."

"It shouldn't be. Where's the wind generator?" Amy said as she swung herself out of the truck. Lexa had spotted it too and was already out of her truck, heading for the station itself with a flashlight in hand.

"Wait," Lorn's voice called out, bringing them both to a stop. He was carrying a flashlight as well. He pointed it at the door, which swung loosely in the night breeze. "That was deliberate. Better let me go first. Luke?"

"Right here," Luke replied. He had his dagger drawn and followed Lorn forward. Spider came up with her bow in hand. Daniel had his sling out, waiting.

They were back in a minute. They beckoned everyone closer. "They're gone," Lorn said, "and they gutted the station.

"We don't know when this happened. Whoever did this may still be close. Luke and I will check the perimeter to the north. Spider, you take Patrick and check the south; everyone else stay close to the building."

"We can protect ourselves," Mark growled.

"And you can foul up any signs or tracks," Spider growled back before leaving. He glared at her but was silent.

Amy and Lexa went to the building and peered inside. By the dim light of Lexa's flashlight, she could make out rows of empty shelves. Amy had never actual seen the inside of one of these buildings before, but she was sure this wasn't how it was supposed to look. Where was all the equipment?

The scouts were back quickly. "The generator is about ten meters that way," Luke told them. "Looks to be totally stripped. Amy, you and Lexa can confirm that, in the morning. For tonight, we camp close and no fire. Guard detail as well. Whoever did this hasn't been gone long, I don't think."

"They went south less than two hours ago," Spider informed him.

"How can you be sure?" Mark challenged.

"Because there were tire tracks and crushed plants," Patrick told him. "The plants hadn't wilted much so it had to be recent."

Spider nodded.

"How are we going to fuel up?" Daniel asked.

"Well, we do have solar panels as a backup," Lexa said. "The problem is they take eight to ten hours."

"No problem," Shawn said. "They'll be done by morning, right?"

Several voices groaned. "Solar," Lorn explained, "as in the sun."

"Oh."

"I don't like spending the day here with potentially hostile forces so close," Luke said grimly.

"Especially not with our guns miles away," Patrick added.

"How do we know they are hostile?" Kurt asked. "I thought all the bandits and stuff were wiped out long ago?"

"So I would have thought," Lorn said. "We haven't

seen anything like this in years. But looters were once common, and apparently some remain. As to their hostility, I can say only this; you found us reasonable people to deal with, right? These people choose not to deal. What does that say about them?"

"Exactly," Luke said. "They could have bartered or asked for what they needed. They didn't. That either means they couldn't or that they just don't care. Either way, we can't expect a pleasant welcome. Now, Lorn tells me this region is rough. No matter what sort of vehicles they use, they won't be fast. We stay here tonight. Since we are stuck here tomorrow, this is what I propose: I'll leave Daniel in charge. Lorn, Patrick, and I will leave at first light to go scouting. We will follow the tracks until noon. If we haven't found them by then, we'll come back."

"I'll go too," Amy said.

"Not a chance, doll face," Patrick sneered.

"I have to agree this time," Luke replied. "This is no mission for non-combatants."

"Her technical expertise may be necessary if we are to assess their strength properly," Lorn said. "She should go."

Luke met his eyes briefly. Lorn did not look away or flinch. Luke nodded. "Be ready by first light."

A fly buzzed at Amy's face, and she swatted at it for the hundredth time. She tried to ignore it and the sweat that drew them. She struggled in vain to remember why she had wanted to come. Scouting was not what it was made out to be. She wiggled a few more inches forward through the heavy scrub.

"It's them all right," Lorn was saying just a few feet ahead. Amy could not see him; all she could see was

Patrick's leg shifting as he reached for Lorn's binoculars. She struggled up between Patrick and Luke.

"Shit," Patrick hissed. "They're armed, and heavily. We really need those guns now."

Luke ignored this latest jab as he peered through his own binoculars. "It's a show," he said.

"How so?" Lorn asked.

"The lead man is carrying a sawed off shotgun. Point guards have crossbows. The grunts have M-16s. Very suspicious.

"If they had any ammo for those M-16s, the leader would have one, mark my words. I bet the shotguns are all they have shells for. He's got three shells on his bandoleer, and that's a pump action, so it holds five. That means they have a total of eight rounds."

"So that's why Jacob chose you?" Patrick said, astonished. Luke looked uncomfortable at the compliment but said nothing.

"Good work," Lorn said. "Crossbows can be nasty weapons, but they won't do any damage to one of our trucks and aren't much of a threat as long we are inside. They are also slow to reload. What about the shotgun, will it stop a truck?" This last was aimed at Amy.

"Close up with a lucky shot maybe," she replied. "But no, it's not much of a threat to the truck. The people inside might be in danger though. What do you have in mind?"

"Nothing more gallant than running for it," Lorn said. "Patrick, pass her the binoculars. I want her opinion about their vehicles."

Luke beat Patrick to it. Amy was amazed at him. She would have never noticed the bandoleer or deciphered the significance of the shotgun. She set to looking at the vehicles.

"Ford Ranger and a Jeep," she said. "Combustion engines, either gas or diesel, I'm not sure which. Old and showing it, but I can't tell how they run from here, other than those tires won't take much more abuse."

"What about the stuff they've taken?" Luke asked.

"They have several batteries thrown in the back of the pickup. No real order to things, so they probably don't have a clue what they've got. Lexa and I looked at that wind generator and thought the same thing."

"They did a thorough job of destroying it, trying to strip the wires out. If they actually used the technology, it would have made a lot more sense to take the whole thing."

They crawled back out of the scrub and sat down. "Not a bad bit of recon," Luke said.

"I agree," said a voice a few feet off.

Both Patrick and Luke leaped to their feet, hands on their knives.

A man squatted nearby, calmly watching them. He was short with long, dark hair. He wore leather buckskin pants and no shirt. His chest was tanned and muscular. A bow was slung casually over one shoulder, and there was a knife at his belt.

"Owl," Lorn chirped, ignoring the drawn knives. "I haven't seen you in years."

"I have not been in these parts for many years," the man replied. "Nor do I think have you. Let's retire somewhere a little farther out of earshot and talk."

They backtracked for close to a mile before sitting down to talk. Lorn introduced Owl to the others. "This is Owl of the Forestdwellers. They live well south of here. They are the best hunters and woodsmen anywhere. Owl, this is Luke, Amy, and Patrick. They're from the mountains. We're traveling together on an important errand."

"Pleased to meet you," Owl said.

"What is a Forestdweller like yourself doing out in the day anyway?" Lorn asked.

"Ah, it is true that since mankind angered mother earth we have been leery of father sun as well. He strikes at us fiercely and we hide ourselves. But today the mother cries in outrage. I have followed seeking its cause."

"Cut the dramatics and speak English," Lorn said.

"Okay," Owl replied sheepishly. "But don't let the other Forestdwellers know." He adjusted himself in the high grass. "We usually work mostly at night, because of the ozone depletion, you know. But I have been curious about this group. I've followed them for several days. They're up to no good."

"So we have already discovered," Luke said. He explained about the fueling station.

"Not good," Owl agreed. "They've been doing stuff like that since they came out of the south. Most of the stuff they take they can't even use, and they abandon it later. It's disgusting."

"Do you know where they're from?" Lorn asked. "I thought all such people were gone from the earth."

"Only vaguely," Owl replied. "I've been following them for some time. They came out of the Deep South where, yes, such people still exist. It's warmer, and there's a better growing season. There're also more cities, some still mostly inhabitable. We Forestdwellers live down there too, but we avoid them."

"The Forestdwellers are nomadic," Lorn supplied. "They go south in the winter and north in the summer. Have you had trouble with scavengers?" he asked Owl.

"Us? Hell no," Owl replied. "We have forsaken that which angered the mother. No technology, nothing to interest them."

"So you've never had any problems with them?" Luke asked.

"Those people are trouble no matter what," Owl continued. "They don't play nice. They fight amongst themselves all the time. Once in a while, one of us will get caught. They always assume we are spies working for one of their enemies."

"You're lucky you haven't been killed," Patrick said.

"Some have," Owl said. "Like I said, they don't play nice. When I saw these people up this far north, I got worried."

"Do you know what they're up to?" Luke asked.

"Unfortunately. I got close enough to hear them talking about a week ago. The knowledge comes a bit late, I'm afraid. They are seeking the Stewards. They believe they have a great wealth hidden away."

"The Stewards?" Lorn said. "That's nonsense. The Stewards are a monastic order."

"I agree, they would not gather riches any more than my people would technology. But that's what these people believe. They were just wandering when I started following them. Then they discovered an old town that was on their map. Since they've seemed to have gotten their bearings, they've headed straight toward the Stewards. I have been trying to get around them to go warn the Stewards. On foot I can barely keep up with them; there's no way for me to get ahead."

"Perhaps we can help," Lorn said. "We are heading to the Stewards ourselves. We have vehicles and knowledge of the terrain."

"That would be most appreciated. I hate to think of what such people would do to the Stewards if they got to them unawares."

The small team, with its new arrival, made its way back to the camp. They arrived back just before noon, and they quickly explained the situation.

"Shit," Lexa said. "These solar panels aren't going to be fast enough. We will not have a full charge until almost nightfall. If we start out first thing in the morning, we won't make it to the next station until late afternoon. They could easily make it before us and destroy that one too."

Everyone groaned. "Now what?" Luke said, throwing his hands up.

Owl answered. "I could go to the Roan tribe; they maintain these, don't they? They have horses, which are faster on this terrain anyway. If I left my pack, I could easily make it there before evening and be back by nightfall."

Several people nodded their approval of this plan, but Spider spoke up against it. "No. we are carrying toxic waste. We can't just leave it."

"Could the Roans bring us extra batteries?" Amy asked.

"That's it!" Lexa squealed running for her truck. She came back carrying her map and unrolled it on the ground before them. "Owl, you go to the Roans. Find a man named Jodie. Tell him Lexa needs his 'special' charge converter. He'll know what I want. He's to take it to station eight, which is about here." She pointed on the map.

"What do you have in mind?" Spider asked.

"With the charge we have, we can make it that far easily. We will meet up with Jodie there. He's got a quick charger. It'll completely charge our batteries in about an hour or so. We don't usually allow them because they drain the stations something awful, but under these conditions it's called for."

"I think I see," Spider said catching on. "It takes us out of our way, but this stretch here is pretty level, if I remember right."

"Exactly," Lexa answered brightly. "We quick-charge and travel through the night to the next station, here. Then on to here and do it again. By then we should be past the bad guys and booking."

"Just one small problem," Lorn said. "There's no route marked between this station and station eight."

"Oh, that's okay. I know a few things that aren't on the map," Lexa said.

Lorn looked suspicious, but Luke said, "Well, if no one has a better plan, I say let's go for it."

Owl passed his bow and arrows and his small pack to Lorn. In a flash, he was gone, running full speed.

"Do you think he can really run that far?" Spider asked.

Lorn nodded. "If a Forestdweller says they can do something, believe them. They're an amazing people."

"You sound wistful," Spider said. "Wishing you were a Forestdweller?"

"Me?" Lorn said. "I'd love to be that rugged and strong. Who wouldn't? But I know the kind of harsh lifestyle it takes to build that kind of endurance. No, I'll stay a Greenbowe and settle for a little softness."

They set out after lunch. Everyone was nervous. The gauges read barely half power, but Lexa assured them it was enough.

Tonight's run might be as level as she says, Amy groused to herself as she drove on, *but today's run more than makes up for it.*

Lorn, sitting at her side, apparently agreed. "Another creek bed! I think we have crossed every creek and hill for miles about and are going over some twice," he growled. "I am sure this is not part of some accepted route, and I don't want to know how she discovered it."

They reached station eight by dusk. They found a dozen horses waiting for them. Owl ran forward as they pulled up. "I have brought the cavalry," he cried.

A lanky man with dark hair and a thin but muscular body came forward. Lexa rushed to him and they hugged. "Jodie!" Lexa cried.

"Brought you some gifts," he told her, leading her over to the fire pit and introducing the dozen or so Roan tribe members who were there. They had arrived a half an hour before and had a fire started, busy preparing a meal.

Over the meal of meat, vegetables and bread, they presented two gifts. The first was Jodie's quick-chargers. He told Lexa to keep them as long as she wanted. "That way I know you'll come visit sometime," he said, laughing.

Their second gift was five handheld two-way radios. "Traveling with hostile forces about, you may need to communicate," Jodie told Luke.

They thanked the Roans for their gifts, and the Roans in turn thanked them for the warning about the station. They planned to camp for a day and then take a team down to fix it. They promised to have all their stations repaired and in good working order before the mission came back that way.

While the trucks charged, Lorn and Luke consulted. They set a new semi-permanent driving roster, abandoning the rotation. Amy and Lexa were in the lead truck, as the two best drivers. Lorn and Spider drove second to guard the front, and Luke and Patrick drove at the back as rearguard.

They set out just after moonrise. The path turned south, and true to Lexa's word, it was straight and level. In fact, they soon turned down a long ramp onto an ancient highway, still in fair repair.

Amy found it spooky to drive on this road at night, thinking about the hundreds of cars that once went up and down it at all hours of the day and night. At intervals, large lonely signs reared up in the dim moonlight. Behind and to the sides, the broken remains of buildings stared emptily at them.

"When I was a kid I went up to one of those buildings with my older brother," Owl said sleepily. "Out back was this huge truck, must have been forty feet long."

"A semi," Amy said. "My dad drove one for a time."

"My brother told me they had once hauled things all over the country in those trucks, but I wouldn't believe him. I couldn't imagine that anything that big could move." Owl laughed. "I still find it hard to believe, but riding in this truck has made me a believer."

"You've never ridden in anything this big before?" Amy knew it was a stupid question as soon as she said it. She hadn't ridden in anything this big before either.

The truth was that she was a little rattled. Owl couldn't drive, so he wasn't on the rotation at all. When he offered to ride up front with them, she had assumed that Lexa's charm was at work. Lexa was already curled up asleep on his far shoulder, and Owl was showing more attention to Amy than she was either used to or comfortable with.

Amy fished the radio out of her lap. "Bad patch up ahead, potholes the size of a horse." Spider's voice crackled an acknowledgment followed by several others. The radios were already paying off in a surprising way. Early warning from the lead truck was allowing them to travel faster and safer than they could ever have without them.

Owl and Amy continued to converse until the moon stood high in the sky. There was a longer than usual pause and then a slight snore from the man. He barely moved when Lexa and Amy changed places at the midnight break.

Amy woke in the morning to find herself curled against his warm muscular side, his arm casually over her shoulder. She straightened stiffly.

"She awakens," he commented casually to Lexa. They had obviously been awake and talking for some time.

"What did I miss?" she asked, still groggy.

"Nothing but dark skies and empty horizons," Owl said.

"The next stop is just a few minutes away," Lexa added.

Looking into the dawn, Amy spotted the wind generator turning lazily in the morning breeze. They had a quick hot breakfast, a shower, and most importantly, an hour away from the trucks. Then back in for another long haul.

Amy drove the first morning stretch, with Lexa's guidance. They turned southwest on another old highway. This one was not in nearly as good of shape. A low river, more of a stream really, ran parallel to the road. Over the years, its course had shifted, and it had eroded most of the shoulder and at times threatened to engulf the road entirely.

"Oh crap," Lexa said. Amy followed Lexa's pointed finger. At the top of the next hill sat a Jeep. They could see the outline of several men watching them. There was no mistaking the crossbows.

"Everyone see that?" Lorn voice crackled through the radio. There was a chorus of "ayes."

A voice boomed through an old bullhorn. "Pull to the side of the road," the voice commanded.

"No way. We know what they'll do," Owl said.

Lorn's voice echoed the sentiment through the radio, "We are not stopping."

"Let me and Luke through," Patrick's voice said. "We will buy the rest of you some time."

"The tires!" Amy screamed as it hit her. She grabbed the radio from Lexa's mystified hand. "Don't," she said. "Just follow me."

The men saw them rolling by faster. The silhouettes were gone, and the Jeep was speeding down toward them. They were on an intercept course and going twice as fast as the trucks could manage.

"They are going to block us off," Lexa said nervously.

No doubt everyone else is thinking it as well, Amy thought scanning the banks frantically. She spied a low stretch and swerved, hoping the others would follow. The truck splashed heavily into the shallow river.

I just hope it is a shallow as it looks, she thought. *If the water comes up to the engine, we're through.* To her relief, moments later she was splashing up on the other side. The heavy electric truck with its massive torque ground noisily through the mud.

"They're almost here," Lexa said as they cleared the bank.

The smaller and faster Jeep had made good use of the momentary slowing of the trucks as they plowed through the water. It had reached the bank about thirty feet downstream and easily plowed across the river. Then it hit the trap that Amy had hoped for. Being lighter, the Jeep's old tires spun in the mud, gaining no traction.

The final caravan truck cleared the river. There were shouts of glee coming through the radio as Amy pulled up the far bank. A loud retort broke the celebration momentarily. Amy gasped as she noticed a small crack in the passenger-side window, only inches from Owl's face.

In complete defiance of common sense, he peered out the window. Seeing her look of concern, he calmly said, "We're out of range now. They'll not waste another shot.

"Any damage?" Patrick was asking over the radio. Amy could guess who was really asking.

"Window's cracked, but no injuries," Lexa answered. Spider reported the same. Apparently it had been a wild shot, taken at the edge of range.

A mile or so farther on, they took a short stop. After that harrowing close call, they needed a minute to regroup and to plot a new course.

It was decided that they would continue on this side for most of the day. They did not know how long the Jeep would be stuck for, where the other truck was, or if the scavengers had any sort of means of communication. There could all too easily be another trap waiting for them.

By late afternoon, they would have no choice but to cross the river again. They couldn't run the risk of missing the next station.

The day passed with agonizing slowness. They saw nothing but jumped at every shadow. Weighing in the back of everyone's mind was the thought that the scavengers might reach the station ahead of them. Then what would they do?

As they disembarked at the next fueling station, Amy noted the signs of stress and fatigue in every face. They set a guard and stayed close to the trucks while they charged.

"We need at least one more night run before we can assume we are safely ahead of them," Lorn said. "Is that feasible?"

"Should be," Lexa answered. "The route from here on is pretty clear, mostly old highways."

"Now that we have passed them, they will probably push on through the night as well," Luke pointed out.

"They don't know who we are or where we are going," Patrick offered.

"Or that we know what they are up to," Mark agreed.

"In a situation like this, we can't afford to assume," Luke countered. "They may have guessed."

"They will at least have guessed that we are headed in the right direction to run into the Stewards. They will not want any warning of their presence," Lorn said then sighed. "I agree . . . we assume the worst."

Lexa sighed too. "Three days and nights, and we are there, if we can maintain the pace that is."

"Tonight then, at least. We drive through the night, and we decide after," Lorn said. Everyone nodded. As tired as they all were, nobody wanted to stay there longer than necessary.

The next four days were a blur. In the end, they compromised. They had driven all night the first night and at least half the night for the next three. That put them in Steward territory by noon the fourth day.

They knew the instant they reached it. They passed over a hill and found a high metal fence that stretched from one horizon to the other.

13

The Stewards

"Everything beyond that fence is uninhabitable," Owl said, "due to radiation and toxins. It's not deadly all at once; you can cross the fence, but you do so at your own risk."

They left the woods behind and entered a vast land of rolling hills and tall grasses. Except for the fence, there was no indication that the land beyond was dangerous.

Perched on a low hill on the distant horizon was an immense building of concrete and brick. "Almost there," Lexa breathed in relief.

The buildings were contained in their own fence. There was a gatehouse on the north side. They drove straight for it. A well-muscled black man wearing denim overalls and a wide-brimmed straw hat greeted them at the gate. Gray hair at his temples seemed to accent his worried look. He was tall, well over six feet, and had the easy grace of someone accustomed to hard labor.

Amy tried not to stare. She had never seen a black person before.

"Something is wrong, very wrong," Lexa said.

"Why?" Amy asked.

"Look at his belt."

Amy noticed for the first time the heavy black pistol. The man swung himself onto the running board and peered through Lexa's open window.

"Lexa Greenbowe and company," he said, trying to sound casual. "And I see you've picked up an aborigine."

Owl smiled. "Joseph," he said. And to Amy, "Joseph thinks we are all nuts for living in the woods."

"We got trouble," Lexa said.

"So do we," Joseph answered. "And I am guessing it's the same trouble. Let's get inside and we'll discuss it."

He waved them through. In the rearview mirror, Amy saw a woman close the gate behind the last truck. She could not tell if the woman was armed or not.

They pulled into a huge garage on one side of the building. Joseph indicated where to park and jumped off the running board.

Amy couldn't help but feel embarrassed for the expedition, yet again. She had at least made an effort not to stare. None of the men had ever seen a black person before either. They had been raised to believe them lesser. That didn't mean they had to stare at this guy like he was a bug or something.

If Joseph noticed the extra attention, he made no sign. He saw Lorn and went straight to him. "Lorn," he cried happily.

"It has been a long time," Lorn answered.

"Years," Joseph agreed. He patted Lorn's belly, "What happened to the scrawny little kid the Greenbowes adopted?"

"They have fed me well, that's all."

"As will we, I promise," Joseph replied. "And we will provide hospitality as tradition demands. But today, events dictate news first."

"I agree," Lorn said, introducing the others.

They were led to a small conference room. Amy marveled as she went. She didn't know exactly what she expected of the Stewards, but it wasn't this.

No, wait. I do know what I'd expected.

The outside of the building had more or less confirmed it. The Stewards were a monastic order. All the books she had read showed solemn monks in drab robes wandering around dim stone corridors. Instead, the whole inside of the building overflowed with life. Giant pools were overgrown with reeds. Vast glass tanks revealed fish and other underwater life. It was like the pictures she had seen of the botanical center where her grandmother had been married.

The people here defied the usual idea of a monk as well. Many wore loose, flowing robes but no uniforms seemed to be in effect. The closest thing was that those going out of doors seemed to favor denim overalls and wide brimmed hats, like Joseph wore. The clothes were often of bright colors that did not put the word "monk" into mind.

All around was a bustle of quiet activity. Few showed it outwardly, but tension hung in the air. Amy thought she spied one woman crying as she tended to the plants in a tank.

The conference room was drab only in comparison to the rest of the place. An aquarium some twenty feet long took up most of one wall. Plants in stands grew in each corner.

The center of the room was made up of a long wooden table filled with refreshments: water, bread, and raw vegetables. Tired and hungry, they all fell to eating while Joseph, Lorn, and Luke talked.

"We tried to send a warning over the satellite," Joseph told them after they had explained about the scavengers, "but you had left."

"Then you already knew?" Lorn said.

Joseph nodded. "We did not know their location or that you would meet them, but we knew they were in the area. Another monastery in our order sent us warning. They did not want us to get caught unawares. They had already been accosted by these people."

"What nonsense is this anyway?" Lorn scoffed. "Everyone knows that the Stewards don't gather material wealth. Why would anyone try to rob you?"

"You do have a stash of precious metals though, don't you?" Luke said.

"Yes," Joseph admitted. "We do."

"What?" Lorn almost jumped to his feet. "Since when? You are the Stewards. Have you forsaken your vows to protect humanity?"

"That's why you have the metals, isn't it?" Luke said.

"Exactly," Joseph said. "We have not forsaken our vows."

"I am sorry," Lorn said. "I spoke rashly. Of course you would not. I don't understand though. It seems so incomprehensible."

"Is it?" Joseph asked. "There was much wealth in the cities of old. Chicago was a wealthy city once."

"Is that where it is from?" Amy asked.

"Yes."

"So it's radioactive?"

"The bomb used in the Chicago attack was a neutron bomb. In the early days of our order they brought us a number of valuable artifacts removed from the inner part of the city. Even now, the incidental radiation coming off them would kill these men in a matter of days," Joseph said, rubbing his head. "It is not just ourselves we are worried about. We are trying to protect them as well."

"What do you intend to do?" Luke asked.

"They are still a few days away, at least," he replied. "We hope to end this peacefully yet. We must at least warn them of their danger. Likely, they won't listen or believe, but we must try."

"That's more than fair, considering they are trying to rob you," Spider said.

"The council decided last night," Joseph went on. "They will be given three warnings. The first will be in writing, placed on their route. The second will be audio, left on a continuous tape at the last fueling station before they arrive.

"The third was the hardest. We are peaceful people, devoted to serving the good of humanity. We *have* to be certain they hear and understand, even if it means sacrificing our own lives. One of us will try to talk to them in person."

"And the rest of you?" Owl asked.

"Will go into hiding," Joseph said. "And let them take what they will. We can fight if need be, but we are not warriors."

"But you said the metal would kill them," Lexa gasped.

"Yes, it will. What else can we do? Owl here can tell you what these people are like. They will hurt or kill us if we try to stop them. I will not let my people die over this."

"I agree," Owl said. "Serves them right. I wouldn't even have warned them."

"Do you really think it will come to that?" Luke asked.

"Count on it," Owl growled.

"We have already begun to prepare for evacuation," Joseph said. "We will get your trucks unloaded as fast as we can. We do not want to leave you stranded."

"We thank you," Lorn said. "But will that slow you down?"

"It shouldn't," he replied. "We are nearly ready. We will not be able to take much anyway."

"We will help any way we can," Luke said.

"That is a generous offer," Joseph replied. "But today you must rest. We will prepare a bath and food for you. Tomorrow, if you're still willing, I may take you up on the offer."

"How are we going to get anywhere, if we keep stopping to help people?" Mark muttered.

An elderly lady named Jes took them to the bathing area. Lorn explained the ranch member's customs and ideas about bathing. She waved him off. She was old enough to remember the old views on modesty.

The bathing facility here was quite different than at Tir-Na-Nog. The pool area was huge with water plants growing along three sides, tall reeds in front of the windows shielded the bathers from view. Lilly pads grew over almost half the surface.

The men were left to bathe by one pool, and the women were led to a second. The pool was cool. Large south-facing windows let the sun's heat in, and the dark bottom helped to retain it, but it came nowhere close to a thermal well.

Amy found it refreshing. Lexa swam to the middle, splashing gracefully. Amy watched her go enviously, wishing she knew how to swim.

Jes joined them in the pool. She was a mass of wrinkles from head to toe, it seemed to Amy, who had never met anyone so old before.

The old woman swam after Lexa with a strength that belied her age. The two swam a lap and came back to Amy and Spider. They all sat soaking for a long while.

"I will miss this place," Jes said.

"Surely, you will come back as soon as the scavengers are gone," Lexa said.

"The others will come back, yes," the old woman replied. "I fear that they will have much work to do. The scavengers will destroy as much as they can from sheer spite. Still, I guess it is better than fighting and dying."

"What do you mean, the others?" Amy asked. "Aren't you coming back?"

"I am not leaving, child," Jes replied.

"What?" the three younger women said as one.

"Someone has to stay, to try to persuade the scavengers not to do what we know they will do anyway."

"That's crazy," Amy said.

"No, we all agreed that they should be given one last chance," Jes replied.

"I know but why you? Shouldn't it be Joseph?" Amy asked.

"What, a man?" Jes said pointing her finger at Amy, "I'll have you know that I was fighting for women's rights before you were a twinkling in your daddy's eye, child. Don't be giving me that nonsense."

"Of course not," Spider said firmly. "But shouldn't it be someone younger? A warrior maybe, like me or Owl?"

"No, we will not allow anyone else to risk their lives on our behalf. It must be one of our order. And we can't afford to lose Joseph, so don't go putting ideas in his head," she warned.

"From what we have heard, this could well be a suicide mission," Lexa said.

Jes sighed. "Yes, I have thought of that. That's why I volunteered."

"You volunteered?"

"Joseph and several of the others wanted to stay. I forced them to accept me."

"How?"

"Told them I would stay anyway. Besides, as much as they hated it, they saw my logic."

"What logic is that?" Spider asked skeptically.

Jes turned partially away from them. With one hand, she stretched the skin on her shoulder. The shoulder was a mass of little white scars and more moles than Amy had ever seen.

"They choose you for your moles?" Lexa asked.

"That's skin cancer," Jes replied. Amy gasped. "It's nothing, child," Jes said. "I've been having pre-cancerous moles removed since before you were born. I am seventy-nine. That's ten years older than anyone else here. The only thing I care about that hasn't died on me is this place."

Lexa's eyes shown with tears. Jes faced her, fixing her with two calm, brown eyes. "The others have people to live for and the strength to rebuild. I have neither. It would be harder for me to live with this place destroyed than to die. I am staying."

"That must have been a difficult decision," Amy said.

"For me, no," Jes answered. "For everyone else, yes. They agonized over it. I had to threaten to stay anyway before they would listen to me. They know how stubborn I am. I'd do it. So they finally gave in."

After their baths, Jes showed them to the guest quarters. They shared one large common room. Luke and Kurt sat at a long table that was fairly laden with food for their consumption.

"Where is everyone else?" Amy asked.

Luke pointed to the other side of the room. The edge of room was lined in curtains. A few open curtains revealed low sleeping nooks.

"Women over there," Luke said pointing at another wall.

"Sounds like a good idea to me," Amy replied, making for the wall.

"Top bunk," Lexa called, racing past.

There must be a dozen bunks, Amy thought, *why is she calling it?*

Light streamed through the thin curtain. Amy wondered wearily how long she had slept and what time it was. Her stomach growled threateningly, telling her she had slept enough. *All right, I'll feed you,* she thought as she climbed up.

"Hello, sleepy head," Lexa called. "Come get some breakfast before it gets cold."

"Colder," Luke corrected.

Almost everyone was around the table eating. Joseph was there and had brought pancakes. He seemed in good spirits.

"The unloading is going well," he told them. "It should be done before nightfall. By this time tomorrow, you can be on your way and out of danger."

"If it's all the same to you, I think we'll stay," Luke said. The others looked at him.

"Why?" Joseph asked, his head cocked.

"I wouldn't feel right leaving you in danger," Luke replied. "We'll stay and help like we offered, at least until you are evacuated. It's the least we can do."

Amy saw Lorn smile. Patrick, however, scowled. "Our mission?" he growled.

"Can wait another day or two," Luke replied. "We will not leave innocent civilians in danger."

"Your attitude is commendable," Joseph replied. "But we really are capable. This does not concern you."

"It has concerned us since we encountered the scavengers," Lorn said. "I agree; we should stay."

Joseph looked away, counting to himself. "I can't say that ten more workers wouldn't be welcomed, if that's truly how you feel."

"Ten? Don't you mean eleven?" Amy asked. Then she looked around. "Where's Owl?"

"He left this morning," Lorn told her.

Amy scrunched up her brow. He'd just left? She thought he'd be eager to help. Seeing her expression, Joseph added, "He went to place the first sign. He signed on to help last night." Amy breathed a sigh of relief. She hadn't misjudged him.

After breakfast, Joseph showed them around.

"This place is amazing," Amy told him as they wandered around a pool larger than the one they had bathed in. "Not at all what I expected."

"We hear that a lot," Joseph replied with obvious pride. "When you build a place on the edge of desolation, people expect it to be, well, desolate. In fact, we work hard to make it exactly the opposite. The whole place is a vast biological filter. These trailing plants along this wall convert carbon dioxide to oxygen, but also filter a lot of airborne pollutants out."

They crossed into a vast hall with many large water tanks. "For water, this is the first step in purification," Joseph explained. "The algae and plants in these tanks are fast growing and use a lot of nitrites. But the real secret is here." He reached his arm into one tank and came up holding a tiny snail. "As these snails grow, they use minerals to build their shells. The quality of the minerals matter little to them. A lot of heavy metals can be removed from the water in this way."

Amy got lost as Joseph talked about various pollutants and various levels of purification. But one thing was clear. Once again, a seemingly primitive place was, in fact, complex. By the time the contaminated water left the graywater system, it was pure enough to drink.

Joseph left them in the garden. The Stewards were frantically harvesting as much as was edible. They did not know how long they would be gone or if any of would be left when they got back. A young woman showed them where to start, and they spent most of the day gathering small carrots and radishes.

Outside on the desolate side of the fence, life abounded as well. The Stewards had a larger version of their graywater system in the form of several ponds. Water moved slowly from pond to pond. Unlike the one inside, this one would continue to function without any interference.

In the lower end of the system, where the water was pure, they raised fish. Several people were wading through, netting as many as they could.

By evening, word had returned from the advance party. The first message had been placed by Owl. He estimated the scavengers were less than two days away.

"Your offer to help will not slow you down much," Joseph told Luke. "We will be leaving before noon tomorrow."

The monastery had twenty-five members. They quickly loaded what few personal possessions they had into twelve electric vehicles along with all the food they had harvested. That night they celebrated a somber farewell feast.

As they prepared to depart the next day, they went down a long, slow line, each hugging Jes in farewell. She tried to wave them off, but they would not budge. Amy, Spider, and Lexa went down the line as well. They barely knew the woman but felt drawn to her courage. Luke, Kurt, and Daniel came after them, shaking her hand. Joseph was last of all. He hugged her tightly for a long time. Tears ran down his face as he gave the order to roll out.

They traveled for two days alongside the tall fence. Rolling plains passed by. The mood was bleak and somber.

After traveling for two days, they reached the small hostel that would serve as their hideout. It wasn't much as hiding places go, but then again, they weren't the targets: the gold was. The hostel was too small for even the Stewards and many had to camp out. The expedition members were used to that anyway.

They remained with the Stewards. No one even talked about abandoning them now. After two days, Amy heard a shout from the lookout station. She ran immediately to the base of the tower where Patrick and Luke sat with their binoculars.

"It's Owl and the advance party," Luke told her. Moments later, she could see them for herself as they raced toward the hostel in an electric buggy.

The entire group quickly gathered around and listened as Owl described the events of the last four days. It was nothing unexpected.

The scavengers had ignored the first two warnings. Owl had hidden himself near the monastery to witness the final confrontation. Faces fell when Owl told them how Jes had been struck by the lead scavenger. They rose slightly when he told them how she had produced a battered revolver and shot him in the foot. They fell again as he described how the last defense of their home had ended on the end of a crossbow quarrel.

The only good news seemed bleak after hearing about Jes. The scavengers wasted little time on the monastery itself. They apparently knew what they sought was deep in the desolate region in a storage bunker. They had crossed the monastery and disappeared.

"We wait here until they have returned," Joseph said. "We will send the advance party back to watch. It could take them weeks to find the right storage area, but I doubt it. They seem to have some knowledge, though how, I don't know."

"I will go with the advance party," Owl said. "And I will track them when they leave. I would see this to its end."

"Thank you, Owl," Joseph replied. "I had hoped as much." He turned to Lorn and Luke. "You guys have really done as much as you can. We do not anticipate any confrontation now. We have truly appreciated the help. We really can't keep you from your mission any longer."

"We will only use up what little food they have," Lorn said to Luke.

"And we have a mission to complete," Luke added.

14

Jake

It was a solemn farewell. No one wanted to leave, but Lorn was right; they were only wasting resources that the Stewards would need. The scavengers had already signed their own death warrants. If they didn't receive a lethal dose of radiation in the desolate lands, they would from the metals they had come to steal. There was no need for the mission to stay.

The next week passed uneventfully. Everyone worked mechanically, and they soon fell back into the routine.

"I miss Rowan the most," Lexa sighed. She and Amy were heading back from the showers at yet another almost identical fueling station. "Though I'd give almost anything just to have Daisy yell at me. I know I leave home a lot, but not like this."

Every night for over a week, it's been the same thing, Amy thought sourly. *A simple "I miss them" should be enough, shouldn't it? Next, Lexa is going to start into a graphic account of Rowan in bed.*

"Can we talk about something other than your family?" Amy asked.

Lexa sighed and then brightened. "Hey, did you see that Jameson at the Stewards's? He was cute. Of course, Joseph is totally hot, even if he is old."

"They're monks," Amy said, scandalized.

"So?" Lexa replied, "It's not like they take vows of celibacy."

"They don't?"

"Of course not," she said. "I was rather looking forward to getting there, but then with the circumstances and everything, nobody was in the mood. So sad."

"Correction," Amy said. "Can we talk about something other than sex?"

"Can a girl help it if she's horny?"

"You are as bad as the guys, I swear."

"What's wrong with liking sex?" Lexa asked.

"It just shouldn't be like that," Amy said, embarrassed.

"Well, how should it be?"

Images of the love stories her sister read went through Amy's mind. She quickly rejected that notion as well. "How the hell should I know?" she burst out. "I was raised on the hick ranch, remember? All I know is that your incessant talk about sex is . . ." *Wrong? That sounds ridiculous. Tempting? I don't even want to think about that.* "Driving me nuts."

"Oh, so I am supposed to become celibate because you can't face your sexuality?" Lexa huffed.

"Fine, go sleep with anyone you want. I'm not stopping you," Amy shot back.

"Maybe I will." Lexa stomped off.

Amy sulked through dinner and most of the evening by the fire. Lexa sat on the opposite side and flirted with Mark.

Not that asshole, Amy thought darkly, *anybody but him.* She glared at Lexa. She knew her face was burning, but she didn't care. Lexa glared back out of the corner of her eye, and then returned her attention to Mark.

Amy got up from the fire early and stomped off to the tent she still shared with Lexa. She lay down, but sleep eluded her.

The camp fell quiet as soon as the darkness fully set in. She heard Lexa's voice as she and Mark talked. She could not hear what they were saying, but she heard Lexa's voice rising and Mark's deepening.

After a moment's dark satisfaction, her anger wavered. No one deserved what Mark was capable of. She had just convinced herself to go out and investigate when she heard Mark's distinctive voice go "Oof." There was a heavy thud as a body hit the ground.

Boots stomped up to the tent. Amy feigned sleep as Lexa threw herself in and into her sleeping bag. After an uncomfortable silence, Amy rolled over. Lexa's eyes were open and wet.

"Don't you dare say you told me so," Lexa said, pointing her finger. Amy could only shake her head. Then Lexa was in her arms crying.

"I am sorry," Amy said over and over.

Finally drying her eyes, Lexa looked up, "*I'm* sorry. Sorry I didn't believe you about what an asshole he is, sorry I goaded you about my family, sorry about everything."

The next morning Mark smirked as she watched him walking rather stiffly, glaring at Lexa. He said nothing and neither did Lexa. *Good for her.*

"Good falls," Spider told Amy as they headed back toward camp. "Your break-falls are really improving."

Amy smiled. After three weeks of regular practice, she still felt choppy and rough, especially compared to the fluid movements of the other two women. She was improving, but she still envied them.

"I am nowhere as good as you," Amy replied.

"She's had fifteen years of practice," Lexa said.

"Yes, but you haven't, and you are way better than I am."

"Am not."

"She's done yoga and dance," Spider said to Amy. "She's more flexible, is all."

"I just want to be good enough that no one can overpower me," Amy said.

"And you're getting there," Spider said, encouragement in her tone. "You are progressing as fast as I have seen any student go, but there are no shortcuts."

It had been two weeks since they left the Stewards. The fueling stations were closer together now. They passed many abandoned towns and occasionally saw other traffic on the road.

"How much longer do you reckon?" Kurt asked for the hundredth time as they joined the men at breakfast.

"Another day or so," Lexa replied.

"What are the Cyclers anyway?" Luke asked. "And what are they like?"

"It's short for recyclers," Lorn explained. "They make

their living recycling technology from the old cities. There is not much left, but they are an inventive bunch."

"They are very barbaric," Lexa sneered. She looked around at the men. "You should fit right in," she added. Amy fought back a giggle.

"They are not so bad," Spider put in. "They live closer to the old cities, so they tend to stick closer to the old ways, that's all. They use more technology and live more like pre-collapse society."

"Lexa's right," Lorn added. "You should fit in just fine."

"That should be okay then," Mark said.

"What sort of technology do they have?" Luke asked.

"Oh, all sorts," Lorn said. "Of course, most of the obviously useful stuff has been scavenged long ago. They still do a brisk trade in converting old machines to new purposes."

"Yeah," Spider put in. "We Greenbowes were heavily invested in electric vehicles even before the collapse, but many tribes had to survive on old golf carts until EV production picked up afterwards."

"What's a golf cart?" Shawn asked.

"It's a game, dummy," Patrick said. "My grandfather used to play." Patrick gave a brief description of the game.

"The point is," Lorn interrupted. "That they drove these little electric carts around. Now a cart can't haul much, but it is better than nothing."

"And the cyclers can provide everything we need, right?" Luke asked.

"They say so," Lexa answered, "or a workable alternative. They have lots of stuff, despite what Lorn said."

Lorn looked indignant. "It is a well-known fact that

they are running out."

"In ten, twenty years," Lexa replied.

"That is still running out," Lorn insisted.

"He's right," Luke said. "When we get back, we need to start immediate discussions about obtaining more renewable technologies like the Greenbowes have." Luke looked around at the faces staring at him.

"What?" he said defensively. "Okay, maybe this supply run will last us another thirty years, maybe not. Either way, we eventually will have to come back down. Who knows if the parts will all be available a second time? Besides, now that we know it's over, and there is a stable civilization down here, why shouldn't we start trade and whatnot?"

"Let him lead one mission, and he talks like he is in charge of the whole ranch," Patrick said.

"I am not," Luke insisted, flabbergasted.

"Seems like he is capable enough, with a few more years' experience," Lorn commented. Luke went about three different shades of red.

"Like hell that pip squeak is going to oust old Amos Deaton," Mark growled.

"I cannot comment on how you select leaders," Lorn replied, "only on the suitability of this one."

"You don't understand us at all," Patrick sneered.

"Guilty as charged." Lorn said with a slight bow.

Two days later, they rolled into the largest town any of them had ever seen. There were massive buildings on either side of the road. In the distance, even taller buildings reared up, masses of steel and glass many stories high.

"Skyscrapers," Lexa told Amy as she gawked, "from

before the collapse, obviously. Only specially trained cyclers go near them anymore. Between years of neglect and looting, most are not terribly stable."

"I would love to see one close up," Amy said. "Or better, from on top. I can remember being allowed up into the second floor of the community hall back home as a kid. You could see the whole valley. I can't begin to imagine what the view from one of those would be."

"Horrible," Lexa told her. "The first time I came here with my mom, they let me up on a ten-story hospital building. I climbed to the very top. I don't know what was worse, the height or the view. I was so high up that if I fell I would be no more than a puddle when I hit. But then I looked around and saw miles and miles of empty buildings. All those buildings used to be full of people, all dead now. It's horrible." She broke off with a shudder.

The Cyclers lived on the edge of this desolation.

The trucks rolled down recently paved roads for the first time in their trip. It was just after noon when they rolled up to a heavy metal gate.

A man came out to greet them. He was heavyset, balding and maybe fifty-five years old. He was dressed in denim jeans and a T-shirt with a welder's apron over that. He eyed the trucks with a professional manner as he approached.

"Must be the Greenbowes," he said as Amy rolled down her window.

"That's right," Lexa called out. "I am Lexa Greenbowe, and this is Amy of Freedom Ranch."

The man consulted a clipboard. "Ten visitors and five trucks," he read. "All right, everything seems in order. You want James Armstrong, fourth building on the right." He waved at the gatekeepers, who obediently swung the gates open for them.

"That was businesslike," Amy commented.

"I told you they were barbaric," Lexa said. "No sense of hospitality at all."

The fourth building on the right turned out to be a large warehouse. There was room for all five trucks to park inside. Inside along the far wall were row upon row of shelves. Amy recognized some of what was on the shelves. There were tractor parts, auto parts, and a partial compressor system for a refrigeration unit.

"Is that our order?" she asked.

"Goddess, I hope not," Lexa answered.

"Why?"

"Because if it is, they are way behind, as usual," Lexa snorted, getting out of the cab.

A tall rail of a man with bulging muscles and thin, sandy-brown hair strode toward them. His denim overalls were faded and covered in oil stains. He wiped his hands on a filthy oil-soaked rag as he came forward. Amy had been called a grease monkey more than once in her life, but she hadn't a clue what that really meant. Now she did.

"Lexa Greenbowe," the man cried gleefully, sweeping Lexa into a giant hug. She went into his arms willingly but seemed none too thrilled about it. "It is wonderful to see you again," he said, letting her go.

"Is that our order?" Lexa asked, pointing at the shelves.

"Is that any way to greet someone who might be your father?" he scoffed.

"Hi, Dad," she replied, her voice rich with sarcasm. "Mom said your math is off anyway."

"How many men could your mother have slept with

between here and Tir-Na-Nog?" he shot back.

"Apparently, you don't know Lexa's mother as well as you think," Lorn chuckled as he approached and shook the man's hands. "She was well known for taking the scenic route wherever she went. You must be James."

James laughed uncomfortably and turned toward the shelves. "Yes, that's it, all right," he said changing the subject. "We are a bit behind, unfortunately. Been short of manpower right now. That, and salvage is farther and farther from our home base, you know. Well, we do the best we can."

"You mean they are not ready?" Patrick blurted out as he approached with the others.

"Now, now," Lorn intervened. "I am sure they are doing their best, aren't you?"

"Oh yes," James replied. "It will all be ready in just a week or two."

"Meaning a month," Lexa muttered.

A month? Amy thought. *We need to be back by then, not just leaving here.*

"Perhaps, we can be of some assistance?" Lorn offered. "We have three people with some technical knowledge." He pointed at the three women, "and several others who are more than happy to do grunt labor." None of the men looked terribly happy at the prospect, but no one complained.

"Well, Lexa I know. If she's half as good as her mom, she'll be a great help. And Spider is it? You've been here before?"

"Once," Spider said, "but I fill in at the light electronics and solar factory back home."

"Great," James said, "but most of this stuff is old world

tech. I really need someone who knows that stuff, old cars and whatnot."

Amy raised her hand and waved. "My dad was a mechanic as well as an engineer. He drove a rig before the blast and maintained the ranch's cars and tractor for years."

"Damn, I might be able to fill this order yet." He smiled. "Good, I will put you to work first thing tomorrow. Sorry, we aren't much up on your 'hospitality' thing, but we'll put you up and get you settled in for your stay."

He turned around and bellowed at the top of his lungs "Jake!" after a moment, he muttered, "Where has that scrawny little devil gotten off to?" And then he yelled again, "Jake!"

"Aye aye, Captain!" came a shout from somewhere deep in the rows of junk. There was the sound of scrambling.

What came out of the rows could not have possibly fit either description of little or scrawny. He was just over six feet tall with broad shoulders and brawn to match Shawn's. His face, however, was as different as possible from the black hair and the dark scowl that Shawn wore. He had sandy-blond hair, a touch lighter than his father's, worn at shoulder length. It fell loose around his face. He had the barest hint of a scraggly beard. His sky blue eyes were wide and gave him a good-natured look of perpetual astonishment.

"Jake," James said. "Get over here, boy. These are the people from the mountains I was telling you about." He gestured at the expedition. "Take them up to the guest houses and get them settled in. You can have the rest of the afternoon off if you look after them."

He saluted his father. "Roger, Wilco."

319

He bounded up to them. "Hey, Lexa."

"Hey, Jake," she replied coolly.

He studied the trucks briefly and then turned to the expedition members. "Well, I suppose you should get what you need out of the trucks. We'll leave them here for loading. I'll take you up to the guesthouses and show you where you will be staying. We usually use individual showers, but if you want, I can take you up to the pool."

"No," Lorn said. "Just show us where we will bunk and get us some food." The men all looked relieved.

"Lorn turn down hospitality?" Spider whispered in amazement.

"Pool is not heated," Lexa whispered back, "and none too clean. That's why Lorn hates it down here."

They got their packs out of the trucks. Jake grabbed Lexa's and Amy's packs from them, one on each shoulder. "M'ladies," he said as he led the way.

Lexa just rolled her eyes, but Amy thought it was a nice gesture. Not to mention an amazing one. He strutted along with the heavy packs as if they were nothing.

Outside the warehouse was an old, rusted school bus. Jake opened the door and gestured them inside. "We have had this on hand for a couple of weeks, anticipating your arrival," he said.

They piled in and sat down. Jake jumped in the driver's seat. They were all startled when he cranked the engine. *It's diesel*, Amy thought as it roared to life. She had all gotten so used to the quiet EVs that she had forgotten how loud a vehicle could be.

The low earthen houses of the Greenbowes blended into the forest where they lived. The houses at the ranch were mostly underground houses built into the slope. Amy was familiar with only one old-fashioned wood house, the community hall back home. That fit in because, well, it had always been there, at least in Amy's mind. Now watching row upon row of wooden houses go by, she couldn't help but notice how they seemed to stick out unnaturally. *They are ugly*, she decided.

She turned her attention to their driver. She could see his muscles bulge under the T-shirt he wore. She could not see his face from this angle, but that left her free to study his sandy hair and broad shoulders without embarrassment.

"Almost there," he called, looking back. He smiled at Amy, and she quickly looked away.

They pulled into a parking lot surrounded on three sides by a collection of long wooden buildings. Each was rectangular with six matching front doors.

"Townhouses," Jake explained, "all unoccupied and ready for travelers such as you. Take whichever you want. They each have two bedrooms, one kitchen and one bath. There's enough you can bunk up or have separate quarters."

"Separate quarters?" Shawn gasped. "Cool." Shawn's family lived in a tiny house on the edge of the ranch. Amy had never been inside his home, but she was pretty sure this was Shawn's first experience with his own room.

"Let's bunk up," Lexa said to Amy, who nodded in agreement.

"Hey, everyone," Jake said. "Me and Dad live in that white house on the corner there. Get yourself settled in and then come over. I'll nuke us some grub."

"What did he say?" Patrick asked as he watched Jake's retreating back.

"I believe he offered us food," Lorn replied.

"I'm not eating anything radioactive," Shawn said.

"That one look okay?" Lexa asked, pointing at one of the doors. Amy shrugged. They all looked the same to her.

The others were hoisting their packs and selecting places as well. Patrick, Mark, and Shawn were each taking their own place on the left. Lorn, Kurt, and Spider were next to each other on the right. Luke and Daniel were going to bunk up in one of the middle houses.

"So, you know James and Jake?" Amy asked nonchalantly, she hoped.

"Sure, I have been coming here with my mother for years," Lexa replied. "Jake and I used to play in the piles of junk when we were kids."

"Is James really your father?" Amy asked.

"No. Rude is what he is." To Amy's quizzical stare, she added, "A father is someone who raises you, takes care of you, not some bloke your mom has fun with occasionally."

"What about what Lorn said about your mother?"

Lexa shrugged. "Mostly true, as far as I know. Big appetite."

"That's an awful thing to say about your own mother," Amy gasped.

"Is it?" Lexa wondered. "I always thought it was a compliment."

"You're kidding."

"She used to always say, if you have to leave 'em, leave 'em with a smile."

"Are you saying that she enjoyed being . . . being . . ." Amy stammered over the word, ". . . a hussy?"

"We don't use words like that anymore," Lexa said crossly. Amy felt bad. "I thought we had all that stupid ranch talk out of your head." Amy blushed, but she figured she had it coming.

"Down here," Lexa explained, "if you're happy and they're happy, it's no one else's business."

"I guess that makes sense."

The townhouses were spacious compared to most of the places they had stayed. Amy deposited her bag in one of the rooms, and they went back down to wait for the others. As soon as everyone had gathered, they made their way to the Armstrong house.

"Howdy partners," Jake called as they approached, "come on in." Many glass jars of soup were set out on the kitchen table. "Who is hungry?"

"Me," Shawn replied, muscling his way forward.

Jake opened a jar of soup and dumped it in a bowl.

"We usually heat our food," Shawn said, crestfallen.

"Never fear my friend," Jake replied. "We'll nuke it."

"I don't eat radioactive food either," Shawn grumbled unhappily.

Jake just laughed. "Not that kind of nuke; this kind." He pointed at a metal box on the counter. With a push of a button, he opened the door and placed the bowl inside. He twisted a dial.

The machine came to life and lit up. It emitted a humming noise. After a minute, Jake cried out, "and . . . *bing!*"

The machine binged as promised. He opened the door and pulled the bowl out. It was steaming hot.

"Wow!" Shawn gasped. "What is it?"

"A microwave," Jake said. "Standard pre-collapse cooking technology. One of the best, no fuss ways to prepare food."

"Yeah," Daniel put in, trying to sound knowledgeable, "My parents told me about theirs. Mom says it one of the few things she misses about the old days."

They all took turns watching their soup get nuked. Amy scoffed at them. *Of all the marvels they've encountered on this trip so far, it just figures this is what amazes them.*

"Any beer?" Mark asked conversationally as he ate.

Jake thought a moment. "Not enough to go around, I'm afraid. We don't drink much." Mark looked disappointed. Then he brightened as Jake said, "Of course the canteen will be open in an hour or so, when the early shift gets off." The men looked excited. They had learned the joys of meeting new people on this mission.

"An hour?" Patrick said. "That gives us time to clean up a bit first."

Jake gave them directions to the canteen as they devoured their soup. The whole village was laid out along three streets. The houses were all pre-collapse, and the community worked together to keep them in order. It was a strange setup. The village was only a tiny fraction of the city. When a new person came into the community, or a child came of age, they simply worked together to repair the next house down the lane and the person moved in.

The store and the canteen were along one of the side streets that connected the village. Anyone who worked in the community was welcome to an equal share in both. Jake assured them that as visitors they could visit the canteen for free tonight, but tomorrow they would be working.

"Well, I for one have no interest in carousing," Lorn said, "but there is an abandoned library not far from here."

"Yeah, it's on Deal Avenue," Jake said. "Just five blocks down. We put a new roof on it a few years ago so that nothing would get destroyed."

Lorn nodded. "I saw it briefly on my last visit here, years ago. I promised myself that I would look it at more closely someday. I think that day has finally come."

"Sounds interesting," Luke said. "Mind if I come?"

"Not at all."

The rest of the men excused themselves to leave as well.

"Beware," Jake shouted at their retreating backs. "KC is a wretched hive of scum and villainy."

Amy gave Lexa a quizzical stare.

"What are you on about?" Lexa asked Jake.

"See, that's the problem with you," Jake replied amiably. "You are ignorant of the great cultural achievements of our ancestors."

Lexa rolled her eyes and gestured around the room. Junk was everywhere. There were electronics with parts hanging out, machines and appliances of every possible description, and open technical manuals on every available surface. "You can really see that Jake and his dad are true connoisseurs of culture," she said.

Amy laughed. "Actually, this place reminds me of home."

"You're kidding."

"My dad was a far better mechanic than housekeeper," she told Lexa. "Better handy than neat, he'd always say."

"Exactly," Jake replied.

"Well, I am going to bow out of this cultural discussion and get some sleep," Spider said with a laugh. "These old bones don't handle camping like they used to. I have been dreaming of a real bed for over a week."

That left Amy, Lexa, and Jake. "How about I introduce you two to some of the best of pre-collapse society?" he asked, "Like *Star Wars*."

"I don't remember that being mentioned in history," Amy said.

"No, it was a movie. Come on."

Lexa looked at her. She shrugged and followed Jake into the next room. She was glad to have any excuse to stay with the gregarious man.

The back room was a large sunken den. As with everywhere in the house, there was junk piled everywhere. At the bottom of the sunken den was a large entertainment center. Pillows and cushions were spread in a half circle in front of it. The wall with the entertainment center was covered from floor to ceiling with shelves of what appeared to be small plastic books. Amy went to inspect one. It had a hard plastic cover with title and picture, but no pages that she could find.

Jake took the plastic book from her hand and showed her how to snap it open. Inside was a single round shiny disc. "DVDs," he declared, "state of the art technology."

He put it back and pulled out a different one. "This is *Star Wars*." He went to the entertainment center and fed the disk into a machine. The TV crackled to life.

"The best things about DVDs," he told them, "is that even after thirty years, there is no corruption. They are as crystal clear as the day they were recorded . . . still will be in hundred years."

"Really?" Lexa remarked as she looked at the fuzzy screen.

Jake banged the side of the TV and the picture cleared. "Wish I could say the same for the equipment that plays them." He laughed. "It's getting harder and harder to find replacement parts for TVs anymore. Luckily they are not exactly a survival necessity, so most of the other Cyclers leave them alone."

By the time the movie was over, Amy was stiff and her eyes were sore. She felt vaguely dizzy and disoriented.

"Nothing to worry about," Jake told her. "You get used to it after a while. I have the rest of the movies in the series, if you are interested. There are six in all."

Amy groaned.

"I, for one, need a break," Lexa said. "TV makes my eyes hurt. I don't understand how you can watch it so much."

"Call it a talent," he answered.

"I'll call it something," Lexa muttered as they gave their farewell.

Amy and Lexa left him and walked to the store to get something for supper. The storekeeper was already aware of their visit and told them to help themselves. The small store shelves were mostly lined with vegetables in glass canning jars.

"The Cyclers live mainly off trade with outlying communities. They don't raise much of their own food; hence everything in jars," Lexa said, grimacing.

"At the ranch, we grow all our own food," Amy told her, "and for most of the year, this is how we eat, from our own canned goods. That's why we need this mission so badly. We can manage without electricity or without vehicles, even though it would make planting a bitch. But without more canning jars and without the refrigerator running, we'll starve."

"We can some stuff as well," Lexa replied. "You can't

avoid it in this climate. I suppose up the mountains, your growing season is shorter still. But we have had the advantage of some of the best gardeners and botanists in the world. Between proper timing of successive crops, cold frames, and greenhouses, we grow stuff almost year round."

In the end, they selected some pasta and canned tomato sauce for their dinner. One glance at the canteen across the street told them that they would be dinning alone. The welcoming party was already in full swing.

Amy splashed the water despondently. Ever since seeing their sleeping quarters, she had been looking forward to this: a bath by herself, like at home. Privacy had been something of a luxury on this trip. As soon as they finished dinner and Lexa crashed on the sofa, she had gone to take a bath.

But it was not the luxury she thought it would be. For one thing the tub was too small. Her knees banged the sides, and the water did not quite cover her. Not that the tub was any smaller than the one she had at home.

The water went cold too quickly. She had to let some out and put more hot water in, a tedious process. For a while, it would be too hot, then too cold again. It was infuriating.

Most importantly, she was bored. She could hear the faint sounds of Lexa snoring in the other room. She wanted desperately to talk about the day, about the Cyclers, and most importantly, about Jake. Lexa seemed to know him well. They tolerated each other but didn't exactly get along. What was their story?

In her mind, she could see him clearly. The big puppy-dog eyes stared at her. She saw his muscles flex under that too-small T-shirt. She wanted to go back over and talk to him some more, see him again, but that was silly.

In the end, she climbed out of the bath, toweled off, and went to bed. She slept fitfully. She was no longer used to a regular bed, with its too squishy springs. But mostly she kept dreaming of things too long repressed.

She woke to a knocking at the door. She climbed hurriedly out of bed and began pulling her clothes on. She heard Lexa answer the door.

"Thanks for the wakeup," Lexa was saying to Luke's retreating back as Amy opened her door.

Lexa turned and held up a small jar of oatmeal and a half-full egg basket. "Luke brought us breakfast."

Amy laughed. "That's Luke's idea of breakfast, all right."

"Oh well," Lexa concluded. "It was a nice gesture, and I can use some of the canned veggies in the cupboard to make omelets while you shower."

"I bathed last night," Amy said. "I'll cook the omelets while you bathe."

"Thanks."

A half an hour later, they were outside on the front yard with the others. Most of the men were bleary eyed. Amy wondered if some of them had gotten any sleep at all.

"Good morning!" Lexa shouted. Mark and Patrick both winced.

"Did you have fun last night?" she continued in the same loud voice, smiling wickedly at Amy, who suppressed a giggle.

"Knock it off, Lexa," Lorn told her.

"You're no fun," she said, but quieter.

"I've seen you there," he replied.

"Not every stinking chance she got, though," Amy muttered.

Jake and James Armstrong were the last to arrive. They all loaded themselves onto the bus, and James talked while Jake drove. "All right," he said. "We have tentative assignments drawn up." He consulted a clipboard. "Amy will be with me and Jake in the auto salvage." Amy cheered mentally. "Lexa and Spider, you two will join the electronics shop. They have plenty of work for you there." Lexa nodded. Amy felt torn momentarily. She and Lexa had worked together for weeks now. "The men will be going with the building salvage crew. It's pretty much brute labor, so you should be able to handle it all right." The men groaned.

Amy, Jake, and James piled into an old pickup truck and headed to the salvage yard.

"It's about two miles away," James explained as he drove. "As more and more people turned to electric, we just didn't have the call for those parts. We had to make room around here, so they went."

Jake pulled a small case out of the glove compartment. It was full of more of the round shiny discs.

"What, a DVD in here?" Amy asked.

"No silly," he replied. "CDs."

She gave him a blank stare.

"Same thing, only music." He put one into the dash of the car.

"Not too loud," James warned.

"Oh, Dad." The music blared to life. It was nothing like anything Amy had heard before. If Jake hadn't told her already, she would have been hard pressed to call it music.

It was entirely unlike the music they played at the ranch. It had a driving beat, like a lot of the music the Greenbowes played, but more mechanical and jarring. The high-pitched female voice sang so fast that Amy couldn't make out the words. Nevertheless, she was sure from the beat alone that Minister Posch wouldn't approve.

"Don't worry," James shouted over the music, sarcasm in his voice, "it gets much worse."

"Dad had a crush on her when he was young," Jake told her.

"I wasn't the only one," James said. "She was very popular. It's hard to imagine now . . . you guys grew up never knowing MTV or superstars or any of that." He shook his head.

"Dad's always talking like that," Jake informed her. "Don't worry; he's just old."

The salvage yard was a vast wasteland of dead and dying cars. Amy's presence quickly proved an incredible benefit. The ranch had just over a half dozen vehicles. Amy had seen them every day of her life. While the others had to read the make and model on each car, she had only to look around for familiar cars.

"There," she said, and they pulled up alongside a car.

As they got out, James pulled a toolbox out of the back of the pickup, and Jake, a boom box. He put in a different CD, one that was, if possible, more jarring and pounding. He jumped up and down, his hair flying as he shook his head wildly. He held out his hands and mimicked playing a guitar.

James shook his head. "I told you, it gets worse."

That music is awful, Amy thought, *but I'll never tell him that.* She watched his arms and chest flex to the beat. It was hypnotic.

Those thoughts were soon buried under grease and sweat. The sun beat mercilessly on them. James was only slightly less merciless. A strong, hard-working man, James simply didn't understand little things like taking breaks or stopping for lunch.

By the time they went back to base, it was midafternoon. Amy felt filthy. Jake walked her home and asked her over for the evening. "I have way more music and stuff," he said. "I'll stop at the store and get a few beers."

"More mellow music, maybe?" Amy asked with a hopeful smile. The thought of spending the whole evening with that jarring stuff was too much. She had a headache as it was.

"Sure," he replied with a mystifying twinkle in his eye.

"Boy, you are filthy," Lexa greeted her as she came in the door.

"Thanks," Amy responded dryly. "Good to see you too."

"Oh, I didn't mean it like that."

"I know. I am just beat."

"How bad was it?"

"As bad as I look."

"Ugh!"

"Yeah, but on the upside, all we have left is to strip an old refrigerator tanker for a better compressor unit. Won't take long. But right now, I need a bath."

"Want some help?" Lexa asked. "Or are you happy to be some place where people still bathe alone?"

Amy was unsure how to answer at first, but feeling her hair clinched it. "I'll never get this grease out by myself," she moaned.

"Daisy can always get it out of my hair," Lexa answered. "I'll just have to remember what she does."

While sitting in the tub as Lexa scrubbed her hair, Amy said, "Oh by the way, Jake invited us over to listen to music tonight. Even said he'd get a few beers. What do you say?"

After a short hesitation, Lexa said, "Sure." She didn't sound thrilled. "I thought you didn't like to drink."

"Once in a while is okay."

When they arrived at Jake's house a little later, he didn't seem any more thrilled about Lexa's presence than she was about being there, but he accepted it in his usual good-natured way.

Upstairs was his bedroom, if one could call it that. His mother had died while he was still young, and James had perhaps been a bit too permissive in his fathering. At any rate, some time in his early teens, Jake had systematically removed every non-load-bearing wall in the second floor, making the whole thing his room.

One corner was a dance floor. Jake had removed the carpet and sanded the wooden floor smooth. Over this hung a glowing ball. "A disco light," he beamed, pointing at it.

"A disco," Lexa explained, "was a sort of dance club. And dance clubs, as near as I can tell, were the only redeeming feature of pre-collapse society."

Jake flicked a switch and a set of colored lights came on. The ball swung, and a strobe light started up. The effect was dizzying. "Lexa loves to dance," Jake said. "She helped me build this."

He started for the stereo system, but Lexa raced after

him. "I pick," she called.

Amy was grateful for the move. *Jake's idea of music makes my head spin.* Unfortunately, Lexa's taste was, if anything, worse. She liked something called techno—all electronic sounds and driving beat.

Lexa closed her eyes and began moving to the beat. It was, Amy decided, like a cross between the seductive "Middle Eastern" dance that Daisy had shown her and someone having an epileptic fit. Even so, it had its own strange appeal.

"I could never dance like that," she muttered enviously.

"Sure. It's easy," Jake said.

"Oh right."

"Just watch." He jumped onto the dance floor and began to shake wildly in a very poor imitation of Lexa. Amy laughed so hard she nearly fell over. He blushed and Amy felt sorry him, but she couldn't help laughing all the more.

"I see you have wowed her with your awesome dance moves," Lexa teased. Jake laughed sheepishly.

Lexa took Amy by the hand. "Come on, it's easy. If you are not a doofus, that is," she added, glancing at Jake.

"He was cute," Amy protested, which made Jake look a lot happier about being the butt of the joke.

"Just close your eyes for a moment," Lexa said, ignoring the last comment, "and feel the beat. Once you got the rhythm, the rest is easy."

Is not, she thought to herself as she tried in vain to follow Lexa's graceful movements. They danced for a long while.

"Who's up for a beer?" Jake asked as he staggered off the dance floor.

"Me," Lexa and Amy answered together.

Amy swayed as she left the floor.

"You okay?" Lexa asked.

"Those lights and that music," Amy answered. "I haven't even opened a beer and I feel half drunk."

"I know, isn't it great?" Lexa said.

Jake opened three bottles and set them on a ledge by the dance floor. Then he went to the stereo again.

"Amy said she wanted something a bit mellower," he said as he selected another CD.

Lexa looked at her. "We listened to music all day," Amy explained. "And it was starting to give me a headache."

"I think he has a different idea all together," Lexa replied, nodding at Jake, who came across the dancefloor as the slow song started, arms outstretched toward Amy.

"I'm not a good dancer," she warned him.

He ignored her comment and drew her in close. Closer than any dance that was allowed at the ranch. Then it hit her. *He invited me, not Lexa and me. On top of that, I'd asked for mellow music and . . . oh god, what does he think?*

Well, it was pretty obvious, now that she thought of it. Did she want him? Truthfully, yes, but it wasn't that simple. It might be down here, or for the men, but not for her.

"Ouch," he said.

"Sorry, I told you I am not very good. Hey! Ouch."

"I'm sorry," he said. In the background, Lexa laughed.

After several more ouches and god knows how many stumbles, Lexa broke them up.

"You two have four left feet," she laughed. "Come here, big boy." She took Jake around the waist and counted aloud while they danced. "Are you watching?" she asked

Amy.

"Yes," Amy replied, hoping the envy didn't show in her voice.

"Good, then you can do it." Lexa swung away from Jake and practically fell into Amy's arms. She leaned in close and whispered into Amy's ear, "One, two, three."

After several awkward steps, she fell into the rhythm. "Good," Lexa told her then broke away. "Now, you two," Jake and Amy moved together. Lexa counted aloud again. They made a few halting steps before Jake tripped her up.

"I can see this is going to be a long night," Lexa said, taking a drink from her beer. She pulled Jake in close again. "Just relax and listen to the music."

The sky was dark as Lexa and Amy wove their way back to their apartment. This time, it was not the lights or the music that had her dizzy.

A figure crossed the parking lot ahead of them.

"Kurt!" Amy cried. "Kurt, how are you doing, old buddy?"

"You're drunk," he grumbled. "I thought you were too good for that sort of thing."

"I am not drunk," she declared boldly, patting Lexa on the chest. "Lexa is drunk. I am . . . I am . . . what was that word?"

"Plastered," Lexa supplied.

"That's it," Amy agreed.

"Well, I am going to bed," Kurt said.

"Want to come to ours?" Lexa asked. Kurt looked shocked.

"She's just teasing," Amy told him.

"Was not," Lexa insisted.

Kurt left them there, arguing.

Amy woke to knocking the next morning. She rolled over and ran into Lexa. "Stop stepping on my toes, Jake," Lexa mumbled. She rolled over and fell off the bed.

Amy drug herself to the door. Spider peered in at her. "Aikido in thirty minutes," she said. "Big class here. You've got to come."

Amy mumbled something about being there and shut the door. She stumbled back to wake Lexa and get ready.

The class was worth it, despite her aching head. They had practitioners of every rank, even several higher ranked than Spider. They were phenomenally good. Most were eager to work out with someone new and only once during the whole class did she work with Lexa.

While Lexa had her pinned to the ground, Amy told her, "If I ever tell you a beer once in a while is okay again, use this move on me."

"Deal," Lexa replied.

Between the early morning exercise and a good breakfast, she felt almost normal by the time they headed to work.

She saw Kurt and hurried over to apologize. "It's okay," he told her. "I wasn't mad at you. It was kind of funny really." He shook his head and moved on, still looking upset.

"What do you think is his problem?" she asked Lexa as he left.

"Well," Lexa began delicately, "I have said these guys are barbaric. One of the things they share with your people is their sexual attitudes."

"They don't go for casual sex?"

"No, that's one thing. They understand about open relationships and preventing inbreeding and all that. It is homosexuality in particular they object to."

"And if Kurt didn't know that . . ." Amy finished. "Oh my, that must have been nasty."

"Yeah, that's another one of the reasons Lorn doesn't like it here. One of the many reasons, that is."

At the shop, Jake looked a little green as well. As they drove out to the work site, his father joked, "What? No music?"

Jake groaned but didn't answer. "Here let me," James continued, reaching for the knob.

"Not if you value your life," Jake replied, blocking the move with his hand.

By the time they were finished for the day, Jake had recovered his usual good humor and even suggested another round. Amy vetoed this firmly. They met Lexa and Spider as they walked toward their mutual homes.

"Spider has found something to make Lorn happy," Lexa said to Amy and Jake.

"Yeah," Spider explained, "this lady, Tara, has a hot tub."

"What's a hot tub?" Amy asked.

"Well," Spider pondered momentarily, "I guess it's like a cross between the public bath we have back home and these guys' private baths."

"It's about this big," Jake explained, gesturing wide with his arms. "And it's full of hot water, and there are jets to move the water around. I've been in it a few times. It's fun."

"Anyway, she offered that I could bring some people over. It's big enough if you guys want to come along."

"Sounds good to me," Lexa replied. "What do you say Amy?"

Amy shrugged. "Sure, I'm game." She turned to Jake.

"Count me in," he said cheerfully.

They went their own separate ways for dinner. Tara wasn't expecting them for a couple of hours. Her house was just a few blocks away, so they planned to meet up and walk down together.

As Lexa and Amy left their townhouse, they saw Luke heading for his. He stopped and hurried over smiling, his face bright. "I have great news," he said.

"What's that?" Amy asked.

"I think we have a recruit."

"A recruit?"

"Jake," Luke informed her. "I just got done talking to him, and he's interested in coming up to see the ranch. I hadn't thought about it until he asked, but we will be getting back just in the nick of time. Getting everything installed and working is going to be a big job. He can help with all that."

"That sounds . . . nice," was all Amy could get out. It was a startling thought, Jake at the ranch.

"You mean he wants to go live up there?" Lexa asked.

"I don't know," Luke replied. "I am not sure if that's allowed. I don't think he even knows if that's what he wants. He said he had his own vehicle and he could come with us and help us get everything set up. Then he could decide if he would stay or go."

"Why would he want to come all the way back with us?" Amy pondered. Lexa gave her a look she couldn't read.

Luke just shrugged. "He's curious about us. Also, he wants to get away from here for a while, so why not? I can't wait until we see their faces back at the ranch. A second mechanic. Marlin can take some time off if he wants. Or he can keep working with an assistant. Imagine that."

"An assistant," Amy said dryly. "Imagine that, my dad with an assistant."

Luke realized too late what he had just said. His face blanched, and he backtracked hastily. "I didn't mean it like that. I know you've always helped out as best you can. But that's not the same as having an actual mechanic."

"Just stop while you can," Lexa said condescendingly. She patted him on his head. He blushed fiercely but held his tongue.

Amy just stood there, not trusting her voice. Lexa wrapped her arm around Amy's and led her away. As soon as they were out of earshot, Amy exploded. "Who does that moron think he is?"

"He's not thinking," Lexa answered with surprising vehemence. "Seems to be a common problem up there. Must be something in the water that addles the brain."

"What on earth does that mean?" Amy asked, taken off balance.

"It means Amy, my dear, that you are about as dense as a brick."

"What are you talking about?"

"Why does he want to go all the way back there?" Lexa mimicked.

"Well, why then?"

Lexa rolled her eyes. "Oh, have you really managed to miss how he stares at you? How he fawns on you? How he practically groped you last night?"

"We were dancing." Amy protested. Lexa just shook her head.

"You think he likes me?" Amy asked.

"You really don't know?" Lexa said in amazement. "The guy's been hitting on you since we got here and you really missed it?"

Amy blushed. "Well, I thought, maybe, but I didn't know . . ." She threw her hands up in despair. "How should I know? I am new to all this, remember? All I ever knew was that Luke and I would end up together because, well, he's not horrible."

Lexa shuddered. "That's terrible."

"What?"

"That you would marry him because he's not horrible."

"Well, if you put it like that," Amy protested.

"I didn't. You did."

Amy paused. "Okay, but you know what I mean. You've seen the others."

"Yes, and I would choose Luke, too," Lexa agreed. "But you ought to have a real choice. Maybe find someone who likes you and who you like."

"Like Jake?"

"Not necessarily. You could meet lots of people."

"You don't like Jake do you?"

"It's not that," Lexa griped. "I have known him for years. He's fun, a good guy, and a good friend. But he's goofy and, well, there might be someone else, you never know. You shouldn't just take the first guy that comes along, you know."

Spider and Lorn were coming down the street toward them, so they stopped their conversation for the time being. The four of them chatted idly about their day while waiting for Jake.

Once Jake arrived, they made their way to Tara's.

Spider did the introductions. The hot tub was out back, behind a privacy fence. Tara had several extra swimsuits and promised that she could find something to fit everyone.

Amy looked suspiciously in the mirror as she tried hers on. It left nothing to the imagination. Amy was just sure she couldn't possibly have cleavage like what she was seeing.

"What's wrong?" Lexa asked.

"This barely covers anything."

"So?"

"It's just weird. Why is it more embarrassing to wear this than to go nude like they do at your home?"

"That," Lexa replied sagely, "is one of the great secrets of life."

Lexa spun in front of the mirror. She was wearing a hot pink bikini that was nearly two sizes too small. Even her small breasts seemed to spill out. "I say, if you got it, you might as well flaunt it." With that, she strode out of the room.

Feeling more than a little apprehensive, Amy followed. As they approached the tub, Jake caught sight of her, and his jaw dropped.

They all climbed into the tub. Amy sat next to Jake. He continued to stare. She found herself reveling in his attention, constantly distracted by the downy hair on his chest. She wondered what it would be like to run her fingers through it. They chatted, but Amy could only follow about half the conversation. Sitting this close to Jake made her mind scatter.

The hot tub was wonderful. Hot jets of water massaged Amy's back. Tara provided cold drinks: beer and, thankfully, iced tea.

Tara bowed out first, telling them she had an early day tomorrow. She insisted they all stay as long as they wanted. They could let themselves out whenever.

Lorn and Spider went next, leaving it just the three of them again. The water was becoming uncomfortably hot, so they moved onto the porch. Jake sat almost painfully close to Amy on the bench, and for a long time, they talked about nothing in particular.

"I think I am going, too," Lexa said, her voice flat.

"Are you okay?" Amy asked, concerned.

"I'm fine," Lexa snapped, looking the other way.

"Do you want me to come?"

"I said I'm fine." Lexa disappeared inside the house. Amy started to rise, but Jake put a hand on her shoulder.

"She said she was fine."

Amy sat back down, her shoulder on fire. She looked up into those blue eyes and wanted to melt, but fear still held her back. He brushed her cheek with his hand, and she shivered.

"Cold?" he asked, moving even closer.

She shook her head no, not trusting herself to speak. Her heart was racing as she lifted her hand to his cheek. He rubbed his soft face into her palm, watching her the whole time.

She dropped her hand, and her eyes went to his chest. She needed to be able to think. "Jake," she started, "I like you . . ."

"I like you too," he said. With one hand, he raised her chin so their eyes met again. Looking into those blue eyes, her resistance melted. She met him halfway in a deep, passionate kiss.

The kiss sent shivers down her spine. Her whole body cried out for him. She threw both arms around him and fed at his lips like a woman half starved. He wrapped his arms around her and lifted her easily onto his lap.

Amy had no idea how long the moment lasted. In her mind, it seemed an eternity. It was broken by the sound of the gate on the fence banging shut. She turned and looked straight into Luke's stricken eyes.

He turned quickly and fumbled with the gate. "Luke," she called, but he didn't answer.

He managed to get the gate open at last and was gone without a backward glance. "Luke," she called again. She stood and was going to race after him when she realized what she was wearing.

She ran back into the house and changed quickly, leaving the stunned Jake without an explanation. Still, she was not quick enough. She wandered back toward the guesthouses, straining her eyes to spot him. Luke was nowhere to be seen.

She knocked on the door of the townhouse that he shared with Daniel. Daniel, bleary-eyed and sleepy, answered. He said that he had not seen Luke since earlier that evening.

She wandered for what felt like a long time, hoping to run into him, but saw no sign of him. She did see Jake heading home with a look of puzzlement and pain on his face. He didn't see her, and she kept quiet until he was inside. She couldn't bear giving him an explanation, not tonight anyway.

She gave up and went home. Lexa was sitting on the couch. She looked startled when Amy came in. Her eyes were red, like she had been crying.

"I didn't figure you'd be home until late," Lexa said, trying to sound normal.

Amy sat down and began to cry.

"What's wrong?" Lexa's eyes narrowed. "If he hurt you, I'll kill him."

"No," Amy wailed. "It wasn't him. We didn't even do anything. We were just kissing . . . then Luke walked in."

Lexa whistled. "I'll bet he's pissed."

"He took off, and I can't find him to tell him it was not what he thought."

"Are you sure it wasn't what he thought?"

"No. Maybe. I don't know," Amy cried. Then she stopped, seeing a look of pain cross Lexa's face. "Oh my god, you have feelings for Jake, don't you?"

"No," Lexa insisted.

"I swear I wouldn't have done anything if I knew."

"I don't have feelings for Jake!" Lexa yelled, throwing her pillow. "Sometimes you can be so fucking dense." She stomped out of the room, crying, and slammed the door.

Amy retrieved the pillow and lay on the couch, feeling miserable. Eventually, she fell asleep. Late that night, Lexa woke her. "I'm sorry," Lexa cried. "You and Jake are good for each other. Just ignore me."

Amy hugged her. "It's okay," she repeated over and over until they both stopped crying.

The next day, she spotted Luke on her way to Aikido class. He looked like he hadn't slept at all. "We need to talk about last night," she said.

"There's nothing to talk about," he mumbled, trying to turn away.

"Like hell there isn't," she said, grabbing his arm and pulling him back. "It wasn't what you think."

"And just how do you know what I think?"

She let her hands fall. "You're right," she said, "I don't know."

"You want to know?" he demanded. "I'll tell you. I expected this of Mark, or Shawn, or Patrick, possibly even Kurt. I would have even accepted it from Daniel. But you? Never in a million years would I have thought—" he broke off, tears in his eyes. He shook his head to clear them.

"I guess I know now why Jake wants to come back with us. I should have guessed," he spat out. "I am such a fool."

"It's not like that," she insisted. "It was just a kiss." Even as the words came out of her mouth, she knew it was a lie. If he hadn't walked in, it would have been a lot more.

"Oh, just a kiss?" he replied coldly. "And how many other 'just kisses' have there been? At the village? At Tir-Na-Nog? Did that hussy let you 'just kiss' her husbands?"

Amy saw red. "Lexa is not a hussy. You take that back!"

"You haven't answered the question."

"Fine. No, there haven't been any others, not that it is any of your business."

"Not my business?" he retorted. "Not my business? You're mine."

"I am not anyone's property!"

"You know what I mean."

"Yes I do, and I am not anyone's." She turned to go.

"If it was just a kiss, why were you half naked?" he shouted at her back.

She spun around, flabbergasted. "That's what you are *supposed* to wear in a hot tub!" she yelled at his now retreating back.

When she got to the shop, Jake acted sheepishly. He

pulled her aside. "Hey, I am sorry," he said. "I didn't know you and Luke were a thing. I mean, he treats you like his sister or something."

"We are not a thing," she declared. But that was a lie, and she knew it. "Well, we are, but it's complicated."

"How complicated?"

She fumbled for an explanation. "It's like you and Lexa maybe. We've known each other for years, since we were kids. We pal around. He thinks that means there is more now that we are grown up."

"But you don't?"

She shrugged. "I'm not sure. Until recently, there weren't any other choices. I'm not even sure there is one now."

Jake nodded sagely. "Yeah, Lexa and I had a fling once. It was just like you said; I assumed since we had been such good friends that, well, you know. It was weird though. We knew each other too well, I think. We've gone back to being just friends, and that's cool."

James called them over to the pickup, and they were off. They didn't have much chance to talk the rest of the day. They had all the auto parts they needed. Some Cycler had several well pumps they'd salvaged, and Amy had to pick through and find two to take back.

"You and Jake had a fling?" Amy asked Lexa over supper that night.

"Who told you that?" Lexa asked sharply.

"He did."

"Blabbermouth." Lexa shrugged. "It's ancient history, trust me. I really don't have feelings for him."

"I believe you," Amy said, throwing up her hands in

surrender. "I'm just glad you're not mad at me anymore. It has been an awful day. I don't think I have ever cried as much as I did last night. It's not like me."

"Not even when your boyfriend catches you Frenching some other guy?" Lexa teased.

"That's never happened before," Amy protested. "Still, I don't usually go around blubbering under any circumstances and— Oh shit!"

"What? What's wrong?"

"Count it out: one week to the Stewards, three weeks since then . . ."

"Are you always so regular?"

Amy nodded fearfully.

"Oh, I am so over that," Lexa said to Amy's relief. "But do you know what this means?" she inquired menacingly.

"What?"

"You have once again missed your civic duty, young woman!" Lexa said with a glint in her eyes. Amy laughed.

They spent most of the evening indoors. Jake came by. Amy was undecided as to what she wanted to do, so Lexa met him at the door and said that Amy was ill.

Later on, they decided to get some fresh air. They found Shawn sitting on a park bench beside the parking lot, a wide grin fixed on his face.

"Hey, Shawn," Amy greeted him. "Didn't go drinking with the others?"

He shook his head no, the grin never leaving his face. There was a distant metallic whine.

"Got plans?" Lexa inquired, curious.

He nodded yes, still smiling. The whine grew louder and became a roar. A Harley Davidson motorcycle, similar to the one that gathered dust in the back of her dad's garage, came around the corner and pulled into the parking lot.

Perched on top was an almost unbelievably small figure in black leather. The helmet's faceplate slid back to reveal a tiny, bright, feminine face framed by blond hair. The grin matched Shawn's.

"Lily Scotsdale!" Lexa said in surprise.

Lily ignored her. "Hey, big boy," she said to Shawn, "want to go for a ride?"

With a soft grunt of glee, Shawn crossed the parking lot and got on behind her. He wrapped his arms around her, impossibly huge compared to her slim waist, and they were off.

"That was Lily Scotsdale," Lexa said as they departed.

"So?"

Lexa thought a moment. "Well," she said slowly, "I guess the easiest way to explain this is it's like your reputation back home."

"A dirty old grease monkey?"

"No, with regards to men."

"A frigid bitch?"

"That's Lily's reputation here," Lexa said. "Most of the men think she's a lesbian, but she's not."

"How would you know?" Amy teased.

Lexa inspected the ground very closely. "You can't blame a girl for trying."

"Lexa!"

"I was bored," Lexa protested chasing after Amy. "And besides, she is cute."

15

The Bitter End

Late that night, Amy awoke to the sounds of arguing. She went to her window. It was Patrick and Mark.

Patrick was holding Mark as he puked. They were both obviously drunk.

"You have got to knock this shit off," Patrick was saying.

"None of your business what I do," Mark snarled as he came up.

"If I have to drag your sorry ass home every goddamn night, it is," Patrick shot back. "And I am not bailing your ass out again, old buddy. Just get that through your head right now. You either control yourself or else."

"Or else what?" Mark sneered. "You will go and tell on me to Luke." He gave a crude laugh.

"Shut the fuck up," Patrick snarled.

"Oh come on, you just love old Captain Luke," Mark went on. "You want to kiss his ass."

Patrick shoved him away. Mark tottered unsteadily on his feet. "I should kick your ass for that," Patrick said. "Not to mention all the trouble you could have gotten us into."

"That bitch will keep her mouth shut," Mark said. Amy's blood ran cold.

"You had better damn well hope so," Patrick replied. "What I don't get is that you have a wife at home. You can do whatever you want when we get back. Why do you have to pull this shit down here?"

Mark just shrugged.

Patrick pointed his fingers at the other man. "You stay away from the booze and the broads, or I will personally kick your ass. Understand?"

There was a deadly silence as the two faced off. Mark gave an almost imperceptible nod. Patrick stalked off. After he left, Mark muttered, "Who does he think he is, my father?" He stumbled off toward his house.

Amy went back to bed, but she lay awake a long time wondering what it all meant.

"Look, I don't want to get in the way of you and Luke," Jake told her the next day as they wandered a deserted hospital corridor.

"I don't want Luke."

Jake looked relieved. "I really do like you."

"Is that why you want to come back with us?" she asked.

"No. Well, okay. That's what made me think of it," he admitted. "But I really just want to get away from here for a while. They don't need me." He turned to her. "I'll go no matter what you decide, but if you'd have me, I will stay."

"Thank you."

"So does that mean you want to pick up where we left off the other night?" he asked slyly.

"I can't, Jake."

"Oh," he said crestfallen. "You and Luke have to sort things out first, do you?"

"Well, yes, but it's not that. It's just, well, a bad time."

"What? Oh." They left it at that.

That afternoon, as she walked home with Lexa, she saw Jake and Luke talking. She was momentarily afraid, but they weren't fighting. Normally, she would have left them alone, but she had to talk to Luke.

They broke off their discussion as she came up. "I've got to get going," Jake said. "I'll let you two talk."

"Hi, Amy," Luke said nervously, but at least he didn't seem angry.

"We need to talk."

"I know."

"Not about that," she replied. She told him about what she had overheard the night before.

Luke nodded. "I'll look into it. Not that either of them will likely talk to me." He looked away and then back. "We need to talk about something else too."

"Yeah, I suppose we do."

"Look, Jake explained the whole thing," he said. "And I can understand." Amy was caught between surprise at Luke's reaction and anger that Jake had taken it on himself to talk to Luke. Both dissolved into rage as Luke went on. "He said it was nothing, just a kiss. If he had known that we were a couple, he wouldn't have done anything. He said it won't happen again."

What is going on? It isn't like Luke to lie. Why would Jake say such a thing? "I need to talk to him," Amy said, very tight lipped. She turned and strode off down the road. Luke watched her go with a puzzled look of suspicion.

"Jake!" she cried as she pounded on his door. "Get your ass out here and talk to me."

Jake opened the door sheepishly. "Yes, Amy?"

"Don't play innocent with me," she fumed. "What did you tell Luke?"

He looked on the verge of tears. "That he could have you," he said in a small voice.

"I am not a play thing to be tossed back and forth. You have no right to give me to him, or anyone," she screamed.

"I'm sorry."

"Why? That's what I want to know. Why?" Her anger was slipping, giving way to tears and grief. "I thought you wanted me. You said so this morning. What happened?"

"I do want you," he replied hugging her, "more than you know. But he deserves you more."

She pushed him away. "Bullshit! Try again."

"There are things he can give you that I can't."

"Like what?"

"I'm sterile," he said in a small voice.

She pounded on his chest with her open palms. "Damn it, not you too! What do I care?"

"But you're fertile," he insisted. "You have to have kids. How else will the race survive?"

"I don't care about the race," she fumed. "I care about you."

He held her as she cried. "It's okay," he told her.

After a bit, she pulled back. "You know, at the ranch

they don't think like that. Nobody would say anything."

"They wouldn't say anything down here," Jake replied. "But we heard the lectures when we are kids. We must try to save the race. I never thought I cared either, but I guess I do."

"Don't give up on me yet."

Out of the corner of her eye, she could see Luke coming down the road. Not caring that he saw, she leaned and kissed Jake.

Luke was waiting for her in the parking lot. "I guess, it's not over," he said, the pain showing in his voice.

Amy immediately felt sorry. "No, Luke, it's not. I am sorry. I didn't mean to hurt you. You've been my best friend for years. I just don't know what I want."

Luke hung his head. "I know what I want. You. I love you."

"You like me," she corrected. "I never understood the difference until recently."

"I know we would be happy together," he insisted more firmly. "But I can't make you love me. You'll have to choose."

Amy looked away and saw a group of Cyclers coming their way. Lorn was with them, and they all looked grim. Luke followed her stare.

"We need to speak with Mark," Lorn said when they approached. Luke nodded and headed for the townhouse. Amy hung back with Jake, who had come out to see what was going on. Lexa came up to them. "What's up?" she asked.

"I don't know, but I have a suspicion," Amy said. She told them about the conversation she'd overheard.

"Over here," a voice said. James was beside his pickup.

"No need to have too many people gawking," he told them.

Mark came out into the parking lot. He circled clear of the crowd nervously. Patrick, every muscle bulging with pent-up anger, stalked out to him. They spoke in angry whispers.

Luke approached the two of them, his face white with rage. In a loud clear voice, he said, "Mark, you stand accused of having forced yourself on one of the women here."

"So?" Mark shot back angrily. "We are not part of this community. They can accuse whatever they want."

"As commander of this expedition," Luke went on, "I have given them permission to treat you as they would one of their own. You will stand trial and, if found guilty, be punished."

"You can't do that," Mark yelled. "Just because Jacob said, you don't have the right to order me about. You should have seen how the hussy was dressed. She asked for it."

A ripple of anger went through the crowd.

"Luke," Patrick pleaded, "tell them to leave him to us. We'll see that he gets punished back home. Amos will take care of it. Anything but this."

"What's Amos going to do?" Luke exploded. "Make him marry this one too? Hush it up? Bullshit! He's going to get punished for real this time."

Three men broke from the crowd and moved forward.

"You can't do this," Mark squealed. "You can't." He produced a handgun. The men froze.

Luke jumped back, shocked. "Where did you get that?"

"None of your business," Mark growled. "Just back

off."

"Put it down Mark, you can't win," Luke said, his voice low and cautious.

"Fuck you," Mark said hysterically. "Fuck you all."

Everyone dropped to the ground as the first round narrowly missed Luke. One of the men was too slow and the second round caught him on the shoulder, slamming him back and down.

Amy looked up and realized that James was still standing. He had retrieved a crowbar from the back of the pickup and was eyeing Mark. He heaved the bar through the air.

Mark turned toward the whistling sound, but it was already too late. A bone-crunching thud sounded across the parking lot, and Mark fell.

Patrick was by his side in a moment, followed closely by Luke. Lorn and Spider made for the injured Cycler.

"Is he dead?" someone in the crowd asked.

"No," both groups answered. Luke added, "But its damn close."

Patrick rose and glared at James. Fire burned in his eyes. A gun appeared in his hands. "You killed my friend," he growled, pointing the gun at James.

"No!" Lexa and Amy cried together, pulling James down.

Luke reacted first, leaping to his feet in front of Patrick. He swept his hand in a vicious sweep, striking Patrick's wrist with a stunning blow. The gun flew from his hand.

Patrick fell back into a ready stance, but Luke was already moving in. He stepped in and swept Patrick's supporting leg out from under him. He followed him down, his elbow landing squarely in Patrick's face. Patrick jerked and went limp.

"Sergeant Hall would be proud," Kurt said as he came up to Luke.

Patrick regained consciousness quickly. Shawn and Lily arrived moments later. Lily, who was a friend of the girl, punched him upside the head, knocking him unconscious again.

The two injured men were taken to the doctor. This man was a real doctor, unlike Dr. Pritchard back home. He declared the bullet wound clean. A few stitches were all the intervention he would need.

When the still unconscious Mark was brought to him, it was a different story. Nobody expected otherwise. It was obvious that he had a cracked skull from the blow from the crowbar and had not much longer to live. The doctor gave him a shot of medicine and made him as comfortable as possible.

Luke and Patrick left with the Cyclers as the rest of the expedition gathered in Luke and Daniel's townhouse. A very subdued Jake stayed with Amy and Lexa. Lily stayed as well, comforting a sobbing Shawn.

It was late when Luke returned alone. Shaken by the day's events, Patrick had given a full account. He took responsibility for the guns. He claimed that he had pulled Mark off the woman and thought that nothing had happened. He had dragged Mark away and gotten the woman to promise to keep quiet, or so he thought. He had taken Mark home and thought that would be the end of it.

While no one quite believed the story, it did agree with the woman's on one major point. It had been Patrick that ended the assault by dragging Mark away with dire threats to both of them. For this one redeeming fact, the Cyclers would allow Patrick to return to the ranch to face whatever punishment they would mete out there.

I can guess what that will be, Amy thought darkly. *Amos won't care.*

Since Mark wouldn't live the night, there was no point in talking about his punishment. The rest of the group was held blameless, as Patrick had been clear that no one else knew about the woman or the guns.

James, Luke said, had acted in self-defense and the ranch held him blameless.

As a precaution, the Cyclers requested the group stick to their own quarters and avoid the canteen. At this pronouncement, Daniel looked around the room and laughed. "Anyone here been to the canteen after the first night?" he asked. They all shook their heads no. Mark and Patrick were the only two big drinkers anymore anyway.

"Where's Patrick?" Kurt asked.

"I sent him to his room," Luke said. "As far as I am concerned, until we get home he is under arrest. What Amos Deaton will do is up to him. I just don't want any more problems."

"You'll have none on our account, sir." Shawn said.

Amy looked up, startled. She had never heard anyone, least of all Shawn, refer to Luke as "sir."

"Thank you, Shawn," Luke replied. "I think I can trust the rest of you on that score."

The next couple of days passed quickly. Mark died quietly in his sleep the first night. The men took the afternoon off from working to bury him in the Cycler's cemetery. Amy surprised herself by feeling more grief than she expected over his death. She'd hated him for years, but she never wished him to die.

They returned to work the next day. Their order was mostly full, and they would be heading back soon. Amy and Lexa passed the evenings with Jake; they watched movies, listened to music, and talked.

On the way home after the second evening, Amy commented, "You know the worst thing about this time of the month?"

Lexa shrugged, "What?"

"For the first time in my life I really want to, and I can't."

"Horn dog," Lexa teased. "You're getting as bad as me."

"Not that bad," Amy laughed. "So you are really not upset? About me and Jake?"

"No," Lexa replied. "I am way over that. Jake's a goofball, but I got eyes, girl. He's a beau hunk."

Amy laughed and let the matter drop.

The next day, they started loading the trucks. Shawn arrived for work with Lily. They walked up to Luke hand in hand.

"She wants to come back with us," Shawn declared defiantly, as though daring someone to disagree. Lily nodded.

Luke paused, considering the two of them. Then he extended his hand to Shawn. "Congratulations," he said. He shook Lily's hand as well. "Welcome aboard."

They all stopped to greet their newest member. While Daniel and Kurt were busy slapping the grinning Shawn on the back, Jake strolled up.

"I'd still like to come too," he said lightly, but there was nothing light between him and Luke.

After several long, hard moments, Luke said, "I said you could come, and I won't go back on my word. Heaven knows, we could use another mechanic."

So it was settled. They had lost one but gained two. They would leave at daybreak the next morning.

16

The Choice

In the morning, Lorn came to them, a look of puzzled concern on his face. "The Cyclers have received a message from the village of Bullhaven, asking about your location. They want to know how soon you can be back."

"Is there a problem?" Luke asked.

"Apparently," Lorn answered, "but it's not something they want to discuss over the computer."

"We are headed back now anyway," Spider shrugged. They'll get there when they get there. There wasn't anything else to say.

The trip back to the Stewards was uneventful. Several of the men had discovered Amy's newfound interest in Aikido and, to her surprise, asked if they could start too. Soon the whole camp was working out every morning.

It provided a break from the monotony. Between the message from Bullhaven and the need to return to the

361

mountains before fall, they were hurrying as much as possible. They drove long, hard stretches every day.

Amy's love affair with Jake went unfulfilled. There wasn't enough privacy, and they were pushing so hard during the day. Besides, now that the first rush of puppy love was over, she was having second thoughts. He was gorgeous and fun to be around, but he seemed perpetually immature.

Luke, on the other hand, was maturing rapidly. The men now treated him with respect. He talked frequently about the future, how they would start building new houses, open trade and relations with others. He even spoke of finding the other communities in their group, what happened to them.

He had told Amy shortly before they left the Cyclers that she would have to choose: him or Jake. He would leave it in her hands and hope she made the right choice. The pained look in his eyes told her that he knew which choice he felt was the right one. She alternated between terrible guilt and bitter anger.

True, they had been friends for a long time. True, he had shown her respect when no one else had. Did that give him the right to expect her love? Despite his new maturity, she could not imagine a future with him.

Now that she had admitted to wanting sex, Lexa teased her constantly. One night as they lay in the tent, Lexa described her one encounter with Jake in graphic, awkward detail.

"Knock it off," Amy groaned. "I'm trying to sleep."

"Go right ahead, I'm not stopping you," Lexa replied innocently.

That night Amy dreamed of Jake. In her dream, she

and Jake made love while Lexa lay on her stomach next to Amy, chatting casually about her day. Amy woke tired and vaguely disturbed.

They reached the Stewards's hideout and found it empty. "I assume this is a good sign," Lorn said.

"We'll find out tomorrow night," Luke replied. They intended to rise early and make the trip in one big push.

"We will find out right now," Lexa called, waving a note she had found. It told them that everything was okay. The scavengers had come and gone quickly. The Stewards had returned to their monastery and were busy rebuilding.

When they reached the monastery the next night, they were greeted by an enthusiastic crowd and a late feast.

"Everything went perfectly according to plan," Joseph told them. "With Owl's help, it took less than a week to track them and retrieve the gold."

"And Jes?" Amy asked.

Joseph looked away. "We buried her in the gardens, like she wanted. I'll show you in the morning, if you want."

She took his hand and squeezed it. "Yes, I would like that very much."

They stayed with the Stewards for one day. They all would have loved to linger, but the message drew them on.

When they departed the next day, Lexa offered to keep Jake company in his electric buggy. That left Amy riding with an increasingly thoughtful Daniel.

"It is sure one strange world we've stumbled into," he said, obviously wanting to talk.

"Yes, it is," Amy replied. "I would have never thought about coming, but I am glad I did. What about you?"

"It has given me a lot to think about. Did you hear Joseph yesterday? He was going on about the tanks and how they purify the water. Fascinating stuff."

"I missed it, but I remember some from our first trip through."

"And the way they talk about Permaculture?" he went on. "Everyone at the ranch talks about gardening like it's boring. These people make it so much more. They're incredible, really. They have some weird social customs, though. I guess to each his own."

Amy had things she wanted to talk about too. She wasn't sure who to talk to, but suddenly she saw her opportunity. "About their customs, what do you make of it?"

Daniel shrugged. "Some of it's weird, but they're okay people. That's the odd thing. Back at the ranch, they would tell you that behaving like that is evil. But these people don't seem evil."

"Have you caught that they talk a lot about fertility?" Amy asked.

"How can you miss that?" Daniel said. "That first night at the Greenbowes, this woman gave me this whole speech about how it was her fertile time and what an honor it would be." He shook his head.

"Did you?"

Daniel blushed. That was all the answer she needed.

"I'm sorry, I didn't mean to be nosy. I don't really care."

"Not since Jake came along," he snorted. He gave her a sideways glance. "Did you?"

It was Amy's turn to blush. "No. All right, maybe I wanted to, but . . ."

"So who's it going to be?" Daniel asked. "Luke or Jake?"

"Does everyone know?"

"It's a small group," he replied, "and pretty obvious."

"I don't know. I can't decide. Okay, if we are going to get personal . . . the lady at the Greenbowes, did you love her?"

"It wasn't like that."

"Just a fling?"

"Yeah, I guess. Not like Shawn and Lily."

"Do you think they are really in love?"

Daniel rolled his eyes. "Have you seen them lately? At every stop, he's picking flowers. Shawn. Picking flowers." They both laughed.

"Okay, but back to the point. Fertility. Do you really think it's that important?"

"For me, yes," Daniel replied with a sudden vehemence. "I'll find out when I get back to the Greenbowes, see if that woman is pregnant or not. There was a woman at the Cyclers too. She said she'd send word. I have to know."

"If you're fertile? Why?" Amy felt a little betrayed by his vehemence. She had spent so long trying to argue that it didn't matter. But he thought it did.

"Just between us?"

"Okay."

"It was Joseph's idea." That startled her. What did Joseph have to do with this? "It was his condition."

"Condition on what?"

"Coming back, joining the Stewards. They don't take anyone who is fertile."

Amy's head spun with the shock. "You're going to join the Stewards? Not go back to the ranch?"

"The ranch is a failure," Daniel griped. "We all talk about freedom, democracy, and the American way. But this is where it really is, down here. We turned our backs on the problem and tried to pretend we were better than the people who did this. We *are* the people who did this. I want to be part of the solution. I don't want to go back and hide from it for another thirty years."

Amy looked at him in stunned silence. He shuffled uncomfortably and blushed. "I suppose you think I am being silly."

"No," she replied. "In fact, I think that's most noble thing I have ever heard. I am impressed."

He smiled shyly. "Besides, Kurt says he's staying."

"Really?"

"With the Greenbowes," Daniel said. "Though he won't explain why."

"I am not surprised."

"No?" Daniel replied. "It's all he talks about, when he talks at all. We used to talk a lot, but now he mostly talks to Lorn. I'm not really mad or anything. I just want to know what's going on."

Amy was uncomfortable. She knew why Kurt wanted to stay, or at least assumed she did. What would Daniel think? Did she even have the right to say?

In the end, she decided that she didn't have the right to say anything. Kurt had never told her directly. Truthfully, it was just gossip, even if she believed it to be true.

That night, she told Lexa about their conversation. "I am not surprised about Kurt," Lexa said. "But Daniel is a bit of a shock. Do you think Luke will let him stay?"

"I don't think he'll have a choice when it comes right down to it," Amy answered.

"What about you?" Lexa asked.

"I haven't decided yet." Amy groaned as she rolled over. "They both stare at me. I can sense their pleading. The longer it goes on, the harder it is."

"I know," Lexa said. "When we get back to Tir-Na-Nog, we will set up a test. Rowan is about Luke's size, and Luther can stand in for Jake. That way you can try both and see which you like better." She laughed.

"Why do you always throw your husbands at me?" Amy asked, exasperated.

"I am just teasing." Lexa said. Amy looked at her, really looked at her as she hadn't since before the Cyclers.

She reached out and hesitantly brushed Lexa's cheek. "What is it?"

Lexa's eyes filled with tears. "Damn, you weren't supposed notice," she muttered. She took a deep breath. "Well, I thought maybe . . . well . . . you know Kurt's staying. Now Daniel is staying. Why can't you?"

"Me?"

"And if you won't stay for me, maybe you would for one of my husbands. I know you aren't comfortable with . . . well, it's really not about sex anyway. You've become like the best friend I ever had. I've never cared so much about someone, and I don't want you to go." She was rapidly dissolving into a sea of tears.

Amy wrapped her arms around Lexa. "I'm so sorry. I really am dense."

"Yes, you are," Lexa said in a tiny voice.

After a time, Amy laughed. "What?" Lexa asked, drying her eyes.

"Are you seriously suggesting I could join your family?"

"Daisy practically said as much before we left. They'd all have to decide, of course. Everyone thought you were great. Nobody would object, I am sure."

"I can't marry six people at once. What would they

think back at the ranch?"

"Since when do you care what they think?"

She had Amy there. Amy was forced to admit it was an excuse. What would *she* think, being married to six people at once? She wasn't sure she could contemplate such a thing.

As the journey went on, Amy began to feel out of sync with everyone else. Everyone was ready to be home again. Shawn and Luke talked constantly about building new homes at the ranch. Spider moaned for a real bed again. Patrick, when he talked at all, hissed how glad he would be to be away from these strange people.

Only Amy seemed to want the trip to go on. She dreaded the decision she had to make. As if it weren't hard enough already, now she had images of herself and Lexa traveling up and down these dusty roads in an old electric truck, fixing windmills, going from village to village, arguing, laughing, and talking the whole way.

Just when you want time to stop, Amy thought darkly, *it goes faster.* They were already pulling into Tir-Na-Nog. She had barely gotten out of the cab when Daisy bear-hugged her. After that, she didn't have time for anymore foul thoughts.

"Oh my Goddess, but what an adventure you two have had. It's amazing that you survived at all. We heard most of it over the satellite, of course. A run-in with scavengers; a bold rescue of the Stewards . . ."

"Don't try to convince her we didn't do anything," Lexa said. "She'll never believe you anyway."

"And that horrible incident with that one fellow, Mike, was it? I thought he was a bad apple, when you were here."

The whole of the Robin's Nest family was there to greet

them. They immediately took the two girls to the bathhouse for hospitality. Amy was so happy to see everyone that they were already soaking in the hot water before she remembered that she should have been embarrassed.

They plied both Lexa and Amy with questions all the way back to their house and well into the night. They knew most of the big events, but they were hungry for every detail.

Early the next morning, Luke was on their front step. He was clearly troubled. Amy hurried out to him. "What's wrong?"

"We are leaving," he replied. "Today. Now."

"Why?" She was suddenly afraid. Had something more happened?

"Let's just say I found out what happened at the village. I have to get the others. Get packed and meet up at the workshop. I'll explain when everyone's up there."

"Lexa!" Amy cried running inside.

"She's already at the workshop," Luther told her.

"Wexa at work," Ewan agreed happily.

Amy dressed quickly and threw her few things into her pack. She had known they wouldn't be here long, but it was disconcerting to have to leave so suddenly.

Lexa was waiting for her at the main workshop. She had heard the news. She ran into Amy's arms crying.

"You have to leave already?" she cried.

"I'm so sorry. I wanted to stay, but I can't."

"I promised myself I wouldn't make a scene," Lexa sobbed, "but just look at me."

"It's okay." Amy held her tightly.

Luke was coming down the path, scowling. Several of

the others were following him. The two broke off their hug.

"What is going on?" Amy demanded as he passed.

"The men have gone nuts," Luke replied gruffly.

"What men?"

He turned and faced the expedition. "Jacob and the others. The villagers sent some people out to check on them. Jacob wouldn't believe them. He thinks we've been kidnapped or something. He took hostages and is refusing to let them go until we are returned unharmed."

"It is true," Lorn said coming down to meet them. He too had his pack. "The village has a whole contingent out there now. They have been in a standoff for several weeks. I will be accompanying you out that far, to see if I can help in any way."

"We will be leaving as soon as you all get your packs loaded. Needless to say, we need to make haste," Luke said.

"Where's Kurt?" Daniel asked.

"He's not coming," Luke said.

"What?" Patrick flared for the first time since they had left the Cyclers. "What do you mean, not coming?"

"Not coming," Luke repeated. "The rest of us are leaving in five minutes, understood?"

As Amy loaded her pack, she found Daniel at her shoulder. "Two negatives," he whispered.

"So are you staying too?" she whispered back.

He nodded toward Luke. "He needs me right now. For Luke, I'll go back. I have already sent word to Joseph. He'll be expecting me back next spring."

"That's great, Daniel," she said, truly happy for him.

The next two days passed in a blur. Luke pushed them

at top speed to reach the village before anything worse happened. When they reached there, they stopped only long enough to refuel and then pressed on.

Amy spotted the Akiras's house in the distance. She longed to stop and talk to Ruth. If anyone could help her with her decision, Ruth could. She also wanted to tell Ruth everything they had experienced. But there was no time.

By noon on the third day, they arrived. A harried looking Johnathan Quimby rushed out to greet them. He was obviously relieved to see them.

"Maybe now that they can see you, they'll calm down," he said.

"Take me to them," Luke said. He had Patrick's pistol strapped to his waist. The others hung back, but Amy followed the two men.

The villagers had dug a low trench as a barricade about thirty feet from Liberty Farm. Jacob and the others left behind had taken some shots at them, but nobody had been hurt yet.

The villagers had made no hostile moves. This was partially out of their peace-loving nature and partially out of respect for Luke.

"It's my fault," Luke admitted quietly. "I thought that sending the map and a note in my own hand would be enough. I should have known how suspicious Jacob can be sometimes."

"No one blames you," Johnathan replied. Amy wasn't sure about that. She had seen some dark looks at them as they came in.

"Still, it's my responsibility," Luke replied. "It's my mission. Let's go have a talk with them. They won't shoot me." Amy hoped he was right as he went up over the barricade and started walking slowly toward the farm. Taking a deep breath, Amy followed.

As they approached, Amy saw the end of an M-16 sticking out of one windowsill. Her heart raced. She was sure the shooting would start at any moment. Less than six feet from the door, Luke halted.

"Who goes there?" a familiar voice called out.

"You know damn well who goes there, Horace," Luke replied.

"Luke? Is that you?" The door opened slightly. "Come on in." Horace appeared and beckoned them in.

"Luke, it is good to see you. And you, Amy. Are the others with you?"

Luke nodded as he and Amy entered the room. William had pulled the M-16 in from the window and was watching them.

"Thank god, you're back," he whispered. "Jacob's gone nuts. We all believed the note, but he would have none of it. The doctor they sent out was of Asian extraction, but he thought she looked Arabic. That made her a terrorist, as far he was concerned."

"He had some trouble when he lived down here, you know?" Horace whispered. "That and the illness . . . I think it's finally unhinged him. He ruminates constantly. He's not sane."

He broke off as Jacob came into the room. They were all wearing the same faded fatigues they had worn all summer, but Jacob's were even dirtier than the others. He was unkempt and unshaven. He carried an M-16 over his shoulder, a bandoleer of ammo around his chest, and a large knife in his belt.

His eyes burned with a wild sort of look. They narrowed suspiciously as he saw Amy and Luke. "Luke!" he said. "They finally let you go, son. Now if they can provide us with the others and the supplies we need, we will think about releasing some of these damn hostages."

"You haven't hurt anyone, have you?" Luke asked.

"I'll ask the questions, boy," he sneered. "What's your report?"

"My report," Luke replied with the same ice, "is that we were never held. The message I sent was true. We bartered with the village for what we needed, but then had to travel some distance to get it. We now have the supplies and are ready to go home, sir." He drew the last out until it was almost an insult. "Now can we let the hostages go and get a move on?"

Jacob looked angered and confused. Beyond him, Amy could see the hostages in the next room, tied to chairs. Other than that, they looked to be okay.

"Where are the others?" Jacob demanded.

"Down by the trucks," Amy responded, "with the supplies."

"How do I know it's not a trap?"

"Daniel!" Horace cried as Daniel stuck his head in the room.

"We're back," Daniel told Horace. Apparently most of the crew had taken advantage of the distraction to cross the barricade.

"It's over," Luke insisted to Jacob. "Let the hostages go."

"Watch that tone, boy," Jacob growled. He started to lower his M-16. "I am in charge here, not you. This is my mission, and those hostages stay where they are until I say

373

so, understand?"

Luke caught the M-16 by the barrel. Patrick's gun appeared in his hand, inches from Jacob's face. "No, it is my mission. You gave it to me," Luke responded. "And I did it, even though it meant babysitting a bunch of immature punks for two damn months, negotiating half a dozen deals, and god knows what else. I did it. And I am going to see it through, no matter what. I did it without violence. I did it by being fair and making trades. You, apparently, think the only way to get what you want is to take it. Fine, if you are going to insist on violence, just hold on to that gun while I count to three, and we'll do it your way."

The gun slipped from Jacob's shocked grip before Luke even took a breath.

"You are out of line," Jacob warned.

"No, you are," Luke returned. "Taking hostile action against civilians despite ample evidence that they meant no harm. Even now, with us back and telling you, you still refuse to believe the truth. You gave me this mission and the full authority to see it through. I am in charge until I say otherwise. That will be when the hostages are released and we are away from here."

Confusion crossed Jacob's face. "You really weren't taken prisoner?"

"No sir."

"You have the supplies?"

"Yes sir."

"Very well, but this is still insubordination."

"We'll let Amos decide when we get back home."

"Fine," Jacob replied turning away.

"What's happened?" Shawn asked from the doorway.

"Luke's grown up," Horace said, laughing as he took the gun Luke handed him.

"He was getting way out of line, Luke," Willie kept saying. "We never thought of mutiny, though."

Luke appeared startled at the word.

"Don't worry," Horace laughed. "We'll stick up for you when we get home. He'll give you no trouble, nor will Deaton."

"So what do you think of Amos Deaton's chances now?" Lorn remarked from the porch.

Amy looked up in time to see Shawn's toothy grin. "I think a lot of things will be changing when Luke gets back."

"Who's that?" Willie asked.

"That's Lorn."

"And her?"

"That's Lily."

There was going to be a lot of explaining to do. Amy left them to it and slipped into the other room. She found a knife and freed the hostages herself.

They spent the rest of the day at the edge of the farm. They alternated between catching the older men up on the trip and trying to mend the gap with the villagers. Luke seemed to be doing a fair job at both. True to their word, the older men were now on their best behavior.

Amy wandered back and forth, lost in thought. The villagers were sending a runner back with news. Wren, who had been one of the hostages, was ticking off names of various lovers who needed to be informed in addition to her husband. The runner shook his head ruefully as the list grew and grew. *Daniel was right about one thing: it is one strange world we have stumbled into*, Amy thought.

That night she dreamt, again, of a flat plain, the horizon clear and the blue sky like a bowl over them. In her dream was the redheaded girl again. This time, Amy recognized the place around her and the girl as well. "Hey sister," Lexa said, holding out her hand. Behind Lexa, Amy saw trees and long, low earthen houses within. Tir-Na-Nog. They were waiting there, on one of those wide porches: Luther, Merlin, Rowan, Daisy, Winnonna.

"We have no right to expect anything of you," Merlin had said at their farewell. "But if you are ever back, for a short time . . ." he had paused, fixing her with a meaningful look, "or a long one, we would be honored to have you in our family again."

That morning, she pulled Jake and Luke aside. "I have made my decision," she told them.

They both looked at her expectantly. "And?" Jake blurted out.

"I'm staying," she said.

"Here?" Luke asked.

"At the Greenbowes."

"You can't," Luke declared.

"Why not?" she challenged.

"The ranch needs you."

"No, they don't. They need a mechanic. Jake will do."

"He might not stay."

"Lily was raised by the Cyclers. She's as good as Jake."

"The ranch would never accept a female mechanic."

She just looked at him.

"Right," he mumbled. "What about your father?"

"It hurts to say it, but we both know he's dead. He didn't have a week to live when we left. I said my goodbyes. Besides, if anyone would understand, it would be him." She sighed. "You'll have to tell Elisabeth, though. She likes you, you know. With Kurt not coming back . . ."

She left it unsaid but saw the understanding through the pain in his eyes.

"I don't want you to go," Luke persisted.

"I know, and I'm sorry."

"I love you." It was barely a whisper and Luke didn't look up as he said it.

Amy sighed, "I know." She reached out and touched his cheek. "But even if I felt it too, I'd never be the wife you want. You know that."

"You could learn."

She rolled her eyes. "No. All I want to learn is what it's like to live somewhere where people don't expect me to be a certain way."

ABOUT THE AUTHOR

Ms. Eliason is both a writer and a fan of deeply immersive science fiction and fantasy novels. She loves writing about diverse characters in unique situations. She loves to share with her fans the worlds she is creating, and the ones she is discovering.

Her books can be found on Amazon or anywhere books are sold online. Check out these other books, or check her website: rjeliason.com for more information.

The Bear Naked series:
Bear Naked
Bear Naked 2: Wolf Camp
Bear Naked 3: The Hunter and Hunted (coming soon)
The Gilded Empire:
The Mage Chronicles